PRAISE FOR C

"The Hunter's Gambit is an intricately crafted, heart-pounding, blood-thirsty, spicy vampire romance, which will linger for the reader far after they've finished. Regardless if the book is full of dangers, I've never wanted to disappear into such a lavish and delicious world before. From page one, Pierlot sweeps the reader away, keeping you ensnared until the very last. This is the type of book that you go back to over and over. Just brilliant."
    – Ben Alderson, author of *Lord of Eternal Night*

"Pierlot's novel is an exciting space romp full of suspenseful chases and daring space jumps, action scenes, and rebel groups that lurk behind the scenes… *Bluebird* is entertaining, with rich world building, and will attract all lovers of queer space stories."
    – *Booklist* on *Bluebird*

"Read for a lesbian gunslinger fighting spies in space who attracts the best ragamuffins to join her."
    – *BookRiot* on *Bluebird*

"Rebellion, redemption, romance, and cinematic action: *Bluebird* is an imaginative space opera with a fantastic blend of heart and heroics."
    – K. Eason, author of *Nightwatch on the Hinterlands* on *Bluebird*

"Ambitious worldbuilding, spycraft, and the aforementioned gunslinging promises a space romp that's both thrilling and thoughtful."
    – *Lit Hub* on *Bluebird*

BY THE SAME AUTHOR

Bluebird

Ciel Pierlot

THE HUNTER'S GAMBIT

ANGRY
ROBOT

ANGRY ROBOT
An imprint of Watkins Media Ltd

Unit 11, Shepperton House
89 Shepperton Road
London N1 3DF
UK

angryrobotbooks.com
twitter.com/angryrobotbooks
Hunter Becomes Hunted

An Angry Robot paperback original, 2024

Cover by Ciel Pierlot and Sarah O'Flaherty
Edited by Dan Hanks and Gemma Creffield
Set in Meridien

ISBN 978 1 91599 817 0
Ebook ISBN 978 1 91599 818 7

Printed and bound in the United Kingdom by TJ Books Ltd

9 8 7 6 5 4 3 2 1

*Dedicated to everyone
who read* Twilight *and thought:
"Why are these vampires so Mormon?"*

DRAMATIS PERSONAE

Humans

KAZAN KORVIC: Blacksmith and liar

JOSEFINE RASK: Head Sales Broker of the Merchants' Guild

SPENCER: Professional bouncer and bodyguard for Josefine Rask

TRAVERS: One of the Wardens; a prestigious group who hunts vampires and guards humanity

Vampires

HOUSE GAMBIT *of the southern fields and marshes*

AISHREYA SUTCLIFFE: Seneschal of House Gambit. Former Baroness of Cairemere and Steward of Pearlwood

DASAR: High Lord of House Gambit. Master of the Citadel. Oldest and most eccentric of his kind

ISIDORA WOODRIDGE: Unwilling and unskilled lady in waiting

KRESSWORTH: Nobleman

WILSON: Soldier

PETYR RANKIN: Guard

WESSON: Steward of Cairemere

HOUSE MOONCLIFFE *of the northern mountains and glaciers*

ADRIUS DE VERE: Seneschal of House Mooncliffe. Sole remaining member of the De Vere family line; a now-fallen human noble house

EZELIND: High Lady of House Mooncliffe. Master of Glassdow Castle. Sister to Weisz

MARTA GARNER: Slightly more skilled lady in waiting

HOUSE ROCKFORD *of the western coasts and moorlands*

AMELIA: Seneschal of House Rockford. Weisz's only heir and commander of his armies

WEISZ: High Lord of House Rockford. Master of Saltrock Keep. Brother to Ezelind

JACQUELINE DAWSON: Soldier, and Amelia's unwitting rival

GIA MONTANARI: Former Queen of the Vampires

MATTHIAS: Nobleman. Montanari's lover.

One Year Ago

It takes less than five minutes for the man to stop screaming. That must be a new record, Adrius De Vere thinks. He breathes in the smell of blood, fresh and filled with fear. Below the gilded staircase on which he stands, his fellows are busy consuming the last of their meal. Three days of impatiently waiting has stirred most in the Citadel into a voracious blood lust. What had once been a luxurious ballroom now resembles a carrion pit, fine silks and gems obscured by glittering blood-spray and fragments of snapped bone. The human among them has been torn apart, quite literally. The head is fought over with the wild frenzy of dogs fighting over scraps.

Adrius turns away from the gruesome scene, seeking refuge in an upper gallery overlooking the main ballroom. The smell of the unwilling human's rapidly cooling body is becoming cloying, nauseating, and altogether gauche.

A woman occupies the gallery with him, a glass of wine in her hand and a sour twist to her mouth.

She glances up as he approaches. "Lovely evening, is it not?"

"You needn't pretend with me, Reya." Adrius leans against the wooden railing next to her, his back to the scene below. "For all your efforts coordinating this, you appear to be enjoying it as much as I am."

With a forced, casual attitude, she shrugs and tosses her excessively long dark hair over one shoulder. "When I was baroness, I always preferred wild boar to suckling pigs. Raising something expressly to act as food does a disservice to both hunter and prey."

"You'll hear no arguments from me. There are numerous ways we could go about this that don't involve an ostentatious charade. It's an unnecessary distraction from events of actual importance."

A salacious grin spreads across her bright red lips, the shine eerily reminiscent of the blood spilt down below. "Would you like me to provide a different type of distraction?"

"Oh, I *would* – but that can't have been the only reason you asked me to drop by."

She sighs, the sound one eye-roll short of an overdramatic huff. "Yes, yes, business first. It's always nice to know someone appreciates my skills as a spy."

"You do so adore showing off."

She snickers. "Guilty. I – ah – overheard that my dear Lord Dasar is sending a few patrols over the northern border tomorrow. The usual. Some silly insult has riled him up and now he has an excuse to snatch more territory for himself. It's petty, but if they die, it'll weaken his forces."

"Consider it taken care of. I have the strangest feeling that they'll go missing before they can accomplish their task." He hesitates, weighing the troop strengths in his head and, as always, coming out with an undesirable answer. "It isn't enough, is it?"

"I wish it were. We have to wait for him to weaken himself further before we can risk bolder strategies. Next year, maybe," she muses.

It has been "next year" for decades. It is a good thing, he reflects, that they are immortal. The passage of time scarcely touches them, though it doesn't make him any less impatient.

"I suppose we'll wait and see," he says. Then focusing on happier matters, "Remember though, after I kill Dasar for you, I get to take my Lady Ezelind's head as well."

Reya drifts back from the golden lights and dazzling splendor of the ballroom below. A cheer rings out as someone licks the last smear of blood from a femur, devouring the final traces of this year's unfortunate Vampire King.

All guile slides off her face like a silk shift sliding off bare shoulders. "My dear Adrius, I wouldn't dream of robbing you of your vengeance."

DAY ZERO

Chapter One

An unfortunate fly struggles in a net of silken threads. Its pitiful flutterings achieve little more than to briefly inconvenience the spider tying it up.

Kazan Korvic feels a touch of kinship with the fly as she picks and tugs at the laces on her bodice, tightening them until she too is snugly wrapped. She fastens the final buttons, presses a thin sheet of rouge paper between her lips, and slides an additional pin into her bun for some much-needed structural support.

Over in the corner of the room, the spider has begun to gnaw on its meal. Kazan watches, morbidly entranced, as the fly dies, the faint tremblings in the web fading away. Then, she crushes the spider under her heel as she leaves.

The majority of her house is not a house at all, but a forge with a tiny storefront and a flat above. It's a quaint sort of place, with floorboards that perpetually smell like charcoal from the forge below and a ceiling that perpetually smells somewhat damp from the frequent rain showers of the region.

She heads down the creaking stairs to the storefront where a long, slim box awaits her on the counter. Double checking that the contents are as pristine as she left them, she tucks it under one arm before stepping outside into the evening air and locking the door behind her.

Her destination tonight sits in the city's center, surrounded by other estates of those rich enough to afford space in the heart of Upper Welshire and social enough to not be parted from the hub of commerce. Around the center are the markets, the Warden's outpost, and more places to grab a drink than she can count. With the abundance of bloodthirsty vampires, haunting geists, and treacherous landscapes, there's no shortage of people needing to get drunk in Mavazem.

Nearly a dozen carriages pass her by the time she arrives in front of a stately manor. At least she is not alone in carrying merchandise – she spots more than a few guests directing the unloading of crates.

She is stopped as soon as she reaches the manor door.

"Pardon me, miss," the stationed butler says, his hand held out to prevent her from entering. "I'll need your invitation, please."

Kazan reaches into the pocket of her ballgown and holds up her invitation for him to inspect, eager to be out of the chill and into the warmth of the party inside. After a brief examination of the gilded card, his eyes go from the box she's carrying, then up to her face, his expression becoming more and more apprehensive.

"There are no weapons allowed," he informs her. "If you will be so kind as to leave that with me, I can deliver it to Madam Rask directly."

"Fine. Don't lose it, damage it, or otherwise let any harm come to it," she warns.

His head bobs up and down as he trips over himself to nod. "I understand, miss. It will be well taken care of."

She holds out the case she's been carrying and hands it over, gently letting it sink into his grip. As soon as she lets go, his arms sag with the box's weight and he stumbles a half step backwards. His voice becomes somewhat strained as he continues, "Thank you kindly, miss. Please proceed to the coat check."

She casts a concerned look at her abandoned case before heading inside. There is indeed a coat check, although the woman in the entry hall seems to be checking far fewer coats and far more secretarial work. Every time someone approaches, she makes a notation on their invitations. Kazan stops there as requested and waits while the woman politely avoids looking at her face and scrawls a number out on her card. Number thirty-one.

"Excuse me," she says to the woman, "what is this?"

"Your appointment number, miss."

Appointment number thirty-one? Unacceptable. To get to thirty-one would take all night, all morning, and possibly until noon the next day. Frankly, she doubts that Rask will bother taking appointments once the night reaches its end. As well-known as Rask is for her extravagant parties, she also has a reputation for shutting them down before dawn. Kazan's lips wrinkle in the effort to push aside a frown. She'll fix this soon enough.

She thanks the woman, and steps out of the entry hall into the main ballroom.

Renowned merchant and popular socialite Josefine Rask is synonymous with the most lavish of parties. Tonight proves to be no exception. Chandeliers drip from high ceilings, the chains lowering the circles of wavering golden light down past the upper stories of the room so they can sit above ground level and make the ballroom glow. Dancers whirl across the room like jeweled birds fluttering around in a brightly colored flock. Two levels of balconies frame the chamber, with ornately carved wooden staircases leading to them, each guarded by a marble statue of a lion, and a diligent manservant. Candelabras are alight on plinths in the room's corners as the sun starts to dip outside, a red glow beginning to burn across the sky.

As Kazan makes her way through the ballroom, she tries to keep to the edges, avoiding being swept up in the dancing or the mingling, or the gentlemen in elegant coats who are busy pretending they're not gambling. At times it feels like a game of sorts, to weave through the world without being noticed.

She should really learn how to dance. If she intends to continue doing business with Rask, the Head Sales Broker of the Merchants' Guild, she will need to become accustomed to the parties that Rask insists on using in order to conduct her deals behind a curtain of distraction.

Kazan starts surreptitiously scanning the other guests. Her memory has always been impressive, if she may say so herself, and when she focuses, she can recall the faces of those who were in line ahead of her. There were five people in the foyer when she entered, and so she rules them out. If the attendant was going in numerical order, those five wouldn't give Kazan any substantial advancement. A few in the ballroom have their invitations tucked into breast pockets, some in dainty drawstring purses, others held in their hands. One, however, rests temptingly in a back pocket, only half hidden by a tailcoat. She wanders through the crowd towards her mark and stands back-to-back with him, disguising the movement as a turn to avoid a passing server. In a smooth motion, she plucks the invitation from his pocket, and before he can notice, strides off to examine her prize.

Number twenty-three. She groans. Oh, for the love of…

"My invitation!" the man cries out, turning around like a dog chasing its tail as he pats down his pockets. His jaw flaps open in panic. "Darling, have you seen my invitation?"

His companion shakes her head, and by now the commotion begins to attract attention. Time to make a convenient getaway.

As Kazan looks around for one, she sees a familiar face lurking on an upper balcony. That will solve her problem.

She hastily waltzes over to the staircase and ascends to the second level. It's just as crowded up here as below. Fewer people, but less space. Shuffling between guests, she makes her way towards a woman leaning against the balcony railing.

The woman is easy enough to pick out. She's not particularly muscular, but she's lanky and looms above everyone else by a good couple of inches, and her visible forearms and face are covered in an eclectic assortment of scars. Spencer. Rask's personal bodyguard and Kazan's former paramour, for lack of a better term.

"Spencer," she greets, giving her a polite nod. She casually rests her weight on the railing, the cool metal pressing against the small of her back. "Might I have a moment of your time?"

When Spencer speaks, her mouth is a study in harsh lines. "Kaz... Why do I get the feeling you're about to ask for a favor?"

"Goodness, such instant distrust. And we've been over this. 'Kaz' is only allowed in my bedroom, and you haven't been there for several months. How are you?"

"Get to the point."

She jerks her head ever so slightly to the office door that Spencer's guarding. "How many appointments does Rask have tonight?"

"Why?" Spencer asks. "What number are you?"

Kazan doesn't even blink as she replies, "Four."

"Wrong lie. I just met the guy who was number four and trust me, you're not him."

Fair enough. Kazan shouldn't have instinctively jumped for the soonest appointment. Spencer is well-acquainted with Kazan's casual relationship with the truth, and although that had eventually squashed their own brief relationship a few years back, it hadn't bothered her once sex was no longer on the table. Or on the mattress, as it were. That is the pattern that Kazan usually follows – meet someone willing to tumble in the sheets with her, then eventually they discover she lied about something or other, usually not anything important, and then it's over.

"I promise I won't take too long," Kazan says, giving the impression that butter wouldn't melt in her mouth. "All I want is to discuss selling one tiny little item. I wouldn't even have to tell her that you pulled some strings for an old friend."

Spencer gives her a distinctly unimpressed look.

"Blackmailing before I've given you what you want? Bold move."

"Oh, no," she says sweetly. "See, I'm not trying to blackmail you, I'm trying to *bribe* you."

Kazan taps her fingers up the lines of her corset. She only has one dress for parties, but she has made several alterations to suit her purposes. There's a slit in her dress along her right side, disguised by a line of lace. Her middle finger catches on a thin metal ring and she pulls it free. A flat wide knife, two inches long exactly, is attached to the ring, the entire thing forged from the same bar of steel.

The glint of metal catches the light, drawing Spencer's eye to her hand. It's easy for Kazan to spin it around her finger a few times, twirling it and tossing it in the showiest manner she can.

Spencer clears her throat and tries to look like she isn't surprised. "Someone should have taken that off you at the door. No weapons and no fighting at Rask's place, remember?"

Kazan ignores the reprimand and adds, enticingly, "It's quenched in blessed water." She flips the weapon in hand, catching the blade and holding the blunt ring section out to Spencer, a clear invitation.

"Seriously?" Spencer's open jaw could catch flies. "You know better than I that it's not cheap."

"If it were cheap, I wouldn't be bribing you with it." But the knife didn't cost Kazan much to make. She'd filled an order for a set of ten over a month ago. The one she shows to Spencer was the spare she'd made in case one had warped irreparably after quenching. All the material costs have long been paid for by the Warden who originally commissioned her. "Besides, I like to think that my time is valuable as well."

Spencer reaches for it, snatching it up and secreting it away in her pocket. "I'm beginning to see your point."

That's better.

Kazan forces a thin smile onto her lips. "I'm next. If you don't mind."

"Deal. I don't really like client number four anyway. It will still be a while, but I suppose that's better than nothing. Someone will be sent to fetch you when Rask is ready for you."

"Thank you very much."

They shake hands, Spencer's grip strong enough to crush her fingers. When they go drinking and Spencer has a few too many, her embraces are enough to make Kazan's spine pop in all manner of painful ways. Back in the days when they'd slept together, those embraces had left far more scandalous evidence.

Now that she's gotten what she came for, she breaks the tight hold Spencer has on her hand and strides off, meandering along the balcony.

A passing server offers her a glass of white, which she politely declines. Wine has an unfortunate tendency to get her laughably drunk after a few glasses. She prefers whatever cheap ale happens to be on tap at the pub two blocks away from her house. That's where she first met Spencer – the two of them are some of the few in the entirety of Upper Welshire who are capable of drinking such swill and actually enjoying it.

She stops in front of a gilded floor-length mirror decorating the hall. Half of her bun is beginning to fall out of its updo. Did she pin it wrong? She's far too used to simply tucking it all beneath a kerchief and leaving it to its own devices. A quick glance confirms that no one in the surrounding throng of people is giving her more than a passing glance, affording her the opportunity to shove her hair back into place with her fingers, not unlike poking an unruly cat away from a chicken dinner.

There's no helping the rest of her reflection, however. She stares at herself in the mirror, and the smooth scar bisecting her face stares back. It has faded some with age, but is still prominent in a way that occasionally bothers her. One of the reasons her friendship with Spencer is relatively painless is because she is the only other person Kazan knows who is just as visibly scarred as her, if not more so. It's pleasant to have everyone's attention go straight to Spencer's rough, patchwork skin instead of her own face. People tend to like a pretty face, and that's why most of her relationships fail. She's never been able to provide that.

Someone brushes past her. Her skirts shift a little *too* much. She tenses up, hastily reaching for the invitation she'd tucked into her pocket, and part of her isn't surprised to find that it's now gone.

Oh no they *don't*. Some idiot has just picked the *wrong* person to pickpocket. She doesn't care about the invitation itself, but her pride rankles at the thought of someone stealing from her and getting away with it. With narrow eyes, she casts her gaze around the crowd, looking for someone walking away from her, for anyone appearing even remotely suspicious. She prowls away from the mirror, itching to give whoever stole from her a verbal smackdown. Were she not under the peaceful roof of Rask's manor, she'd be more than happy to make it non-verbal.

Before Kazan can get very far, a hand presses against her waist.

Her heart skips. Instinctively, she goes to reach for another hidden blade, but instead, a cool glass is placed into her open palm. Wine? But why? With her free hand, she goes to the one on her waist with the intent of snapping fingers.

A calm voice murmurs in her ear, "There's no need for that."

She spins on her heels to find herself face to face with a stranger, far too close for comfort.

Wealthy is her first thought. Noble too, by the curve of his back and the casual elegance with which he holds himself. He's an inch taller than her, with neatly styled hair that's so blond it's almost white. Although he is quite obviously up to no good, there's something else about him that whispers *danger*. Something around his eyes is a little too acuate, something on his smug lips is a little too inviting.

"My apologies," she replies, giving him her most confrontational and insincere smile. She lifts her new cup in false gratitude. "May I have the privilege of your name?"

"Lord Adrius De Vere. No need to introduce yourself." He reaches into his breast pocket and retrieves her stolen invitation. "Sir Richard Littman of Drumcaster. Pleasure to make your acquaintance."

"My brother's invitation. Drumcaster is lovely in the summer."

"Don't bother." He tucks the invitation away once more. "I know who you are, my Lady Blacksmith. As a rule, I do not take kindly to someone cutting in front of me."

Ah, so he's client number four – the man whose place she just took.

"Then I owe you my apologies once again," she says, unwilling to give up her new spot in the queue. "Enjoy the party while you wait, won't you?"

De Vere seems almost taken aback by her complete refusal to heed his unspoken request, drawing himself up another inch and sharpening his voice like a blade against a whetstone. "I have pressing business with Madam Rask. I would appreciate it if we could part ways without much unpleasantness."

"Unpleasantness?" The closeness between the two of them pulses in Kazan's veins, a scant few inches separating them, her skirts brushing his boots. His hand is still on her waist. "Why, do my ears mistake me or is that a threat?"

"I would *never*," he replies, faking a look of indignance without any real effort. "I just thought to inform you of what might happen if you refuse to heed my request."

"Oh, not to worry. I have a few good theories already."

"Really?"

She places her glass of wine on a passing servant's tray. As if she would ever be so stupid as to drink it. "Poison is frowned upon in polite society, Lord De Vere."

His eyes are brown, she notices. Pale, shimmering brown and

she can't look away from them as he stares at her. "Poison?" He gives her an analytical once-over and then asks, "Why would you assume something so... permanent?"

"Madam Rask deals with all sorts of clients and the Merchants' Guild can be quite literally cutthroat."

For the briefest of moments, so brief that she almost thinks she imagined it, those pale brown eyes of his flash. "Then I suppose it was a reasonable suspicion. For the record, it was drugged, not poisoned. Clever first guess, though."

"A strange man handed me a glass of wine. I'm not fool enough to drink something when I can't see where it came from."

"How sensible of you." He steps in closer, his breath ghosting over her ear as he threatens, "Now I'm going to have to ask politely once more, that you rescind your place in the queue. Or if you'd prefer, a few acquaintances of mine can escort you from the premises. I can't imagine that option would be very... *pleasant* for you. I suggest you make the more sensible choice."

The close quarters work in her favor this time. Faster than he can react, she draws her hidden blade and presses it between two of his ribs, digging the point into the fabric of his coat just the tiniest bit, catching a single, delicate thread.

"I'm afraid I'll have to decline both offers," she whispers. "Have you ever been stabbed, Lord De Vere? I can't imagine it would be a *pleasant* experience for *you*."

His free hand reaches between them, and his surprisingly cold fingers clamp down on her wrist. "I would advise against that."

"Oh? You could, of course, back off. You could stop trying to threaten me, get whatever goons you have to stand down, and we can part ways with all afforded dignity."

"No," he says, aristocratic voice unusually rushed, "I'm trying to tell you that man over there just saw your knife."

Chapter Two

De Vere pointedly tilts his head in the direction of an elderly gentleman pushing his way through the crowd, shooting panicked looks at the two of them over his shoulder as he rushes towards Rask's office and the guard outside it. De Vere *is* worried. And reasonably so. Fighting is strictly prohibited at any and all gatherings of Madam Rask's. That's been the tradition – and the law – for as long as she has been running her business. Kazan is screwed for pulling a knife, and Rask's zero-tolerance policy will screw De Vere over just the same. Not even her association with Spencer will afford her leniency.

If they're caught in a conflict like this, the both of them will be kicked out and told firmly to never return. She cannot risk that, and she doubts De Vere can either.

Were Kazan not holding a knife, she would start chewing her nails down to stubs. "He's heading towards Spencer. I can't be caught instigating a fight!"

"And *I* can?" De Vere demands. "I still have a half-full vial of narcotics in my pocket, do you really think that will look good for me?"

She and De Vere exchange a look. No spot in line is worth losing business entirely.

"Truce?" she quickly offers. "That man doesn't know us – he can't identify us by name."

"If we hide, we won't get caught," he finishes.

They pull away from the crowd, bolting down a quiet

corridor. Few people are back here, the hallways around the main ballroom unofficially roped off.

De Vere finds an unlocked door and pulls it open, ushering her inside before shutting the both of them in.

They find themselves in a study, a desk and a bookshelf decorating the small room, with far fewer lit candles than the glowing ballroom outside. The two of them go dead silent as they wait for trouble. De Vere presses his back to the door, listening for movement in the hallway, and Kazan grabs a chair from behind the desk. With a practiced motion, she shoves the chair under the doorknob and jams it in there until it's snug. Even with a key, no one should be able to get in.

A voice, muffled by the door, rings out, "...just here, I swear it..."

Her breath catches in her throat.

Footsteps pass them by. Surely her heartbeat is loud enough to hear. She forces her breathing under control and her body to relax. All that matters is avoiding being noticed and staying quiet. Then she'll be fine.

De Vere seems to have mastered that art; he's standing a hair's breadth away from her and yet she can't hear the slightest sound from him.

"...don't have time for this. Go back to the party..." That's Spencer. Her voice recedes into the distance along with the beat of her footsteps. "...trouble over nothing... let me know if you see them again..."

"But..."

Kazan and De Vere both sigh in relief before she remembers that they are hardly allies and raises her knife once more.

"Really?" He holds up his hands, palms out and open, the universal gesture of peace. "I doubt that bodyguard of Madam Rask's is far enough away that a fight won't draw her attention again. Besides, well-armed though you may be, I can guarantee that you won't be able to beat me."

Just because it didn't work earlier doesn't mean it's not

worth another shot. Although, she has to admit, he's right about attracting attention. She purses her lips and asks, "Do you have a better method of resolving this?"

"We can share the slot, if you're willing. Conduct our business with Rask at the same time? I assure you," he says pleasantly, "I'm very good at sharing."

"That makes one of us."

He raises an eyebrow and quips, "I'm guessing you're an only child?"

"No," she automatically lies. "I have three brothers and a sister."

"Older or younger?"

"Younger."

"As someone who *actually* had a brother, I don't believe that for a second. If you did," he taunts, "you would have been more specific about the age differences between those numerous siblings."

"Oh *fine*." It would seem she has no choice. Losing the chance to speak with Rask would throw her career into jeopardy that she might not be able to recover from. She holds up the knife, letting him see as she flips it around to grip the handle and slide it back into her pocket. "I agree to share the slot. It'll do."

Stiff tension still grips the two of them and then he dips into a shallow yet elegant bow. "I suppose we'll be enjoying close quarters for a while, so I offer my apologies for the unpleasant manner of my actions earlier. Shall we try for a second start?"

Why not? They are rather stuck here. She has time to kill before they can speak to Rask and leave this party. He's also the most interesting person she's spoken with today. It's rare to meet someone who has no qualms about admitting an attempted drugging. Most people she deals with in her job provide her with interesting work, but not interesting conversation. Threats of physical harm certainly are a deviation from her usual days of hunching over a forge with a hammer in hand.

Besides, De Vere's apology has been surprisingly sincere, and thus she considers her pride placated.

"Since you asked so nicely," she allows, and finds that the words are almost chipper.

He takes her free hand and lifts it to his lips, his breath barely brushing over her knuckles. A shiver runs down her spine. "It's truly a pleasure to make your acquaintance, my Lady Blacksmith. Usually when someone pulls a knife on me it ends up being a rather dull affair."

Although he holds on for far longer than is proper, it still feels all too soon when he relinquishes her hand. Something about that tantalizing touch gives her pause. A band of steel sits on his right ring finger. It's a simple ring, but the sharp engravings on it catch her eye. It has been spelled, she'd bet her lucky hammer on it. Cogs in her mind turn and if her curiosity wasn't piqued before, it unquestionably is now.

"The pleasure is all mine, my lord. Please, just call me Kazan."

"Isn't that rather forward?"

"You drugged my wine, I'm sure you can be so bold as to call me by my first name."

"Then I would ask you to return the favor and call me Adrius."

"Alright, *Adrius*," she replies, drawing out his name. "How do you propose we pass the time until any attention is safely away from us?"

"Besides your previous attempted murder?"

"You strike me as the sort who enjoys a little death at his party."

For a second, she thinks that perhaps she has stepped a tad too far with the comment, but then he laughs. It's a short bark of a laugh, as though she's surprised the noise out of him. "I must say," he says, "I'm amazed I haven't seen you at one of Rask's events before. You deserve to be the life of the party."

"Please. We both know I don't fit in here. I'm not exactly

titled, like you are, or half as wealthy as the rest out there. And that's before we get into the physical reasons." She makes a vague hand gesture towards her face.

"I didn't mean to offend."

"Oh? Then what did you mean?"

"To flatter," he tells her simply.

When Kazan inspects the look in his eyes, she sees only sincerity. That, almost more than anything else, is what draws her in. "Most people aren't interested in flattering me," she tells him frankly.

"Then most people are boringly superficial."

"And you're not?" she replies. "We have only just become acquainted, after all."

"Perhaps we could change that."

There's a spark in Adrius's expression that she wants to chase, a draw that she doesn't think she wants to resist. "If you'd like to get to know me better," she says, giving him an invitation she hopes he'll take, "I'm open to suggestions."

"I do have *one* suggestion you might be interested in. However, it may be a bit..." he pauses, not out of hesitancy, but as though to tease suspense from her, "forward."

She inches the slightest bit closer. "How forward?"

"Hopefully, just the right amount."

"Well then, in that case, I'm all yours."

He holds out his hand, and she's not sure what he's requesting. "If you would do me the honor of letting me borrow your knife?"

Not quite the type of forward she had been expecting, and she hesitates. "That depends a good deal on your intentions."

"Educational purposes only."

She's interested, she cannot deny it, but there are few reasons to trust him and a great number of reasons not to. Reaching into her secret pocket, she draws the blade again, keeping it safely in her hand.

"Show me whatever you like, *my lord*," she says, stressing

the title. Charming though he may be, she's not an idiot. She won't drop her guard simply because he makes her heart skip and gives her the privilege of using his first name. He needs to be reminded of that. "But if you think I'm going to let this blade leave my hand, you're not as clever as I think you are."

He laughs. It's quiet and almost suppressed, but it's unmistakable. "Oh, my dear Lady Blacksmith, I promise that I can show you a great deal while your knife remains in your grasp."

"Prove it."

He wraps his hand around her wrist. She can feel her heartbeat keenly in her chest as he directs her movements with barely any pressure behind his grasp in a way that makes her crave a firmer touch. They're close, so close, and she's more aware than ever of how his body should be warmer than it is. He positions the knife so that the tip of it brushes against his coat, gliding up the tightly woven fabric thread by thread. Rib by rib. The blade comes to a stop. They must have drifted closer together because the tip now presses into the material.

"Your aim was off," he tells her softly.

Her mouth seems to have dried up. "Huh?"

"When you drew on me earlier, your aim was off. You needed to be one rib higher to pierce my heart."

"Oh. I–I didn't notice."

"Your instincts are good, and you hold a knife like someone who knows their way around a weapon, but you must lack practice on living opponents."

She laughs, feeling oddly winded. "I'm good with my hands."

With his hand wrapped around her wrist, she notices again that his skin is surprisingly cold, perhaps from the chill outside. No, that's not entirely correct. His *hand* is cold, but the ring on his finger is warm like a midsummer's day.

Ah-hah.

Vampire.

For a split second, she's furious with him. Flirting while maintaining the deception, it rubs her the wrong way. She's not particularly fond of his *kind* either. But at least the last time she encountered one, they were upfront about their nature. And yet.

"Well, well, well," she says, sharp and sarcastic. Even irritated, she's unable to truly quash the enjoyment she feels at having finally, properly figured him out. "It would seem that you have quite the surprise up your sleeve, don't you? Or on your finger, as it were."

The slight tension in his eyes is barely visible but it's unmistakably there. He relinquishes her knife as though it has burned him. "Now, Miss Kazan..."

"You're taking quite the risk coming here, aren't you?"

Shock has settled over his face like a sheet of snow. Thin, blank, and definitely hiding something underneath. "You're making the assumption," he says, voice betraying no emotion at all, "that Rask doesn't already know."

Somehow, that wouldn't surprise Kazan. "Profit is profit with her, I'm assuming?"

"Indeed it is."

"Even when it comes to dealing with *vampires*," she sighs. With a deliberate slowness, she lowers her knife and puts it away. "I *am* human, and I can't say I hold any affection for vampires in general. However, if you tried to drink my blood in this manor, you'd be banned from business with Rask and likely a similar ban would extend to whichever bloodline you're from. After you went to such efforts earlier to ensure that your business with her would be successful, I doubt you would risk that. I'm in no danger from you for as long as I'm under her roof."

"Unlike some of my kind, I don't hunt for sport," Adrius firmly informs her, as though personally offended by the implication. "And as you said, I would never risk such a thing here."

"Then I don't intend on making it a problem. Do *you*?"

"I wouldn't dream of it. I admit, I'm impressed you figured it out. What gave me away?"

She entwines her hand with his, running her thumb across his ring. "Most people wouldn't notice, but *I* know the look of spelled steel. When I felt the heat coming from it, I realized whatever enchantment was placed on it was currently active. I'm guessing it's a glamor to hide your true nature. That's also why you waited until I was away from the mirror to properly approach me – the silver backing of the mirror wouldn't have reflected the glamor. Though I must say, you were rather impulsive when you kissed my hand. I'd never have figured out the ring was actively casting a spell if I couldn't feel that it was warm."

"You were – you were *guessing*?" His mouth curls up into a surprised but undeniably delighted smile. "And here I was, worried that I had made some critical error in my disguise. I must admit, Miss Kazan, you're the most interesting person I've spoken to all year."

"I aim to please."

"It truly doesn't bother you?"

"Currently? No. Although now I'm dying to know what you look like without the glamor. Do you have giant fangs?" she teases. "Slitted eyes? Pointed ears?"

"Nothing so ludicrously stereotypical, I assure you. The change in my features is only slight – enough to reveal me in a crowd, however. I have to say I'm surprised. I was expecting judgment, not curiosity."

"I've spent almost my entire life studying your kind. Everything short of cutting one of you open to figure out how you work."

"And yet you've never seen a vampire without a human disguise? Rings like my own are extremely rare. If you've ever come across a vampire before, I'd be shocked if they appeared human as I do."

"I encountered one once," she says slowly, "but it was a long time ago, and I can't trust my memory of the event."

That is only half a lie. It was indeed a long time ago, and she never quite managed to see the vampire clearly enough to pick up on all the potential details, but she remembers every second of that encounter with precision clarity. The memory has been burnt into her mind, not only with the sharpness of fear but with bright-eyed reverence.

"Ah." Adrius likely picks up on the implication of that, and returns to the subject at hand, running his thumb over the surface of the ring. "Well, far be it from me to deny you the answer to a tantalizing mystery. Would you like to see?"

They're standing so close now that she's certain he can feel the excited thud of her heartbeat. She's heard how seductive vampires can be. And how terrifying. Her own brief experience in the past had been an excess of both. Will he be terrible or beautiful to behold? Either way, this is probably her only chance to find out without the threat of death.

"I would," she confesses. "If you don't mind, of course. I wouldn't want to insist."

"Your wish, my command." He removes the ring and with a shimmer like a sheet of water, the glamor falls off him.

Beautiful or terrible. Adrius, free of the trappings of glamor, is both. Black pours into the whites of his eyes like ink into water, and his irises shift into something bright and golden. The brown becomes amber, making his gaze on her all the more piercing and unquestionably inhuman. His light hair turns pure silver, cold as ice, color desaturating as she watches. The pale, nearly luminescent undertones of his skin, the way everything about him seems sharper, more intense – it takes her breath away.

On a whim, she grabs his hand and splays out his fingers.

"Ex*cuse* me?" He's almost adorably indignant. "Is there a *point* to this?"

She examines his nails. "Curiosity." She gives him what

she hopes is her most winsome look to make up for rudely grabbing him. "I confess that I'm disappointed. Where are your claws?"

His fingers flex and long claws plunge out of his fingertips, the keratin thick and gnarled. Bits of paper-thin skin cling to the base and the smooth round tip cracks into a keen point. It's easy to imagine them scoring flesh and drawing blood. She's tempted to touch them, to see if they are exactly as sharp as she remembers vampire claws being. Not the stinging sharpness of a razor or the rough edge of broken glass. A smooth sharpness, needing naught but the slightest whisper of pressure to open flesh.

"You said you'd seen a vampire before?" Adrius asks, and his voice has an abominable softness to it.

His claws retract and he reaches out to caress her cheek. It's impossible for her to completely repress her instinctive flinch. Nevertheless, she meets his gaze as though it's a challenge. The tip of his thumb brushes against her scar in a silent question.

A creative and suitably alluring story is on her lips before she's certain of how much of a lie she wants to tell. A whole one? Something close to the truth? Most people ask about her scar at some point or another. She knew, even from a young age, that her scar garnered pity, but the whole truth only resulted in odd looks. But pity, she learned, could come in many useful flavors, so long as it was spun the right way. Telling the same story over and over again got boring, and before she hit fifteen, she began using misdirections, then entertaining variations of the truth, then flat out lies for her own amusement. After her sixteenth birthday, she never told the truth again.

Perhaps because Adrius is a vampire, or perhaps because she's relatively certain that she will never see him again after the party, she opens her mouth and finds the truth coming out.

Or as much of the truth as she ever tells. Which is *never* the full truth.

"I was quite young," Kazan begins, "and it happened at

night, so neither my memory after the fact or my vision at the time can be considered entirely reliable. A group of vampires – your fellows, I'm sure – attacked. Most of the adults in the village went to fend them off, but I was tiny, easily overlooked, and rather confused, so I hid in a barn. A vampire found me. They came up to me." A lie sneaks in. "They pinned me down and I was so weak, I couldn't move at all."

"A vampire's strength is a challenge for fully grown humans to match. It's not a surprise that a child wouldn't be able to escape."

"Mm," she replies noncommittally. "Then they…"

She reaches out, mimicking his earlier gesture. With her palm against his cheek, she carefully, sensually, slides her hand up so her fingernails brush against his right temple. And just as she had all those years ago, he leans into the touch. She watches the way his throat bobs as he swallows, his eyes staring straight into hers with a nearly unbearable intensity.

"They had me right where they wanted me and yet they didn't kill me. I don't know why. Maybe they wanted to toy with me or watch my reaction when I found out that the rest of the village was dying at that very moment. I won't apologize for assuming the worst about a vampire. Whatever they had in mind, they didn't get the chance to actualize it. A Warden burst in, and –"

With a flick of her wrist, she draws a diagonal line through the air from above his right eyebrow, down to the hollow of his left cheek.

He catches her hand before she can lower it, his thumb casually caressing the meat of her palm as he keeps her close. "The Warden startled them, I assume? Did you know that it was an accident? As a child, I mean."

"I knew."

"Did the Warden know that they were indirectly responsible for your injury?"

Now *that's* a vampiric question, through and through. "I

don't believe it ever occurred to them. In the Warden's defense, I don't think they could see me properly until after they'd put a stake through the vampire's heart. They probably assumed I was cut before they arrived."

"I suppose you hold a particular dislike for my kind then?"

"Like and dislike are such *simple* words," she teases. "I don't like how much I like you, and I dislike how difficult it is to completely dislike you." He gives her an odd, evaluating look, and she quickly swaps the subject to something that has been lurking in the back of her mind. "Do you have fangs?"

"Fangs? I would think that's obvious," he replies, voice low and heavy despite the somewhat violent subject matter. "But if it would assuage your curiosity, you're more than welcome to find out."

With that invitation, kissing him is simply the inevitable next step.

It takes him barely a heartbeat to kiss her back and when he does it's soft, as if savoring the first sip of a particularly fine wine. For her, it's not nearly enough. She's too attracted, too *intrigued*, and a part of her mind hates her for those two emotions. He *does* have fangs, she finds to her delight. She runs her tongue against them, the sharp points scratching her. She can feel him pause every time, careful to avoid actually drawing blood. Maybe it would be better if he did cut her, maybe she would deserve the pain as just recompense for her obsession.

When she pulls back the slightest bit for breath, she asks, "Are things with you always this fun, or did I simply catch you on a good day?"

"Being around humans is one of the scant few times I can truly relax and be myself," he admits. "Will you blame me for my impulsive overindulging?"

"I would never."

It was a very good kiss, and she's keenly interested in a second. However, before she can act, the grandfather clock sitting on one of the bookshelves chimes.

"We should probably get back to the party," she says with a sigh. "Spencer will be sending someone to fetch me for my appointment with Rask. I doubt either of us wants to miss that."

"Seeing as we went to such trouble earlier..." he adds wryly. From his pocket, he withdraws an embroidered white handkerchief and offers it to her. "Your lipstick is smudged."

"Thank you," she says gratefully as she takes it in hand.

It is pure white, trimmed with lace, but it's the insignia masterfully stitched on the corner that stands out. Beautiful needlework forms two swords, one silver and one blue, crossed over each other, surrounded by elegant scrollwork. As she examines it, he puts his ring back on. The illusion of humanity returns to his face, the black and gold fading from his eyes. He blinks and it disappears entirely.

"I've never seen this sigil before," she says, tracing the insignia. "What is it?"

"A coat of arms," he replies. "The crossed swords are the symbol of Mooncliffe, the House to which my bloodline owes allegiance. The scrollwork around it signifies the De Vere line." His expression darkens. "For whatever that name is now worth."

"Ah." She rubs the corner of her mouth that he points to, leaving a smear of light red on the white fabric. "Isn't Mooncliffe a city in one of the far northern parishes? I'm sure I've heard the name before."

"I honestly can't say which was named first." He pulls the chair aside and then offers her his arm. "Ready?"

She takes his arm with a smile, sliding her hand into the crook of his elbow. "Lead on, my Lord Adrius."

The hallway is empty when they step out of the office. Muffled voices of people ahead drift down through the corridor, guiding them back to the lights and hub of the party. They easily slip back into the throng of partygoers without so much as a ripple of disruption. Everyone around them is too caught up in their own chatter to notice two people quietly moving through the crowd.

Kazan looks across the balcony, spotting the far away figure of Spencer standing at her guard post. As she should be.

"Can you see the man that caught us fighting earlier?" Kazan asks.

"Let's see..." Adrius leads her to the railing, looking down at the swirl of dancers in the sprawling hall below them. To her eyes, it's near impossible to pick out such an unfamiliar face amidst the revelry. "Ah, there he is. He's dancing with a woman in a rather scandalous dress. I doubt he's interested in looking for us anymore."

"Excuse me, Miss Kazan Korvic?"

The two of them turn to see a butler smiling blankly at them.

"Yes, that's me," Kazan replies. "I take it Madam Rask is ready to see me now? Would it be acceptable to bring an associate with me to share my appointment? We will be swift, I assure you."

He bows. "It is your timeslot, miss. You may do as you wish. Please proceed to her office when you are ready."

She smiles at Adrius. "Shall we?"

Chapter Three

Even though Kazan has been inside Rask's office once before, the sheer opulence of it never fails to make her breath catch. It is more of a sprawling study than a simple office, walls lined from floor to ceiling with bookshelves. There are books aplenty in the room, but the spines are illegible to her, unfamiliar markings scrawled over them as part of whatever complicated notation system Rask uses. Here and there sits a curiosity – faintly luminous stones, a knife embedded in a skull, a silken handkerchief with a lipstick kiss. There are cases of perfect red rubies, a box of shimmering gold bars, a diamond necklace laid out on display. It all lends to the impression that much of the contents are either a stunning demonstration of wealth, or evidence that Rask prefers to keep her liquid assets close at hand.

Madam Josefine Rask herself is just as extravagant. From the decadent layers of satin and jewels that make up her flowing gown, to the ornate curls and pins keeping her blonde hair in an elaborate updo, she radiates luxury like a sun. On anyone else, it would be gaudy and overstated, but there is something about the way she holds herself that implies it's nothing more than a trifle, really, and wearing anything less would be akin to wandering around in a nightgown.

Rask rolls up a well-marked map that was sitting on her desk and greets the two of them with a polite nod. "Kazan Korvic. Always a pleasure. And Lord De Vere, what a surprise. I was unaware the two of you knew each other." It's not phrased as a question. "No matter. To business, shall we?"

"Thank you for your time, madam," Adrius says. "I believe all that you need from me is my signature?"

"Ah yes." Rask withdraws a stack of papers from a desk drawer. She flips through them, pointing to lines in the dense text. "Sign here, and initial wherever you see an 'X'. A couple of my men will hand your order off to your associates as soon as we're finished here."

"Certainly." Adrius takes a seat on the other side of her desk. His elegant fingers grab a quill, and he begins to go through the papers.

Rask opens a side door that has, until now, been hidden by a bookshelf. After a moment of rustling noises, she returns with the long, rectangular box that had been taken from Kazan at the door. Kazan breathes a sigh of relief to see it safe and undamaged. Placing the box on a side table, Rask opens the lid and peers at the contents. She reaches in, brushes the protective straw aside, and holds the object up to the light.

It is a standard arming sword, perfectly straight and balanced, tucked into a polished sheath. Rask slides it just an inch out of its scabbard to see the glint of white – pure silver wire inlaid in a deep fuller on both faces of the sword. The silver runs down, loops around the crossguard, and then twists around a pale, off-white wooden hilt. Two wires spiral parallel around and around each other until ending at the pommel, a separate piece of the same wood formed into a wicked spike. The blade's edge shines like moonlight.

Quenched in blessed water, covered in burning silver, and hilted with rowan wood. The perfect blade for killing vampires and the finest weapon Kazan has ever forged. The gentry might pay her for ornate daggers, village watchmen might buy her sturdy spearheads, and hunters might come to her for a well-balanced axe, but this is what she truly *excels* at.

She can hear Adrius's sharp intake of breath as he sees the

weapon, and then a quiet crack as his fingers grip the quill too tightly and snap the shaft.

"Hm," is all Rask has to say.

"I was hoping you'd have a buyer in mind. It's very fine work," Kazan stresses, "and it would fetch a hefty price."

The flat of the blade shimmers as Rask turns it around to examine it more closely. "It is. Truly, I have never seen its equal," she agrees, and the banal tone of her voice instantly tells Kazan their conversation isn't going to go how she wanted it to. "However, I doubt I could sell this. I've been able to sell some of your personal projects in the past to collectors or local Wardens, but this is far out of their price range."

Kazan's jaw stiffens and her lips go cold as she presses them into a tight line. "I see."

Rask sheathes the blade, hiding the glossy steel once more, and nestles it back into the straw. The lid shuts with a solemn finality.

"I'm afraid I can't take it," Rask declares.

"Surely you know someone who would be interested." Her teeth bite down on a *please* that she refuses to vocalize. She won't beg. But she *needs* the money. Desperately. "Anyone at all."

Rask moves to her desk and begins scrawling something onto a piece of parchment. "I know you and Spencer used to be close, so as a personal favor to her, I'm going to write you a letter. Deliver it to Baron Medies in Luthow and he'll be able to put you in touch with the High Warden. That should guarantee you a buyer."

"Luthow?" Upper Welshire is far from remote, but Mavazem's capital isn't exactly a short distance from here. "The travel time alone... I appreciate it, I really do, but I don't even know when I could safely make the journey."

Rask withdraws a second sheet of parchment and continues writing. "Fortunately, *I* do. I'll write out the details for you." With a knowing look, she adds, "I'm certain that if you have the High Warden promenading your work around Luthow, you'll never want for money again."

If Kazan *can't* sell this sword, then she'll have wasted an exorbitant amount of money on materials, to say nothing of the time spent crafting it. But if she *can* sell to the High Warden, then she'll have Wardens from the eastern capital to the western coast clamoring to get their hands on her work. And then she will never have to beg for clients again. She'll never have to slash her prices, or pretend as though the materials cost less than half of what they do in order to keep customers from walking away, or smile at the bastards that insist she work her hands bloody and raw in order to meet absurd deadlines.

Soft yellow wax drips from a candle onto the letter, and then Rask stamps it shut, leaving behind a seal with an elegant *R*. Kazan takes the letter when prompted and tucks it into her skirt before picking up her sword crate.

Rask holds out her hand to Adrius. "Done with those?"

He surrenders the paperwork and the forms are quickly sorted into one of the many stacks on her desk.

"Thank you for making this quick, I really do appreciate it," Rask says, one painted finger pointed politely towards the door. "Enjoy the party. And Kazan, feel free to commandeer one of my carriages whenever you choose to leave. It will be getting dark soon and as I'm sure you know, there's interesting company around tonight."

Taking that clear dismissal for what it is, Kazan casually takes Adrius's arm again as they leave. The crate isn't particularly light, but she's strong enough that she can tuck it under her other arm.

Spencer merely nods at her as they pass by on the way out. Adrius however, gets a very suspicious glare that he brushes off, paying the bodyguard no attention as the two of them step out of Madam Rask's door. Does Spencer know of Adrius's nature? Presumably, given that Rask does. Even if Spencer knows, Kazan is safer with Adrius now than she was before, what with the weapon she now holds.

There's a hint of something new to Adrius's voice, a new depth of respect, as he sincerely remarks, "I must say, my Lady Blacksmith, I am thoroughly impressed."

"You have an eye for weaponry?"

"Indeed, but even if I did not, from the moment that blade was unsheathed I could practically *feel* it burning me from across the room."

"I'll take that as a compliment."

"You should. I intended it as one."

She frowns. "Really? I would have thought you'd be less... *appreciative* of a weapon designed specifically to counter your kind. It hardly sends a friendly message."

"You're not wrong, exactly. Most of my kind would be far from thrilled. However, I am both impressed by the weapon itself, and understanding of the human desire for self-preservation. We are predators, after all. Learning that our prey can defend itself isn't inherently threatening, at least not to me. It's perfectly natural. With that taken into account, it's easy for me to appreciate the objective beauty of the blade."

"Aren't you worried I'll attack you with it?" she asks, although just as banter and without any real malice. "I could kill you."

When he laughs, it is soft and dangerous and makes her toes curl. "Oh, my Lady Blacksmith. I can say with all sincerity that I would *love* to see you try."

Perhaps he's certain she'll lose, but Kazan thinks she would have a decent chance. For she doesn't simply forge swords, she learns them too – how to hold them, how to swing them, how to cut with them. Wardens often pass through the city, and she watches them practice with one another. Asks them for a lesson when they have the time. Most are either amused, bored, or kind enough to show her a few things, and she practices religiously every chance she gets. She has no intention of ever being caught unarmed or defenseless again.

"I suppose we'll agree to disagree." Turning the conversation back to him like swinging around the point of a crossbow, she asks, "So tell me, what were you purchasing from Rask?"

"Hm, I suppose there's no harm in your knowing. I was purchasing blood." The frank matter of this confession makes her stumble more than the words themselves. "Rask is a go-between for my House and a discrete supplier. A vampire associate in Astcombe pays humans in exchange for a small amount of their blood. No one dies, so they're able to get by without attracting the Wardens' attention. They're apparently well studied in a few arcane arts, so they put the blood in magical stasis for shipping."

She blinks. "That's surprisingly humane."

"It's practical."

"True, but vampires simply don't seem to be the practical sort. No offense."

"None taken. Some of us are. Some of us aren't. Same as with humans, I should think." She admits he has a point there. He continues, "It also provides a surprising amount of safety for the human populace there. If a relatively inexpensive source of blood is available, then many vampires in the area don't bother hunting. Of course, some hunt simply for pleasure, but most are lazy enough to sit back and let their meal come to them."

"And if you don't get that meal, what do you do?" she asks. "Or do you eat… well. Human food that isn't *humans*."

"Yes and no. We can consume human food and enjoy it well enough, but it doesn't provide any sustenance. For that, only blood will do. And that tastes better than anything else."

"So… you waste human food for no reason other than enjoyment?"

"It isn't as though most of us care if humans starve." He shrugs in a manner that could be considered apologetic if she's exceedingly generous. "And resisting luxuries isn't something our kind is known for."

"Really? Don't take this the wrong way, but vampires have always seemed rather too *beastly* for that sort of thing."

"That's only one aspect of our kind. Let me put it this way; the common belief is that geists are sorrow personified – the remnant despair that humans try to hide from the world. If you follow that school of thought, vampires are the personification of repressed desires. Our kind overindulges in everything. Blood, obviously, but also sex, alcohol, human feasts – we are even known to enjoy frequent afternoon naps, although we require less sleep than humans." He laughs and adds, "Though, I've never seen hide nor hair of a geist myself, so perhaps my metaphor needs adjustment."

"What? Obviously I've never seen one in the wild, as it were, but the church in Lower Welshire is blessed with a saint, and I've seen it during a sermon once. Everyone knows saints are amicable geists."

Adrius laughs, a quiet huff of a noise. "Saints aren't special types of geist, they're just humans who lived and studied long enough to gain a rudimentary grasp of magic. Parlor tricks, not on the same level of the ritualistic blood magics that the most powerful of my kind can craft, but magic all the same. You people simply decide to venerate them once they're dead."

"Visit the church in Lower Welshire sometime, you may be pleasantly surprised."

"I'll consider it, as a favor to you if nothing else."

They make their way downstairs. She's content to hang off his arm, the cold that radiates from him dimmed with both the reapplication of his glamor ring and the layers of thick fabric between them. It's a little disappointing when she notices that night has begun to fall outside. She's still tempted to stay, for a little while longer, to enjoy Adrius's company. But she can't remain here the entire night, and she's eager to see what instructions Rask has given her.

"Fascinating as this is, and it is truly fascinating I assure you, I should probably leave soon," Kazan admits. "Time is money."

Her own regret is clearly reflected in his eyes. "Of course. My associates and I have to be departing Upper Welshire tonight as well. We have business, of a sort, to attend to. Though I cannot say I am happily anticipating it. Let me at least escort you to the door before we go our separate ways?"

A chill wind blows outside. Darkness creeps across the sky like a blanket; cloud cover muting any rising stars. It will be pitch black shortly. With a quick word, Kazan sends one of the footmen to fetch her the ride that Madam Rask had promised.

"My carriage isn't far," Adrius suggests, ever so slightly hopeful. "I could offer you a ride to wherever you wish to go. It would be no trouble, I assure you. Indeed, you'd be doing *me* a favor. While the merchandise I was here to pick up cannot be delayed, that urgency doesn't entirely extend to myself. An exception could be made."

Under Rask's roof she might be safe. In a carriage owned by Adrius, there's no telling where she would end up, if she even made it to her destination alive. She gives him a short smile. "We both know why I can't accept that."

"I know. You have your duties to attend to and… I have mine."

He relinquishes her arm and gives her that second kiss she'd been hoping for, his lips sweet but not quite soft against her own.

Wheels clatter on stone as the carriage pulls up behind them, like a belltower tolling out the quintessential denouement of midnight.

Adrius sweeps into a bow, taking her hand and bringing it to his lips, an echo of his earlier seduction. "Thank you, Miss Kazan, for a most memorable evening."

"I won't be forgetting you any time soon either, my Lord De Vere," she replies, savoring the cool touch of his lips before they part.

She lets the footman help her into the carriage, pulling her crate onto her lap as she takes her seat. The door shuts, the driver stirs the horses into action, and she begins to roll away. Before Adrius is completely out of her sight, she has a final burst of audacity and turns to blow a cheeky kiss at him through the window. From his surprised and amused expression as he watches her leave, she can tell he saw and appreciated it.

A memorable evening indeed.

Chapter Four

As the carriage bumps and rolls through the city streets, Kazan pulls out Madam Rask's letter and slides her thumb under the still slightly warm wax to break the seal. The first sheet of parchment is addressed to her – the instructions – and the second sheet is sealed with another wax stamp – the letter of recommendation. That she leaves untouched.

It would seem that Rask has a thoroughly detailed plan indeed. Kazan admires her ability to whip information out of her mind at a moment's notice and piece it all together into a comprehensive itinerary.

Apparently, a Warden-led caravan leaves Upper Welshire tonight, heading south. They will cross through the Vildenmarr, the dense and dangerous forest that blocks the parish off from southern travel. Between the wandering paths, the threat of bandits, and the rumors of geists beneath the dark boughs, every journey through the Vildenmarr is a risk. Doing so during the night certainly wouldn't be Kazan's first choice and she wouldn't dare pass through it alone, but with a Warden leading the way, she would be afforded as much safety as one can have.

Kazan calculates quickly in her mind. As long as she packs her things and gets to the city gates by midnight, she will be able to catch the caravan. Rask's itinerary has her scheduled to arrive in Luthow in no more than a week, providing there are no delays.

She leans back in her seat and lets out a long sigh, like placing down the bellows after hours stoking a fire. Her foot taps out an impatient beat as the carriage rolls through the city. Part of her rush is legitimate, but mostly she itches to burn off the energy still curling inside her. The sooner she's back to business and on the road, the better. A trek through the Vildenmarr is just what she needs to cool down. She will likely be dead tired by the time they hit the southern border in the early morning, and then she can rest at the first town they reach outside of the treacherous forest.

When her carriage comes to a stop, she jumps immediately outside, grabbing the crate before the footman can open the door for her.

"Thank you very much," she tells him, before marching towards her home.

The sign on the door has been flipped around to display 'Closed, return later' and she smiles to think it will be that way for a good while longer.

Lights are still flickering inside. Her candles haven't yet burned out; she hates coming home to a pitch-black house. She leaves the crate in the main shop, propped up behind the counter. She briefly steps through the back door, checking the quiet forge for any sign of tools out of place, then briefly locks up a few of her more valuable cabinets before heading up the creaking stairs to the landing above her shop.

There are a few things in her kitchen that will travel well. She fills a skein with water and grabs an assortment of foods – hard cheese, dry crackers, and dried fruit. Going from kitchen to bedroom, she tosses it all into a knapsack. She changes into traveling clothes – breeches, a vest, a heavy coat to ward off the night air, and a pair of well-worn leather boots. Two short daggers slide into her boots and the knife from her dress is moved to a sheath on her belt. Most people taking the Warden caravans through the Vildenmarr go unarmed, trusting in the Warden's expertise to keep them safe. Kazan knows better.

In the downstairs storeroom, she retrieves a band of leather and straps it around the sword crate so that she can sling it over her shoulder. She grabs her hat from the peg by the door, tugs it down over her messy bun, and then locks up.

It must have rained briefly while she was getting ready. Water drizzles between the cobblestones, pooling in dips in the road and splashing against her boots. The noise of the city has died down with the sun, but a few distant shouts of merchants echo through the streets and the occasional horseback rider passes her. All doors are shut and locked by midnight in most cities; guards patrol the streets during the night, keeping a watchful eye out for any suspicious activity.

The stars and waning crescent moon cast a dim pearly sheen upon the world as she makes it to the city's gates. Torches line the walls, red and orange lighting the one part of Upper Welshire that never sleeps and never stops watching.

Kazan tips her hat to one of the guards posted at the gates. "Good evening, Emil."

The greeting catches him by surprise, and he jolts upright, nose twitching. "Mm, yes. Evening. Have a um… good time?" He tips his hat in return. "Good evening again, Miss Korvic."

Just outside the walls of Upper Welshire is the promised caravan. A few wagons are slowly being packed up, torches lit and strapped to anything that can carry the flame, while men and women mount horses in preparation to leave. She's made it, and right on time, it would seem.

She nods in greeting to people as she passes them. It looks like more than one Warden guards this caravan, as three of them linger near the back and one at the head. That seems strange. Usually, the most she sees with groups this size is two.

She makes a beeline towards the Warden leading the caravan. "Excuse me, sir!"

The lead Warden is a grizzled looking man, patches of white beginning to enter his short beard. Thin metal plates his upper arms and chest, and he carries a sword at his waist that has the wear of something that has seen years of action.

He glances at her before returning to fixing his horse's saddle. "Good evening to you, miss."

"My name is Kazan Korvic. I'm here to join your journey. Sorry for the late arrival."

"Warden Travers. And you're right on time. Give me your hand."

She holds out her palm for him. The Warden tugs a four-pointed silver star from his belt and presses the pendant into her skin, waiting a moment to see if her flesh burns. Despite the spiritual connotations of the symbol representing the four brightest stars humans use for navigation, the shape is not what matters. It is the silver that would reveal her as a vampire or geist-possessed, even if she were disguised as a human.

The star, obviously, comes away clean.

He tucks the pendant back into his belt and then shakes her hand. "Good to have you with us."

One of the extra Wardens from the wagon behind them passes a burning torch to Travers. "We're ready to head out," she informs him in a gruff voice.

"Alright." Warden Travers lifts the torch into the air and speaks up. He possesses that lucky ability of not needing to yell at the top of his lungs to be heard across distances, and his booming voice easily carries to the back of the ragtag group of wagons, riders, and foot travelers. "Attention! We're moving out! We should reach the Vildenmarr shortly. From there it's nine hours till the parish's southern border. We'll stop in Belsire by morning light."

A few people cheer; those who look more tired merely nod.

Kazan holds out her hand to the Warden. "Sir? Let me take the torch for you. Use both hands for the reins."

"Much appreciated."

He passes her the light and climbs into his saddle. His horse, a calm chestnut mare, easily responds to his slight commands and starts trotting forward. On his signal, the entire caravan beings to follow, heading steadily away from the city and towards the dirt paths sloping down into the valley. It's an easy enough speed for Kazan to keep pace by the side of the Warden's horse.

Upper Welshire is nestled snugly between the Epilade mountains. Only one path leads safely south, a road that slowly dips down towards the sprawling branches of the Vildenmarr. Kazan has taken this path six times before, three trips there and back – twice to Belsire for business and once all the way to Luthow for a fete week. In the end, she'd determined that while it was a fun festival, it had far too many people for her liking, both on the journey there and in the city itself. As such, she's not found a reason to leave Upper Welshire in years.

"Will we be taking the Faebower, sir?" she asks the Warden.

He nods, his beady eyes focused on the gentle decline, as if danger were already upon them. "I know the Faebower better than the back of my hand. It may go through the center of the Vildenmarr, but it's certainly an easier path than skirting around by Rivervale. That'd take us an extra day at least and the road is uneven." He frowns and then looks down at her. "Are you traveling alone, miss?"

She pointedly looks over her shoulder towards the group behind them. "Not really, wouldn't you say?"

Whatever levity she'd been hoping for falls flat under his stern look. "Hm. You'd best stay close to me then. If I've learned anything in my years doing this, it's that everyone here is only looking out for themselves. Even you."

"What about *you* then?"

"I've sworn my life to protect the people. That trumps any instinct of survival. I've long since accepted that dangers such as nighttime or geist activity matter little in the world of coin. This is the last, and very delayed caravan heading south before the fete week in Belsire – this lot would be heading south tonight with or without us. We're just along to ensure your survival, as is our duty." He tilts his head towards her sword case. "If that box of yours gets too heavy, you can always double back to one of the wagons and take a brief rest. It's going to be a long walk and a longer night. Don't feel as though you need to keep pace the entire time."

"Thank you for the offer, but I'm not going to risk resting so long as I have this on me. If someone were to take my work while I wasn't paying attention... Let's say I'd ensure it ended badly for the thief."

"If I were you, I'd worry less about the people here and more about the forest."

"You're certainly a cheerful person, Warden Travers."

He jerks his chin towards the valley ahead. "I've lost chunks of my flesh to vampires multiple times in the Vildenmarr – I know full well that death lurks in those trees."

Her previous trips through the forest have all been uneventful, but she would be a fool to ignore any tidbits of wisdom the Warden has to offer. "I'll assume your paranoia has something to do with the additional Wardens? I've taken the path before, and I've never seen more than two per caravan. Four seems excessive."

"There's always... *something* this time of year. We don't know what, but there's often increased vampire activity this month."

It would seem the Wardens are well informed. There is indeed vampire activity in the area. She does, however, have a handy piece of information that they don't. Adrius, presumably along with the rest of his vampire friends, is already leaving the borderlands and heading back north to Mooncliffe. And given his apparently pressing business, she imagines he left in rather a hurry. If the Wardens intend to catch them, it's too late.

Kazan shrugs. "I'm not particularly worried about vampires."

Travers laughs – a gruff, unfriendly thing. "With that bravery, you'd make a decent Warden."

"You would think, wouldn't you?" she muses, more than a little sour. That hits a sore spot. "It's a shame that the rest of your organization didn't agree."

"Oh?" He raises a bushy eyebrow. "You wanted to hunt vampires?"

Not precisely. "Yes."

He gives her a second look, glancing at her sword case and then settling where most eyes settle – her scar.

The Warden she'd spoken to in the past said she was too young. Fair enough, she was six at the time. So, she took an apprenticeship that she thought would lend itself well to a combative lifestyle. She learned how to swing a sword and forge an axe, and then when she was fifteen, she went down to the local Warden outpost and asked again. That time they said she was too old. Later, she'd found her mistake was learning a craft first – the Wardens try not to recruit those who practice a valuable trade.

Practical, of course. Albeit irritating.

"When I asked to be a Warden, they told me that because I had no family to vouch for me or support me through my training, I would have to come back once I had someone to sponsor me." Another lie, but one designed to cut at the Wardens. If they wanted to shun her, she would insult them all she liked. She shrugs. "Your loss, I suppose."

"That's a shame," Travers says, frowning. "I didn't know that so many of us still held such archaic beliefs. I apologize on behalf of my organization. You shouldn't have had to deal with that."

She knows it's petty, and more than a bit childish of her, but his apology is a balm on her twice-scorned injury from the Wardens. That is something else she learned from a young age – the truth gets you scraps and vulnerability; lies get your needs met. It doesn't matter to Kazan if the result means no one can get close to her – not when it gets her a roof over her head and clients through her front door.

The caravan hits the valley floor. Lush, twisted trees become more and more common and then, within minutes, they enter the domain of the Vildenmarr. Roots plunge out of the path.

The soft grass of the valley road recedes to stone and moss and various lichen. Despite the overgrown plant life, the path is clearly visible. Branches have been removed from the way and the stones are well trodden, proof that the road leading forward sees frequent travel.

"The Faebower," Warden Travers says as the canopy envelopes the sky, leaving only thin cracks of moonlight shining through. "Beautiful, isn't it?"

Oh, it's beautiful alright. In Kazan's opinion, however, a more appropriate word would be 'eerie'. The further they move into the forest, the thicker the trees around them become. The branches grow denser, as if the leaves themselves are stained a darker color. Even with the bright torches lighting their way, an unnatural gloom seems to permeate every inch of the forest.

Not to mention that it's strangely still. Although Kazan hears noises of wind and animals – a fox's screech, a barn owl's hoot – she finds it difficult to tell from which direction anything comes. From the uneasy murmurs of the people behind her, it seems she's not the only one unsettled. She tightens her grip on the torch.

Her nerves are slightly assuaged when they pass a milestone etched with protection spells. She doesn't know much about stonework, or any such magics, to be able to determine what effects it has on the forest, but she reasons it likely guides travelers through the more treacherous paths of the Vildenmarr. A closer look reveals a chipped etching of the saint who created it when they were alive. One of the group – a clergyman in white robes – stops to offer a brief prayer. He kneels by the stone for a minute, touching the four-pointed star tattooed on his forehead.

"How often do you take this pass?" Kazan asks.

Warden Travers shrugs, gently brushing a hand over his horse's mane. "Oh, maybe twenty times a year. I tend to circle around south for a while before making another trip north.

There's a number of Wardens who make the trip through the Vildenmarr, I'm hardly the only guide around these parts."

Without being aware of it, she finds her thoughts drifting to the northern parishes. As Adrius travels north tonight, where will his final destination be? Humans cannot make it to Mooncliffe in one night, but could a vampire? Or will he stop somewhere closer to Upper Welshire?

"How far north have you been?" she asks.

"Savis. Never been further than that. It's mostly just snow and ice-covered mountains from there on out. There's a bit of a geist problem in the forests up there – I'm often called on to escort a larger party through safely."

"And vampires?"

Travers's frown is a heavy-set sag of his features. "Yes, there's vampires in the far north. They're everywhere. And aside from some churches, you never see geists without a vampire somewhere in the area. We don't know why, but it's a correlation we can't deny. Most vampires up there tend to haunt their remote manors. It's worse by the northwestern coast. That's where the really vicious bastards are. I had a run-in with one of them two years ago – Axeclere bloodline. They're nasty. She killed two of my fellow Wardens and left a series of scars on my back before the lot of us could drive a stake through her."

Kazan flinches. By the saints, she got lucky with Adrius. He'd been kind, charming, interesting. And yet, she cannot discard the possibility that if they had met under less favorable conditions, he may very well have killed her, despite his dislike of hunting for sport.

After a half hour of walking, the caravan stops in a small clearing for a short break, just a few minutes to water the horses from a creek that runs through the forest. Then they're back on the road. The same clergyman who stopped and prayed earlier offers Kazan a water pouch which she then offers to the Warden. She doesn't trust the people here any more or less than she trusted the guests at Rask's party. Her own skein full of water sits in her bag. If she needs to drink, she'll do so from a safe source.

Perhaps calling the Warden paranoid was a bit hypocritical of her.

As the wagons roll across the forest floor, this time she asks Travers another question, "What do you think of the High Warden?" On a whim, she embellishes with a quick lie, "I've got a contract to serve him as a blacksmith for two years and I'm curious to see if he'll be a good person to work under."

"You don't see many elderly Wardens as a rule, miss," Travers replies bitterly. "We serve till death – the High Warden leaves a bad taste in my mouth, sitting in his rich home and calling himself a leader."

"He must have been good though, to get promoted?"

"During his prime, he was incredible. I once saw him and the former High Warden – Elara – deal with an entire coven of vampires along Astdrum Coast. Of course, that was a good few years ago and Elara died in Dunmoss from geist possession shortly after." He sighs, an almost reverent look on his face, as if he's a priest during sermon. "No one was ever quite as good as Elara."

"I remember hearing about her," Kazan muses. "She was famous for never giving up on a hunt no matter how long she had to track down a vampire."

"Her endurance was faultless." Travers pats his hip where a wooden stake hangs in a leather sheath. "She grew up on a vineyard. Knew her way around trees better than anyone, and knew how to keep rowan wood alive for a damn long time. If a hunt dragged on, most of us would start to worry about whether our stakes were fresh enough to have any effect, but not her."

That is the only problem with rowan. Like all living things, wood doesn't live forever after it is cut and carved. Once its power slowly fades away, it does nothing to a vampire. Kazan's own sword will need the handle replaced every year or so for it to retain its potency.

They trek deeper into the Vildenmarr. Last time she made this journey, she wasn't nearly so uneasy. It could be her imagination, but it feels as though they are not alone. The thickness of the forest begins to feel suffocating; a cold wet mist rolls across the ground, soaking into her trousers, chilling her to the bones. While the mist does nothing to obscure the lines of the Faebower, it hides stones and tree roots that sneak out to trip them up.

They haven't seen a protection milestone since the one at the edge of the forest. It's been long enough. They should have come across another one by now.

The horses are skittish. It's near silent in the forest. No animal rustlings. No flutter of bird wings. A couple of the wagon horses start to whiny, tugging at the reins, pawing at the ground nervously, hooves kicking up clumps of dirt and scattering tiny stones.

Travers pats his mare's neck, trying to sooth the animal. He raises his voice to the rest of the caravan behind them, "Keep together and keep moving!"

"What is it?" Kazan's free hand unconsciously reaches for her sword crate. "What's wrong?"

Instead of answering, he signals something to one of the Wardens at the back of the caravan, his hand forming a series of shapes that she can't decipher. "Not your concern." His sharp tone conveys quite clearly that he's in full business mode, and, not being a Warden, she is not part of that business. "Keep your head down, and your feet forward."

The Warden in the back steers their horse away from the rest of the caravan and steps off the Faebower, galloping into the forest.

"Where are they going?"

"Scouting the perimeter," Travers replies. "Now, keep back."

Dark shapes flit through the trees, just far enough out of

sight to be formless, just hard enough to spot that they could be nothing more than shadow. Her heart begins to tighten even as she forces her footsteps to remain even and steady. She knows what she sees can't be an illusion. It's too quiet. Something is creeping around them.

The crack of a snapping branch sounds – just one, as if done on purpose to scare them.

At her shoulder, Travers quietly draws his sword.

Something flashes in the darkness – was that gold? Did she see gold?

"HELP–!"

The aborted scream comes from the back of the caravan. Kazan whips her head around fast enough to crack her neck just in time to see one of the Wardens guarding the rear being dragged into the bushes by –

"*Vampires*!" Travers cries out, his yell shattering through the forest.

Chapter Five

"Stay together –!"

A man with an open mouth full of fangs leaps from the trees like a wild animal, tackling Travers around the waist and throwing him off his horse.

Panic descends.

Screams erupt from every direction. The horses break free of their restraints, bolting off into the woods and abandoning their riders. Everyone in the caravan scatters – into the bushes, down the Faebower, tripping over themselves on the road, chasing their horses. Spooked like common prey.

A scream dies in Kazan's throat as fear digs its claws into her.

On the ground, Travers presses his silver star into his attacker's face. The vampire recoils, screeching in pain from the burn on his forehead and Travers has enough time to get to his feet and pull a stake from his belt. It's over so fast. One moment Travers is down, the next he has plunged the wood through the vampire's chest and killed him.

Kazan throws her torch onto the dead creature, letting it catch and send a pyre up through the night.

But he isn't alone. A white-faced woman stalks towards them, dropping the dead and bleeding body of a merchant to the ground. Blood is streaked across her mouth like a smear of lipstick.

She lunges at Travers.

From the darkness, a hand hits Kazan across the back and

she falls into the dirt, knees scraping against one of the ancient stones that make up the Faebower. Her bag tumbles over the ground beneath her. Her hat tears on a tree root and is yanked from her head.

Her sword. She needs her *sword*.

Her assailant stalks forward, looming over her and grinning, fangs barred.

Travers throws aside the woman he's fighting; her shrieks pierce through the screams of the rest as she dies.

"Stay back!" Travers orders.

Sword in one hand, stake in the other, he faces down the vampire attacking Kazan.

Simple steel won't do the trick. The vampire just laughs as Travers's standard Warden blade slashes a bloody line across his chest. The vampire's shirt is torn open and his skin parts, but then, through whatever strange magics of immortality his kind possess, the skin and muscle and sinew begin to regrow, knitting back together until his chest is entirely unmarred. So that's how vampires regenerate. She's always wondered.

Clawed hands rip the Warden's blade asunder. The steel lands ten feet away in the bushes.

Kazan fumbles with the straps around her sword case. Why did she have to wrap the stupid thing with leather? She can't reach it quick enough, her fingers scrambling to get purchase. At last her nails dig under the straps and she pushes the leather aside.

Travers lunges forward with his stake in hand. It's not fast enough. The vampire steps to the side, grabbing Travers's wrist easily and *cracks*. The Warden screams in pain as his wrist snaps like a twig, and the wooden stake slips from his fingers into the dirt.

She sees the whites of his terrified eyes as the vampire sinks his teeth into Travers's throat.

Oh fuck – *fuck* –

Her hands slip over the cloth wrapping and then the sword

is in her grasp, a steady and well-carved grip, a weight that she knows in her heart, a blade that she now has to trust with her life. How good is she *really*? How well does she know her craft? She can boast all she wants about making weapons designed to kill vampires, but now she has to test her own work.

White fangs blur in her vision as the vampire drops Travers's still-breathing body and steps towards her instead.

She rips the sword from the scabbard and *swings*.

The steel meets no resistance as it cleaves the vampire's head from his body. If she didn't know better, she would say there is surprise in his golden eyes as his head hits the ground.

Unsteadily, her entire body shaking like a leaf in a storm, she stumbles over the corpse and looks behind her. Carnage has splattered across the Faebower. Bodies litter what remains of the caravan after those who could run, have. Some corpses lie over the wagons, limbs strewn out as though making angels in the snow, most of them being fed on by a hungry vampire. A handful of humans remain alive – the lucky or the skilled – wielding axes and spears to keep the attackers at bay, relying on slashing and hacking faster than the vampires can regenerate to buy themselves time to flee.

Travers is badly bleeding, but he still lives. In theory, she could do something for him, even if she doesn't know what. One of the three other Wardens had been killed and her eyes fall on the two that remain. A woman in armor fends off two vampires at once, stake in one hand and silver star in the other, a fallen sword at her feet. Deep gouges have been clawed out of her leg and every lunge or bite she dodges makes her falter. The last Warden takes Kazan a moment to locate. He has become a few pieces of strewn-about armor, a smear of gore, and hunks of flesh that a group of vampires are devouring with fervorous hunger.

None of those who still live will last much longer. Neither will Kazan if she stays.

With a handful of dirt and grass, she wipes the dead vampire's blood from her sword and slides it back into its sheath. The silver is too bright; it will shine in the moonlight and make her visible to anyone looking.

Without a second thought, she abandons the rest of the caravan and runs.

She leaves everything except her sword, none of it valuable enough to find, and the weight of it would slow her down. Vampires block the Faebower, but she trusts in her sense of direction enough to know that if she runs through the uncharted area of the Vildenmarr, she can find her way south. Upper Welshire is north and probably closer, but it's uphill. She would tire before the vampires got bored of the chase.

Blood rushes through her ears as she races through the forest. Her feet tear up the underbrush, nothing important to her beyond the knowledge that her only chance is to run as far and as fast as she can. Speed is her only hope – she doesn't have a chance at silence, not against a vampire's keen hearing.

A man with glowing golden eyes comes at her from the right and she's forced to run to the left, unwilling to stop and fight lest she be overpowered by multiple attackers. As Adrius had so casually proved to her earlier this evening, she cannot beat a vampire's sheer strength.

Her pounding heart drowns out everything else. If she just keeps running...

Within minutes, another pursuer chases her from the left.

She is being herded.

The trees part and she stumbles into a clearing; bright warm lights startle her eyes after the darkness of the forest. But the group she has stumbled into isn't human.

Regally dressed vampires sit astride pitch-black stallions. They turn to stare at her as she crashes into the open. Some of them are distracted, a couple are feeding on a less fortunate man who is still pointlessly moaning in pain. There must be at least fifty vampires in the procession, maybe closer to a hundred. The light that had so distracted her comes from the glow of elegant glass lanterns affixed to resplendent carriages.

A few armored vampire knights turn their spears towards her. She spins around, boots sliding over the grass, to find her two pursuers are *right there* on her heels.

"Stay back!" She holds up her sword, still in its scabbard, the sweat on her palms threatening to make the lacquered wooden sheath fall from her grip. "I'm warning you!"

They – they *laugh*.

She slowly turns around in a circle. They haven't moved closer to her, keeping a distance of a good dozen feet. There must be a way out, someplace where there are fewer guards, some sort of opening for her to exploit. There *has* to be.

Her yell has attracted the attention of the nobles as well as the soldiers. One, a blonde woman wearing a bronze velvet cape, strides towards her. The line of guards parts as she approaches, letting her pass into the circle like a champion gladiator entering an arena. There's a sword on her hip but she pays no attention to it. Clearly she doesn't think she'll need it to deal with Kazan; she thinks this will be an easy win. How *dare* that vampire think so little of her.

"How pretty!" one of the other vampires crows.

They snicker at her, watching eagerly as she panics.

The blonde noblewoman gets closer, and more are drawn over. Kazan looks to the carriages in the hopes that she might steal a horse or something, and she sees –

Adrius.

Firelight flickers over Adrius De Vere's frozen features. He is without his glamor, staring at her with unreserved shock in his eyes. Something in her stomach twists unpleasantly. She'd been perfectly content with never meeting him again, with parting ways after an enjoyable night. Was that his game all along? String her along, let her make a fool of herself for his amusement? How he must have been *laughing* inside as he lured her into kissing him. How bloody *thrilled* he must be to see her in this trap – *his* trap.

"Stay. Back," Kazan grits out through her teeth, returning her attention to the woman approaching her.

The noblewoman snickers at her. "Oh, this one's funny."

This one's going to fucking kill you.

Anger and terror run through her in equal parts, making her heart race and setting fire through her veins. Battle lust, fear, whatever it is, it wants to rip off heads to get to safety.

"Let me go!" Kazan spits out.

"We've got most of your group already, I think we'd prefer to take the complete set." The blonde vampire keeps getting closer – one step – another –

She puts her hand on Kazan's shoulder.

Kazan slams her sword's pommel into the vampire's right eye.

Claws scratch her coat as the woman stumbles backwards, more from shock than pain at first, as if stunned that a human would have the audacity to strike her. Then a faint curl of smoke drifts from her bloodied eye socket as the silver and rowan come into effect. She clutches at her ruined eye and a scream rips from her jaws that is as much a banshee's shriek of rage as it is the horrified wail of a child experiencing their first scraped knee.

"Lady Amelia!" someone cries.

A twisted mess of dark flesh and white ooze is all that remains in Amelia's eye socket, fluids dripping from between her trembling fingers. The skin around it bubbles up and burns, blackened shreds still smoking.

"You filthy human!" Amelia's scream must shred her vocal cords. "You *filthy miserable human*!"

Guards scramble to help her, two of them grabbing her by the arms and hauling her out of the circle. Dirt and blood streak her pretty cape as she shrieks in agony and hisses out garbled, nonsensical insults.

Another one of the monsters who chased Kazan through the woods rushes towards her. She spins around as he leaps on her, claws out, flashing in the firelight. Her body tells her what to do: her thumb flicks against the guard of her weapon, releasing the blade and revealing a flash of the silver that runs through it, and she doesn't so much draw the blade as throw the scabbard desperately to the side.

The vampire falls on her sword and the blade sinks deep into his chest.

He coughs sticky blood onto her coat as he dies, clawing at the sword handle and burning his hands in the process. Before anyone around her has the chance to react, she pulls the sword from his heart and brandishes it wildly in front of her. There is no elegance in her movements, just a frantic whirling around, pointing the tip at whichever vampire gets too close. The silver shines like a star in the moonlight and faint wisps of smoke rise from the blood smeared over the blade.

"I *said* stay the fuck back!" she cries, rage rushing through her voice, covering the fear. Her hands shake and she grips the blade ever tighter until her knuckles are as pale as the silver. "I already killed one of your friends in the woods – that's two I've killed now. Do any of you really want to be the third?"

The vampires circling her don't look afraid, but they do wait. Not on her, however.

"She's *hilarious*. Let's take her, shall we?"

The voice belongs to a man with brown hair that shines like copper in the firelight. He's tall and reedy, dressed in a velvet coat of rich purple. Gold jewelry pierces his face, a ring on his lower lip, more gold hanging from his ears, the entire affair sparkling under the torches. Thick dark circles sit under his eyes and the grin on his lips is like a crack in a mirror, one step out of sync with the rest of the world.

Oh, she'll show them *hilarious*.

He waves at Adrius. "Why don't you give it a go? Although I would take care not to be as overly enthusiastic as Amelia."

Adrius bows deeply. "Yes, Lord Dasar. Right away."

Kazan raises her sword immediately and lowers her knees, an opening stance as familiar as breathing. All those years of frustrated practice in the hope that one day she would be welcomed into the Wardens' ranks – now she has a use for all that wishing and training. She embraces the rush of terror and rage flowing through her, lets it seep into her muscles and bones until it radiates through every inch of her body, like swallowing burning coals. She glares straight at Adrius, unwavering though all instincts beg her to flee.

He calmly walks towards her, not sparing a glance for Amelia who still clutches her eye on the ground and whimpers.

With a delicate hiss of steel, he draws a beautiful rapier with a point fine enough to pierce Kazan's heart even through her many layers of clothing. That veneer of restraint is still painted over his face as he circles her. One hand behind his back, the point of his sword low to the ground, in a poised and practiced stance. At least he treats her like a legitimate threat. At least he affords her this one dignity after everything he's done.

"You needn't make this difficult, Miss Korvic," he says, eyes trailing over her in a revolting mockery of their earlier encounter. Then he had meant to flatter. Now he picks apart her weaknesses. "I'd prefer not to fight you, but I will if you force my hand."

"And here I was thinking you'd be thrilled by this, you backstabbing bastard!" she snarls. "After all, didn't you say you'd *love* to see me try and kill you? Will you still love it when I shove this rowan through your *fucking skull*?!"

He almost looks taken aback – and then the expression vanishes from his face completely.

With a scream in her chest, she rushes him.

He's fast – faster than she'd thought he would be. The first desperate swing of her sword is deflected with a tap of his own blade, and when she uses that parry to whirl around and strike from the other direction, he doesn't even blink at the silver coming for his head. A glint of steel in the firelight is her only warning as he elegantly dodges her blade and steps into her attack, bringing his rapier up to pierce her shoulder. She turns her run into a slide, skidding under his sword on her shins, dirt and grass staining her breeches. Low to the ground, she slashes her sword at the backs of his knees, hoping to cripple him.

With a quick, neat flick, he snaps his blade back to block hers, a clear ring of metal on metal as they collide. She throws herself to the side to avoid his next downward strike. Her knees scrape across the rough ground as she rolls and comes up into a low crouch. With her free hand, she grabs the small knife tucked into her belt and throws it at him. It flings through the air, true as day.

For a second, she thinks it will connect, but then he merely tilts his head to the side and it goes flying past him.

The blade hits a carriage, quivering as it embeds in the wood. It missed a woman's head by scant inches. The vampire's elaborate hairdo loses a few strands but she doesn't look worried in the least. Instead she... she claps.

Fucking *claps*. Like Kazan is a pet performing a particularly impressive trick.

She throws herself at Adrius with a furious cry, stabbing straight at his head; vibrations ripple through the metal as he deflects the blow with his rapier. Momentum throws her past him and then he slashes right through her defenses. The tip of his blade barely brushes over her chest as she jumps back just in time. She twists her sword around in her hand, bringing it up to block his follow-up strike.

Every fluid hit, every successive collision of their weapons, sends shockwaves running up her arms. It feels almost comforting, the same sensation as repeatedly striking a hot billet of steel. The sort of stress she has dealt with for years. If he expects her to tire, he will be sorely disappointed.

She drops to one knee, sword held in a high guard above her head to block. When he brings his blade down, she flings the blow away with all her strength and then rolls to her feet, striking up in a quick slash that she hopes will get through while his sword tip is thrown to the side. He's stronger than her but she counts on getting one hit – one good hit from her blade, and the silver and steel will do their duty. She has no doubt that the pain would be enough to cripple him as it did Amelia. That's all she needs. A single hit.

The way his wrist bends as he slides through her attack is near impossible, rapier circling around her sword. She barely has enough time to bring her crossguard up to catch his blade before it cuts her hands.

The move is seamless. He tips his handle up, blade down, and cuts a circle in the air around her weapon. Pain flares through her hand as the hilt is wrenched down. With that one neat little move, her sword is ripped from her grasp. It flies through the air, blade sinking into the dirt where it stands upright in the soil like a grave marker.

Indescribable loss guts her. It's not just that her best tool to survive has been taken from her, but her dearest creation too. She has to push down the panic and do something. If she can find a weapon, she can *hurt him*, and she craves that with a frenzied, boiling passion. She makes to run for her fallen sword, hand reaching out, fingers so close and yet so far.

Not quick enough. Adrius flips his rapier in his hand and slams the dull hilt into her stomach. Air is shoved out of her lungs, agony blooming in her chest while white spots dance in her vision and she gasps for oxygen. He throws her body off his sword, sending her crashing to the ground five feet away with a pained grunt.

No, damn it, *no*!

She pushes herself out of the dirt onto aching knees, her entire body protesting, and grabs both knives from her boots, one in each hand. She swings out with one of the knives, aiming to stab straight through his thigh, only for him to snatch her forearm before she can strike. His clawed thumb digs into her pulse point, forcing her fingers to spasm around the hilt until it falls from her numb hand. Pain lances through her arm and, praying for whatever miracle the saints will afford her, she tries again with her second knife.

Adrius brings his boot down on her other wrist. A scream wrenches its way out of her throat as he grinds her hand into the ground, breaking her grip on the dagger.

"That's enough," he tells her flatly.

One of the guards picks up the fallen sword. *Her* sword. The man offers the blade to the gold-pierced lord who ordered her death, wrapping the hilt in protective cloth. "Lord Dasar. The woman's weapon, if it pleases you."

Dasar's spider-like fingers clasp the hilt –

"That's *my* fucking sword!"

A burning, cruel possessiveness overwhelms her. She rips her hand out from under Adrius's boot, ignoring the way it scrapes practically half her skin off, ignoring him completely, ignoring everything except for the fact that some rich fucking vampire holds the best damn piece she's ever made in her life. That's hers. *Hers*! How *dare* he hold it!

A guard buries his fist in her gut before she can so much as try to get close to Dasar. After having Adrius slam his sword hilt into her stomach, the additional blow makes stars of pain burst in her vision. Iron floods her mouth and she forces herself not to spit out the blood, some distant part of her mind remembering that she shouldn't make them hungrier than they already are.

A half-dozen vampires mob her while she chokes on silent screams and bitter blood. Hands grab her wrists, pinning her arms behind her back. A foot slams into her knee, forcing a cry from her and bringing her to the ground.

All the madness of a captured animal rages in her. She shrieks and howls, clawing at the vampires that hold and press her into the dirt, trying to kick and punch without skill, just wild fury. Her head twists to the side and she opens her jaw, sinking her teeth into an attacker's arm until foul, cold blood bursts in her mouth. It's disgusting and filthy but she bites down harder until the man rips his arm away then backhands her, dirt and blood smearing across her cheek.

"Kazan." Adrius stands in front of her, staring down with emotionless eyes. "It would be best if you stopped fighting."

"Fuck you!" she screams, spitting the mouthful of blood at him, both her own and that of the man currently holding her down.

Adrius grips his blade in a reverse hold. "Very well."

The pommel of his sword flashes towards her head and she can't move out of the way –

Everything goes dark.

Chapter Six

Warm lights swim in front of Kazan. Pain throbs in her temples, an ache in her hands. She forces her heavy eyelids to crack open and her eyes attempt to take in her surroundings.

The first thing she can focus on is her hands. She sits upright at a table, and a couple of gem-encrusted rings rest on her fingers, rings that she has never seen before. White lace falls over her hands, attached to plum-colored sleeves made of a rich silk, and she wears a dress.

Why is she wearing a dress? She didn't put one on. Is she hungover? She has been on ill-advised benders before, but normally finds herself on her bedroom floor or in someone else's bed, head spinning. Unfamiliar dresses were not usually part of the experience, no matter how wasted she was.

Memories flood back in a choppy sea of images. She had been in the Vildenmarr – there was a caravan ambush – Adrius.

By the saints, how is she still alive? They beat her, she had no way out, she should have... Her mind goes cold, ice creeping into her skull. She should have been killed.

Pain shoots through her left hand as she tries to move her fingers. She shifts to see a bandage wrapped around her wrist, and she can feel the sharp sting of exposed flesh beneath it. Her right hand still aches from where Adrius stepped on it, but this sharper pain is something new.

An object sits on the table in front of her, set where a dinner plate should be. A crown. An old, slightly tarnished, golden crown. A fat, glossy ruby is set in the center of it, and still-tacky blood is smeared across the surface. Her blood? As she stares at it, that smear fades into the gemstone and the ruby darkens, as though drinking in her blood with the same gluttony as a vampire.

She tears her eyes away with disgust and looks to the rest of the room. It's a banquet hall, of all things. It's massive, so large that she can't even begin to imagine how much money was spent in its construction. Overhead stretches a ribbed vaulted ceiling from which dozens of gilded chandeliers are hung, heavy from gold and covered with so many melting candles that threaten to snap the petite chains holding them up. In the middle of the ceiling, a circle of clear glass allows the night sky to shine down into the hall, a crescent moon above like the imprint of an ivory thumbnail.

A sea of people spreads out before her, decorated in a rainbow of colors and glittering with jewels, blindingly bright under all the candles. People cluster at tables covered with platters of foods so exotic and decadent that she can't identify half of them. And there's wine, everywhere wine, bottles upon bottles adorning every table in all colors of glass known to man. No, it's not wine, she realizes. Or at least not all wine. It's blood. These aren't *people* sitting around here. They're vampires, every last one of them.

Don't panic, she tells herself.

"Ah!" an excited voice next to her declares. "She's awake!"

A cheer rings out through the hall.

Kazan blearily blinks and turns to look at the speaker: the man from the Vildenmarr, the one who told Adrius to fight her. What had Adrius called him? She can't recall.

"What…" She trails off, not even sure where to begin asking questions.

Hands reach out from somewhere, and another vampire picks up the crown and places it on her head.

Still adorned with gold and with an ecstatic glow in his eyes, the man beside her raises a goblet full of a liquid so deeply red as to be almost black. "To Kazan Korvic! The Queen of the Vampires!"

Cries of excitement ring out, vampires cheer and clap, some even laughing. Queen? No. They couldn't have turned her, could they? She runs her tongue over every single nook and cranny in her mouth, searching for the feel of fangs. There's nothing but normal human teeth. So, if she's still human...

It's a *show*.

A show where she's somehow the star and has no idea what on earth is going on. She thinks to run, but realizes she wouldn't know where to run *to*. And in a room full of predators, it would be pointless.

Fear sends her heart racing and her mind can't begin to comprehend what's happening around her. She still tries to wrap her head around why she didn't die in the Vildenmarr, and everything else is waiting to catch up with her.

Don't panic, she tells herself again, firmer this time.

The man offers her a goblet, this one full of wine. "A queen should give a toast at her own party."

"I'm not a queen," she replies, her tongue finally deciding to function properly. "Who the hell are you?"

"High Lord Dasar, sovereign leader of House Gambit, at your service, Majesty."

"Don't call me that. What's going on?"

"Every year we pick one lucky human to host this little party. It's a tremendous honor! We have three days of feasting and dancing, and you'll have all the finest things to eat and wear, and you'll meet all the most important people –"

"And after three days?" Kazan can barely hear herself – can barely hear *anything* over the roar of blood in her veins. "Then what?"

Dasar grins at her. "Then... you're the feast! But don't think about that right now – just have *fun*!"

That axe of a sentence hits her. Her stomach twists like it

has been kicked out from her chest. She chokes, her throat burning. They're going to kill her. They're going to taunt her for three fucking days and then drink her blood and she can't... she has no way to stop them.

What can she do? There has to be something. She doesn't want to die. Not here, not to these bastards, not ever.

Don't panic, she keeps thinking, *just don't panic*. She must try and come up with something, some clever way out, some way to trick them into letting her go. They're not infallible, there must be *something*.

But there's so many of them. Even if she fools one, she can't fool them all. She has no sword, no way of killing them or fighting her way out.

Don't panic, don't panic.

She's going to die. Isn't she?

Don't panic don't panic don't panic don't –

DAY ONE

Chapter Seven

A blonde man caresses Kazan's cheek with his claws, turning her head this way and that as he examines her. "Oh, she's an adorable thing, isn't she? A bit flawed, what with this unfortunate mess on her face, but, on the whole, yes, very quaint. I can see why Dasar chose her. He does so love polishing up broken things."

"Don't get too close," a tall woman with heavy makeup warns.

The woman stands nearby, hovering by the man's shoulders, part of the crowd of vampires trying to get a better look at Kazan. Some of them just chat in the background, others have bowed to her in false and overly theatrical supplication, snickering all the while as their friends goad them on, wanting to play with the new human. Almost all of them have remarked on how they hope she will taste. Not merely on what they want from her blood. Some have said they hope her bone marrow is soft enough to slurp, some want a satisfying chew from her muscles, and one memorable vampire had waxed rhapsodic about the variety of flavors found in a human spleen.

"If Dasar's to be believed, she killed two soldiers and took Amelia's eye when they captured her," the woman informs the blonde man, quieter for only him to hear. No one cares if Kazan hears. "For the first time, I regret skipping Dasar's flamboyant hunting parties, if only so that I might have been there to chastise Amelia on the spot."

"Poor Amelia," the man coos. "I was wondering why I haven't seen her yet, her absence has me *quite* put out. Is she pouting in her chambers? Did Her *Majesty* wound her pride?"

"Don't bother talking to it. The little thing hasn't spoken since she got here."

The claws on Kazan's cheek dig into her skin.

He leans down to get a closer look at Kazan, dragging his claws until he has one finger lifting up her chin. He stares at her with lidded eyes, lips ever so slightly parted as if preparing to sink his teeth into her.

"Careful, my dear Weisz," Dasar's chipper voice says. "She might bite."

The claws pull back and the man, Weisz, is all false smiles and syrup. "If she bites, she'll be right at home here, wouldn't you say?"

Dasar's laugh is like jolly windchimes. The depth she'd expect from a man with a heavy belly and round cheeks, mixed with the airy giggliness of someone blowing through a reed. "And this is why I have the best taste in regents." He slides an arm around Kazan's shoulders, far too close but not enough to break through the haze keeping her still as a statue. "Allow me to introduce the darling High Lord Weisz of Rockford, and his astringent sister, High Lady Ezelind of Mooncliffe. You did just take the eye of Weisz's seneschal, but that's water under the bridge now, isn't it? Far more delicious courtly intrigues are on offer than a wounded underling."

Weisz puffs up with the indignation of a child denied a toy. "Amelia's mutilation is *not* yours to make fun of. It's mine."

Ezelind pets her brother's arm to hush him. "Now, now, don't take offense. Just another of Dasar's jokes, *isn't it?*" she says, as though the words are a spear she's pointing at the two. "We were just saying how much we love your pick this year, weren't we, Weisz?"

His pick. Kazan. She's a *pick*. She doesn't want to hear Dasar's reply. She doesn't want him to speak his thoughts about her worth or her value. He doesn't deserve to *have* those thoughts at all. Normally a thousand retorts would be flying out of her lips, but right now her tongue is made of lead and all words remain trapped in the pit of her stomach.

"Your approval means oh-so much to me, my dear," Dasar says, either entirely serious or his grasp of sarcasm is so masterful that it's undetectable.

He removes his arm from Kazan and reaches to his hip – to her sword. He has her sword. He stole it from her in the Vildenmarr. Deep inside her, spite flares. Panic had crusted her bones over like a glacier engulfing a mountain and extinguished almost all emotions. But now, a tiny crack forms. All it takes is that little possessive tap of Dasar's gloved finger on her weapon.

He took her sword; he took her dignity. She refuses to let him take her life too.

Somehow, her body moves.

"Lord Dasar." She pushes drunkenly to her feet. The crown on her head feels unpleasantly heavy and she removes it, placing it softly down on the table. Her voice is flat, dead, just as dead as she'll be in only a few days. "I am going to retire for the evening."

I want out.

"Oh," Weisz remarks, raising an eyebrow. "Would you look at that. She speaks."

Dasar looks thrilled even as he replies, "But Highness, it would be such a tragedy to leave your own party so soon! Is your human flesh so weak as to require rest *already*? No, no, you simply need a bit of freshening up." Regrettably, he hands her sword to a nearby attendant who scurries off with it, and she watches it disappear. He gestures to one of the many hallways off the massive center hall. "Let me show you to your rooms."

He places her hand on his arm as though they're old friends and leads her from the hall. Every vampire they pass lights up to see her, calling out greetings and laughs, but at least Dasar's presence seems to keep them from touching her. Lights and music dazzle the part of her that isn't still frozen glacier, the sounds and sights of the main hall threatening to sweep her away if she lets them.

That chipper grin of Dasar's doesn't fade as he guides her through the twisting maze of halls off the main hall and leads her through many doors and up stairways, drowning her in the labyrinth of the castle. If only he still had her sword; she would steal it from him in a heartbeat. Rip it from his spindly hands. Tear it from him, belt and all. She would sever his head from his shoulders and spill his blood all over the embroidered carpet.

The palatial building is confusing, but she knows he predominantly leads her upwards. Her footsteps are mechanical and dull, like the lifeless ticking of a clock. Dasar takes her up ten flights of stairs until she feels sure they are on one of the highest floors above the banquet hall.

"I've set out all the best jewelry for you, my sweet Highness," Dasar says pleasantly. "Tell me, do you prefer gold or diamonds?"

"Silver."

"What a darling mouth you have." He says it with reverence, not sarcasm, and that makes it worse. He finally ends her march and gestures to the ornate set of double doors in front of them. "Your chambers, dear Majesty. I'll send up your lady in waiting shortly and she can explain your fun-filled schedule for the next three days. I do hope you like her."

The thought of a vampire hanging around her constantly makes her blanche. "I don't need anyone."

"There's no harm in playing along. You might even come to see the amusement of it. We do, after all."

She can't stop herself from hissing, "I won't let you do this."

"Every human thinks that at first." He pats her cheek, and she wants to bite his hand off. "This party has happened every year for two hundred and fifty-three years. Even if the Wardens have noticed one mere human vanishing per year, they've never gotten within spitting distance of my abode. There's no convenient human assistance coming to your rescue and nothing you can try that someone else hasn't already attempted. Why not simply take what enjoyment you can from the next three days?"

She spits at his feet.

"How delightfully undignified," he says, grinning.

She cannot take another damned word from him. Reaching behind her, she fumbles for the doorknob until her unsteady hand grasps the bronze latch. She yanks it open, stumbles inside, and slams it shut in Dasar's unbearable face.

A series of sprawling rooms greets her. A sitting room, a bedroom behind it, a bathroom behind another door, and every inch of the place covered in red velvet, plush carpeting, marble, and more fucking gold chandeliers.

She takes a few tentative steps forward and comes to stand in front of a loveseat, rich crimson velvet over an elaborately carved frame of dark wood. This is the sort of finery she sees at Rask's parties, not in a room she's expected to live in. This sort of opulence is something she always dreamt of having for her own home but accepted that such things would never happen. Instead, it lies wasted in some horrible vampire mansion, housing a sacrificial lamb before a slaughter.

Alone, finally, she sits down and allows herself to sink into the excessively comfortable cushions. But the moment she sits, she realizes her mistake. In the banquet hall, her back was straight, her skirts starched stiff, and her expression stoic. But now that she has broken that rigidity, even slightly, she can't stop breaking. Like glass shattering in on itself, sharp pieces compacting and squeezing, filling her lungs and choking her. The glass claws at her insides, shredding and tearing and crushing.

She presses her hands over her mouth, determined to

prevent any sound from escaping. Something wet and hot runs down between her fingers. Her eyes sting. The room around her blurs and darkens, swimming out of focus into a nebulous void of confinement while she suffocates in slow motion.

She needs to stop this. She needs to stop this right now and pull herself together. If she doesn't, she will die in three days. It's just a fact.

Many humans die young. Another fact of life. Kazan remembers the ringing of the village bells and the way her father had grabbed a shovel from the garden when vampires attacked, all those years ago. At six years old, she had been too young to remember anything solid, and was left only with vague memories of her father's dark hair as he sang and the warm smell of his shirt when he put her to bed at night.

She is used to being on her own. She has been alone practically her whole life. She's always been fine with that, by necessity if nothing else. But, in this moment, she wants...

She rocks back and forth in her seat, tasting tears, a helpless cry for her father tearing up the back of her mouth.

Is this what they've reduced her to? A sniveling mess blubbering for a father she cannot properly remember? Something white hot and *angry* blooms in the void that's taken over her body.

Damn them all! She will *not* let them do this to her. She's *better* than this. She *will* escape, no matter what. *Damn* the odds.

Her hands betray her, shaking as she wipes her tears away. Two hundred and fifty-three years. Two hundred and fifty-three victims. Surely, she can come up with something that two hundred and fifty-three people haven't already tried? A thousand shingles can form a roof, but it only takes one sliding out of place to let the rain in.

Focus, she thinks. Look at the problem like looking at tiles of bloom steel that need to be properly stacked together – the high-carbon and low-carbon laid out into something neat and orderly and precise.

She fists her hands into the fabric of her skirts and forces herself to consider the situation rationally. What does she know? From what she saw on her way here, she knows there must be several other wings of the manor – it is simply too tall for it to not be wider as well. Her mouth twists into a scowl as the map begins to form in her mind. She must be closer to the heart of the building, given that her room has no outside windows. As traditional and predictable as it is, climbing out of a window is the first escape attempt that comes to mind.

What else does she have?

When she casts her gaze about the room, the mantle draws her eye. Not for the way it's been ornately carved and gilded, but because she has a *fireplace*. They climbed ten floors to get here, how high up is she? How close to the top of the manor, how short is the chimney?

She gets down on her knees. The grate is difficult to remove with just her fingers, and black ash rubs off on her hands as she sets it to the side. She pokes her head into the fireplace and finds the chimney flue is maybe a square foot wide. Even if she squeezed, her shoulders would never fit. Damn it. It was probably a stupid idea anyway. Two hundred and fifty-three people before her. How many of those tried the chimney first? What methods will be expected of her, what are they prepared for?

"Excuse me, Your Highness."

Kazan barely avoids banging her head against the brick. She gets to her feet and dusts her skirts off, looking as dignified as she can for someone who just had their head in the coals.

The intruder is a young woman, soft brown hair and skin tinged with that bloodless look of all vampires. The woman gives a stumbling, petite curtsey that implies her biggest concern in life is figuring out which utensils are used for which dinner course. "I'm Isidora Woodridge, your lady in waiting."

"It's an insult to you, isn't it?" Kazan guesses, intending her words to cut. "A vampire being forced to tend to a human like this. You're not playing the game like they are; you're being made to do the gritty job."

Isidora's cheeks turn a bright red. "I – well," she mumbles.

"Which of them forced you into this? Dasar?"

"He – he has that right. He's my lord, I do as he instructs."

"Don't you *hate* him for it?"

She squeaks like the world's tiniest piglet stuck with a needle. "I – erm – that is…" She clears her throat. "May I assist you, Highness? Lord Dasar has instructed me to tidy you up and acquaint you with your… um, your duties."

"Duties?"

"Well, there's a lot for a queen to do. A number of people who um… want your time. My Lord Dasar is inclined to show you around his Citadel." Isidora chews on her lower lip and tentatively adds, "I'm sure you'll find it pretty here? And there are dances and feasts and rituals, of course…"

Kazan's eyes narrow into slits. "Rituals?"

"That is –" she says, floundering. "Well, I mean to say… Highness, may I please assist you in tidying up?"

"And what does that mean?" Kazan demands. "Do you mean to polish up my skin? Perfume my neck? Leave me in nothing more than a shift to make me easier for consumption?"

"I'm supposed to fix your hair and makeup," Isidora mumbles.

Oh. Well, in that case… She gathers up her ridiculous silk skirt and plops down in front of the vanity. "Get on with it then, I haven't got all day."

Chapter Eight

As Isidora helps turn Kazan's hair into a work of art and paints her face, she goes through a list of things that Kazan is expected to do. The mess of partying and events with Dasar go unelaborated upon. Those rituals, perhaps? Kazan has no idea what Isidora could be referring to, but considering how many times she dodges the subject, they must be important.

Once Kazan's appearance meets vampiric standards, Isidora ushers her out of the room with a flutter of hands and a few mumbled suggestions. A guard waits outside and stoically follows behind them, a spear clutched in his hand to discourage Kazan from doing anything rash.

The party remains in full swing. Unfortunate, as it means an uncountable number of people buzz around her the moment she enters the main hall in a sea of leering faces and sneering giggles.

As people push past Isidora to paw at Kazan and pay her cruel compliments, she ignores the admirers and instead tries to search the crowd for a familiar face. Dasar is twisted, Isidora insipid, but despite everything that has happened, she knows Adrius is at least rational. She would sooner trust a ravenous bear than place her faith in him again, but he still owes her answers. Answers she intends to get, even if she must rip them from him one by one. The bastard deserves it.

"I want to talk to De Vere," she tells Isidora. "He's here, isn't he?"

Isidora freezes up and nearly trips over her own feet. "De Vere? You... But he's... Highness, I couldn't possibly."

"You're not very committed to this charade, are you?"

"I am! It's simply that De Vere is... *dangerous.*"

As if she doesn't already know that. "In what way, exactly? Because I'm uncertain if you've noticed, but *everyone* here is dangerous to me."

When Isidora says nothing further, Kazan turns sharply on her heel and reaches out for one of the many vampires whirling around her. She grabs a man by the cuff of his sleeve, and he doesn't hesitate to face her, a grin on his lips and a shine in his eyes.

He plucks her hand from his sleeve and is about to kiss her knuckles before she yanks her arm away. Without pause, he says, "I'm honored to have your attention, Majesty. Would you care for a dance, or perhaps a drink?"

"Do your highness a favor," she demands, "and tell me where I can find Adrius De Vere."

The man draws back as far as he can without leaping away. "De Vere? What could a lovely lady like yourself possibly want with someone like him? No, no. Best to stay away from such unsavory company. Remain here with us, my friends and I will treat you with all the delicacy you deserve as our queen."

Isidora tries to step between the two of them, though her courage fails before she can get even halfway. "Sir, please. I'm supposed to bring her to my Lord Dasar..."

"Oh, well, in that case..." The man gives Kazan a pompous bow as though he's dismissing her instead of being dismissed himself. "Enjoy your party, Highness."

With a fumbling apology, Isidora continues to clear a path through the crowd. Though Kazan looks over every inch of the hall, Adrius doesn't magically appear. Is he keeping his distance from everyone? If so, she can't help envying him.

Dasar lounges at the high table where Kazan had previously

been forced to sit, a gaggle of revelers surrounding him. He lights up the moment his eyes land on her.

"I've brought Her Majesty back as –" Isidora tries.

He waves her off before she can finish. "Lovely, simply lovely! What excellent work you've done, Isidora dear." Though he addresses Isidora, he doesn't look away from Kazan, his gaze heavy on her shoulders. "Such red lips compliment your scar. Now, as much as I hate to let you leave before you've finished your dinner – or is it breakfast now for you humans? – the most acerbic Lady Ezelind has requested your presence. T'would be tragic indeed to deny her, no? Especially after she seemed so… *enamored* with you earlier."

A bit of disappointment would be healthy for this lot, Kazan thinks. She's about to vocalize that thought when he beckons for one of the revelers to attend him.

"Be a dear and scurry off," he tells the newcomer, who nods enthusiastically to his every word. "Find my darling Sutcliffe and have her send someone to prepare the basement for later. As for you, Isidora, you'll find Ezelind skulking about my menagerie."

Isidora curtseys. "Yes, my lord."

"When you say Ezelind has requested my presence," Kazan demands, her jaw shaking as she stands her ground, "how much of my blood has she requested as well?"

Dasar's eyes widen in a show of surprise that borders sarcastically exaggerated or honestly overdramatic. "Why, Highness, I would hate for you to think that I've mislead you. When I said that you would be the feast on the third day, I meant it. This is my Citadel. My domain, my rules, and as such Ezelind wouldn't dream of supping upon your lifesblood till then." He flicks his wrist at her. "Run along now."

Isidora escorts her away without further argument, their armed guard still trailing after.

As they skirt around the vibrant center of the manor, the sounds of partying echo through the walls, everyone enjoying the promise of laughing at and eventually killing Kazan. That mix of panic and hatred flares up again, a familiar combination to her now. She desperately wants to grind every single one of them into the ground, preferably nose first.

The menagerie is misleadingly named. She had expected to be taken outside, perhaps, or to some other place where beasts might be safely kept. Instead, the place is not unlike a museum or a library. Thick curtains fall from the high ceiling to the polished floor, turning the room into a labyrinth that muffles the noise of their footsteps. A musty smell, like old paper, floats among the honeyed wood, and dust motes drift through the air like flakes of gold.

Kazan looks over her shoulder as they enter, watching the guard take up post at the doorway. But what truly captures her attention is what hangs above the entryway. A drawing, easily twice as long as she is tall, is framed upon the wall. Faded ink displays a detailed drawing of a manor perched atop a rocky hill, next to a map that appears to be the same shape as the manor.

"Is this... Dasar's Citadel?" she asks. "As in where we are now?"

Isidora leaps at the opportunity to parrot off, "Oh yes. He commissioned it quite some time ago from a human cartographer, a woman he took a liking to and um... well, he didn't end up having her, but he kept the map as a token."

The manor appears to be in roughly the formation of a lowercase 't', with the main banquet hall in the center, as well as what Kazan thinks are her chambers. Below that are the kitchens and dungeons and an area marked as 'livestock (human)' that she tries not to think about too hard – there's little she can do about it and she would prefer not to make herself sick imagining it. The longest arm of the manor stretches to the south, where most of the permanent residence chambers are located. Below are servant quarters and storage rooms. There's more, of course. Statuaries and galleries and dance halls and parlors, but those are scattered everywhere as though the architect had more rooms of leisure than they knew what to do with.

"Why don't I show you more, Highness?" Isidora says, moving away from the map. "I know Lord Dasar would um... be pleased to know you are seeing the best he has to offer."

Isidora doesn't wait for an answer and continues to walk along as she rambles off information about how glorious the Citadel is, the entire thing sounding as though it has been drilled into her skull like a teacher instructing students on mathematics. Clearly, she has found a far more comfortable niche to be in than answering Kazan's questions.

Kazan remains quiet and begins to commit as much of the map to memory as she can. Knowing which way to run is key to getting the hell out of here.

After a few minutes, Isidora's droning voice begins to fade as she continues her recitation unaware that Kazan is no longer following her. After burning an image of the map into her brain, she turns to the rest of the menagerie. She walks in a different direction from Isidora, making her way through the halls of curtains. The place seems to be filled predominantly with pedestals, each covered in glass and in all manner of sizes.

The menagerie is so large that she can't even see where it ends. She could likely retrace her steps to the door she entered from, but from where she stands, it appears an endless expanse of curtains and plinths and low, warm lights from a smattering of candelabras. At first, it feels terrifying, to know that it could swallow her whole, but then she finds it comforting. She could escape into it.

As she goes further into the depths, the display plinths become more and more numerous and more and more dirty. Despite what appears to be the occasional effort on someone's part to keep the place clean, circles of dust lie around the plinths, as though servants are afraid to come too close to them. When she takes a closer look at the stained glass covering a plinth, she sees something inside, something metallic. A gauntlet?

It *is* a gauntlet. As she steps closer, she can read the small, tarnished plaque beneath its glass casing.

Armor of Grand Warden Claire Laurent.

Grand Warden Laurent. Under her oversight, the Wardens ushered in a full decade of relative peace and safety. Until Laurent was slain in a vampire attack, her forces scattered, and her body torn apart. That was over a hundred years ago. Why would a piece of her armor be in a vampire manor? Why would it be on display?

She darts to the plinth across the way. This one is a tall case, covered with so much dirt that she can barely see through the yellowed glass to glimpse the shadowy object within – a tattered but still intact cloak, the leather faded and metal clasps no longer shining.

Cloak of Hunter Tess, the Bogwitch.

While Kazan doesn't know the name, she recognizes the title. It's more of a myth, but rumor has it that hundreds of years ago, a woman patrolled the marshes and bogs in the southern parishes, forging paths for human travelers that needed safe passage to the rest of Mavazem. She became known as the Bogwitch for her uncanny ability to make rowan trees grow in the marshy climates in defiance of their natural habitat.

Morbid curiosity propels Kazan from plinth to plinth. Here, a set of bronze earrings. There, a wooden longbow. She realizes after a dozen or so, that they are *human* trophies. All of them. Dasar's menagerie of victories. Heroes who dedicated their lives to saving people, to ensuring peace and safety wherever they could, who died to help others. Something that, deep down, she knows she would never do. That great, selfless sacrifice that all these people embodied. And now what's left of them has been condemned to an afterlife of entertaining an eccentric vampire. Is that what's going to happen to her? Does Dasar keep a list of every one of his kings and queens? Will he take her bloodless bones and display them in an unvisited corner of his menagerie?

"Poor you."

She shrieks.

A man... a person... a *thing* stands before her, all gangly limbs and sunken eye sockets but a distinct lack of vampiric eyes. Yet he's not human. His skin is a pasty paint splatter of green and white and it flakes off his body in places, leaving behind white bone beneath tattered clothing, like a dead fish washed up on a riverbank. As she watches, a piece of skin hanging off his jaw falls, the papery thing floating to the ground with the slowness of falling leaves. His body is fading at the edges and if she squints, she can partially see through him, his image superimposed upon the library behind.

A horrible realization dawns on her and she stumbles backwards until her hip smacks into the painful edge of a plinth.

"You're a geist," she whispers.

She has seen a saint before, although despite her confident proclamation to Adrius earlier, she hadn't gotten a particularly close look at them. But as she ogles this geist, she can see the similarities, the same pasty shroud hangs over it, just like the saint. But this is no friend to humanity. It is a wild thing, one of the dangers that lurks in the mountains and the nights of Mavazem.

The thing walks up to the trophy case she'd been examining. Although he moves his legs, his feet don't touch the ground, as they disappear halfway down when she looks. "You won't be."

"What do you mean?" she asks. "I won't be a geist?"

He drifts towards the longbow contained in the case, hands passing through the glass as though it's made of water. "You won't be."

Footsteps patter through the halls.

"Human!" Isidora must be worried if she's momentarily forgotten the pretense of this entire charade. When Kazan

turns to her, she skids to a stop in the corridor. "I mean –
Majesty. Are you alright? I heard you scream."

"Am I *alright*?" She gapes at the geist, still hovering there,
and then turns back to Isidora. "What kind of stupid question
is *that*?"

"I mean –"

"She can't see me," the geist whispers.

Kazan makes a split-second choice. Usually in a hostile
situation, she tends to favor secrecy, and she has no reason to
tell Isidora about the geist. "It's nothing," she says sharply. "I
was disgusted by this foul display of Dasar's. Now get out. I'll
be along to satisfy Ezelind's whims in a moment and I want to
take a closer look at this."

Isidora turns as red in the face as vampires possibly can,
which merely stains her cheeks with a purple tinted rouge.
"Right. Well. I suppose I'll… five minutes, yes?"

She gives a bouncy curtsey and then turns away, heading
down the long rows of curtains until she's out of sight once again.

"What did you mean?" Kazan demands once Isidora has
gone, although this time she keeps her voice as quiet as she
can. "Why can't she see you? She can't hear you either, can
she? Is it just Isidora who can't, or is it all vampires?"

The geist sighs, and the sound is filled with dust. "They can't
see what they create."

"You're not making much sense, you know."

He merely sighs once more.

She resists the urge to stomp her foot. "Are you going to
answer me or not?"

"He won't," a different voice says. "He's too old."

Even though this time she knows it's another geist, she can't
stop herself from whirling around again. If she keeps getting
surprised like this, she's likely to break her own neck. Sure
enough, a second geist lurks around the corner of the next
plinth. This one looks like a woman, a ragged gown floating
around her transparent body as though underwater. Limp

strands of hair hang down in front of her face and tangle in her teeth when she cracks open her decaying jaw to speak.

"We forget. When we get old," the geist explains. Or rather, attempts to, given the vagueness of the statement.

Kazan glances back at the first geist who drapes himself over the longbow. "How old is he?"

"Oh, I don't know. Older than me. He was already here when I was brought in." This new geist floats through the stacks towards a different plinth, this one displaying the shiny badge of a human soldier. She lazily drifts around it. "Some of us get lucky and are bound to the place where they died. Some of us aren't. I'm tied to this. When Dasar brought it here, I was forced to come along too."

"Did Dasar kill you?"

The geist nods, the movement causing a strand of her loose hair to stick to her eyeball.

"What did..." Kazan glances over her shoulder. "What did your *friend* mean when he said Isidora couldn't see him? Something about how they can't see what they create?"

"The vampires see us while they eat us, and then they don't once they've finished."

That must be why Adrius has never seen a geist, and why he claimed he knew no one who had either. Neither he nor his fellows *could* see geists, even if he walked straight through one. If he should ever take her advice and seek a saint, he would only see a church of humans staring at nothing.

"So," she asks, thinking it through, "geists come about after a vampire kills a human?"

"It's so hard to explain," the woman bemoans.

Kazan inches closer. "*Try.*"

"Vampires can fill their fangs with venom when they wish. It makes it easier for them to eat, but it's also the first step in turning a human. If a vampire gives someone such a cursed bite and drains all their blood without destroying their body, then they become stuck like this. Trapped in between vampiric

eternity and sweet death. Two of my..." She shrinks back and
tilts her head to the side. "I don't know. Two of my... family,
I think? I can't recall. Two people were with me when Dasar
killed us. He drank me dry and left me, and now I'm like this.
But the two others were torn apart and their flesh was eaten.
They passed on."

"Is that why he said I wouldn't become a geist?" Kazan asks,
leaning in as the geist shies away towards the plinth. "Because
they won't –" She stops as her guts churn. "Because they won't
kill me in the necessary way?"

"Mm. They always do something wrong to the special
humans."

"What do they do? Are they going to –" a silent retch "– eat
my flesh as well, or is it something else?"

The geist drapes herself around the badge. "I've not seen it.
It doesn't happen down here. All I know is that the human
servants don't see any of the special humans after they die."

Human servants? Of course, when Kazan thinks about it,
it makes complete sense that the Citadel would have human
servants. It's not as though vampires would lower themselves
to do even slightly menial work. Snobbish, arrogant bastards
that they are.

"They come down here, sometimes," the geist adds,
cheerfully morose. "Most are too scared to say much, but
occasionally they speak. Sometimes," and here her dead voice
turns low which draws Kazan in closer, "they are silly. Silly
and stupid and they get so close that we can *touch* –"

A rotting hand snatches towards Kazan.

She throws herself away, slipping on the floor, heart
pounding in her throat. With a frustrated shriek, the geist claws
at empty air, throwing herself against some invisible barrier,
a molar falling from her mouth as she hisses and struggles.
Trapped, less than a foot away from Kazan. Her flaking form
is tugged like a fishing line, reeled in back to the tarnished
soldier's badge displayed on the plinth.

Kazan pants for air and realizes, "You can't get far from that thing you're bound to, can you?"

"You were so *close*," the geist bemoans.

"Not close enough." Pride tugs at her lips. "And you won't get a second shot at possessing me, I can assure you of that."

There are footsteps again. Isidora's coming back.

Kazan turns away from the geist – who now has her head pillowed on her arms and is brooding on the plinth – and faces Isidora. "Let me guess, my time's up?"

"Yes, Highness," Isidora says. "Lady Ezelind is here. She's um… she's not one who appreciates being kept waiting."

"Fine."

She casts one final look at the geist. The eerie figure lets out another long sigh, watching Kazan leave with undisguised longing in her rotting face. A hungry hope that she would get close enough for the geist to possess her body and use her like a puppet till she died.

Kazan scowls. Just another thing that thinks of her as nothing but an object to consume and discard. She grinds her teeth until her jaw aches.

Chapter Nine

Ezelind awaits. She stands behind an empty pedestal at the far end of the menagerie, her clawed hands resting on the sides of the freshly polished stone as she stares down her nose at Kazan. There's an electricity to her, something cold, deadly, and able to lash out at a moment's notice.

Without breaking eye contact with Kazan, she orders, "Dismissed."

"Oh. Um, yes. My lady." Isidora fumbles for a moment before leaving, heading towards the far away entrance where the guard waits.

"Why don't we have a little chat?" Ezelind snarls the moment Isidora is gone.

Kazan steels herself. "And if I say no?"

"That's not an option. Listen to me, *Highness*," she hisses out the word. "I don't give a damn what you do during your remaining time in the land of the living. Party, cry, sleep. Whatever you wish. I'm sure there's a plethora of people here willing to chat you up and give you their advice as to what you should do."

"If you're so ambivalent to my fate," Kazan retorts, "then *back off*."

"In a moment. As I was saying – do as you will. However, you'd best heed this warning for I won't give it twice." She tilts her chin up, staring down at Kazan. "Stay away from my enforcer."

This makes even less sense than she thought it would. "I haven't the faintest idea who you're talking about."

"Oh?" She laughs, a snap of a sound. "Did De Vere not tell you? He's my seneschal, and unlike Dasar, I don't have my second in command balance my books or order my clothes. I send De Vere out to break fingers. And I *don't* appreciate it when he goes out of his way to be deplorably soft on a human."

"Soft? You must have noticed that he hasn't exactly been rushing to help me. I haven't seen him for even a second since arriving here."

"Are your fingers broken?" Kazan refuses to answer the obvious and so Ezelind quickly continues, "As I said. *Soft.* You're barely bruised from your fight in the Vildenmarr. Furthermore, it's obvious he knew you. How else do you think we found out your name?"

"He can turn to dust for all I care." Especially since he clearly has no interest in caring about her either – at least not enough to help her survive. If he truly gave a damn, he would have let her go.

"Know this," Ezelind presses, "you are nothing more than food. Entertaining food, but still food. You have no power and no escape, and if your flailing distracts my enforcer, you will find that as bad as things are for you now, they can always get worse. I don't care how you know De Vere. I don't care if you bumped into him in the street once or if you've been close for years. He's always done what is necessary, and if I ordered him to kill you, he would do so without hesitation."

"Fine! As I said, he can turn to dust. But your threats don't scare me."

Slowly and pointedly, Ezelind splays her fingers out across the center of the pedestal. "There is one more thing I want you to know. I may not be personally inclined towards barbarism, but I have no such boundaries when it comes to those who cross my brother. Amelia is Weisz's dear seneschal, and though she was careless enough to lose her eye to you, she still belongs to my brother. In payment, I shall take *your* eye." She caresses the stone beneath her. "And I shall place it here, to waste away with the rest of Dasar's toys."

Kazan scoffs, and she wishes she were truly as confident as she makes herself sound. "You're Dasar's guest and this is *his* party. His party, his rules. There's nothing you can do to me until the three-day mark has passed."

"I wouldn't rely so heavily on Dasar's protection if I were you. You never know when it might *disappear*. He may rule the southern valleys and marshes, but my brother and I rule the west and the north, and I will not hesitate to leverage that power. And don't forget, Dasar cares far more about the Citadel than I do."

She frowns. "What does the Citadel have to do with my death?"

"It's amusing how little you know," Ezelind replies, though there's not a shred of amusement in her expression. "Play your part and you will get the entirety of your allotted time. Upset my carefully built order and your eye may end up here far sooner than you'd like."

Kazan inclines her head with a short, sharp jerk. "Noted."

"Then we're done here." Ezelind raises her voice and calls out, "Girl! I've finished with Her Highness. Get her out of my sight."

With that, she stalks off, the click of her heels on the floor following her out of the menagerie. She doesn't deign to grace Isidora with any sort of acknowledgement, forcing the girl to scurry out of her way.

"Ezelind's a bastard," Kazan says aloud, just to see what Isidora will do.

Nothing interesting, as it turns out. She merely squeaks and nervously double checks to make sure their silent guard still shadows her. Kazan hadn't noticed at the time, but the guard had stayed away while Ezelind was in the menagerie, and her interest peaks. Is that because Ezelind is strong enough to handle herself without assistance, or because the guard knows to afford these vampiric rulers a measure of privacy? If the latter, Kazan has discovered a blind spot she can likely exploit. Dasar, Ezelind, and from what she can gather, Weisz as well.

Another guard awaits them outside the menagerie, dressed in the same purple-toned raiment of her current escort. The newcomer doesn't address her or Isidora, and instead turns to the guard trailing behind them and pulls him aside to speak in hushed tones. Kazan strains her ears, but she can only pick up a few words, Dasar's name chief among them. A vampire's hearing must be a tad more sensitive than a human's, for Isidora leans towards them with rapt attention.

For a brief moment, none of the three people look at Kazan. If she remembers the map of the Citadel correctly – which she *does* – then there should be a stairwell two halls to the left, leading to a set of smaller corridors that she guesses are designed for servants.

Kazan looks to the left. She looks to the right.

She takes a tiny, shuffling sidestep to the left and holds her breath, steeling herself. One of the guards mentions Dasar again, their conversation seemingly turning towards some sort of disturbance in the schedule they have planned out. She inches another step to the left, her heart pounding away in her chest as she sees a faint glimmer of hope. Isidora starts responding to a question one of the guards asks her.

Shifting her weight to the balls of her feet, Kazan tiptoes away at breakneck speed.

She has already turned down the next hall by the time she hears Isidora's shocked squeak and panicked shout of, "Highness?!"

Speed over silence. The pervasive fear, as if she's back in the forest again. She can feel thin branches catching at her clothing, her blood rushing in her ears. She runs down the second hallway and finds the stairwell entrance the map had promised. The air is cooler here, and she leaps down the stairs two at a time, then three at a time, all but throwing herself downwards. What else had the map shown in this area? What exits, what hidden doors, what places can she hide?

Two seconds after she catapults off the last stair, she crashes into someone.

The figure lets out a pained groan as Kazan's knee bangs into their shin and stumbles back. Their hands grab her shoulders. Are they trying to drag her away? Her hand curls into a fist and she prepares to throw a punch when the person instead steadies her and helps her back on her feet.

The person she's just accosted is a woman, dressed simply. A *human* woman, whose eyes get wider and wider as she takes in Kazan's appearance. A servant?

"You're…" The woman gulps and yanks her hands away, clutching them to her chest.

Kazan presses a finger to her lips, her hand trembling with adrenaline, and whispers, "Shhh! You never saw me!"

The woman's eyes grow wider still. Her jaw shakes with the effort of keeping it shut.

"Where's the nearest door out of this damn place?" Kazan demands.

"It's…"

Footsteps come from the stairwell above and the woman panics, her mouth gaping open to yell, "She's down here! Guards! She's here!"

"You absolute *bastard*!"

The metal footsteps sound right behind her. One of the guards grabs her around the waist with an unshakeable grip, not so much as flinching even as she claws at the armored plates on his arm and kicks out, bruising her heels on his metallic boots.

"You sold me out to one of *them*?" she screams at the servant woman. "Does being human mean *nothing* to you?"

The woman merely shakes her head back and forth as the guards drag Kazan away, continuing to stare at her with those large, scared eyes that mirror her own. "I... I'm sorry," the woman mumbles. "But you'd have done the same."

Chapter Ten

Kazan is practically frogmarched by the guards to somewhere in the southern wing, into a beautiful parlor with a golden tea service set for two on the center table. They don't shove her into the room, but they certainly aren't gentle as they let her go.

Dasar is lounging on a burgundy chaise, casually sipping from a teacup. "Ah, Highness! Please, come in, make yourself comfortable. Isidora, run along now. Go enjoy the party."

Kazan's entourage obeys him instantly. So, she thinks, she's right about the guards giving Dasar and company their privacy.

When she remains standing, Dasar gestures to the lounge across from him. "Please, Majesty, do take a seat."

She does, with no small measure of reluctance.

"An escape attempt already, hm?" he remarks. "I commend your efforts!"

That's it? All her desperation amounts to is a commendation? "I find it hard to believe that you'd want me to escape."

"Oh, I don't, but I do so love to watch you try. Here, have a sip and tell me what you think."

Dasar pours her a cup of tea, holding it out for her. She pauses briefly. Is it poisoned? No, Dasar is allegedly rather set on waiting three days before killing her. She's safe. It's a rose tea, and her first sip is delicious beyond belief, certainly the finest she's ever had. She wonders if he drinks from the same pot, or if his cup contains blood instead.

"Not bad," she says after she finishes half her cup.

There seems to be a constant levity shining in Dasar's eyes. "I'm so glad that you enjoy it. Help yourself to anything at the table, really, I insist."

The spread of bite-sized sandwiches and scones tempts her, her stomach protesting the fact that she hasn't eaten in who knows how long. The hunger outweighs the fearful knots in her belly and she grabs a sandwich, shoving it indelicately into her mouth. "Why did you wish to see me? If I remember Isidora's rambling explanations earlier, I'm supposed to be in the middle of that party of yours."

"Why, I want to get to know you, of course! It would be so terrible if Ezelind beat me to that particular punch." He takes a deep sip from his cup before elaborating, "Humans are *fascinating*. For food, that is. I always love taking the opportunity to learn more about your kind during these parties. It's so fun, wouldn't you say?"

Not really, no.

"If we're so fascinating to you," she replies curtly, "why eat us?"

He laughs as though that's the funniest thing he's ever heard. "Yes, right there, that's exactly what I'm talking about. How do humans describe it? Gallows humor?" He continues with her question completely ignored, "So, tell me about your previous life. Where did you live before we found you?"

"Upper Welshire," she tells him. If Adrius told everyone her name, she doesn't want to risk the chance that he had also mentioned where she's from. And if Dasar catches her in one lie, he'll catch her in another.

"Ah yes, that explains your passage through the Vildenmarr. It's a lovely little forest, isn't it? I've gone hunting in it more times than I can count, although it's always more enjoyable this time of year. Given that they are... *technically* my equals, Ezelind and Weisz are supposed to join me, but they never do." His sigh involves an overdramatic sinking of his shoulders.

"Instead, they send their seneschals, and it's fine, I suppose, but you saw how unsporting Amelia turned out to be." He takes a sip of whatever mystery liquid he's drinking and seems to remember that he had other things he wanted to discuss instead of simply complaining about his fellows. "What is your parish like? I've visited it many times myself, but I'm curious as to how one actually lives there."

"It is as all human parishes are."

Dasar seems disappointed that she doesn't want to play his game. "How was your life there?"

"Not long enough."

Cue laughter. Damn him for taking her life so lightly. "Why did you leave? What made you travel through the Vildenmarr? As far as I know, most humans don't tend to travel far. Or am I mistaken?"

"We travel more than you might think. I've been to an uncountable number of other cities across Mavazem." It's an automatic lie. Not for a reason, but out of habit. A comfort.

"And how are you liking the southern lands?"

"Currently? It could be better."

He grins again. Does he really find her so entertaining? He refills his cup from the same pot that he used to serve Kazan. So he *is* drinking tea. "You're very amusing, my dear."

Vampires keep telling her that. Amusing. But Adrius had found her *interesting*. That shouldn't matter, but as soon as she thinks it, the thought refuses to stop itching at her.

"Weisz called me an 'adorable thing' if that's what passes for a joke here," she recalls. "*I* wasn't amused."

Dasar shrugs. "Weisz is an acquired taste."

"If only that statement applied to me."

That comment he seems to find especially hilarious, sending peals of over-the-top laughter across the table. "It truly is a shame that so many of my fellows fail to appreciate your kind's sense of humor." He helps himself to a scone once he stops giggling, smearing cream and jam over it before plopping it into his mouth. "Tell me about your family. Back in Upper Welshire."

No one. No one to go looking for her when she's declared missing.

"I have an elder sister whose wife comes from old money. My mother serves the church as a keeper of saintly relics and my father is an influential Warden. What about your family, my lord?" she asks, wanting him to feel just as poked and prodded as he makes her feel. "Do you have siblings? What about your parents? Do you have you a spouse?"

He shakes his head. "Tragically, I never married. Commitment has never been my style. As for parents, well. You wouldn't recognize her name even if I told you, she's been dead for so long. My sire had many progenies, but ultimately, I emerged as the holder of my bloodline's title. That was so long ago, and since then many of my siblings have died and others have become so irrelevant that I've completely lost touch with them."

"How old are you?"

"Who's to say? Older than my two fellows, certainly. I lost track somewhere in the three hundreds. All the years look the same after that."

"It must be nice, knowing that you'll live to see the end of the week."

"It can get dull, at times."

She grits her teeth together until the grinding hurts her ears. How she'd *love* to have the problem of living for long enough that life itself becomes a chore. She'd gladly trade places with him. Maybe he'd find being in *her* situation fun, *hmm*?

"These murder parties shake up the years, do they?" she demands, anger flaring. "Is that why I'm here? Why you're going to kill me?"

Dasar's thumb absently twists his golden lip ring. "Yes, Highness, and no. While I admit these parties are the highlight of the year, they're not without purpose. You see, two hundred and fifty-four years ago, there was an *actual* King of the Vampires. But he was rather dreadful at the end of the day, you know, and we weren't overly fond of him. Houses Gambit, Rockford, and Mooncliffe came together and attacked the Citadel. It was a splendid showing on all parts, and at the end of a three-day battle, we killed the king." He gestures to the manor around them. "This is a sort of... reenactment, shall we say? It's awful fun, too."

"Have you heard the saying 'all good things must come to an end'?"

"A human phrase applicable to human lives."

The teacup rattles under her hands as she sets it down in her lap. She can feel those glass shards in her throat once more, her lungs collapsing like pressed billows.

Dasar grins at her.

"Why are you –" She grinds her teeth together in frustration. "Why are you looking at me like that? I'm not even *doing* anything."

"Of course you're doing something. Even inaction is action," he says, smiling at the contradiction as though its illogical nature is especially tantalizing. "What will this year's majesty do? What will they not do? How do they act? How do they do something as simple as drink a cup of tea? My fellows think that humans only have a few reactions to trying circumstances, but I find that pressure can elicit all manner of beautiful responses in humans It's all action, dear pet. All equally fascinating –"

"I am *not* a pet!"

"Anger? Hm, that's less novel than your earlier witty banter, I must say. Not nearly as entertaining." That damn cheerful smile plays on his lips, blank and vague and *clinical*.

She doesn't realize she's leapt to her feet, but is extraordinarily aware of throwing her teacup onto the table, shattering it into an angry mess of porcelain and brown liquid.

"Look at me!" she screams. "Look at me like I'm a *person*!"

He bursts out laughing.

Her hands are around the teapot before she notices, the hot porcelain burning her numb fingers. She raises it over her head and –

The door opens.

"Pardon the interruption, sire," a guard says in a flat and remarkably bored tone, in no way concerned by the fact that she's about to smash a heavy piece of pottery into Dasar's face. She knows it wouldn't harm him, but still. She wants them to at least *blink* at the violence. "Lord Weisz is requesting Her Highness's presence at a wine tasting party. As the preparations you requested have yet to be completed, I did not deny his request."

Kazan drops the teapot, letting it shatter. Hot tea splashes over her skirts and the table and the neat little trays of sandwiches and cakes.

"Thank you for the conversation, my lord," she snarls. "You'll have to excuse me."

Dasar sighs, a fluttering, butterfly-esque noise of indulgence. "Snubbing me already, Highness? Very well, go enjoy yourself with Weisz. My wine cellar has some fantastic bottles in it, if I do say so myself."

Steam comes out of her ears as she stomps away from him, following the guard as he leads her to wherever Weisz is.

A swift death is too good for Dasar. If only she had her sword... Her hands curl into fists. If only, if only. Vivid images of ripping it out of his greedy hands and cutting her way out of this place fill her mind, gory and satisfying.

She had never thought of herself as a particularly violent person before, but she is, was, and always will be, *desperate* to survive at all costs. She refuses to go the same way as her father. She will not succumb to the all-too-common human fate of being killed by creatures of the night. She must prove she's better than that.

She *will*.

Chapter Eleven

This guard is a much more pleasant guide than Isidora. He doesn't say a word, and that's worth a lot in Kazan's book. The walk through the candlelit corridors of the Citadel is blissfully silent. It appears she's still in the same wing of the manor, merely descending several steps to one of the lower floors. Weisz's party must be situated closer to the wine cellar.

When the guard finally comes to a stop two floors down, he opens a large, elegant door that leads into a similarly large, elegant room. Cold light fills the space, the candelabras placed throughout the room flickering eerily, the fireplace burning with wavering flames. The light reflects on the overabundance of glasses and bottles that cover the tables. A single window has been curtained off by heavy velvet shrouds. Just under a dozen vampires mill about the room, jewelry weighing down their necks and ears, lace spiderwebbing off wrists, and everywhere those unnatural black and gold eyes. Eyes that all turn to her the moment she is pushed through the doorway.

Weisz flutters to the front of the pack, blonde curls bouncing as he moves, and smiles like tree sap. Oozing, impossible to get rid of, and hoping to catch flies. "Highness," he simpers. "Do come in."

Another nudge from the guard sends her into the room.

Weisz's cold hand clamps down on her shoulder. What is it with these people and manhandling her? "Welcome to our party within a party. I would introduce you to my friends, but I don't think you particularly care about their names."

No, she doesn't. "Why am I here?"

"A queen is always a treasured guest," one of the vampires chimes in, an echo of Isidora's earlier words.

Another adds, "We love the opportunity to see what a human's tastebuds prefer."

With a sweeping gesture, Weisz motions to a table filled with half-drunk bottles and dirty glasses. Dozens of pristine glasses are set up in a line down the center, each containing about an inch of wine in them. Did they really invite Kazan here simply to get her drunk and see what wine she likes? She rather expected 'wine tasting party' to mean something more nefarious.

As Weisz draws her into the room, the vampires move like water to crowd around her, blocking her off from the exit. More effective than a padlock over the door. She has no choice but to be pushed towards the table. Her only other option is throwing punches, and then she'd have to contend with a vampire's unnatural strength.

"Here," says a woman with a particularly elaborate coiffure. She holds out a glass of a lighter red wine. "Try this one first. It's my personal favorite."

Kazan raises the glass and takes a sip.

"Well?" the woman says expectantly, leaning in with a grin. "What do you think?"

She shrugs. "It's fruity."

Someone in the group claps with unabashed excitement. "An unrefined palette! How wonderful. This is a spectacular opportunity to perfect your taste." They are the next to hand her a glass of wine. "Try this one!"

The next glass Kazan proclaims as oaky.

Luckily for her, their intent doesn't seem to be to get her drunk, as glasses are pulled out of her fingers as soon as she's taken a single sip and stated her thoughts on it. That said, with little food in her stomach beyond a tiny tea sandwich, the alcohol will likely make an impression upon her a good deal earlier than it normally would have. That's not even considering her low tolerance for wine in particular. After half a dozen testers, she can already feel it sitting unpleasantly in her stomach.

She tastes twelve different wines, some darker, some lighter. Words that she doesn't understand like 'tannins' and 'racking' are tossed around by the assorted vampires. They don't seem to care if she understands or not. Even though she knows the wine won't do anything to hydrate her, she can't help the desire to quench her thirst. Her tiny sips turn into large gulps.

"Here," Weisz says on glass number thirteen, pushing one into Kazan's hands. His fangs are prominent as he smiles. "*This* one."

Kazan drinks.

It's oddly warmer than the others and… and it's too thick and slick and salty and filled with iron bitterness. Revulsion and disgust overwhelm her.

Her throat involuntarily convulses and her stomach turns itself inside out. She falls to her knees and wretches. The blood they fed her comes up, along with wine and bile and the bits she's managed to eat since arriving here. Chunky, sanguine purple splatters on the polished stones. Her stomach heaves again, acid burning up her throat, her lungs desperate for air.

Laughter scours her ears.

Her nails scratch against the stone floor as her hands curl into angry fists, but she can't yell and cry at them solely because there's no breath in her and it's not *fair*!

"How disgusting." Weisz's laugh is high pitched, haughty and mocking. "See?" he remarks to his companions. "Didn't I say she'd be funny?"

A ragged gulp of air finally makes it into Kazan's lungs and she uses it to scream, "*Get out!*"

More laughter.

"Let's give the prissy highness a bit of space," one of the men says. He scoffs in disgust. "And send a cleaner in here or something. I'm not that picky, but even my sense of smell objects to this stench. Oh no, don't worry, my Lord Weisz, it was *very* amusing, I'm only saying that the aftermath requires a mop."

Someone giggles. "Usually the aftermath doesn't –"

"– because we don't leave a drop of blood behind!" someone else finishes, equally chipper.

The room clears while Kazan does her utmost not to cry. It takes more willpower than she would have imagined to force her desperate gasps and dry sobs to stop. She must stay in control. Who knows how long she has before Weisz and the others return, and she refuses to give them any further satisfaction. Shame turns her stomach as much as the blood.

She pushes herself up, careful to keep her skirts from getting in the mess. A jug of water sits on a nearby table and she staggers towards it. She grabs it and a napkin lying nearby. She drinks straight from the jug, cold porcelain soothing against her lips and the water not nearly wet enough. She swirls it around her mouth and then spits it out, clearing the sour taste from her gums. Dunking a corner of the napkin in the jug, she uses the damp cloth to wipe her mouth. At least she can regain the dignity of cleanliness.

A series of candy tins are littered about on the table; one of them contains small slivers of candied ginger. She shoves a piece in her mouth and chews until her stomach settles and her mouth tastes like fresh ginger instead of acid.

There's a mirror hanging on the wall, and she double checks her reflection to make sure there's nothing else smeared on her face. The flickering candlelight and surprising amount of tarnish on the mirror's surface makes it difficult to get a clear image, but she seems clean enough.

She sees something else in the mirror. The dark, velvet curtains.

This might be the perfect opportunity. She strides over and throws them open, her heart soaring as she reveals the window hiding behind it.

Apparently, they haven't been completely lax in their security measures. There's a lock on the window. Fortunately for her, it's merely a tiny pivot lock, and the metal is poor enough quality that she easily bends the pins with her fingers and yanks them out. The first inch of the frame needs to be worked up gently to avoid any noise, but after that it slides as if it has been oiled not an hour ago. She shoves the glass all the way up and relishes her first breath of fresh air in what feels like years.

Dasar's manor is in the mountains, on top of a tall, spiraling peak, with lush green forests far below. So far that it looks like a dark blur to Kazan's eyes. The drop is terrifying, even though she's on a relatively low level of the manor. Where the walls finally meet the ground, there are well-groomed bushes and gardens. If she should slip and fall, that's where they'd find her body, a tangled corpse among the roses.

No, she can't think about that.

Besides, it's not as though she will be any less dead if she stays. She has the perfect opportunity to climb out and scamper down the mountainside as fast as she can. She's a decent runner and her stamina isn't bad.

But she couldn't outrun them in the forest, and she reluctantly knows that they will pull her back as soon as she reaches the ground. It will take her longer to climb down than it will take them to notice she has attempted another escape and send guards to retrieve her.

Perhaps, she thinks, if she went up instead of down it might work. Lead them astray, make them run in the wrong direction? There would still be the risk of running too close to a guard tower, but if she were to double back through the Citadel and head to the ground another way, she could dodge the guards. She knows somewhere within these walls her sword lies waiting for her to take hold of it again...

Wind tugs her sleeves back and she looks down at the bandage wrapped around her left wrist. It's stained, the former bright crimson now a dingy brown, and the wound beneath it still stings. When she removes the bandage, she can see a thin red line across her pulse. They can probably smell the blood, but she can use that to her advantage.

She tosses the blood-stained piece of fabric out the window. It flutters down gently, eventually landing in the bushes below.

Kazan stands up on the windowsill.

It feels exactly like climbing a tree. Her hands pull her up, finding vines to grip onto and gaps in the stone, leading the way for her feet to follow. The stone scrapes her skin and she has to be careful not to reopen the cut on her wrist.

Folds of fabric catch under her feet. Damn this dress... It is not made for scaling a building and she cannot afford it getting in the way.

The soft soles of her shoes are not designed for climbing any more than the dress, and they nearly cause her to slip twice, but she manages. Up here, with the constant menacing reminder of a deadly fall, the wind seems twice as loud as it should be.

In the end, the climb goes more quickly than she had feared. She makes it up ten stories before her absence is noticed. She can hear from down below the sound of someone's panicked shout, "She's gone!"

She pushes open the window in front of her and tumbles inside as fast as she can, landing quietly on her unsteady feet.

"Well, *hello* there."

Kazan practically jumps out of her skin at the shock.

The speaker is a woman – a vampire, of course. She lounges on a four-poster bed, a sheet of parchment in her hand, wearing nothing more than a scandalously thin shift, her extraordinarily long dark hair doing more to hide her figure than her clothing. Her golden eyes slowly trail all the way up from Kazan's dirtied shoes to the final strand of hair pinned atop her head until she feels far more naked than the woman herself. She fights the urge to squirm.

The woman leans back on her hands and smiles. "I wasn't expecting a personal visit from Her Majesty. Is there... something I can do for you?" *Something*, in this case, is said with such a smooth purr as to imply a great many things, and one very specific thing at the same time. "Or are you merely passing through?"

"Taking a casual stroll," Kazan fires back, having recovered from her initial shock.

"More's the pity. Have a good afternoon, Highness."

Is that it? "You're... you're just going to let me leave? I climbed in through your window."

"I noticed. And yes." The woman gestures to the door. Amusement dances in her gold eyes, surprisingly devoid of the mocking jeer of most vampires. "I'm curious to see how long it will take the guards to catch you. A spontaneous training exercise every now and again is good for them."

"I hope you won't be too disappointed when they fail," she spits out.

"Forgive me for saying so, Highness, but the odds are astronomically against you." She picks up a sheet of parchment. "Now, I'm going to return to work and forget that you ran through my room, hm?"

This is a trap. It has to be. "I could escape, I could steal my sword back, I could even kill Dasar."

"Well, it certainly would be interesting if you did." Her red lips turn up at the corners. "Don't I get a thank you?"

Kazan can hear loud footsteps clank outside the bedroom. The rush of armored guards clattering through the halls. A few of them shout. Some laugh.

Someone yells, "Search the rooms!"

Kazan's heart skips a beat. Her eyes dart from the door to the woman and back again. If she leaves now, she'll be caught and dragged back to Dasar. If she stays, she'll be caught the second the guard enters. She hears a door slamming open. How many rooms away is that? How long does she have?

The footsteps become louder and louder. They're right outside.

With so little time to think, she seizes the first thing that flits through her mind and just runs with it.

She scrambles onto the bed, pushes the woman down, and smashes their lips together. It's hard and clumsy and were she actually trying to seduce the woman, she would be extremely embarrassed by her own inelegance. The woman squeaks in surprise and Kazan's half convinced that she will use that unbeatable vampiric strength to push her off and send her flying across the room. But as she hears the door handle being turned, the woman grabs a fistful of Kazan's hair and tugs her down, sliding her tongue into her mouth.

The door is thrown open.

"My lady, there's –" The guard's gruff voice hesitates. "… There's been an escape attempt?"

As suddenly as she reciprocated, the woman breaks the kiss, turning those sharp eyes to glare at the intruder. "As you can see, I have things well in hand. If she'd meant to kill me, she already would have thanks to your rather dismal response time. Now, I'd like to have things *more* in hand, so if you wouldn't mind…"

"Of course. Sorry for the interruption, my lady. But Lord Weisz was asking for her to be returned to him."

"Tell him he's had his fun already," the woman replies. "Let me have mine."

"Yes, my lady." The door shuts behind him.

"…Sorry," Kazan says awkwardly as soon as they have some privacy.

"Oh, don't apologize," the woman drawls, her eyes lidded. Her tongue licks her lip as though she'd rather like to eat Kazan – though in what sense of the word, she has no idea. "Now where were we?"

Kazan pushes herself off the bed before she thinks twice. "I was leaving."

"Mm... but there's a whole host of more enjoyable things you *could* be doing," the woman replies, running a hand down the curves of her body as she sits up, pointing out her many inviting assets. "In my experience, people who are as good with a blade as you tend to be equally good with their hands. Why not stay awhile? As much as I'd love to see you escape my Lord Dasar's clutches, you won't in the end."

My Lord Dasar. Something about those three words breaks through the confusing attraction like a boot at high velocity breaks through a glass window. Unexpectedly and with an unignorable bang.

"Apologies," Kazan says, this time without even the slightest trace of sincerity, "but I have more important things to do than *you*."

The woman gives her a smoldering look and smiles. "You wound me. You certainly have a wicked tongue, don't you?"

There's nothing Kazan can think of to say in response, and there's silence from the halls. It's a perfect time to get the hell out. She casts one final look at the woman, gently eases the door open, and starts to move.

Her shoes are abandoned quickly in favor of silent bare feet. Before, she'd needed speed over stealth. Now, she needs the opposite. In fact, the more time, the better. With that gorgeous woman having, essentially, called off the search, it will likely take a while for the guards to return to their usual posts and Kazan doesn't want to be caught in the middle of that shifting around.

Fear begins to get to her again, and she forces her heartbeat to still, forces her breathing to remain even. If she fails, she'll need to come up with a new plan, and her time is limited. Which means she can't fail. Simple as that.

She turns a corner, and finds herself scurrying down a hallway lined with paintings. Some are sprawling landscapes, some are portraits so detailed she swears that the eyes follow her. But there is one painting...

A geist is sitting beneath it.

This one looks less decayed than the others in the library, his flesh mostly intact and his body slightly more opaque around the edges. He is young then, both in terms of his undeath and physical appearance. She guesses the geist is around the same age as her, if not a year or two younger. His hair is pale and close cropped, his cheeks round and lined in a way that suggests a history of smiling, though all traces of even the memory of mirth are absent from his face.

Then she looks at the painting he sits in front of, and halts in her tracks.

The painting is Adrius De Vere. On canvas, he appears not as the stern vampire she fought in the forest, but as the lighter man she met at Rask's party. While there is no open levity in his features, there is undeniably the echo of a smile on his lips and a warmth in his eyes. A warmth to his skin too, persisting through the thin layer of dust on the canvas. And his eyes are a plain, normal brown. Was this painted while he wore his glamoured ring, or when he was still a human?

The geist's eyes slide from the painting to stare at her. "Ah... a new queen. Can you help me?"

"How do you know who I am?" she demands. "Who are you?"

"The magic of the regency is already on you." His voice is thin and whispery, as though speaking through holes in his throat. "It's begun, and it will end with your death."

How does she even respond to that? It feels almost foolish to argue with an only semi-coherent geist, so she feels disinclined to waste her breath.

"Help me and I'll help you," he offers.

Not a chance. She learned that lesson in the menagerie. "You're out of luck, I'm afraid. Another geist already tried that trick on me, and I'm not about to be fooled twice. Even if you *did* mean to help, and this isn't all a ploy to get me too close to you, there's nothing you could do that doesn't involve possessing my body. Better luck with the next person to come along."

"Please," the geist says, but it's too late, she has already run off again.

Recalling the map in her mind, there should be a series of rooms up ahead that aren't too far from a guard tower. She can hide in there for a few minutes to make sure the last of the guards have run off and then sneak in to get out. She waits outside that set of doors for a moment, double and triple checking to make sure the coast is clear before she slips through.

One door seems to lead to a bedchamber, the other to a washroom, and the other to another smaller sitting room –

"Ah, Highness." Dasar is sitting in a plush armchair, giving the impression that he has simply teleported up from the parlor, minus his tea set. A smile stretches from ear to ear, the grin so wide that it appears someone has sliced his cheeks like a filleted fish. "Come for some more diverting conversation?"

Chapter Twelve

"How did you know I'd be here?" Kazan demands.

"Why, where else would you go?" he replies cheerfully. "Haven't you come here for that sword of yours?" He wiggles a single finger at the room around him, indicating the numerous golden ornaments and plush drapery. "I know far better than you the decadent drug of possession."

Every instinct in her body tells her to run, to find her sword, to cut him down, but she stands frozen. His amused, transcendental gaze fixes her in place like a needle pinning a butterfly to a cork board. The pendulum between her fight or flight reflex has been swinging around wildly ever since the Vildenmarr, and is currently stuck somewhere in the middle. She watches him watch her, and his smile only grows.

"Come now, Highness," he says at last, rising to his feet with all the grace of a peacock sweeping its tail across the ground. "Let's return to the party, shall we?"

"No. Where's my sword?"

He tuts in the manner of one dealing with a stubborn child. "Highness, there's really no need for all this fuss."

"If I *am* your queen," she says, and she wants it to be a loud and proud declaration, but her voice betrays her and comes out as barely more than a mumble, "then you have to do as I say. I want my sword and I want you to let me go."

"Oh *Highness*." He sighs and places his cold hands on her

shoulders. "It's far too late for that. Your regency has already begun."

That's what that geist had said to her. The magic of her regency. "It's a spell of some kind, isn't it?"

"A tad more complicated than a mere spell."

Another memory comes to the forefront of her thoughts. They had cut her wrist before the banquet and smeared her blood on the crown. "Blood magic? Isidora mentioned a ritual."

He beams with delight. "Ah, *very* clever of you! This –" and he looks about the entire room as if to indicate *everything* "– is indeed framed by blood magic. Decorated by it, if you will. As a canvas decorates a painting." She doesn't get the chance to tell him that simile doesn't make sense before he steers her towards the door. "Come along now."

"Not without my –"

"Your sword, yes, yes. Don't worry your lovely head over it. I promise you that it will be well taken care of, as befits such exquisite craftsmanship."

"Will you put it in your menagerie?" To sit forever alongside all those other foul trophies that he's taken? She can't allow that, she just can't, and that's another reason to get out of here before she's killed. Get out, save herself *and* her sword from this fate. "I won't let you."

"Now that's a wonderful idea." He steers her towards the door, all enthusiasm and airy energy. "I will be a bit disappointed if you say 'over my dead body', Highness, as that's rather the idea."

"Over *your* dead body," she snarls instead.

"That's the spirit!"

About a half dozen guards are either standing outside the door or currently running up to it when she's forced outside. One of them salutes, pressing a gauntleted fist to their chest. "Forgive me, my lord. Lady Sutcliffe gave us the impression that the queen was... *contained*."

How were the guards *slower* to arrive than Dasar, given that there must be guards on every single level of the Citadel? She would have assumed that Dasar would be flouncing about at his party instead of quietly waiting in his room.

The thoughts are pushed from her mind when she spots Adrius. Her mind goes blank, and then very slowly, anger starts to leak in. So *now* he deigns to show himself?

He heads up the corridor towards them, rushing in a way that doesn't involve outright running so much as speed walking. Although the guards remain at attention, they shift away from Adrius as much as possible. Cowards. She stands her ground and pins him with the most pointed glare she can muster.

"Lord Dasar," Adrius says politely, giving Dasar a bow. "Is everything alright?"

Dasar brushes it off with a smile and a wiggle of his fingers. "Perfectly lovely. Her Majesty just stopped by for a pleasant chat, isn't that right? I must say, I'm quite impressed that you ignored Lady Sutcliffe's stand down order in favor of continuing to search for our errant queen."

"Call it instinct," Adrius replies cryptically.

"Well, you certainly have fascinatingly good instincts. You can go tell your Lady Ezelind that there's no cause for concern and that she shouldn't get her hopes up about my death just yet."

Adrius's mouth becomes a thin, emotionless line. "I'll pass on the message. Although I am obligated to assure you that she doesn't desire your death."

"Now, now, no need to lie, we're all friends here."

"I'm sure my lady will appreciate that sentiment." Now that she's trying to make eye contact, Kazan can tell Adrius is purposefully avoiding looking at her. "If that's all...?"

Another flippant finger-wiggle. "Run along and enjoy the party."

"Of course."

Again Kazan actively tries to meet his eyes but to her

irritation he continues to avoid her, turning around and walking off before she can scream at him.

Placing a hand on the small of her back, Dasar escorts her down the hall. The retinue of guards moves to follow until he waves them off. That confident, is he? She hates to admit it, because she desperately wants to cut that stupid smile off his face, but she doesn't think the guards would do him any good anyway. If she were a vampire, with their unnatural strength, maybe she would be a threat. Without her sword, she is not.

She can feel Dasar's claws on her back as he says, "Let me indulge your curiosity and show you some lovely blood magic, Majesty. I *was* saving this for later, but since you've gone and skipped ahead in the order of events, as it were, there's no harm in showing you now. By the by," he adds, "do be careful of De Vere. If there are any fanciful ideas of revenge in your mind, I bid you discard them."

"You think I'm not aware I can't beat him?" she snaps. "I *was* there in the Vildenmarr."

"Highness, he left you as intact as you are because I wished it. Test him, and you'll find he's far more dangerous than you think." He brushes a clawed finger down her cheek until she turns her head away from him. "Take my advice or leave it, dear, it's your choice in the end."

She merely grits her teeth and doesn't bother to respond.

Despite many hours passing since she woke up, drugged and dressed in her ridiculous gown, the party hasn't stopped raging for even a minute. As Dasar leads her through a series of corridors, she spies a games room filled with revelers laughing over cards, a parlor room where a suspiciously long pipe is being passed around, and a smaller dance hall filled with so many people that it appears more like a meat grinder than a celebration.

She's uncertain where Dasar means to take her, and that morbid curiosity keeps her from fighting out of his grip. Ignoring the various crowds that call out for the two to join them, he continues downwards, taking staircase after staircase until the noises of the party have become distant and echoing, a vibration in the walls around them. It's pleasantly cool down here, but then two levels further down it's horribly cold. Goosebumps rise on her skin, and she wishes that her dress was made of wool.

The stairs go from carpet, to polished wood, to rough stone. At last, the endless decent ends, and they can go no further.

A heavy granite door stands in front of them. With a bit of futzing, Dasar removes a key from inside his coat. It's a thick, wrought iron thing, the bits twisted and rusty from age. Dim light has managed to make its way down here from the upper levels, and the faint illumination reveals an indentation of a keyhole in the stone. He inserts the key and steps back, letting it sink completely into the lock.

Reluctant, scraping groans emanate from the stone door as it begins to tremble. Before Kazan's very eyes, it starts to slide downwards into the floor until it has vanished completely, revealing an open doorway into the lowest level of the Citadel.

"Come along, Highness," Dasar says, striding into the darkness before them.

Her toes curl on the cold stone floor. She takes a hesitant step over the threshold and, slowly but surely, follows him into the dark.

Exposed brickwork and icy air greet her. A high ceiling arches overhead, and although it is too dim to make out the details, she can see patterns carved into the supports. Cobwebs cling to the pillars in the distant corners of the room, and dust coats the floor. She can feel some sort of pattern to the tiles beneath her bare feet, but it's so worn down that she can't make it out. If vampires here rely on human servants to do all the dirty work, then clearly they must not be allowed down here to clean. Something in this cellar is too important to risk interference.

Golden flame flickers to life in the darkness.

First, she can see Dasar's sharp profile, and then as her eyes adjust, she begins to make out more of the room. The vampire stands in the center of it, and the light radiates from a single candle stuck in the middle of a twisted and ornate candelabra that he now holds. The wavering light illuminates the room and gives slight clarity to the strange pattern on the tiles – an intricate spiral, continuing outwards into the gloom.

Dasar holds out his free hand. "Come here, sweet one."

Another few steps closer. Something else catches the light. It looks like a table. A small, round table the likes of which would support a single vase of flowers or perhaps a decorative lamp. As she gets closer, she can see that it's carved from stone, the legs of it connected to the floor and the same spiral patterns running down from the top of the table into the ground.

"What is all this?" she asks, her voice echoing in the chamber.

"It's time for the next part of our festivities, Highness." Dasar once more grips her by the arm and pulls her the final few steps, until she stands at the middle of the spiral with him. "You're such a clever thing, I'm certain you remember what I told you earlier? Two hundred and fifty-four years ago, when we fought a spectacularly daring, three-day battle to overthrow the former King of the Vampires?"

"I *am* capable of basic information retention," she snaps.

Dasar leans close, placing the candelabra on the stone table so that she can see the spiral carvings atop it. "Of course. You see, we *did* win. But the Citadel itself was in shambles. Our beautiful stronghold, all caved in, and all its treasures buried under rubble. You can understand why we couldn't bear such a horrendous thing, can't you?"

"Honestly, I don't care."

His voice crawls inside her ear like a fuzzy spider. "You *should* care, Highness. You see, we took the still-breathing king and a single human, and we brought them down here, to the base of the Citadel. I confess that my specialty was transformation magics and not these rites of blood, but myself, along with the previous rulers of Mooncliffe and Rockford, weaved the most glorious of magics together. Complicated hours of rituals and filigree spells. You should have seen them as they died, the two lying together with their blood mingling as though there was no difference between human and vampire. When their bodies lay exsanguinated, we three gathered their blood into a ruby and used it to restore the Citadel to its deserved glory. Then, we *ate* them."

"Fascinating."

Her knowledge of magic is limited – as is true of most humans. The saintly magics utilized by the church are rather mysterious to her, having never been a member of the clergy or even particularly devout. She's heard tales of vampiric magics, however most of those were unsubstantiated beyond the basics. Preservation of blood, for example, is something she knows is possible without being aware of any details. All she has is a hazy impression of grimy blood magic, stories of turning invisible – she's pretty sure that one's false – and one drunkard's promise that he saw a vampire turn into a bat and fly away.

"But the magic couldn't last forever," Dasar continues, "not with a spell as powerful as the one we used. So, every year, we find a special, lovely human to make both vampire ruler and human sacrifice, and over the course of three days, we use them to restore the spell."

A chill, more than simply the basement air, runs down her spine. Hence her sacrificial murder. Does it make it better or worse that there's a concrete reason for all this besides mere fun?

"Look closely now, Highness."

Dasar points to the table, at the center of the spiral that's carved into the stone. Despite the faint light, she can see a slight reddish-brown tinge to the spiral grooves. It's faded away almost entirely.

"The remnants of last year's king," he tells her. "All but gone."

For a brief moment, her curiosity outweighs her fear. Dasar uses that moment to tug her sleeve back and drag his claw over her wrist, reopening the barely healed cut from last night. Fresh blood wells up.

"What do you think you're –"

"Shhh. Watch."

He turns her wrist over so that her blood falls into the center of the spiral. The pain is almost polite, waiting a moment before kicking in, and she doesn't really feel it as three drops of her blood splash onto the stone.

Those three tiny drops turn a bright, unnatural red as they sink into the stone grooves. It's as though the blood gets eaten up, soaking the stone, and then spreading. Just like the ruby in the golden crown. Red paints the spiral, curving out and out and out until crimson is curling up the walls and onto the ceiling and all she can smell is the stench of her own blood. Her wrist throbs now, each beat of her heart pulsing where he'd cut her. Red swims in her vision and she stumbles, her head light and heavy at the same time, and she leans against Dasar –

She's lost control of her body to the point where she's *leaning against Dasar*.

"Aren't you *beautiful*," Dasar croons. "Such a lovely addition to my castle."

"Damn your castle," she murmurs, still not fully in control. That familiar combination of anger and panic burn against the pain in her wrist. She has to be in control of herself, she can't let herself slip.

With a colossal effort, she rips her arm out of his loose grasp. "Damn it and damn you. Say goodbye to your precious Citadel because I'll be long gone before day three."

"Oh, *Highness* –"

Whatever else he says falls on deaf ears as she flees on shaking legs.

Chapter Thirteen

Kazan staggers off the last stair into a gloomy foyer, the stone hard and brutal on her bare feet. A candelabra sits on a plinth, flickering like in the basement, shining on the next set of stairs that leads up and out of this dark pit of Dasar's. She's never been prone to claustrophobia, but now she swears the walls of the Citadel are literally closing in, that crimson spiral of blood magic compacting the entire manor into a tiny sphere around her as her blood runs through the bones of the Citadel. Isidora's mention of rituals, Ezelind's threat about her apathy towards the manor, Dasar's assurances that they wait three days before killing her. No wonder they won't let her go. She's the coal for their bonfire.

Unsteady feet slow her down, and it seems as though barely a minute has passed before she hears someone following her.

"Highness, would you please stop this little tantrum?" Dasar's voice calls out. "I really *hate* running."

Her stomach lurches and she fears she may be sick again. She has to get away from him, she can't stand to listen to his voice crawling into her ears for another second. It doesn't matter that her head is fuzzy and her bones sluggish. Panic spurs her past that.

Raucous noise from the party hits her ears once she makes it out of the basement foyer and she keeps going up, grabbing the rail to stop herself from slipping. A distant part of her mind is aware enough to remind her not to leave a blood trail. The rest of her is far more focused on getting the fuck out of this place.

A gaggle of vampires take to the staircase behind her and so she veers off the moment she can, picking a direction at random and hurrying down it. This corridor is at least empty, and the plush carpet beneath her still-bare feet is far more comfortable to walk on than the cold stone. She takes the next left, then right, running without thought until she feels certain she wasn't followed. If she's lucky, she can find an out of the way stairwell and get far enough from anyone that could stop her. Surely a place this big has access to a stable or something, some place where she could steal a horse and get away before being chased down and caught.

An open door up ahead reveals a warm, well-lit room that draws her attention. A place to hide? It's some kind of game room, presumably lit up in preparation for whatever partygoers happen to be in the mood for cue sports. Inside, there's a fainting couch against one wall, a box full of cigars sitting on a table, and bookshelves filled with tomes that appear more ornamental than practical. A grassy-green billiards table sits in the center, the polished wooden balls set up in a neat triangle in the middle and a series of cue racks stationed nearby.

She has always loved swords. And knives. Blades, really, are very nice, as a category. Always her preferred weapon. But as she grabs a billiards cue and feels the weight of it in her hand, she is filled with the joyfully vicious realization that regardless of what the cue was originally designed for, its *true* purpose in life is inflicting blunt force trauma.

Come and get me, Dasar.

"I truly don't understand why you think all your running about is worthwhile."

Adrenaline and panic jolt through her at the sound of Dasar's voice. How the *fuck* does he keep catching up to her so quickly? She'd seen no sign of him for at least two or three halls.

"If you wanted to play a game," he says pleasantly, running his fingers over the soft felt of the billiards table as he drifts towards her, "all you needed to do was ask. I'd be happy to put together a group."

Unlike the previous time he snuck up on her, right now she's fueled with nigh-unlimited cue-given confidence and bloodthirst.

The expression on Dasar's face as she swings the billiards cue at him is one she'll treasure for eternity. His jaw drops and he stumbles backwards without a single hint of grace to avoid getting his nose broken. A downright childish petulance puckers his brow, and his eyes are wide with shock.

"Highness, this is *unnecessary* –"

"I'm not some candle for you to burn through!" she screams. "This place deserves to be reduced to rubble!"

She swings again. The cue whistles as it cuts through the air, its weight building a viscerally satisfying momentum. This time he manages to raise his hands to protect his face and the cue impacts his forearms with a beautiful *crack*. Sharp splinters burst like a blooming flower as the force of her blow snaps it into two pieces, leaving her holding a messy, fractured spear.

Not unlike a stake.

It's not rowan, but it will do. In the fraction of a second it takes her to realize the power of the weapon in her hands, in the span of that single heartbeat, Dasar's petulant expression darkens into something furious and dangerous. His eyes flash like the warning flicker of a rattlesnake's tail.

His hand darts out, grabbing the broken cue and ripping it from her grasp before she can so much as blink. The next thing she knows, his fist slams into her solar plexus and white spots of pain burst behind her eyes. She's vaguely aware of being thrown onto the fainting couch and before she can scramble away, she finds herself caged by his arms. Her instinct to escape presses her flat against the sofa to put as much distance between them as possible.

"Don't. Break. My. *Things*," Dasar hisses.

She tries to slap him. It's stupid and rash and *of course* it doesn't work. He grabs her arm before she can even get close to clawing his cheek, and then she's pinned down in two ways instead of just one. His thumb digs into the wound on her wrist as she struggles.

He smiles. It isn't friendly. He runs the tip of his tongue over his fangs, the gold ring on his lower lip glistens. "A warning, Highness."

The bright amber of his eyes is mesmerizing from up close, the way it highlights the copper in his wild hair, the jewelry hanging from his ears, and she can't deny the way he shines like a flame in the dark. And for that one heart-pounding second, she's frozen in place.

He bites her wrist.

Pain shoots up her arm and through her spine; she thinks being stabbed would hurt less. Something burns in her wrist, something more than just pain, an acid in her veins. She yanks her arm, trying to shake him off, to do anything at all to make it stop, but she can't. His lips are sealed over her skin, his teeth buried in her flesh and grinding against her bones.

Her lungs fill with air, and she tries scream, to cry out for help, to…

It doesn't work. Her tongue is fat and numb in her mouth. Slow sludge flows through her bloodstream and her bones turn into floppy cartilage. Her body slumps on the sofa, lying placid and obedient. The beat of her heart is sluggish. While she can breathe and blink, there's nothing else she can do. No matter how hard she tries, she can't make her fingers do more than pointlessly twitch. Forming a fist is a pipe dream.

Her arm is limp in Dasar's grip as whatever venom or poison he's given her keeps her pliant. She watches as his throat bobs, swallowing down her blood in deep, savoring gulps. Occasionally his tongue darts out to lick up a drop that threatens to roll down her arm, and then he returns to the source, teeth chewing up her flesh as he slots his fangs back into the original punctures.

Even the pain begins to fade. A cloying fog has seeped into her arm from elbow to fingertips. But it is somehow worse now she can't feel it. Pain would make it sharp, would cut through this haze.

Peripherally, she's aware of the door opening.

"My Lord Dasar," a familiar voice gasps, shock pushing the breath out of her words. A woman's voice. Where has Kazan heard it before? "Save some for the rest of us, won't you?"

Dasar withdraws his fangs from Kazan's wrist and stands up. The moment he's no longer holding her arm, it flops down, sticky blood smearing her dress. "Of course, my dear, how unspeakably rude of me," he says to the newcomer, all upbeat charm and smiles once more as he wipes his mouth off. "I've finished here and there's no lasting harm done."

"Let me go clean her up, shall I?" the woman says. "I'll bring her back to the party once she's a bit more presentable."

"Thank you, dear, that would be much appreciated."

Footsteps sound as the woman walks around the sofa and stops in front of Kazan. Oh yes, she *does* know this person. It's the half-naked woman she inadvertently stumbled across when she climbed in through the window.

The woman wraps an arm around Kazan's waist and effortlessly hauls her up, supporting her as her knees refuse to function properly. "Come along, Highness."

Chapter Fourteen

Kazan is little more than a ragdoll as the woman carries her out of the study and into the main hall. Fortunately for her dignity, the woman immediately turns into a smaller corridor and up a set of stairs that lead away from the more populated areas. It's a stupid thing to worry about, but with everything lying in tatters at Kazan's feet, she cannot bear any further humiliation.

"I am sorry about Dasar," the woman remarks, helping her stagger up the stone steps. "He can be a tad… *indulgent* at times, even by my standards. And don't worry about the venom. It burns through a human's system remarkably quickly."

Makes sense once she thinks about it. It wouldn't need to last long, as she imagines most humans are cut off from the source of it only after they've been thoroughly exsanguinated.

"Where're…" Kazan swallows. It's a surprise when her throat functions. "Where're you taking me?"

The woman glances down at her ravaged wrist. "Somewhere you can get that looked at."

"What's the point? I'm dead already."

"Don't count your chickens until they're beheaded, Highness. And just because your time is almost over doesn't mean that having an open wound is in any way comfortable. Once Dasar's venom wears off and you can feel the pain again, you'll thank me."

The woman leads her to a set of private quarters belonging

to someone likely important by the abundance of space and thick carpeting. For the second time now, she is deposited into a chair, but with far more delicacy than Dasar utilized. The woman takes the time to prop Kazan's still bleeding wrist up on a beaded pillow to help stop the flow. She pulls out a handkerchief, gently wrapping it around Kazan's wrist, bandaging the wound as best as possible.

"Who are you?" Kazan asks.

The woman's glossy, crimson lips form each letter with distracting precision. "A friendly colleague of Lord De Vere. More specifically, I am Lady Aishreya Sutcliffe, former Baroness of Cairemere, Steward of Pearlwood –" Kazan knows that last name; she buys gold from the Pearlwood mines "– and Seneschal to High Lord Dasar of House Gambit." She bends her head to press a soft kiss to Kazan's knuckles. "But *you* may call me Reya."

Reya ties off the handkerchief. Kazan's voice cracks as she whispers, "Get me out of here. Please."

"I must beg you not to ask that of me, Highness. I love giving people answers they want to hear. If I reply, I'd either be giving you an unpleasant answer or lying. And I don't particularly want to lie to someone as pretty as you."

"I don't care what you want. I care what you *do*."

Reya winces, and then the expression vanishes. Despite having finished with the handkerchief, she continues to delicately hold Kazan's hand. The venom in Kazan's body still runs strong, too strong to let her pull away from Reya and her neatly painted fingernails and her smooth skin. The touch is gentle, almost caring, and that makes it worse. A slap would at least feel honest.

Kazan wets her lips and asks, "Why help me?"

Reya runs her thumb over the bandages covering Kazan's knuckles. "Ah, another difficult question to answer. If I say it's because you don't deserve what Dasar did, you'll call me out for the discrepancy in helping you now only to let you die later. If I say it's because you're beautiful, you'll think me vapid or a liar. But in the end, I suppose it's because you gave Adrius a decent fight. I was there, you know. In the forest. I watched you stand toe to toe with him for longer than I would ever have guessed a human could. It was quite… breathtaking."

Earlier she used Adrius's surname, and now she uses his given name. What exactly is their relationship? 'Friend' can encompass a wide spectrum, including whatever political alliances and rivalries that must be present in the upper crust of vampire society.

There's a near silent creak as the door opens and Reya quickly rises to her feet, rushing to see who it is.

Although Kazan can't turn her head to look, she can easily hear Adrius's voice accompanying his footsteps. "What happened?"

"Dasar happened," Reya replies, dry as one of the wines Kazan tasted earlier.

Adrius approaches, and fiery anger struggles to win a fight against Kazan's paralysis. He reaches for her hand to examine her wrist and she twitches, trying her damndest to pull away. But her arm barely moves despite the furious nature of her desire.

"Don't touch me," she snarls, the words faint and flimsy.

Adrius bites his lower lip but takes a deliberate step back, holding his hands up in peace. "I only want to help. That's not going to get any better if you let it bleed out, and to be frank, I wouldn't advise walking around a vampire manor with an open wound."

Much as she hates to admit it, he's not wrong. "…Fine," she mutters.

"I'll be gentle, I promise."

Adrius heads straight to the long desk at the edge of the room. These must be *his* quarters. He runs his hand along the decorative scrollwork carved into the wood until he presses down on one of the whorls. It clicks as it recedes into the desk, and two latches flick out at the sides of the desk. When he slides them back and pushes up the entire desktop, it reveals a hollow interior. He retrieves two objects from the trick compartment – a blunt quill and a stone inkwell. With his other hand, he grabs a jug of water and a clean cloth.

"I'm sorry you had to wait this long," he says, kneeling in front of her. "If I'd known, I would have come sooner."

"I didn't know how to get a message to you." Reya's standing back, her polished thumbnail trapped between her teeth as she watches. "Not without leaving her alone. I doubt Dasar will try anything again. Making the same blunder twice isn't his style and he so rarely loses his temper enough to bend the rules of his own party. But someone else might, and she can hardly do anything to stop them while inhibited by his venom."

Adrius wets the cloth, removes Reya's hasty bandage, and starts cleaning as much blood from Kazan's wrist as possible. He removes the stopper from the inkwell and dips the quill nib into it. "This is a tincture of yarrow and water from Savis's moonpools." He holds out the quill for her to get a closer look at it; a tiny thing, a small shimmering blue feather that's almost black. "And this is a magpie feather. Now stay still, please."

The tincture smells fresh and sunny when it touches her skin. He uses the quill to draw a series of complicated symbols and lines in a circle around the wound on her wrist.

"I have a basic knowledge of healing magics," he explains as he works. He dips the quill back into the tincture and keeps drawing. "It's a common misconception that you need non-human blood to perform magics, but in reality, all you need is time. Humans rarely have enough to learn anything more than parlor tricks in their last years. Or invocation, although in that they're merely a conduit for the lingering magics of whatever saint they're worshiping."

"Why healing?" she asks.

He shrugs in a way that loudly declares he has no desire to talk about it. "It seemed interesting."

"What else can you do?"

"Me? Nothing. Others of my kind have studied different magics, but in general, putting forth such effort is not popular. I've heard that Dasar used to study transformation magics and could take the shape of a bat whenever he wished, although we suspect he's forgotten how, this past century. As a more concrete example, my disguise ring was made by one of our kind, an illusionist from Faireway Hill."

Reya, still lurking, gives a twitchy smile when Kazan questioningly glances at her. "I've dabbled."

Design apparently complete, Adrius stoppers the inkwell and sets the quill down. He places his thumb over the center of her wound and *presses*. Pain, sharp and present and beautifully alive cuts through her and she struggles not to cry out.

Then the pain becomes overshadowed by a warm, humming sensation. Her lips fall open in a silent gasp. The tincture vanishes, and a thick, grizzly scab starts to form around the bite mark. It's far from healed, but the bleeding has stopped. And the unpleasant fuzzy sensation rapidly exits her bloodstream.

"Oh." She swallows. "That's – thank you."

He cleans the area again, removing the last smears of red. "There. It should scar over within the next few hours. Let me know if it still hurts and I'll see what else I can do."

She twists her wrist experimentally. "No, it doesn't."

"I'm glad to hear it. Lady Sutcliffe, would you take her back to Dasar when she's ready? I should be –"

"Don't you *dare* leave," Kazan hisses. "You owe me a damn apology."

He flinches, unable to meet her eyes. "I... regret what happened in the Vildenmarr. Had Dasar not ordered me to do so, I wouldn't have fought you, no matter what I might have joked about at Rask's party. And whatever you may think, I *am* sorry. If you hadn't fought back, I wouldn't have hurt you."

"Are you really trying to tell me this is *my* fault? If I could move my arm, Adrius De Vere, I would slap you."

"I wouldn't stop you if you did," he quietly replies. "I phrased that poorly; what happened was in no way your fault. I simply meant that I tried to injure you as little as possible and wouldn't have hurt you at all had I the choice to avoid it."

"Better. I still don't forgive you."

"It would be unfair for me to ask that of you." He lets out a slow, dragging sigh. "You've lost a lot of blood, you should rest. I know that is not exactly possible at the moment, but feel free to stay here as long as you need. Lady Sutcliffe can find a way to distract Dasar for an hour or so."

"I am quite practiced in that art," Reya quips.

Kazan sags in her chair. If only it were that easy. "What's the use? If I don't show up to the party soon, Dasar will simply find me again."

"Find you again? What do you mean?"

"He keeps following me around. I run and there he is. He's unbelievably fast too, especially for someone who doesn't look like he would lower himself to move at a pace quicker than an arrogant saunter."

All the smoldering allure of Reya's resting expression ignites, turning into a cold and furious glower. "Sometimes I really can't stand that man."

"You believe he's…" Adrius trails off.

Reya nods.

"I'll search her." He hesitates for a long minute before saying, "Pardon me."

He places the supplies down on the floor and turns up the cuffs of Kazan's sleeves. Apparently the lace and stitching is of great interest to him, for he examines it with a keen eye. After a minute, he moves on, checking the rings on her fingers. One by one, he pulls them off, turning them over carefully, and then once he's done, replaces them on her hands. She doesn't bother asking what he's doing. She's exhausted from all of this, and her curiosity has temporarily receded, too tired to do anything other than watch.

He stands and checks her hair next, delicately picking over the pins holding it in place. Then he removes her necklace and presumably examines it as well. Once he replaces it, he slowly circles her, a deep frown narrowing his eyes and pinching his lips.

"It must be somewhere," he mutters to himself.

To her mortification, Reya remarks, "Check her underthings."

"Tell me," he asks, "are you – I'm sorry to ask such a question – but you're wearing a garter, aren't you?"

"Yes. No stockings though." Which is rather odd, when she considers it.

His expression sours. "How very like Dasar." He drops to one knee in front of her and she suddenly knows where this is going to go, although she has no idea why. "I'm truly sorry about this," he says, and then pushes her skirt up.

Denying that she'd thought about this at Rask's party is a waste of effort, but she must confess that she could never have imagined the circumstances correctly. His cold fingers move up her thigh, barely touching her, as though determined to maintain a firm boundary between the two of them. She feels the garter around her left thigh loosen and then the soft fabric is gone. His touch similarly vanishes, leaving goosebumps on her skin.

He stands again, hastily letting her skirts fall back down. A crimson ribbon is clasped in his fingers, and he holds it out to the light, turning it over in another careful examination.

"There it is." He glares at the ribbon.

Reya's nose wrinkles as though someone has offered her a plate of molding cheese. "A tracking spell," she says. "Dasar's never quite as foolish as he acts. Although that doesn't explain how he's moving through the Citadel as fast as he has been... He knows this manor better than anyone, and I won't deny he always manages to be exactly where he wants to be, but I suppose I've never seen him *need* to get from one place to another so quickly."

Adrius shows Kazan the offending object.

Strange symbols have been stitched into the garter's fabric, and when she reaches out to touch it, it feels warm in the same way his disguise ring had been – the mark of a spell at work. He strides over to the nearest candle, pulls back the plate of glass in front of it, and burns the ribbon. It doesn't char and smoke in the way she expects, instead it bursts into flame within the blink of an eye. It crumbles into ash, leaving no trace of its existence besides a dark dusting of soot on the table.

"That ought to do it," Adrius declares.

He picks up his healing supplies and returns to the desk compartment he'd initially retrieved them from. As he finishes putting away the quill and inkwell, Kazan turns towards the window. If he and Reya intend to leave her, could she climb...?

"There's no point," he says, glancing over his shoulder and catching her gaze.

"There's *always* a point," she stubbornly counters.

He leans against the window with a sigh, beckoning for her to come over. "Take a look."

Standing is difficult, but Kazan manages. Reya inches forward, hands held out to help her if she needs it, but she refuses to accept the kindness. She edges towards him, unwilling to consider how easy it feels to be close to him compared to Dasar. Outside the window is near the same scene as earlier when she climbed up to Reya's rooms. Nothing that unusual, as far as she can tell.

"I'm looking," she says. "Tell me what I'm supposed to be *seeing*."

"Say you manage to make your way to the ground floor and by some miracle you are not spotted either inside the manor or climbing down the walls," Adrius asks. "What then?"

"I run down the mountain. Or steal a horse."

"And then? How do you avoid all the soldiers patrolling the grounds? How do you get past the gates?"

She glares out the window, refusing to acknowledge his words by answering them.

"How do you make your way down the mountain in the first place?" he continues. "Do you scale the sheer cliffs and break your legs doing so? Do you take the sole safe path that remains patrolled at all hours? You're standing in the tallest building – the highest vantage point – for miles around. How do you avoid being spotted and hunted down?"

She doesn't even know where she is, in the grand scale of things. If she made it to the forest, how could she avoid being hunted down again as she was in the Vildenmarr? And yet this manor must have a way out, it must. There *must* be an escape route for her. She has always been able to save herself in the past, no matter what. This *needs* to be the same. *She* needs it to be the same. Panic claws around in her insides, shredding and freezing everything in its grasp as she stares out the window and tries to think.

"Every prison can be broken." Is she telling him that, or herself? "There has to be a way out."

He avoids her eyes. "Do you really think you're the first human who has tried to escape? Everything, and I do mean *everything*, has been attempted and still no one has ever been successful. Fleeing the Citadel is impossible."

"No," she insists, her hands clutching the windowsill. "There has to be an escape route."

Maybe she could try and sneak out with someone leaving the manor – but who would be leaving? The party isn't over yet. And if she's noticed to be missing for even a second, they would raise the alarm and halt everything from leaving the moment she vanishes from sight. Even if Dasar can no longer track her, it takes time to hitch a ride without being discovered and she wouldn't be able to make it that long.

"Kazan..." Reya hesitates before finishing, "This castle was designed for more than mere parties. It took three days and hundreds of vampire soldiers to breach the walls. One human doesn't stand a chance."

Kazan attempts to take a deep breath, only to find her

lungs a bit more stubborn on the matter. Think. There must be something. What part of this puzzle is she missing?

When she doesn't say anything further, Reya shifts away towards the door. "I'm sorry. For this, and for my Lord Dasar's unsavory action earlier. I'll... go provide that promised distraction, shall I?"

After a moment's hesitation she leaves, and the door softly clicks shut behind her.

"Kazan," Adrius begins, "I know I can't fully understand how this must feel, but I *am* sorry." There's something in his voice, not quite pity, not quite disappointment, but some vague sadness, as if a small part of him wishes things were different.

"If – if there is a way out, would you tell me?" she can't help asking. Reya wouldn't, but maybe...

He stares at her for a long time, his lips parted ever so slightly while he tries to answer. "No," he says at last. "Not if there was even the slightest risk that anyone would discover my assistance. And there would always be such a risk. My reputation is miserable enough as it is. An error such as that would very well result in my fellows attempting to put a knife in my back. And I do mean that literally."

Of course he won't help. She shouldn't have expected he would say otherwise. He might have had fun with her at Rask's party, but it clearly meant nothing to him. Whatever it might or might not have felt to her... what a fool she was to expect him to care about her emotions, even a tiny bit. She's on her own. She's *always* on her own. Furthermore, contrary to his demeanor at the party, here he appears to be dulled. As though the color has faded from him. She would have expected him to be in high spirits surrounded by his fellows, but instead, a dreary shroud of fog and melancholy drapes over him.

"Reya will help me," she tries.

The use of Reya's first name makes him draw back, confusion pinching his brow. "I didn't know you two were so well acquainted. Even still, the Citadel is the center of our society and it, and its treasures, are among the few things she would not risk. She won't help you any more than I will."

"If there's a way out," she asks, desperation hastening her words, "even if you can't tell me what it is – could you tell me if there *is* one?"

"You're searching in vain," he replies softly. "I wasn't lying to you when I said there is no escaping this place."

"No," she murmurs to herself. "No, there's a way. I can escape this. I can survive this. I just – I just have to figure it out."

"The Citadel isn't a puzzle, Kazan. It's a prison for humans just as much as it is our place of power. Over the centuries, our kind has mapped every darkened corner of this place. Discovered all its secrets. There's no weakness to be found in its walls. Why do you think you're allowed to roam so freely? Because there is nowhere to go."

She feels the truth of his words and they make her sick. Claustrophobic fear grows in the pit of her stomach and slowly creeps up her spine like the many limbs of a large tarantula. No gaps in patrols, no way down the mountain, no way past the gate, no way out of the manor.

Oh, saints help her. She will die if she doesn't think of something. Her mind spins with all the futility of a dog chasing its own tail. She keeps thinking of it like a puzzle that can be solved if only she's clever enough, but if Adrius and Reya are right...

"What do you recommend I do then?" she demands, trying to throw enough anger into her voice to cover the fact that she's all but begging him.

He shrugs. "In the past, the humans who have seemed... better off... were the ones who spent their time rather thoroughly inebriated."

"That's your suggestion? That I spend the rest of my very short life drunk?"

"It's that or spend the rest of your very short life terrified.

I'm not making a decision for you. I'm only telling you what I've seen."

"So – what?" She laughs bitterly, mania threatening to creep in. "Are you telling me that I should just... *surrender*? I don't give up, Lord Adrius De Vere. I'm *not* dying here. I–I *refuse*."

"As I said, it's your choice. But if you keep trying, your escape attempts will eventually stop amusing Dasar. You may find that it is better to keep him entertained."

"To hell with his entertainment. I am not a game."

"To him, and the majority of those here, you are." Adrius holds up a hand when Kazan draws hers back to slap him. "I'm only stating their perception of you. If you choose not to spend your last days in drunken stupor, then you will likely find more comforts by appealing to his sense of humor than you would otherwise."

Even rabbits caught in snares still struggle till their dying breath. Is that all she's doing?

"Adrius," she asks quietly. "You said that you didn't wish to hurt me, but before you leave, I have to know. The Vildenmarr – were you...?"

He shakes his head. "I had no idea you would be there. I can assure you that I was not following you."

"You offered me a ride."

"It was a sincere offer. If I'd intended to capture you, I wouldn't have gone about it that way. If I had known you would end up here, I wouldn't have done what... Well, I wouldn't have."

"Why even make the offer if you were joining Dasar's hunting party?"

Although his face is turned away from her, she can see the way his shoulders tense. "If you must know," he admits, "I was hoping to find an excuse not to attend Dasar's event. While Ezelind would not have been pleased, nothing truly pleases her, and Dasar wouldn't have been offended if I missed his hunt because of a dalliance with a human."

She draws in a sharp breath and chokes on it. If she had accepted Adrius's offer, if she had gone off and had a fun couple of hours, then she wouldn't have read Rask's letter until it was too late to join the Warden caravan. Some other traveler would have been picked up and left in her place, and she would have been blissfully safe with one of the few vampires in all of Mavazem who had no desire to kill her. She had thought she was being clever when she turned down his offer… Instead, she had sealed her fate.

"Kazan, I –" Adrius tries.

"I think," and it's so difficult to speak without her voice breaking, "that you should leave. Don't you think you've done enough?"

He opens his mouth to protest before snapping it shut again. "Of course."

He politely steps out of the room and then Kazan is alone once again.

Her nails pick at the scab on her wrist. As the wound rapidly heals, it begins to itch, and as her mind whirls away like a mouse in a maze, she can't stop herself from scratching. Rough, thick tissue provides a focus in a way, something for her thumb to fixate on. The scab begins to loosen, pushed up by the reforming skin beneath, and she runs her thumbnail underneath the edges of it, sliding slowly back and forth.

Did she truly doom herself? Obviously accepting Adrius's offer would have saved her. There's no way out of the Citadel, she knows that now. Fear buries its claws deep into her, sliding against her bones like her nail underneath the scab. If she doubts herself, if she accepts that this was her fault in even the slightest manner, then she's truly doomed.

Swing the hammer and commit to the blow. In all her years of smithing she has learned that once the hammer comes down, she cannot doubt the angle of the swing or the force of her blow. She must commit. Follow through. Be certain. Everything is a confidence game.

A game or a trap? she thinks. This manor is designed to keep her trapped… and perhaps that's the problem. Every human before her, everyone who has previously tried to escape – that was how they lost. So maybe it *is* a game. Maybe Dasar is right about that. Escaping would mean tossing her cards down on the table and leaving the game behind, not staying and playing to victory.

She can still play to win.

She wants to make them *pay*. She wants revenge, she wants to humiliate them as they've humiliated her. Her mind drags up the image of a boar spear. Unlike most spears with their long blades, a specialized head with protruding wings on the socket that act almost like a sword hilt is needed to hunt wild boar. Once the animal has been skewered, its sheer rage will cause it to claw itself further upon the spear in order to tear apart its hunter. It doesn't attempt to avoid pain or preserve its own life. Instead, it decides that killing itself faster is worth ensuring vengeance.

Yes, she is trapped in here with them. But *they* are also trapped in here with *her*.

Something scratches against her wrist. Her thumbnail slides and slides and the scab finally withers off, falling into her lap. A rough patch of scar tissue mars the inside of her wrist now, like a smear of thick, pale paint. Ugly, but no more so than her face.

She gets to her feet and refuses to let herself wobble.

Abandoning the various bloodstained bits of cloth and tossing the now-ruined beaded pillow onto the ground, she strides out of Adrius's quarters and back into the fray.

"Oh look! It's Her Highness!"

A group of vampires lounge in the corridor, one of them holding a half empty bottle with its contents sloshing around as he walks. Kazan isn't sure if they're drunk on wine, blood, or the excitement of the party.

"Highness," one of the woman coos, "you left the party so early this morning, we were all very disappointed."

Kazan purses her lips. "How tragic."

The man holding the bottle giggles and nudges his fellow in the arm. "You should bow to her. It would be hilarious."

His friend laughs, bending into a deep and exaggerated bow, his fingers almost scraping the floor as he feigns supplication to Kazan. "Majesty," he snickers, as the rest of them cannot contain their mirth.

"On your knees then," Kazan demands.

He glances at his companions, who now howl with laughter – what a sight for them, the false queen being so authoritative, as though she has real power! How funny it must be for them. "As Her Highness commands," he says with a snort.

As soon as he gets on his knees, she plants her foot on his head, shoving his face into the tiled floor. Then, she steps over him as though he were just a stone in her way. His friends burst out laughing once more.

They won't be laughing much longer. She'll make sure of that. She will steal her sword back. She will humiliate them all in return. And she will kill Weisz, Ezelind, and Dasar. She might kill Adrius, too, for good measure. Her mind isn't made up on that point, but it doesn't matter. He does not stand with her, and thus, he is against her.

High above, she hears the Citadel's bells ringing out, ushering in midnight.

One day down. Two to go.

DAY TWO

Chapter Fifteen

Kazan has never been wealthy. Not a single day of her life. Her mother was a tanner, but she died after a lean, hungry winter when Kazan was a year old. So that income stream dried up when she was still too young to help around the house or otherwise contribute. Her father took over the business soon after, but even back then she could pinpoint exactly where she was in the hierarchy of their village – very, *very* close to the bottom.

Being a blacksmith is a steady job, and while she pours her heart into swordcraft, it simply hasn't afforded her many luxuries. So, as much as she despises every single vampire in the Citadel, and as much as she's accustomed to sleeping on her worn-down mattress at home, she *loves* the indulgently soft bed they've given her.

After her revelation, she'd hauled her bloodstained and barefoot self into her chambers and laid down on the bed while Isidora began preparing her wardrobe for the nighttime festivities.

"Highness," Isidora says now, laying a dress down at the foot of the bed. "I, um, well, that is – I thought a nice gold would look alright?"

The gold gown is horrifically ostentatious, laced with a rich purple. The same colors Dasar wears.

"Absolutely not. Get me something in... silver." The color might not burn as the metal itself does, but she likes the idea of wearing something that gives an impression of danger.

"Oh – alright."

Whatever else she can say about Isidora's nervousness and stuttering and fumbling, the woman is an efficient lady in waiting. No sooner has Kazan gotten into bed than she is forced to roll out again. Isidora begins unlacing her dirty gown, unwrapping the rumpled and stained fabric from her body with the professionalism of a tailor. Isidora strips her down and it's not so awkward to be naked in front of her, considering the clinical nature in which Isidora works. After the stripping comes a quick bath filled with fragrant soaps. Once she has dried off in the softest towel she's ever touched, Isidora begins redressing her, layer by layer, moving her arms and twisting her torso.

When the whole affair is finished, Kazan finds herself in a shimmering midnight blue gown with silver embroidery, loose sleeves, and a somewhat daring neckline. Given that it was selected by hedonistic vampires, that last bit does not surprise her.

"You're very pretty, Majesty," Isidora murmurs, draping a diamond-laden necklace around her collarbones.

"The fact that you have to assure me of that disproves your point, don't you think?"

Isidora stammers and stutters for a good while before diplomatically saying, "Well, you see, we – vampires, that is – we don't scar. Usually, I mean. There are exceptions." Like Amelia. That woman will never get her eyeball back, a fact that brings Kazan no small pleasure. "But some of us consider scars to have a certain exoticism to them. Not me, personally. Um, no offense, Highness."

Exoticism. She hasn't heard that one before.

"Highness, can I ask…?"

Kazan resists the urge to roll her eyes. "I have a feeling I know the question already."

"Um. Your scar?"

She sees the hungry curiosity in Isidora's eyes. Ah *ha*.

"Nothing special really." Now what can she say that will get her something from Isidora? "I'm sure you know how rough it is living as a human, and I had a particularly hard childhood. Very little in the way of food. My mother taught me how to hunt in the forests nearby. One day we were attacked by a vicious bear. My mother managed to kill it, but not before it had swiped its paw across my face and gouged me with a single claw."

Isidora gasps, clapping her hands over her mouth. "Oh, Majesty, that's simply awful!" She leads Kazan over to the vanity with fussy, worried hand motions. "Let me try to help, really, I'm sure there's something I can do to make it better. A pretty red lipstick might detract from everything else."

A variety of cosmetics lie on the vanity, and Isidora spends a good deal of time applying powders and paints. On it goes until Isidora is finished with Kazan's face and begins doing her hair. Her dark hair has always been a bit shorter than she would like it to be, coming down to her mid-back but no longer. For so many years, she had tried to grow it out, in a desire to emulate the long, elegant hairstyles that women like Rask can pull off. Her efforts had always been interrupted, though. Sometimes a spark would land on her hair and singe the ends, or something would get knotted in it and she would simply be too frustrated to bother untangling.

As a result, there's not quite enough hair for Isidora to create some of the more elaborate styles that the other vampires have been wearing. She clearly tries her best, pearl-tipped pins stuck in her mouth that pinches into a concentrated frown.

For a moment Kazan's mind wanders to Reya, and her extravagantly long, dark brown hair. All the things that could be done with that beautiful hair, how it could be pulled up to expose that delicate neck or let loose to frame that enchanting face. And... *no*, Kazan is not thinking about that. She has things she needs to do, and that list does not include fantasizing about a woman who refuses to help her. Her interest in Adrius is bad enough.

"There!" Isidora finally declares.

Kazan looks properly in the mirror and something very small inside her heart twists. She touches her unscarred cheek, gently running her fingertips down the soft skin. Bronze darkens her eyelids, and her eyes aren't plain brown anymore, instead they glow in a way she's never seen before. It's... beautiful. *She's* beautiful. She has never been beautiful a day in her life, not with this scar.

Perfectly red lips form shapes in the mirror as she whispers, "Thank you."

"You're welcome, Highness," Isidora mumbles, blushing. "I'm glad you like it. Back to the party then, Your Majesty?"

Kazan's nail presses against the center of her lip, watching the flesh yield to the pressure until she can feel it against her teeth. She can't look away from her surreal reflection and barely pays attention to what Isidora is saying. "Go on ahead, please. I'll be down there in a minute. I'm hardly able to run away now, am I?"

Isidora stutters again for a moment before she curtseys. "Of course. If I may – that is, if it's not too informal of me – you *are* expected. My Lord Dasar will likely send someone to fetch you sooner rather than later. I'll be around. If... if you need me."

It takes Kazan a long time before she can do anything other than stare at herself. Eventually, she puts on the delicate slippers that Isidora set out by the vanity and breathes confidence back into her posture. Isidora's warning about Dasar sending someone to look for her remains at the forefront of her mind, but that still gives her enough time to see if she can collect an ally. If no one is willing to volunteer, then she shall turn her sights to the dead.

She makes her way through the manor, tracing the routes she recalls taking before and overlaying them with the menagerie map she committed to memory.

Everything in the hall of paintings is as she remembers it. Adrius's warm, human features frozen in pigment and the semi-opaque geist resting absently beneath it. The geist's eyes roll up as she approaches.

"Alright." She stands in front of him, crossing her arms in front of her chest. "Let's talk."

The geist tilts his head up maybe one third of an inch. "Oh, it's you again. I thought... Did you not run from me?"

"I was more running from this place in general than you specifically," she clarifies. "But that doesn't matter now. It has been... made clear to me that running isn't the best use of my time. You offered to help me if I would help you in return. What did you mean by that?"

"I meant what I said. You want to leave their stronghold. I want to make them pay. We can help each other."

She barks out a laugh. "Well, isn't this a fortunate coincidence. I've actually changed my goals lately, and it would seem they align with yours. I am more than happy to listen to the details of your proposal. What, precisely, would you want me to do?"

The smile that comes over him isn't so much a movement of his mouth or eyes, so much as it is a slight shift in his translucency. The corners of his mouth form slightly more solidly for a moment, the dead smile lines around his eyes a bit more defined. He looks familiar to her, somehow. Then it's gone, and he's back to a ghastly, semi-opaque, cloud of gloom.

"Someone killed me," he tells her.

"A vampire. Must have been if you're a geist now. Who?" She glances up at Adrius's painted visage. "Was it..."

"I don't know who. I didn't see their face. They came up behind me, bit me, and then I was..." He pauses and stares off into the distance for a moment. "They're here, in the Citadel. I can sense it. If you want my help, then you must find them."

"What can you even do to help me? You're a geist, you can do naught to humans but possess them. You can't even get far from that painting. I'm not particularly inclined to go from being a vampire's plaything to a geist's puppet."

"You want to kill vampires," he remarks blandly, as though commenting on the weather.

"As do you, it would seem."

"We can sense them. We're *bound* to them. We can feel them when they're near and follow their scent like... like fish. Following the water's current. Your body could be my vessel and I could lead you through empty halls to those you wish dead. A captain on the sea." His mouth goes slack, and he tilts his head to the side. "I never sailed a ship. I wish..."

She sighs. Being that sort of hunter is tempting, but it has strings attached. "We all wish for a great many things. Tell me, how would I guarantee that you'd *leave* my body once you did all this?"

"Take me back to my painting. I would stay here, if I could. I painted it, I think... It's so hard to remember." A sad frown makes his face droop and for a moment she pities him, as one pities a dog with only three legs. "Or perhaps when my killer is dead, I will go... wherever it is I'm supposed to go."

"I see. It's all well and good for you to help me hunt these bastards down, but I'll need more before I go tracking down this mystery killer of yours," she says. "Something about your death, something that can help with finding them or that can help me with my predicament."

"There is one name I've heard, a name who knows something about the regency," he replies. "Gia Montanari. Find her, and you'll find some answers, good or bad."

"Gia Montanari." She muses on the name for a moment, scouring her memory for any mentions of it. But no, it's wholly unfamiliar to her. Still, it's something.

His head drops down like a scarecrow's hood flopping over. His eyes narrow as he looks seemingly at Kazan's feet. "Don't trust the black cat."

What the –

Something meows. Sure enough, when she looks down, a tiny black cat is rubbing up against the hem of her skirts. It has sleek fur and a long tail, and looks up at her with a relatively generic cat face; amber eyes and ears that are perfectly triangular. A golden collar is clasped around its neck, the thing practically a necklace, shimmering like water as the cat moves.

"Aren't you gorgeous," Kazan murmurs. "Did your owner put that gaudy thing around your neck?"

The cat huffs.

She looks back up at the geist. "Gia Montanari, huh?"

The geist hums a quiet, affirmative noise.

Alright then. She bends down to let the cat sniff her hand. A rough tongue licks her fingertips and then the cat pushes its head into her hand, as though demanding adoration. She obliges, gently petting its smooth fur while it preens like a peacock. For such an adorable thing, it's a pity it cannot be trusted. Perhaps it belongs to Dasar?

The cat trots away from her, before tilting its head to the side. Does it want her to follow?

She scoffs. "Sorry, sweet thing. I'm on a deadline."

Turning her back on the cat, she begins her march back to the main hall. Isidora had warned her that her time was limited, and she would prefer not to have someone come search for her. Best to make an appearance now and attempt to discern where her sword might be in the meanwhile. That, and figure out who Gia Montanari is and why the woman might be relevant to any of this. And of course, she can't forget to learn more details of her role in all this, and how best to avoid being caught scheming before three days are up.

At least now she's not entirely alone, dead though her company might be.

Chapter Sixteen

A predictably hand-wringing Isidora and a stoic guard are waiting to latch onto Kazan the moment she returns to the halls around her chambers. Given the lack of windows in most of the manor, she can't quite say what time it is. Once she follows Isidora out onto one of the balconies overlooking the main banquet hall, however, she looks up at the glass ceiling and sees the night sky. It's probably around two or three in the morning, and the party down below carries on. At Rask's party, Adrius mentioned that vampires sleep only as an indulgence, not as a requirement, so it's unsurprising to see that while there isn't quite the packed throng of people that had been present the first night, the room is still vibrant with dancing, feasting, and socializing.

She has two goals: Find her sword and find out who killed the geist. Similarly, she has only two clues: Gia Montanari, and the geist's connection to Adrius De Vere.

Although people here seem rather uninclined to discuss Adrius, she may be able to press someone for information. Or find Reya again, given that she seemed at ease with him.

Her stomach rumbles. Alright, a third goal: Eat something.

She makes her way to one of the banquet tables, sits down atop the table instead of bothering with a chair, and picks up the nearest thing she can find. It happens to be an apple, and she bites into it with gusto. Now, how best to proceed?

Regrettably, her solo contemplation is swiftly interrupted. If she remembers Isidora's ramblings correctly, she's supposed to be dancing and socializing by now and thus the vampires are apparently on the lookout for her. A small group flocks over to her within minutes.

"Ooooh, Highness," a ludicrously drunk woman croons, draping an arm over her shoulder. "Aren't you a vision?"

One of her companions laughs, a man who seems slightly more sober, although it's a very low bar. "She's something alright! Certainly got a one-of-a-kind face, doesn't she? I mean," he adds sarcastically, reaching out and patting her face with a clammy hand, "you're *so* pretty, Highness. Absolutely –" He hiccups. "Absolutely queenly."

Kazan reaches out and grabs a cheese knife lying on the table. With one hand she removes the man's hand from her cheek and with the other, she plunges the knife straight through his palm until he's pinned to the table. Blood oozes onto the wood as his friends try to pry the knife from his flesh, and his pained screech is music to her ears. She gives him an indulgently gleeful smile before hopping off the table and striding away.

Luck, for once, decides to grace her with its presence. When Isidora tries to follow her, she gets distracted by the injured vampire and instead starts fussing over that, awkwardly and ineffectively dabbing at the wound with a napkin.

Kazan slips into the crowd before Isidora notices but unfortunately finds herself surrounded by a great deal more vampires. Most want nothing more than to exchange a few light and often drunken words, playing along with their silly little game. A man kisses her hand and a woman strokes her hair. The names go by in a blur, all their simpering remarks to her the same. Some names sound familiar, towns she's heard of or noble human families. While vampires mostly declare themselves to one of the three houses, it would seem they also claim either a vampiric bloodline as a family name or keep their well-known human surnames.

She tries to ask a few of them about Adrius but they all have similar reactions to Isidora. They don't want to talk about him, they try to steer her towards alternative subjects, or they outright warn her away from him. Though they all obviously can't wait to eat her, it would seem they don't want her to come to any serious harm before then.

Movement on the edge of the hall catches her eye – Amelia, and she is not a pretty sight. A silken bandage wraps around her face, covering her mutilated eye socket. Any visible facial features are lined and scowling, irritation has narrowed her one good eye. She shoves at the man she's talking to, and when Kazan eavesdrops as she approaches, she can pick up on what's being said.

"I don't care for your excuses." Amelia talks over the man even as he tries to open his mouth to defend himself. "If our Lord Weisz says he wants something done then we get it done. I have too much on my plate to deal with minutia, so this falls to you. Understood?"

The man, who Kazan now notices is a soldier dressed in the same green and bronze as Amelia, nods so quickly that it gives the impression that his head is barely attached to his neck. "Yes, sir. It will be done. Is there anything me and the rest of the men can do to... well, to alleviate the other burdens he's placed on you?"

Amelia huffs. "I bloody *wish*. Regrettably, this particular task is mine and mine alone. Now, get gone."

"Yes, sir."

When the soldier marches off, Kazan slides in to take his place. If Amelia is Weisz's seneschal in the way Adrius is Ezelind's, then their shared rank might make her more amenable to discussing him than everyone else here is.

Amelia's already sour expression curdles into pure vinegar. "Highness," she says through gritted teeth. "To what do I owe the displeasure?"

"Trust me, the displeasure is mutual," Kazan snaps back.

"What do you know about Adrius De Vere? Who is he?" Remembering his appearance in the portrait, she adds, "Who *was* he when he was a human?"

Amelia folds her arm across her chest and stares Kazan down. "Why do you care? You'll be dead soon anyway."

"Yes, whatever you say," she drawls. "But are you telling me you really can't fathom why I might want to know more about the man who beat me in the Vildenmarr. Besides, no one else in this damn place seems to have enough courage to so much as speak his name."

"Hm." There's a stretch of silence, and right when Kazan has become convinced that the conversation is a dead end, Amelia begins, "I'm sure you've heard by now that De Vere is Ezelind's seneschal?"

"It's been mentioned, yes."

"Aishreya Sutcliffe and I both hold a more traditional version of that title. With De Vere... the position gives him the freedom and authority to do as much of Ezelind's dirty work as she wishes, but everyone knows he'll never lead House Mooncliffe if we see her die. Sutcliffe is skilled and widely liked, even outside of House Gambit. As for me... not everyone likes me, I'll admit it, but my troops respect me and I'm happy to say that my house – House Rockford – is quite fond of me. But no one, and I do mean *no one*, likes De Vere."

"Why not? Has he done something?"

"I'm only going to bother saying this once, so listen up, human," Amelia explains, exasperation and irritation lacing her voice in equal measure. "De Vere might *act* like he's restrained, but don't let that fool you. You probably think that all us vampires are the same, that we're all bloodthirsty bastards or whatever it is that humans say about us, but we do vary wildly in that respect. De Vere, on the other hand, is a wolf one meal away from starving. Ezelind's word is all that holds him back in his cage, yet it only takes one missed dinner, one provocation, and then..."

"Then he bites," Kazan murmurs. "Did that start when he was a human?"

Amelia's sharp eyes scan her features as though searching for something. "What a specific question to ask. No one really *knew* him when he was human, but we know what he did back then."

"Well, don't leave me hanging."

"If you really want to know, I'm not going to shove rose-tinted glasses over your eyes." Amelia shrugs. "De Vere slaughtered his entire family in cold blood. They were humans, of course, so we don't really care about their deaths, however… whatever you may think about us, we take bloodlines *very* seriously. Murders between our kind indeed occur with various frequency, but to kill one's sire or progeny goes against every instinct we have. De Vere viewed family so lightly, even when he was human, and since then he's only continued to fuel that bloodthirst. He was turned by Ezelind's sire, and once he joined our society, he hunted down every single one of his sire's progenies before Ezelind exposed him. He's been safely under her thumb ever since."

Kazan thinks back to the portrait. Was it made before or after Adrius went on his apparent murderous rampage? He had appeared so much *softer* in the painting.

She doesn't get the opportunity to ask, however. At that moment, across the banquet hall, there's a massive *crash*.

All eyes are suddenly upon this new scene. A table has been upended, and a man scrambles out from underneath it with a bruise on his face rapidly fading. Ezelind stalks towards him, fury burning in her gaze and her fingers flexed, claws out, train of her dress sliding behind her like a snake's tail. Behind her, Weisz is perched atop a chair, blinking in surprise at the scene his sister is causing.

"How *dare* you!" Ezelind barks at the man.

The assaulted man scrambles to his feet and Kazan gets a proper look at him. She doesn't recognize him, but he's dressed in the purple and gold that Dasar wears – the colors of Gambit.

He pushes himself to his feet and squares his shoulders despite the danger she presents. "I only said what we've all been thinking. First Weisz's seneschal loses an eye to a human, and then he fops around and lets the human escape. We would have lost her entirely, had it not been for my Lord Dasar's soldiers. Your brother is half a ruler at best!"

"You will *not* insult my brother." Ezelind draws herself up and seems to gain an extra three inches of height at least. "Stand for yourself or pick your champion, Sir Kressworth."

Next to Kazan, Amelia snickers under her breath. "Oh dear…"

"What is it?" Kazan asks.

"A duel."

Kressworth points to a man in the crowd. "Sir Wilson. Will you stand for me?"

As this man named Wilson steps into the circle that's rapidly clearing around the fallen table, it's clear Kressworth chose well. Wilson is loomingly tall, and as he removes his overcoat the thick muscles beneath his shirt become quite noticeable. Someone hands him a sword, and he holds the scabbard with familiarity and comfort. He and Kressworth shake hands, gripping one another's forearms as friends and comrades.

"I'll stand for Kressworth," Wilson confirms, staring Ezelind down.

"De Vere," Ezelind snaps. "Stand."

Revelers all but throw themselves aside as Adrius walks past and faces down Wilson. His rapier rests at his waist, and his face may as well be made of stone for all the emotion he shows. A flash of fear slips behind the black of Wilson's eyes before he pushes it down and meets Adrius's gaze with a firm determination.

Weisz, still sitting atop his chair rather than in it, declares, "I'm the offended party, so this will go till I call it. Five paces, if you please."

Adrius and Wilson exchange shallow bows, turn their backs on each other, and take five steps. Once apart, they face one another again. Wilson unsheathes his sword and tosses the scabbard to Kressworth. He shifts his feet apart and settles into the sort of steady stance Kazan was taught during one of her prized lessons with a passing Warden. Adrius merely rests his hand on the hilt of his rapier.

Weisz grins and calls out, "Begin!"

There's a nick near the hilt of Wilson's blade, and as Kazan watches, he slowly and deliberately slices his palm open on it. Red vampiric blood runs down the fuller and the previously-invisible spellwork glows on the blade. Scrawled markings that she cannot understand shine outwards, like elegant brushstrokes made by a master so skilled that they could create an entire painting without lifting brush from canvas.

There's a heartbeat in which the two combatants stand off. It's shattered when Wilson leaps forward and swings his blade.

Adrius ducks under the attack, the flat of the blade missing the top of his head by a scant inch. His entire body angles forward, right hand tightening around his rapier's hilt. Steel flashes as he draws, nicking his thumb in the same motion, a matching pattern of sickly crimson spellwork fully activated by the time the blade is exposed. They both use the same magics?

Wilson must have luck on his side to avoid getting gutted; when Adrius slashes the rapier across his torso, the only injury he suffers is a tear in his shirt and a button cut off.

Wilson falls back and raises his blade in a defensive position. "Don't think you can intimidate me into conceding, De Vere," he growls.

Adrius merely waits for the next attack. After a moment, Wilson's patience runs out and he charges forward, sword raised. He brings the blade down and Adrius deflects it, sending the tip pointing at nothing more than ground.

It is seamless. In one smooth motion, Adrius turns. He flips his rapier into a reverse grip and plunges it through the side of Wilson's neck.

The flesh burns everywhere the steel touches. Not like the silver and rowan, but a grisly burn that blisters and whitens his flesh, as though the blade is covered in corrosive acid. Blood gurgles from between Wilson's lips. When Adrius slides his crimson blade out, the vampire crumples like wet paper and falls down dead.

So that's how Adrius fights, when he's free to kill his opponent. Swift. Brutal. Kazan's cheeks burn hot with desire. There's something deeply wrong with her.

Adrius doesn't sheathe his sword. "Lord Weisz," he says slowly, each word tense with paper-thin restraint. "Is the match called?"

Weisz is still smiling. "Not yet."

"…Of course."

Spells still active on his blade, he turns to Kressworth. Fear widens Kressworth's eyes and he stumbles backward, trying to escape into a crowd that refuses to interfere with the duel. He makes it perhaps two steps before Adrius slashes his rapier through the air. Blood mists the marble floor. There's a pause, and then Kressworth's severed head slides off his neck and *thunks* onto the ground.

"Called for my darling sister, Ezelind," Weisz decrees.

Those dressed in Mooncliffe or Rockford colors cheer. Those in Gambit's sigh and grumble. Though Kazan tries to keep track of Adrius, he vanishes within moments of the duel being officially ended.

Amelia isn't wrong, no matter how much her tales contrast Adrius's appearance in his portrait. Nor were all those other warnings wrong. Adrius *is* far more dangerous than Kazan had imagined.

Chapter Seventeen

Two unfortunate human servants are brought in to clean up the mess. They carry away the corpses, one handling the bodies with sheer misery making her mouth tremble, the other stone faced and blank. Every vampire in the room keeps a wide berth from the blood on the floor. There's an effort to resume the jubilant mood, but it's slow going and likely won't succeed until every remnant of the duel has vanished.

It takes Kazan more than a few attempts to shake herself into doing something other than simply staring. Once she does so, she turns to see that Amelia has vanished. She had been next to Kazan for the duration of the fight and yet now she's gone.

At first, she thinks *good riddance*. Then she happens to glance up at one of the high balconies and sees Adrius striding away from the banquet hall, Amelia surreptitiously trailing after him. Now *that's* intriguing.

Kazan hesitates. Does she truly want to risk invoking Adrius's ire by spying on him? He'd claimed that he didn't wish to hurt her, but after witnessing the duel, her confidence in that statement has been chipped away. However, when she looks behind her, she sees Isidora bumbling through the crowd in search of her.

Well, that makes her decision easier. Isidora sticks around worse than an unpleasant rash. Kazan quickly abandons the ballroom and heads up the stairs after Adrius and Amelia as fast as she can.

A few partygoers stumble past her on the way, the evidence of Dasar's extensive wine cellars painted all over them. Literally, in the case of one man whose cravat is stained burgundy. They pay her no attention, drunkenly swaggering by and talking too loudly with one another. What a pointless way to waste centuries of life. Were she one of them, she would do something far more useful with the gift of immortality.

She sneaks along, hugging the wall and ducking behind decorative plinths and large vases. She nearly loses sight of her quarry along the way, only the occasional glimpse of Amelia's cloak vanishing around corners or behind doors keeps her from losing track of them entirely.

To her surprise, she finds herself heading towards Dasar's rooms.

Dasar's door is cracked open by the time she gets there, but she can see neither Adrius nor Amelia. From inside, she hears rustling and the occasional curse word in a voice that's very clearly *not* Dasar's. Whichever one of them is in there must have called off the guards. Or, if it's Adrius, he may have removed them in a far more violent manner.

Amelia stalks out of Dasar's chambers. Kazan drops to her knees behind a statue, tucking her skirts in and keeping her breathing silent as the grave.

"Bloody useless waste of time," Amelia mutters as she stomps past.

Right before Amelia rounds a corner and disappears from sight, a figure steps out of the shadows and Kazan has to clap a hand over her mouth to keep from gasping.

Adrius has suddenly appeared, blocking Amelia's path with a hard, unyielding set to his features.

Amelia finches, her hand dropping to the sword at her waist before she sees who it is. "Oh," she says, slowly shifting from being ready to draw to a mere condescending sneer. "I was wondering where you'd disappeared to."

"I was waiting for you to show your hand," he replies.

"Did Ezelind send you to skulk about here? If not, shoo."

"You are Weisz's seneschal and I am Ezelind's," Adrius says, each word dangerously articulated. "Whatever you might care to think, that places us in equal standing and thus gives you *no* authority to give me orders. Now why are *you* skulking about, as you put it? Interested in Dasar's jewels?"

"As you just pointed out, I don't have to answer to you. Out of my way, De Vere," she scoffs.

It happens so quickly that Kazan can barely keep up. Amelia puts her hand on Adrius's chest to shove him out of her way, already having taken half a step forward, a sneer still frozen on her lips. Swift as a hunting wolf, Adrius grabs her wrist and *yanks*. He steps aside and uses her forward momentum to throw her onto the ground like a sack of bricks. Her back impacts the ground with a horrible crunching noise, and she contorts, spine twisting and lungs heaving. A hit like that would take most humans out of commission, but not a vampire.

Amelia gets back on her feet a second later. She reaches for the broadsword hanging at her belt, her thumb sliding between crossguard and scabbard, revealing a glimpse of shining steel as she grasps the hilt.

Adrius is faster. He grabs a fistful of her shirt and slams her against the wall, pinning her in place. His superior height keeps her literally on her toes, the tips of her boots skimming the floor. Before she can fully unsheathe her sword, he draws his rapier. As he'd done previously, he nicks his thumb on the blade and lets the bloody spellwork glow. Whatever that spell is, it clearly allows vampires to bypass their healing abilities in order to kill each other.

In a flash, Adrius has the blade against Amelia's neck.

"Careful," he warns, in a low voice that makes Kazan squirm. "One flinch and I'll give you another irreversible wound to match your eye."

"You rabid son of a —"

He presses the edge of his blade right up against her neck.

The scrawling lines of spellwork on the cold steel *hiss* in gleeful anticipation of shedding blood.

"Fine," she mutters. She releases her sword hilt and holds up her empty hands in a universal gesture of surrender. "I'm not interested in fighting Ezelind's mad dog. Search Dasar's rooms all you want. The sword isn't there. That's what you're here for, isn't it? You wanted me to follow you, put my neck on the line first, didn't you?" She groans and rolls her one good eye up to the ceiling. "Of course. Typical. Weisz asks me to do all the menial work, only for Ezelind to send you out for the same damn thing."

"Perhaps Weisz was under the correct assumption that anything more stressful than the most menial tasks would be too much for you right now," Adrius snaps back.

The sword. They're both looking for Kazan's sword. Or at least, they are on their lords' behalfs, but then that begs the question of why Ezelind or Weisz would want it. Dasar obviously wants it as a trophy, but she can't guess the others' motives. Courtly political rubbish has never interested her, and yet now she has no choice but to give it her most diligent attention. Her life has become their politics.

"If it's to be a competition between us, then know I'll *win*. It's a powerful weapon." Amelia glances down at his rapier, the line of crimson still visible on the fuller. "And *anonymous*. Kill me with that blade you've got there, and people will smell your blood on my corpse. But if I get the sword first and kill *you* with it… well, no one would be able to tell who the culprit was. We both know no one would trust someone of your reputation with a weapon that powerful."

"Do you have a point beyond insulting me?"

"Give up, de Vere. I'll win in the end, but if you stay out of my way, then I won't kill you once I get my hands on it. I might even throw in a good word with my lord's sister for good measure. How about it, hm?"

She drops to the ground when Adrius releases her, and she dusts off her velvet cloak with an indignant huff.

"Very well," he says. "I'll leave the sword to you." There is *something* behind his eyes that Kazan picks up on and she wonders: can Amelia tell he's lying? He sheathes his sword, the blood and spellwork fading away as it slides into the scabbard. "Just remember not to cross me next time. I have that *reputation*, after all."

"Wise choice," Amelia says, all caustic arrogance. "See how much nicer it is when we're not trying to kill each other?"

"I do so love our little chats, Amelia." His sarcasm is so impeccable that it's almost entirely undetectable. "Let's hope Weisz gives you some time off to convalesce after you've fetched his new toy, hm?"

"Oh, shut up."

Amelia's nose wrinkles in disdain before she turns away and marches off. Neither she nor Adrius seem stupid enough to turn their back on an enemy, but there's something between the two of them that suggests a dynamic somewhere between enemies and friends. Akin to disliked coworkers who have long since acclimated to the other's presence.

"One last thing," Adrius says softly, stopping Amelia in her tracks. "Did Weisz mention to you why he wants the sword?"

She frowns, full lips pinching. "No, he didn't. Did Ezelind?"

"No." He sighs. "They won't be able to hide the theft from Dasar for long, surely they know that."

"They're going to kill someone then," Amelia suggests with a casual shrug. "Someone in the Citadel, before the party ends. Ten guesses who?" she adds with a snarky laugh, implying that there's only one obvious victim. Trouble is, Kazan has no idea who they're referring to. "Since I'm assuming they'd never dare kill the perfect Lady Aishreya Sutcliffe," Amelia continues. "Everyone loves her. I wonder if I can use it for myself once they're done with it."

Adrius raises an eyebrow. "And who would *you* mean to kill? After they're done with their own target, of course."

"Hm..." She taps her chin thoughtfully. "I'd kill Jacqueline Dawson."

"I don't know her."

"Rude woman, rather stiff necked. Works for my Lord Weisz."

Adrius frowns. "What have you against her?"

"She thinks herself my equal," she replies, turning her nose up. "Insult of insults, that."

"How unimaginative."

"As if you're so much more righteous. Who would *you* kill, if you had the sword?" She appears to think better of it and rolls her eye again before walking off. "Never mind. I don't know why I bother asking a mindless attack dog these questions."

She strides away and her footsteps fade into nothing. Kazan is pressed so tightly against the statue she hides behind that she can barely breathe.

Alone, Adrius quietly snarls, "Ezelind. I'd kill *Ezelind*."

Chapter Eighteen

Kazan waits for a long time after Adrius leaves to avoid him noticing her. She can't risk being caught sneaking around Dasar's chambers and she *really* doesn't want to be caught by a pissed-off Amelia. Not without a weapon. Not without her sword, which will be in shocking demand if it truly provides an untraceable method of murder as Amelia seems to think.

Alright, so her sword has been removed from Dasar's chambers. It's probably not in the menagerie either. She had inadvertently suggested that to him, and she doubts he'd place it there before she's dead to avoid her finding it. That said, there can't be *that* many places he could secure a weapon desired by so many.

The map in the menagerie had listed an armory. Somewhere designed for storing swords, kept under lock and key, and heavily guarded by Dasar's guards and Dasar's guards alone. That's got to be where it is.

She ducks back into the main hall for a moment, both to reorient her mental map and to keep people from becoming too suspicious of her whereabouts. She allows Isidora to catch sight of her a couple of times while moving around the hall to the north exits. If her memory is correct, and she knows it is, then she can access the armory through the north wing.

Numerous vampires swarm around her as she goes, and she finds herself dodging offers to dance and ducking underneath too friendly hands. Even in the crush of people, she manages to slip away. She ducks around corners and weaves her way through halls to make as direct a line as she can towards the armory. She imagines that once she actually gets there, she won't have such an easy time sneaking around past the soldiers, but for now she is merely grateful for her good luck.

The scent of fresh grass and blooming roses suddenly wafts into her nose. Up ahead is an archway and she remembers, very vaguely, the map mentioning a garden. Faint hope fills her chest as the smell of flowers fills her lungs. She hurries up, rushing through the stone archway and finding herself, for the first time since the forest, standing on soft green grass instead of cold tile. There are rose bushes artfully scattered throughout the garden, quaint cobblestone paths winding between flowering fruit trees and lush shrubs, and glorious moonlight shining down upon it all.

For a moment, she is outside again, unencumbered by any vampiric plots and utterly free to run off into the night. She finds her hands reaching for the vines that creep up along the stone pillars before she looks up and realizes that she is not truly outside. The moonlight is streaming down through a pure glass ceiling, similar to the glass that domes the great hall. She releases the vines with bitter disappointment. She will find no escape here.

She begins to cross the garden and make for the armory, but the moment she takes a step onto the first stone path, something fuzzy curls around her ankle. That same black cat from earlier now sits in front of her, its front paws placed firmly on the toe of her left shoe. It tilts its head to the side, gaudy golden collar shining in the moonlight and big eyes staring straight at her.

"Hello, beautiful," she murmurs. Why would a vampire have a pet, and why would that pet keep showing up near her? "Go run back to your owner. I'm busy."

She gently nudges the cat aside with her foot so that she can continue onwards. The moment she pushes the cat away, it huffs and scampers back in front of her to sit stubbornly on her foot once again.

"Come now, I'm hardly doing anything furtive," she lies. "No need to look at me with that kind of suspicion."

The cat blinks pointedly at her.

She can hear the distant sound of music from the great hall, and she knows that she won't have long until someone else wanders through here. On the far-right side of the garden, she sees a flicker of movement and hears faint chatter as a group of vampires pass by. Far away as she is, they don't see her, but if she had kept going, she would have run into them and been dragged back to Isidora or dropped into Dasar's lap.

The cat rubs its cheek against her ankle, unfairly soft fur brushing against her skin right above the top of her slipper.

"Did you… did you stop me on purpose to prevent me from getting caught?" she asks, frowning at the pet. "You're an odd one, aren't you?"

With a swish of its tail, the cat scampers away.

Sighing at the odd mystery of the cat, she takes another look at the garden. As so many people are passing through, she'll have to figure something else out, some other way of getting to the armory. Maybe it would be a better use of her time to find out about Gia Montanari instead. The only question is who to ask?

She turns around and finds herself face to face with Reya Sutcliffe.

"Excuse me –" she tries to protest as Reya wraps an arm around her waist, steering her towards a patch of cobblestone where the music is clearer.

"Why," Reya says with a smile, "there's nothing to excuse, Highness."

"That's not –" Kazan finds it difficult to pull away with Reya's hand resting on the small of her back. Even through the layers of fabric, there's the faint chill of vampire skin. "Do you need something? Because I've rather had enough of you and your false sympathy."

"I promise, it wasn't false."

The moonlight burns bright and causes her lush hair to shine and the golden jewelry around Reya's neck to sparkle. Delicate chains of the stuff weave through her hair and adorn almost every exposed bit of skin, even spidering across her deep purple dress. She practically *drips* gold, not unlike Dasar, although on her it is undeniably appealing.

That golden necklace makes Kazan look twice and she can't help thinking of a similar collar around that black cat's neck.

"Do you have any pets?" she asks carefully.

"Why no, I don't," Reya replies.

"Are you certain? Not a single one? Not even, oh, I don't know – a small, black cat, perchance?"

"No pets. Care to dance?" Reya says with a salacious smile that sends more than one kind of shiver down Kazan's spine.

"Well, with you I suppose that I wouldn't mind –"

"Wonderful."

Reya takes Kazan's waist and properly directs Kazan's hand to rest on her shoulder. Back at Rask's party, she *had* thought that she would eventually need to learn to dance, although she could never have anticipated these circumstances. It's easier than she thought, although it helps that Reya leads, sweeping Kazan along through the garden in time with the faint music. Her dress is thankfully long enough to conceal the many missteps her unskilled feet make.

The music swells and Reya spins her around, making her dizzy for a moment before she regains her footing.

Unlike Dasar's slightly unhinged grins, Reya's smiles are dazzling and sincerely warm. "So, tell me, darling Kazan, how are you enjoying my Lord Dasar's party so far? Since I had rather a larger hand in the proceedings than I might have liked, I'm curious to see what result my efforts have yielded."

"You set this up?" Kazan pauses. "Actually, that's no great surprise. Dasar doesn't strike me as someone who'd invest himself in the menial tasks of selecting musicians or writing a menu. And no, I can't say I'm enjoying this party in the slightest."

"I apologize." The music switches from one tune to another, and Reya continues to twirl her around with barely a second's pause to adjust their tempo. "I would hate for you to hate me."

She yanks her hands out of Reya's. "I'm getting tired of this, all this – *darling* rubbish and flirting and playing nice. I know you all have such low opinions of humans and I'd rather not spend my last days alive being toyed with."

"Toying with you?" Reya draws back and genuine confusion crosses her pretty face. "I wouldn't do that, or at least I didn't *intend* to do such a thing."

"If you don't want me to hate you, then you can do me a favor. There's someone I want information on, and you're a well-connected woman, aren't you?" Adrius had been surprised when Kazan used Reya's first name, and so she pointedly adds, "If you can't, then I'll simply go ask *Adrius*. He's been ever so helpful since he healed my injury and I'm sure he wouldn't mind helping me again."

Reya's eyes widen. Her voice is uncharacteristically restrained as she murmurs to herself, "Is that so... Hm." Then she snaps right back to her faint and lovely smile. "As it happens, Highness, I have a favor lined up for you already. Let me show you. Don't worry," she adds, "if you dislike it, I can arrange something else for you."

Even though Kazan doubts Reya knows what she wants, her curiosity is piqued enough that she's willing to see what Reya has planned. She allows herself to be led out of the gardens and back the way she had initially came. Reya doesn't get as far as the main hall, instead heading to one of the upper balconies and away from the excess of prying eyes that reside inside the walls of the Citadel.

A woman leans against the balcony railing, absently swirling around a glass of some sort of amber alcohol and looking frustratingly bored. Her red hair is done up in a cascade of curls dotted with pearls, and her silken green gown hugs her form in a way that shows off far more than most of the vampires here. Next to her is a stern-faced woman in more militaristic clothing.

"Oh, I wasn't expecting you." Reya nods to the military woman. "Jacqueline Dawson, isn't it?"

The woman Amelia wanted to kill?

Dawson gives her a short bow. "I see I've been intruding on a private party. Do excuse me. Lady Sutcliffe, Highness."

The woman in green looks more amused than anything else as Dawson walks off.

"Sorry to keep you waiting and interrupt your chat," Reya says. She extends a hand towards the woman. "Highness, I hope you don't mind that I set up a brief meeting with an associate of mine. I heard you were looking for Miss Gia Montanari."

Wait, *what* – Kazan nearly trips over her own feet. "How did you…"

"I have my sources."

"I've not asked a single living person," she snaps.

"Technically none of us are living, Highness, save you," Reya politely reminds her.

Montanari smiles. It's not a reassuring expression. "I'm always happy for a bit of friendly chatter."

"But you're a –" Kazan sputters, "you're a *vampire*."

"Am I really?" Montanari gives Reya a flippant wave. "Thanks for the introduction, but don't you have seneschal work to do? Unlike most of us layabouts, your job follows you to this party. Do excuse us."

With a smile, Reya inclines her head to the both of them and glides away.

"I'm pretty sure I know exactly what you want to chat about," Montanari begins once Reya has disappeared, "but illuminate me all the same. Who knows, you could surprise me."

Kazan doesn't waste time in blurting out, "What do you know about this party? About my position as queen?"

Montanari pushes the glass she's holding into Kazan's hand. "Drink this. I have a feeling you're not going to be thrilled by what I have to say."

Fine. Kazan drains the glass and *damn* does it burn. "There. Happy?"

"Look," Montanari begins with a sigh, taking the empty glass back, "I'm not really supposed to talk to you or anyone about this, but it's also not going to help you now and I don't really like Dasar anyway. I suppose I'm the closest thing to a former queen that there is."

Kazan's chest tightens. A former queen. Does that mean Dasar was lying about no one ever getting out of this? "What do you mean?"

"About fifty years ago, a vampire named Matthias picked me out of the crowd shortly before one of these parties. Obviously, my good looks and charms seduced him in an instant." She flips a strand of red hair over her shoulder. "I have that effect on people. Well, I end up in the Citadel and he's supposed to let me be that year's queen. It was a bit of a messy argument between him and Dasar about the affair and one thing led to another..."

"Did Matthias convince Dasar to let you go?"

Montanari laughs. "Oh, I *wish* Dasar was so lenient. No, Matthias turned me into a vampire before I could be crowned."

"So you only got out of this by... by *preventing* it from happening in the first place?" How is that supposed to help her?

"In a way." Montanari shrugs. "Only human blood works for the ritual this whole thing is built around. Of course, it was all rather a scandal, but a human servant was brought in last minute to be that year's king and the party went on as planned, albeit with hurt feelings across the board. No one had much of a choice, really. Had Dasar kept me in the role of queen, the Citadel would have crumbled into dust when the third day finished, and my human blood hadn't been spilled."

"I don't understand," Kazan mutters, almost more to herself than Montanari. "I don't know how he does it, but Dasar can get around the Citadel faster than should be possible. Couldn't he have stopped Matthias before it was too late?"

"Again, I hadn't *technically* been crowned at that point. If I had been, Dasar would have kept a much, *much* closer eye on me. And besides, it's not usually a slow process. It's simple, really. We have venom in our fangs – when we bite a human, we can choose to release that venom into their bloodstream. Keeps them nice and pliant." A process Kazan is now unfortunately familiar with. "To turn a human, a vampire gives the human a venom bite and then the human consumes that vampire's blood in return. A bit of enjoyable tit for tat. After that, there's no going back. Matthias had his fangs in my thigh before anyone even knew what he was planning."

"Well that's no help at all," Kazan can't help snapping. "They've already made me queen and Dasar's taken my blood for that jewel in the crown and the damn spellwork in the basement."

Another casual shrug from Montanari. "I did say this would not help you now. Even Matthias wouldn't have turned me if I'd already been crowned. No one's willing to sabotage the magic and cause the Citadel to collapse, *obviously*."

"I suppose everyone's desperate for this place?" she scoffs.

"It's our history and our greatest pride. It's filled with enough wealth to buy and sell a hundred human cities. It's the center of our world. Everyone would kill for it." She pauses, and then amends, "Well maybe not Aishreya Sutcliffe. She's too damn perfect."

So Kazan truly can't get out of this in the same way Montanari did. And that would only have happened if she was willing to be turned into a vampire in the first place. She can recall with vivid detail how the vampires in the Vildenmarr tore those people apart, and she has no desire to be the one doing the tearing.

Kazan looks at Montanari. Really *looks*, searching those features for any sign of something beyond her lighthearted recollection. Some sorrow, some regret, anything. But there's nothing behind those inhuman eyes.

"Don't you hate it?" she can't help asking.

Montanari tilts her head to the side. "Hate what?"

"Being a vampire. You *kill* people, you have to drink their blood to survive, you were almost subjected to this same brutal ritual that I'm stuck in. You must see how awful this whole damn thing is."

With an exasperated sigh, Montanari rests her hand over Kazan's and pats her as though speaking to a child. "Listen. When I was human, I owned a bookshop. I wasn't exactly living on the streets, but it wasn't easy either. Always worrying about income, always saving coin wherever I could, well aware of the dangers beyond my city walls."

"I'm a blacksmith, and I grew up constantly in and out of orphanages. I know what it's like."

"Then you should see just how good I have it. I live in Matthias's manor, in the lap of luxury, unconcerned with where my next meal is going to come from. Not to mention the perks of immortality and, frankly, incredible sex. Sure, *blood*, but there's plenty of ways to feed without killing the human in question. And even if one dies occasionally, you get used to it and the benefits outweigh any guilt I felt at the beginning. What do I have to hate?"

"You are *literally* killing people!"

"It's a dog-eat-dog world, and I'd rather be doing the eating."

Kazan draws herself up, ripping her hand away from Montanari's. "You're foul, you know that?"

"And you're so honorable?" Montanari scoffs. "Not even the least self-serving, are you? I heard about the way you were captured. You didn't protect those other travelers – you only cared about yourself."

Montanari's words hit home. Kazan *had* fled the caravan in the Vildenmarr, abandoning her fellow humans to their fate. She had a weapon that could kill vampires, she could have stayed, could have helped. Could have saved *someone*. But she hadn't. She'd picked herself over them without a second thought. And she knows, deep down, that she would do it again without hesitation. Honor isn't her domain. Self-preservation is. Montanari's right, and she hates it.

She spits at Montanari's feet. "Fuck you."

"You're not my usual type, but if you insist, I'm not about to protest."

"That's not what I meant, and you know it!" It's so childish to stomp her feet and huff, and yet she can't stop herself from doing it. Fury has made her cheeks bright hot, and she's not overly concerned with whether or not she's making a scene. There's no one here beyond Montanari to see it regardless. "Maybe I'm a self-serving bastard, I'll admit it. But at least I'm not about to turn on my fellow humans."

"Of course you won't, you won't have any opportunity to do so in the next..." Montanari pretends to think. "Day and two thirds. Give or take."

Day and two thirds. That really *is* all that's left.

Kazan struggles to breathe. "I'm going to be sick," she murmurs.

"No, you're not, that's just the scotch hitting you. I like my drinks strong."

Her alcohol tolerance isn't impressive, that's true enough. "You're a horrible person."

"I told you this wasn't a conversation you wanted to be sober for and you chose to drink without me forcing it down your throat. Chin up, Highness. Oh," Montanari adds, looking over her shoulder at a tall, ticking grandfather clock. "I believe it's time for your next little performance. Dasar's wheeling out tonight's entertainment and I imagine someone is searching for you as we speak."

"I won't do it."

"Highness, you haven't a choice." Montanari flicks her fingers at her dismissively. "Have fun."

Chapter Nineteen

Despite Kazan's halfhearted effort to run away before she can get dragged into whatever grisly event Dasar has planned next, she's caught by about a half dozen guards before she can get more than two corridors from Montanari. One of them gives her a look that quite clearly says she can either walk back with her dignity or be dragged back without it. She chooses to walk.

Cheering and clapping of all decibels hits her ears as she's escorted to the banquet hall's head table. People have flooded back to the party now that all traces of the duel have long since been scrubbed away.

That awful crown they forced on her rests on a dinner plate, waiting like the executioner's axe. She can't tell if it's just her imagination or not, but she thinks the large ruby in it is a little less vibrant now than it was when it first drank of her blood.

A beaming vampire pulls out a chair for her and she's deposited into the same seat as yesterday, forced to sit and face the banquet hall. Someone comes up behind her and picks up the crown, settling it upon her head. She tries to swat them away, but they just dodge her hand. The movement makes her stomach lurch unpleasantly from the alcohol she had downed. The crown doesn't feel half as heavy as it did last night. When she tries to take it off, a vampire laughs and pushes a wine glass into her hand instead and makes her drink it before refilling the cup.

Weisz lounges at one of the other tables, and raises his glass to her. "To the Queen of the Vampires!" he toasts.

Another familiar figure stands out of the crowd. Dasar sits not at, but *on* a table, one leg bent to his chest, the other dangling off the edge. He's in the middle of speaking with a vampire dressed in rather plain clothes when she notices him, and at the sound of Weisz's toast, he perks up.

"Time for her to give a speech, isn't it?" Dasar declares.

A few people whoop and holler with excitement. She's supposed to talk for this? Isn't it bad enough that they humiliate and laugh at her every chance they get? If she opens her mouth, all she'll want to spit at them is vitriol. Actually, that sounds like a fantastic idea. Give them a piece of her mind. It's not like they don't deserve a torrent of insults.

She gets to her feet, swaying slightly, and is about to tell them all which of their orifices she's going to shove her sword into, when someone grabs her by the elbow.

"Don't worry that *pretty* head of yours," Ezelind whispers. She snakes her arm around Kazan's waist, yanking her along until Kazan has one arm pinned behind her back and is forced to lean against Ezelind or else fall over. "It's a scripted speech. You needn't exercise that human brain for even a moment."

"I'm not your fucking monkey," Kazan snarls. "I don't dance on command."

Ezelind's claws extend and bury themselves into Kazan's forearm. The pain hits her, sharp and piercing, and she grinds her jaw to stop herself from crying out. She won't give Ezelind the satisfaction.

"Repeat after me," Ezelind says, digging her nails in just a little bit more, "or else it'll be a lot worse for you."

Kazan feels her pulse in her eyelids. A beat of her heart and the room blurs. Another beat and it clarifies. Focus, damn it. Just say the words, get through this, and leave before the pain overcomes her in front of all these bastards.

"I," Ezelind begins, speaking each word with insulting slowness, "the Queen of the Vampires…"

Kazan opens her mouth and another twist of claws forces her to say, "I, the Queen of the Vampires..."

Ezelind continues, feeding her the lines until Kazan has a complete speech.

"I praise those who were sacrificed to give sustenance to the soldiers," she finds herself saying to the banquet hall and its assemblage. "I praise the swords that were sharpened in battle. I praise the victors and drink to their glory. May their spoils of war stand the test of time and may their realm drink deep of my blood. The gates of the Citadel are thrown open. Come, conquering army, and accept my surrender."

The crown grows hot upon her head. Whatever the words might mean, they certainly are having some sort of magical effect. All part of this damn ritual. How many more steps of this remain? How much more of her blood and her dignity must she surrender before she can beat them all?

A deafening noise rings out. Kazan's head pounds and the room swims, and she has no idea if they're cheering because she did it right or screaming because she did it wrong. Ezelind's claws retract from her arm – the only reliable indicator of success.

The vampires blur as they start clinking glasses with one another and shift around. She blinks over and over to try to clear her vison. Apart from Weisz and Dasar, she can't spot a single familiar face in the crowd. Adrius and Reya aren't exactly her allies, but it might have been nice to see people who don't actively thirst for her blood.

Kazan can hear Dasar's voice calling for something, although there's so much cacophony that she can't make out the words.

Whether or not she could hear it doesn't end up mattering though, as the churning sea of vampires parts to allow two people to enter the newly made clearing. One is a vampire, a woman dressed in the same regal purples and golds as Dasar, with a bright smile on her lips and a sword at her waist. The other is shoved in after her. Tattered clothing and a lack of black or gold in his eyes marks him as human. As prey.

Kazan tilts her head to the side as she looks at him. His clothing looks familiar somehow, even though bandages are wrapped around his neck and torso. Has he been injured? While he stumbles as the vampires push him into position, his eyes slide across the room until they lock onto hers.

No wonder he's familiar. Though she had left him for dead along with the rest of the caravan, fate clearly had other ideas. She stares across the room at Warden Travers, his face pale from the blood he lost in the Vildenmarr and pure shock in his expression as he recognizes her.

Another beat of her pulse throws her vision into disorienting hyperfocus and for one eternal moment, she can see her reflection in the glossy shine of Travers's eyes.

"Champion of the Three House Coalition!" Weisz cheers.

The woman in purple and gold draws her sword, laughing and preening to the raucous and excited audience. Kazan is reminded of a tournament she once attended when she was a teenager, an exhibition for a group of young Wardens about to get their badges and officially go from trainee to servant of humanity. Despite the seriousness of the affair, the young men and women had shown off to the crowd in much the same way this vampire is now.

Weisz's next call is far more mocking, "Champion of the Vampire Queen!"

Someone thrusts a plain broadsword into Travers's bandaged hands.

"Would you care to wager on the odds?" Ezelind hisses, her words right in Kazan's ear, so bright and crisp that they cut through everything else. "I must say, your champion doesn't quite look up to the task."

She watches the vampire champion laugh, twirling her wrist and making her sword flash as she stalks Travers. Sweat drips from his forehead and he stumbles backwards, only to be cruelly shoved into the circle again and forced to face down his opponent. He tries to settle into a soldier's stance, but his injuries don't allow him to move as he should. Terror haunts the edges of his face as he stares down his enemy and then he flattens it out, deep and determined breaths until he projects nothing more than a Warden's confidence. A slightly too deep breath makes his ankle spasm, and the fear takes him again.

Jeers and taunts ring in Kazan's ears and she can't – she *can't*.

What had Adrius said before? The humans who seemed better off in the past were those who spent their time prodigiously drunk? She picks up a glass of wine and drains the entire thing. It is tasteless.

There's a clang of metal against metal, blade against blade. It's like watching a cat bat around a mouse. The vampire parries and redirects and twists out of the way, landing light taps on Travers in return. Enough to leave a dainty cut on his cheek, to nick his shirt, to slice off a few strands of hair. Humiliating him as she draws out his own terror.

Travers slips, foot skidding across the stone floor, his wounded body falling to his knees. Even then the vampire does not end it. She circles him with a fanged smile, patiently waiting for him to stand up. Once he does, she kicks out and sends him falling again.

Kazan tries to leave, but Ezelind shoves her back into her seat.

"Watch," Ezelind's venomous voice whispers against her ear. "Didn't you abandon him once before? This time, you'll stay to the conclusion."

When Travers falls again, he cannot rise back up. His hands are too unsteady, his legs too battered. The vampire prowls around him, her sword nicking his neck a couple times as if to test him. When he doesn't respond with anything more than a weak groan, the roar of the crowd crescendos and the vampire sheathes her sword. For a moment, just for a single moment, Kazan thinks that the fight is over, that Travers will be allowed to live.

Then the vampire lunges down and sinks her fangs into his neck.

At first, there's no blood. But it begins to flow faster than she can drink it, trickling down from between her lips and soaking his shirt. When she rips her mouth away to swallow a chunk of flesh, dark crimson splatters the ground and Travers's eyes roll back in his skull; his pale, exsanguinated face going slack forever.

If Kazan stays for even a second longer, she will be sick all over the table. Muttering something – she's not quite sure what – she scrambles away from Ezelind and the crowd. She snatches a bottle of wine from a passing table and pulls the cork out with her teeth, drinking deeply so that the taste drowns out the memory of Travers grunting in pain.

She falls straight into an armored guard as soon as she puts a single toe outside the main hall.

"Highness!" the guard exclaims. "What are you doing leaving the party so soon?"

She tries to draw herself up. "I," she declares, "need to go."

"I think you need to sit down."

"No, I need to get *out*. You bastards made me queen." Why are words so difficult to string together into sentences? It would be easier if she could get her breathing under control. "And if I'm queen then I order you to let me go. Right now."

The guard laughs. "Come on, Highness, you've had a bit too much to drink. Let's get you sorted out."

"Don't treat me like a thing to be carted around!"

"Whoa, hey now. Settle down and come back to the party."

She spits at his feet.

He's so busy laughing that she slips right past him. Every sound fades away as she runs from the banquet hall; she is consumed by the thud of her own heartbeat and the rush of blood in her ears. Her strides are uneven, her feet refusing to properly cooperate, and she trips a dozen times as she climbs up the first set of stairs she can find.

Corridors and hallways transform into an endless maze. It's all a jumbled mess of dark wood and ornate doors and fuzzy candlelight. Her mind is a mess as well, and she can't think. Can't focus. Can't come up with a destination beyond *not here*. Visions of her sword lying on the floor of Dasar's chambers or in some glamorous armory fill her mind, only to vanish as she tries to grasp onto them. Travers appears behind her eyelids every time she blinks. Her legs move with the intent her mind lacks, and she doesn't even think about where they're taking her until they come to a stop.

The geist is exactly where Kazan left him. Sitting beneath the mysterious portrait of Adrius and doing a mixture of moping and sleeping. Can geists sleep? She has no idea, but it's certainly an interesting nugget of a thought, much more interesting to chew on than what's going on back in the banquet hall.

She leans against the wall across from him, not quite close enough for him to possess her but close enough for whatever company she's looking for. Exhaustion grabs at her, dragging her down till she's sitting, legs sprawled out. She drinks.

"Hello," she mutters.

The geist tilts his molting head up. "Hello... I didn't think to see you so soon. Have you come to fulfill our bargain?"

"I don't know who killed you," she admits. "Not yet."

"Oh."

"I just..." She wants to lie, because the truth is trapped in her throat and clawing at her from the inside out. But when she opens her mouth, the truth escapes. "I don't want to be alone."

To her relief, she doesn't need to elaborate. The geist looks straight at her and agrees, "It hurts."

"Mm."

"To share a body... it would be less lonely."

"Tempting," she admits, before she scoffs and drinks again. "But not time for you to possess me yet, dead thing. Gia

Montanari didn't give me anything useful either, so the clue you gave me was worthless. You're going to have to wait."

It shouldn't be possible for dead eyes to show emotion. Nonetheless, translucent tears glisten in the corners of the geist's eyes and they disintegrate into dust as they fall. "I can help, I promise. Please."

"What, you can't be patient? Not even a bit?"

"No one has been able to help me in years," he admits, the words more dust than his tears. "I have seen so few regents; they are too afraid. A couple have helped me, decades ago, but they never found my killer. The human servants talk but they do not offer help. They know better than to misstep around their masters."

The other geists in the menagerie are far more decayed than this one. Falling apart like moth-eaten curtains, drifting aimlessly around the items they're tied to. One didn't even remember the people who had died with her, if they were family or mere acquaintances. Form and memory, both being lost to time. How old is this geist? Certainly younger than the others. Young enough to remember at least a few details of his death. Perhaps he still recalls his name and his family and all the other bits and pieces that make up the tapestry of a life.

She looks into those sad, sagging eyes and some hazy part of her mind almost wants to laugh at the truth behind his earlier boasting. "You're running out of time, aren't you? Worse than that – you *know* you're running out of time. Counting every chime of the clock until you forget and lose the last pieces of yourself, and then you won't have any way to remember that you want revenge."

One of his lower molars crumbles in its gummy socket as he replies, "Tick tock for the both of us."

"I'm... sorry. How old were you? When you died, I mean."

He whimpers. "No, no I don't want to remember that. Please don't ask me. Anything but that."

Young then. Younger than she thought – she wouldn't have

guessed a day over twenty. "Sorry. I never asked... what's your name?"

"Alphonse," he says, and the name is a barely-there whisper in the wind.

Ally-ally-alphonse, her mind sings. Alphonse and Amelia and Aishreya and Adrius. Everything's coming up A, isn't it?

She giggles, the sound wet and pathetic. "I could've saved someone, ya know. Two days ago, there was this man I met... I could've saved him. If I'd tried. But I didn't. Cruel, isn't it? The only people I can be assed to help are myself and a dead man."

"The only ones I am *capable* of helping... are you and myself. Perhaps that may be enough?" Alphonse murmurs.

The wine has become vinegar now. She feels grateful for her weakness for wine. Everything smooths out at the edges, the world becoming distant and numb. It makes thinking rather more complicated, but it fades Travers's face as much as can be hoped for.

"I'm afraid," she whispers.

"Fear is all we have sometimes."

"You're the best bet I have right now, sure, but no matter how much you claim you'll leave me in peace, I can't trust that." Maybe it's rude to say it to his face, but she doesn't care. "I know geist possession can kill, and that it's worse if the geist has to be forced out. Would be funny, huh? If I do what I need to do and in the end, you kill me before I can force you out?"

"Do you trust me enough to try?"

She drains the bottle and drops the empty glass onto the ground. Pushing herself to her feet, she sighs and says, "Trust or no, this deal is the best I've got right now. I'll be back. With answers. Promise."

"Be bold," Alphonse murmurs in soft parting.

Bold it is then. To hell with sneaking around. She already hinted to Adrius that she's closer to Reya than he might have guessed when she used Reya's first name. And implying that Adrius had helped her seemed to catch Reya off guard. If she can keep playing them off each other, she can get more information than she could by skulking about.

She'll simply *ask* Adrius about his painting, and if he doesn't want to answer then she'll claim Reya will.

As she staggers off, she gives Alphonse a lazy wave. It's a good thing that she has a stellar sense of direction, otherwise she would be entirely unable to remember where in this stupidly big castle Adrius's rooms are. There are so many twists and turns on her way, but her dizzy mind pulls up details – a pretentious suit of armor here, a decorative vase there. She stumbles through the halls without too much trouble, only taking a wrong turn once and only smacking her head into a single open door.

Eventually, she finds it, grabs the bronze handle of Adrius's door, yanks it open, and lurches inside.

There's a noise to her left. She steps into the next bedroom and then freezes dead in her tracks.

Unsurprisingly, Adrius is here. The surprise is that so is Reya.

A lot of bare skin glistens in the candlelight. The two are pressed up against the wall, wrapped up in each other as if being even an inch apart is unbearable for them. Adrius isn't wearing a shirt, the sharp lines of his back muscles shifting as he bends to drag his tongue over Reya's neck. Half of her clothing lies on the floor already, her leg hitched around Adrius's waist, his fingers digging into her exposed thigh.

Kazan's thoughts struggle through surprise, appreciation, and then around to land on the stomach twisting realization that she's been had.

Reya's head falls back against the wall and her lips part around a low moan. Kazan, on the other hand, can barely breathe as she stares.

The moment shatters as Adrius catches sight of her. "Kazan?" he asks, eyes wide with surprise. "What are you *doing* here?"

Reya gasps, lowering her leg to stand on both feet, though she makes no effort to pull her clothes back into place. She blinks, and then her shock fades into a rather sultry and heated gaze. "Well now, this is unexpected."

Kazan takes an unsteady step backwards. "You – you two *played* me."

"Oh please," Reya remarks with a laugh. "You tried to play *us* against each other. You hardly have the moral high ground."

Hurt feelings don't make her burn like this. But humiliation does.

Adrius sighs in exasperation. "That's not exactly helping. Kazan, listen, this isn't what you seem to think it is."

"Oh, this is exactly what I think it is." Anger bubbles up in Kazan's chest and starts to grow. "All your nice words about not wanting to hurt me or wanting to do me a favor, letting me think that just *maybe* –" She chokes on her sentence and snarls, "Flirt with the human, toy with the human, isn't it funny to make the human blush? I get enough of that disrespect from every other fucking vampire in this place, I don't need it from you two. How *dare* you both play me for a fool!"

Adrius holds his hands up as though worried she will hit him – which, actually, she very well might. "Hold on a moment. You're drunk, Kazan, and –"

"Don't talk to me like I'm stupid!" she snaps.

"He's not," Reya chimes in, crossing her arms in a way that pushes her cleavage up and is quite distracting. "We're not trying to play you or whatever it is you think we're doing. Is it so hard to imagine that two people might both like you, like each other, and *also* have there be no resulting conflict?"

Kazan blinks stupidly. "Wait – say that again, but more slowly and with fewer... words."

Adrius wraps an arm around Kazan and a protest is on her lips before she realizes that she had been about to topple over. "Come on," he says gently. "We'll help you get back to your room – Dasar doesn't skimp on the potency of his wine, and you need to sleep this off. We'll talk more once you're sober."

Putting one foot in front of the other is enough of a challenge that she barely hears Reya say to Adrius, "I'll go tell whichever poor sod Dasar made play handmaid that she's in bed. That should keep her from being summoned by someone who can't leave well enough alone for at least a couple of hours."

A couple of hours. Who has that kind of time? Kazan giggles in sheer delirium.

"...you slip out the usual way?" Adrius asks.

Reya makes a faint murmur of dissent and says something that sounds like, "I'll take her to her chambers... you carrying her will cause a scandal..."

Scandal. Cause that's the biggest problem here.

"Reya... I don't want her to..." Adrius's voice begins to descend into slurring and indistinct sounds in her ears. "... we can make our move *this* year."

"I'll see if... can discuss this after she's in bed..."

Kazan's eyelids are too heavy to resist anymore.

Chapter Twenty

Soft firelight flickers in front of Kazan's sore eyes as someone lightly shakes her out of her slumber.

"...'n a minute..." she grumbles into a pillow.

Ugh, how late did she sleep? And who the hell is kicking her out of bed? She lives alone. Cold emptiness seeps into her as her eyes properly open. She's not home. She may never be home again.

"Majesty," Isidora's voice says quietly, "it's early afternoon. You should wake, before the day passes you by."

Half the day –?

Realization of where she is shoots through her as though struck by a bolt of lightning. Time is running out. While she slept, hours passed, leaving her with precious few left. Everything comes back to her in a headache-laden haze. Alphonse, Montanari... Travers. Adrius and Reya.

She sits up, then promptly feels ill from the sudden movement. The soft velvet of the blankets crunches beneath her fingers as she pushes herself up, a deceptively pleasant luxury, like everything else in this damn manor. A stiffness lies in her limbs from sleeping in an uncomfortable evening gown.

She rubs the sleep from her eyes. "I'm awake."

Isidora gestures to a platter on the low table. "I brought you some food since I thought you might be hungry. And there's tea with willowbark, to relieve any pain if your head aches."

The dim light makes Kazan's temples throb more than she

cares to admit. A night spent consuming little more than wine doesn't make for a pleasant wake up. And a wine induced hangover is its own special sort of awful. Her stomach protests as she stands up, making her wonder if she should wait before eating anything, lest it come right back up again.

She looks in the mirror and something resembling a drowned cat stares back at her.

"Shall I help you look more presentable, Highness?" Isidora asks politely.

Kazan just nods, tugging at her mussed hair and trying not to notice the fact that she smells of sweat, dust, and wine.

In record time, Isidora has drawn a hot bath for her, pouring sweet smelling oils and salts into the water until the entire washroom is as fragrant and lovely as a rose garden. Kazan's crumpled dress can't be removed fast enough, in her opinion. It peels off her tacky skin. Did she spill a drink on herself last night?

Isidora delicately nudges her into the warm bath, the sublime water leeching stiffness from her limbs in a way that should make her relax but instead only contributes to the discombobulation she wades through in her mind. Isidora tugs a small stool across the bathroom floor so that she sits behind Kazan's head and tries to bring order to her dripping and tangled hair with soaps and perfumes. If she were more lucid, Kazan would likely smack Isidora's hand away, the feeling of fingers massaging her scalp so unusual and strange. But instead she succumbs to the sensation.

Water still drips from her hair as she is helped out of the tub and then dries herself, the steam filling the room and keeping her warm. There's another mirror in here, fogged over, cloudy, yet still clear enough for her to see her own reflection. The light is white and clear, not the flickering candlelight of the rest of the manor. It cuts across her body without mercy. Without the plush gown and elegant jewelry she had been draped in, without the makeup and powders, she can see all of herself.

Or what's left of her, anyway.

A nasty purple splotch the size of a hand has blossomed around her sternum like an ink stain. Marks from Ezelind's talons on her forearm. Her wrists, her knees, all mottled with bruises that have yet to begin fading. The thick patch of white scar tissue on the inside of her wrist from Dasar's attack looks pasty compared to the bruises caused by Adrius's boot stomp on her hand in the Vildenmarr. With the dark circles under her eyes, she looks like fruit left to rot by the roadside.

She traces the many blemishes with her fingertips. This place has marred her – injured her body, stolen her blood – what else will she be forced to sacrifice before she saves herself?

"Well," Isidora says, nervously chewing on her lip. "I'm, um, I'm certain I can do something about..." She gestures to all of Kazan. "*This.*"

It's easy enough to hide what's happened to her once Isidora gets to work. She cloaks Kazan in satin the color of a cloudy sky, wrings the last dregs of moisture from her hair and pins it up, paints makeup under her eyes to make her look less half-dead, slides lace gloves over her hands to cover up her wrists. When Isidora is done, Kazan looks far more presentable. Under silver moonlight or crystal chandeliers, the illusion of perfection will shine on her.

"Thank you. You can go now," she says. "I'll head back to the party shortly, I just..." She gestures to the pot of willowbark tea. "I'd like to clear my head a bit and rest some more first."

"Of course, Highness." Isidora curtseys. "You're welcome."

Alone again, Kazan rises to her feet and finds herself steadier than she thought, all things considered. She swallows some tea and eats one of the scones Isidora left. When she's finished, she feels perhaps slightly more human.

She catches a glimpse of herself in the mirror. Still flawless, if a bit twitchy at the edges. She takes a deep breath and slowly lets it out. She is confident. She is poised. It's only as much of a lie as she needs it to be.

In a whirl of skirts and shimmering jewels, she turns sharply on the heel of her slippers and marches out.

While servants bustle around to prepare the upcoming evening's elaborate feast, relatively few vampires are out and about in the Citadel's halls. It seems that many of them may be indulging in afternoon naps before another night of pointless debauchery. That, or they're doing their debauchery behind closed doors. Either way, Kazan feels perfectly content to be left relatively alone to process the mess of emotions sitting low in her stomach.

Last time, that cat and Reya's smooth interference stopped her from heading to the armory, but this time she is determined to get her damn sword one way or another. With the Citadel half-asleep, and Isidora under the impression that she's still convalescing, no one is expecting her to be up and about, and thus no pesky guards search for her while she weaves her way to the north wing.

The armory is on one of the lowest levels, marked by a heavy door and flanked by suits of armor. To her considerable confusion, no guard stands outside.

Kazan scans the area before approaching the door. It seems to have a basic pin and tumbler lock. Simple enough. She reaches into her hairdo and removes two pins. She bends one of them and, after checking again to make sure no one is watching, kneels before the door and gets to work on the lock.

However, the moment she presses on the door, it eases open. It was already unlocked?

Sticking her pins back into her hair, she enters, keeping her steps light and quiet. The room is filled with neatly organized racks of spears and swords, all kept in excellent condition and with varying degrees of ornamentation. Shields hang like decorative banners, most of them painted in the purples and golds of House Gambit. This treasury of metal seems infinite, beautifully so.

Someone moves around further in. Kazan sneaks forward

to see that it's a guard, fussing over a low rack made of carven stone. The vampire jolts to attention, whirling around to stare directly at her.

"Highness?" He gapes. "You aren't supposed to be here."

"And I'm guessing *you're* supposed to be standing guard at the door. So neither of us are where we're supposed to be," she replies.

"When I took my shift," he explains carefully, "there was evidence of a break-in. I believe something may have been stolen, though I'm still attempting to locate it. Highness, it would be best if you returned to your chambers. If this theft *has* occurred, it would be reassuring for all of us if you were kept under close watch. For your own safety." She notices a sword sheathed at his hip.

Her shoulders tense. "What's been stolen?"

"I'm afraid I can't tell you –"

"See," she says, a possessive and bone-deep anger beginning to boil up in her, "I have a feeling that someone has stolen my sword. And if they have, it would be in both of our best interests if you simply told me what you've discovered and when the theft occurred."

He takes a step towards her. He doesn't reach for his sword, but the handle is within threateningly close reach of his fingers. "This isn't any of your business."

"*My* sword, *my* business."

By now he is right in front of her, the proximity making her heart beat faster and her chest tighten. He places a hand on her shoulder. Firm, steady. A reminder of how she cannot beat a vampire's sheer strength. And yet he's standing between her and the information she requires.

"I'm going to have to escort you out," he tells her.

Before he can make another move, she grabs the handle of his sword and draws it, sliding it out of the scabbard only to then sheathe it in the guard's chest with all her strength.

He chokes, face paling from shock as he paws at the blade

sticking out of his sternum, shaking hands trying and failing to grasp it. The wound won't kill him, but that doesn't stop her taking an unethical amount of pleasure in knowing that it hurts.

He manages to grip the blade, but before he can pull it out, she kicks him, slamming her heel into the side of his knee and sending him tumbling to the ground. She plants one foot on the sword's pommel and leans her entire body weight onto it until she feels it bury itself into the stone beneath the guard's back.

"What did you find?" she demands, spitting the words as he spits out blood. "When was my sword taken?"

"Don't... know." His cough is an unpleasant gurgle. "Past... few hours?"

"How did they break in? Tell me!"

"I don't..." She leans harder on the blade until it forces him to continue. "Don't know... They must have..." He chokes, blood trickling out of the corners of his mouth, running down his cheeks to mat in his hair. "Must have... ordered... the guards away..."

A hand reaches out from her peripheral vision and grabs her by her hair.

She shrieks as she's dragged away from the guard, digging her nails into the hand and kicking out. Her foot connects with a shin and a surprised yelp sounds from her attacker. Their grip loosens for a second, long enough for her to slip free. When she whirls around, she sees Amelia's furious expression.

Amelia shoves Kazan in the chest and pushes her back until her hip bangs into a rack filled with shields.

"Where is it?" Amelia snarls, her nose less than an inch away from Kazan's. "Where is the sword?"

"I don't bloody know!"

"One more lie and you won't like what I do to you. I have quite a few ideas," she hisses, reaching towards Kazan's face. "I've been meaning to repay the favor and take your eye. Fair is fair, after all."

"Dasar would have your hide if you killed his human sacrifice before it's time." Before this is over, she thinks, she will take Amelia's other fucking eye.

"Oh, I wouldn't kill you. It'd be easy. Humans are so weak after all; it wouldn't take me long. Unless I wanted to draw it out for you. I could just trace your eyelid, a gentle press of my fingers." She trails a finger up Kazan's cheek, the touch freezing on her skin. She finds she cannot move, something about Amelia's voice keeping her pinned in place even as her heart pounds against her ribs like a drum. "Steady, slow pressure until I pop your eye from your skull."

One sharp claw scratches against her skin, just under her lower eyelid. It's enough to snap Kazan back into focus.

She's afraid of Amelia alright, but hot anger burns within her, unquenchable and scorching. She jerks her head backwards and grabs the corner of a shield. She swings it as hard as she can at Amelia's head. The vampire raises her arms in time to avoid getting hit in the face, but the impact still sends her staggering backwards as a tremendous *clang* rings out through the armory.

"I didn't do anything!" Kazan repeats, throwing the shield onto the ground between them. "So fuck off!"

"You stole my sword!" Amelia accuses.

"*My* sword," she automatically corrects. "And I wish I had."

Amelia's eye narrows as she properly takes in the still struggling guard, the empty stone rack in front of them, and presumably the notable absence of Kazan's sword. "If you didn't steal it," she says slowly, "then can you wager a guess as to who did?"

Oh, she *can*. Dasar could order the armory guards away, but she's willing to bet that so could Lady Aishreya Sutcliffe, his ever-popular seneschal. A seneschal who happens to share a bed with one Adrius De Vere, the other person in this manor that Kazan knows for certain is after her sword.

"No," Kazan lies. "But if I were you, I'd try to find out which of Dasar's lackeys would be so desperate to steal it that they'd risk angering him."

"So there *is* some measure of a brain in that human head of yours."

"Occasionally I manage to form an entire thought," she drawls. "Shocking, I know."

Amelia rolls her eyes and grabs Kazan by the scruff of her neck, bodily tossing her aside. "Take this advice, Highness, and stay out of my way."

Looking down at the guard, who has barely managed to grip the sword again, Kazan remarks, "You do know that Dasar will be informed of all this. He believes I'm going to die soon, so I'm no threat in his eyes. But you... you *would* be a threat if you got your hands on my sword."

"An easy dilemma to solve."

Amelia plucks a sword from one of the racks. With slow deliberation, she drags her palm over the nick near the handle until her flesh parts and her blood runs down the fuller. Spellwork sluggishly flares to life, the red light of it falling upon the guard's panicked expression.

She glances back over her shoulder. "Run along, Highness. And don't bother me again."

Kazan flees the armory as Amelia brings the sword down.

Chapter Twenty-One

A couple of drunk, wandering revelers try to catch Kazan's attention as she rushes through the Citadel, calling out or grabbing at her. She ducks under outstretched arms and ignores the pleas for her attention, cutting off any pleasantries with a demand to know where Adrius De Vere is. After more than a few failed attempts, where no one wants to talk about him, she gives up and simply heads straight to his chambers.

She stomps through the Citadel until she stands outside of his door. Back straight and head held high, she throws the door open and enters.

Adrius and Reya are lounging together on the couch, properly dressed this time even if they're still tied at the hip. Adrius's rapier leans against the armrest, and Reya's shoes lie discarded on the floor as she rests her bare feet on the cushions. Their conversation cuts off the moment Kazan shuts the door behind her.

Reya sits up properly. "Oh good. We were hoping you would... Kazan?"

Kazan doesn't respond. She goes straight past them and doesn't stop her determined march until she reaches Adrius's desk. Despite being more than a little preoccupied when he had done this before, her impeccable memory doesn't fail her, and she recalls exactly what he did to access his hidden medical supplies. She presses the right knot in the wooden scrollwork, flicks back the hidden latches, and opens the top of the desk.

Inside, above the normal papers and supplies, rests a long object wrapped in silk. A pale hint of rowan wood peeping out from beneath the shroud. Her sword, at last.

Kazan leans against the open desk, crosses her arms, and declares, "I think it's time we talked."

"You don't miss a trick, do you?" Reya says, smiling. She shifts to the side and pats the cushion between her and Adrius. "Come on." She beckons Kazan over. "Have a seat. It's quite comfortable."

"We won't bite," Adrius says. "Well, *I* won't, at any rate." There's that hint of teasing he'd shown at Rask's party.

"I make no promises," Reya purrs.

Kazan shakes her head and points to the sword. "No, *this* is what we need to talk about. This and other things, but…" First things first. She takes a deep breath before reluctantly admitting, "Maybe you were right in saying that I'd attempted to… that I had implied to both of you, separately, that the other would help me in a way that might not have been… technically true."

"Don't worry," Reya says pleasantly. "I like the lies. They're a lovely puzzle."

No one has ever said that before. Kazan can do nothing more than blink in confusion for a good long moment before she manages to collect her thoughts again. "Well, good, because I'm not going to apologize for it."

"We wouldn't ask that of you." Adrius winces and adds, "I know this entire thing gives you few options."

"Few to none. As I see it, here are *our* options. I can go to Dasar and tell him what the two of you have been up to. I doubt he'd truly care if Adrius were to kill Ezelind, but he would have to do something about it, if only to avoid it happening under his roof. And Reya – the perfect Lady Sutcliffe, Dasar's seneschal, all set up to inherit the Citadel when he dies. I imagine it wouldn't take long for Dasar to put two and two together about why you're involved in this plot."

"Clever as always." Adrius's expression is very carefully neutral even as he stands and takes a single step towards her. "And do you have proof?"

"You've been after my sword this whole time and *someone* ordered Dasar's soldiers away from the armory. Amelia can attest to both – she's furious enough that I imagine she'd do so at the drop of a hat."

"I see. I'm assuming you have a second option?"

"Something more... collaborative." Kazan swallows, her throat painfully raw. "But I just... It may be hypocritical of me, but in this I'm going to demand honesty from you two. I've kissed the both of you of my own volition and I won't deny that I enjoyed it. So there. Those are my cards on the table. I need to know – have I been nothing more than a game for you to play?"

Reya blinks, stunned. "Is it truly so hard to believe that Adrius and I can both genuinely be interested in you while simultaneously being interested in one another?" The surprise on her face shifts into something far hotter. "And I'd prefer to have more than simply your *cards* on my table."

"Reya and I are lovers, that's obvious enough," Adrius carefully explains. "That doesn't mean we don't take others into our beds also, either together or separately. I tend to prefer humans, as they usually have no idea who I am. Her tastes are far more broad, but she's generally uninterested in anyone who bores her. So, I can safely assure you that neither of us were deceiving the other in our interest in you, nor did we find it entertaining to string you along or whatever other less charitable motivations you may have ascribed to us."

A knot inside Kazan's chest unwinds. They care. They actually do *care*, even if it is only the slightest scrap of emotion. If they care, then she has a *chance*. A chance to do something better than just risk it all on the gambit that she can survive possession, that Alphonse will leave her as he claims, that she can overpower him if needed.

"Then, the way I see it," she says, trying to sound more confident and less desperately hopeful, "we can help one another. We all want the same people dead. Give me my sword and I'll kill Weisz, Ezelind, and Dasar. Both for myself, and for your benefit. I will keep my mouth shut about your involvement and take all the blame. In return, you keep me from dying tomorrow. I don't care if you let the Citadel crumble or figure out some way of saving it, it's yours to do with as you will."

Reya and Adrius exchange a glance and, to her surprise, the two of them relax.

"We've been waiting decades for the ideal year to make our move," Reya says, getting to her feet and fluffing out her skirts. "This morning, we decided to go ahead *now*. You're right, we don't want you to die and, as fortune would have it, I believe I may have an idea as to how to keep the Citadel standing while still preserving your life."

"How?" Kazan asks.

Reya chews on her lip and deflects, "Let me worry about that. I'm still not completely certain of the minutia of adjusting the spell."

It's not as though Kazan knows much about blood magic, though she can't shake the suspicion that Reya's hiding something. She turns to Adrius and quirks an eyebrow. "And you?"

"Ezelind will die by *my* hand," he decrees vehemently. "And Weisz must be left alive. The more our leaders die, the more unstable our society becomes and the more vulnerable we are to the Wardens. Apart from that, we're in agreement. The sword stays here until tomorrow night, giving Reya plenty of time to solidify her adjustments to the spell. Then you can kill Dasar as brutally as you like."

"It would seem," Reya says, "that we have a deal."

Years ago, when Kazan first traveled to Upper Welshire, their caravan had gone through a mountain pass. She walked through to the other end and found herself on the edge of a cliff, staring down into the valley below, wind whipping around her and gravity singing to the beat of her heart. This, right here, gives her the same whirling, dizzying elation as being at the peak of that mountain.

With that energy filling her, she strides forward and kisses Reya. Then she grabs a handful of Adrius's coat and kisses him too.

"Deal," she agrees triumphantly.

Reya winks. "Care to seal it with more than one little kiss?"

"Is that an invitation?"

Adrius tilts her chin up and presses a lingering kiss into the crook of her neck and something tight and *hot* curls in her stomach. "It is."

"And I'll live through it?" she asks, only mostly joking.

"I should hope so."

Why the hell not, she thinks. *I've all but won already.*

She leans in and kisses Reya, hard and slow and savors it in a way she hadn't before. The taste of Reya's crimson lips is even sweeter than it had been the first day, and this time there is no pause before Reya returns her affections. Kazan has barely begun memorizing the shape of Reya's mouth before Adrius grips a handful of her hair and pulls her towards him instead, capturing her lips for himself. Reya runs her tongue over the side of Kazan's neck, fangs just noticeable enough to entice without causing pain.

She grins and lets herself be tugged into the bedroom. Adrius's arms are around her waist as she sits on the edge of the bed, and she can feel the solid shape of his torso against her side. Reya moves onto Kazan's lap, her arms draped over Kazan's shoulders and her legs straddling her hips. Her tongue slides between Kazan's lips, burning against her as Reya all but devours her, relentless kiss after relentless kiss. Kazan tangles her fingers in Reya's gorgeous curls, and runs her hands over the exposed skin of Reya's plunging neckline.

"Delectable," Reya murmurs.

Kazan suddenly finds her eyes at the perfect height to stare straight at Reya's impressive bosom and she forces herself to crank her head upwards to instead stare into those golden eyes shining with mischief. All that manages to come out of her mouth is, "Erm."

Adrius smothers a laugh. "Reya, you're going to break her."

"Not yet," Reya purrs.

"Erm," Kazan says again, wishing she were capable of more coherence.

The cold of Reya's hand makes her shiver as she cups Kazan's cheek. "There's no need to be so speechless. I know I have that effect on people, but I rather enjoy your mouth."

"You are not helping," Kazan blurts out.

Adrius chuckles in a way that makes her toes curl. "Now what happened to the woman I met at Rask's party? I seem to recall that she was quite the flirt. I don't believe I ever managed to render her speechless."

"You never sat in my lap," she points out.

Reya leans back an inch as though retreating. "I can move if you're not enjoying yourself."

"I didn't say *that*."

For once, there's no deception between them. No conflict. Only passion.

Adrius pulls her hair back so that Reya can more easily access her neck, the two vampires sandwiching her between them. "This is what I wanted to do at Rask's party," he admits, pressing his lips to hers. "Two hasty kisses weren't nearly enough."

"You have me now. My, ah –" She's briefly distracted by Reya lifting up her skirts a scant but very noticeable inch, "my undivided attention, as well, without being encumbered by business, as it was previously."

"And I benefit a great deal from your earlier restraint," Reya adds with a light laugh, her breath tickling Kazan's skin. She places the tip of her finger underneath Kazan's chin and turns her head. "Do you have any particular preferences? I would hate to scare you off now, when the fun has only just begun."

"Don't you dare bite me," she states.

"Pity, but fair enough."

"And if you pay any special attention to my scar, I'm gone."

Reya opens her mouth, brow furrowed with confusion, but Adrius cuts her off. "Of course," he says quickly. "Perfectly understandable."

"Is there anything you don't want *me* to do?" Kazan asks, toying with the buttons of Adrius's shirt.

She can feel the shape of Adrius's smile against her collarbone. "I think if you manage to surprise us with something we've never done before, we'll be far more impressed than offended."

"Normally I'd take that as a challenge," she says, a little more breathlessly than she'd intended, "but I think I'm out of my depth enough as it is."

Cold air runs down her spine as her dress loosens and slips from her shoulders. The silk bodice sags, still high enough to keep her decent, but only barely, and she can't help the tiny, surprised yelp that escapes her lips.

"You two were busy talking," Reya says cheerfully, continuing to pick at the laces keeping Kazan's dress in place. "I had my mind on other matters."

An excellent point. Kazan shifts so that she can remove her slippers and then laughs, nudging Adrius until he kicks off his boots as well. Kazan caresses one of Reya's legs, starting at one of her smooth calves and slowly working her way up to a soft thigh, savoring the sensation of cool skin.

Kazan has slept with men and women alike in the past, but never at the same time. She finds herself being passed back and forth between the two of them, skilled hands tugging her this way and that. Had they not already told her that they were accustomed to sharing, she would be surprised by the practiced manner in which they arrange her. Her bodice falls off her completely as she leans forward. There's an impatience to Adrius's movements as he tugs her dress down, the fabric pooling around her waist.

"Take this off," he tells her in the sort of commanding tone that never fails to pour heat into her blood.

Her fingers are clumsy in her haste as she loosens the skirts enough to pull the entire silken affair over her head and toss it to the side, leaving her clad only in a thin white shift. Deciding that he's wearing far too much, she pushes insistently on Adrius's coat. The warmth of Reya presses against her back and she reaches around Kazan to assist and then – then he's kissing Reya.

Their intimacy is so very different than it was last night. Last night things had been more than a little blurred by wine and she'd been both furiously confused and just plain furious. Now she sees with unclouded eyes. There's a familiarity between them, a complete lack of the exploration that all early kisses come with. Adrius kisses Reya as though consuming her, and Kazan watches the way the muscles of his jaw shift. Reya kisses Adrius as though every second she spends not kissing him is a waste, and Kazan watches the way her eyelashes flutter against her rouged cheeks.

Reya removes Adrius's shirt, exposing a tantalizing amount of bare skin and defined muscles, and he works at her bodice until it too is removed. Reya slips out of her skirts into that near transparent shift she'd been wearing when Kazan first walked in on her.

Kazan's mouth suddenly goes dry but it's not jealousy. It's raw appreciation.

"You're both…" She struggles to find the words. "You two are so…"

"Speechless again?" Reya's laugh is a light, teasing thing. "You must find us quite fascinating."

"Yes. Yes – yes, that's it *exactly*. You're *fascinating* –"

Entirely out of words, she seals her mouth against Adrius's

and tries to explain it with actions instead. She kisses him violently, every bit of tension and fear and stress that has been building up inside her over the past two days finally finding an outlet. She only pulls back to gasp for air and then kisses Reya just the same, her tongue scraping against the woman's fangs.

It's like a dam breaking: wild river water crashes through her and sweeps her away in the strong current. Since the Vildenmarr, she has been in constant, unmitigable danger; terror always holding her in a clawed grip. But now *she* is the one who has everything under her thumb, who is finally about to come out on top of Dasar and Ezelind and Weisz and Amelia and every single bastard who has dared to laugh at her. And all she wants to do is not think for a minute. To have fun and fuck two very attractive people and it's all so much and she just... lets go.

She paws ineffectively at Reya's shift until Reya laughs again and says, "So impatient. You'll ruin my clothes!"

"Bit excitable, isn't she?" Adrius teases, addressing Reya instead of her.

Reya grins. "I bet I can get her to settle down."

Kazan doesn't even think of protesting when Adrius pulls her towards him, her back pressed up against the hard planes of his chest and her hips between his thighs. His cold lips kiss her neck and one of his hands slips underneath the neckline of her shift to toy with her breast. She moans, heat rushing through her against his chill touch. Questing fingers hitch her shift up and she honestly can't tell who does it, only that the fabric is tugged high up to her waist and goosebumps dot her exposed legs. There's a flash of Reya's rakish grin before she buries her head between Kazan's thighs.

The first touch of Reya's lips is barely a whisper, just enough to make her whimper. The second touch is the most intense of kisses, all tongue and pressure and freezing heat, and Adrius's free hand claps over Kazan's mouth before she can cry out. She can't help bucking her hips against Reya's mouth, another cry smothered as he pinches her nipple between thumb and forefinger.

"I hate to keep you silent, but if you scream, you're likely to draw some unwanted attention," he murmurs, his voice curling around the shell of her ear. "Can I trust you not to scream?"

She nods frantically.

"Good." He removes his hand, fingertips brushing against her swollen lips. "Anything short of a scream is allowed. Encouraged, even. It would be a shame if you were *shy*."

"I'm not – *ah* –" It's a challenge to be coherent as Reya licks a toe-curling line up her sex. "Not fucking *shy* – Mmm…"

Adrius half lets go of her and removes Reya's hand from her tight grip on Kazan's thigh. He brings her knuckles to his mouth and kisses her. As Kazan watches, breathless and nearly dying from Reya's skilled tongue, his thumbnail juts out into a sharp claw and he cuts a tiny line across the inside of Reya's wrist.

Blood wells up over Reya's brown skin and he licks it off with a languid drag of his tongue. A strangled moan vibrates in his chest and Kazan can feel his arousal harden against her hip.

The tautness building in her snaps and she chokes on a cry as she comes. Beautiful, trembling aftershocks run through her. Only now, as she must force her fingers to relax, does she realize that she's completely messed Reya's perfectly styled hair. She slumps in Adrius's embrace and tries to get her breathing back under control, a task not at all helped by the tiny, lingering touches Reya gives her as she comes down from her peak.

Adrius devours a few final drops of Reya's blood before the cut on her wrist heals itself in that unnatural vampiric fashion. When she's healed, he tugs her to her knees, her lips still slick and shining, and claims her mouth hungrily. A tiny gasp slips out of Kazan at the sight.

"I didn't loosen her up any," Reya says in that low, seductive voice of hers. "Can I taste you when you fuck her?"

Without even looking away from Reya, Adrius places his palm on Kazan's stomach and shoves her backwards. Her head sinks into the pillows, her legs tangling between her two lovers. She almost protests at being tossed, except Adrius is sliding a hand up her inner thigh and it's *so* distracting.

"You're unexpectedly polite today," he says to Reya, a heated, intimate familiarity in the way they look at one another.

She smiles. "I know how you feel about... *biting* when there are humans around."

"What's that supposed to mean?" Kazan can't help asking.

Reya leans over her, dark strands of hair forming a curtain around them. "Blood has a thousand different tastes, you know. The slightest variations – not unlike fine wine. Certain sensory experiences... mmm... they translate into flavor. I can literally *taste* his ecstasy and he can taste *mine*." She presses an open-mouthed kiss to Kazan's jaw, one hand slipping up underneath her shift. "I could taste yours too, if you'd let me bite you." She quickly amends, "I won't, of course. I'm *very* obliging."

"So I've noticed," Kazan replies, feeling more than a little dazed, not to mention very distracted by the things Reya's doing to her.

Over Reya's shoulder, she can see Adrius removing his breeches and her stomach twists in anticipation. He notices her staring, pulls her left leg up to rest on his shoulder, and kisses her calf. The drag of his tongue against her skin makes her shiver. Then she can't see him at all anymore, as Reya enthusiastically pulls Kazan's shift off her. A moment later and Reya strips just the same, her shimmying movements all but putting on a show despite her rush to remove her final piece of clothing. That golden necklace of hers is the only thing remaining, the gemstone shining between her breasts.

It's impossible for Kazan to say how grateful she is that

neither of them pause upon the reveal of the myriad bruises littering her body. It's no hardship to imagine that they too understand the need to simply not have to think about their problems or deal with any challenges for a pleasant hour or two. Her world has narrowed and softened into Adrius's broad shoulders and the smell of Reya's perfume.

Adrius briefly pauses. "If you're nervous..."

"I'm not," she replies, and to her surprise, it's not even slightly a lie.

With a faint chuckle, he pulls her hips flush against his and sinks into her. If she'd thought Reya's mouth was amazing, this is indescribably better, that same burning hot ice deep inside her. She's so focused on that all-consuming sensation that she barely registers Adrius's pleased groan as he starts to properly fuck her. The bulk of his chest covers her, and as he leans over her, he grabs one of her wrists. Pins and needles shoot through her hands as he squeezes, making her blood pool in her palm, wrist aching. Claws extending, his thumb caresses her skin. He practically groans as he kisses her wrist, languid, his tongue dragging over her racing pulse.

"Adrius, let me..." Reya's voice almost, very nearly almost, sounds like pleading as she presses up against his side.

He releases Kazan's wrists, grasping her hips instead, and tilts his head to the side, baring his neck to Reya. Canines sharpen and elongate into wicked fangs behind those blood red lips of hers and, with a sigh of pure relief, she sinks her pearly teeth into his neck.

"Fuck!" He gives Kazan a particularly hard thrust that makes her cry out in pleasure. "Reya, *careful*."

Reya pulls her fangs out. "Sorry, sorry."

A drop of blood rolls down Adrius's collarbone and Reya's tongue darts out to lick it away. The noise Reya makes is practically obscene. Her eyes flutter closed, and she turns her attentions to the bite mark on his neck, her hips rolling against nothing and she drinks as though chasing a phantom touch.

Adrius's movements get rougher, faster, and the heat inside Kazan burns ever hotter. There's a sharp burst of not at all unwelcome pain as his claws on her hip pierce her skin and spill her blood. He curses upon seeing what he's done but doesn't stop, instead raising his crimson-stained fingertips to his mouth and devouring her blood off his claws. Reya's muffled moan burns straight through Kazan's veins like fire. Were she to put her tongue to the bite mark on Adrius's neck, or more indirectly through a kiss to Reya's bloodied lips – what would she taste? What does ecstasy taste like?

The heat scouring her veins breaks. A scream burns in the back of her throat as she comes again, her back arching off the bed, her hands grasping the sheets.

Adrius's voice murmurs praises, telling her how good she feels around him, how wonderful she tastes. He doesn't relent, keeps her squirming in a painful bliss as he fucks her, pulling her closer until he's so deep inside her that it almost hurts in the most exquisite of ways. Only then does he reach his own completion, kissing her as though chasing the taste of her. She feels his shout more than she can hear it.

Bliss makes her limbs heavy. She sinks into the pillows, her chest heaving, lungs struggling to catch up.

Adrius gently runs a hand over the swell of her hip, smearing the blood that lingers there. An equally blissed out expression lingers around his gold eyes as he pulls back from her, her legs still spread around his. He turns to kiss Reya, one of his hands reaching between her thighs to caress her. His other hand, stained with Kazan's blood, is lifted to Reya's crimson lips. An indescribably erotic moan slips out of Reya as she sucks and licks away all traces of Kazan's blood and, either from touch or taste, climaxes on Adrius's fingers.

Perhaps, Kazan thinks dreamily, *it's a good thing that the Wardens refused to let me join them. If I had, they would have taken my head for this.*

Chapter Twenty-Two

Kazan buries her nose in the sweet-smelling curls of Reya's hair. Once more she finds herself in the midst of a study in contrasts. The soft curves of Reya pressed against her front and the corded muscles of Adrius resting against her back. Adrius's fingertips lazily dance over her hip and over her waist until she shivers from the chill, heat beginning to desert her. Reya tugs the sheets over them.

Adrius's hands linger on the bruise painted across her sternum, trailing down to brush the ones on her knees, and gently touching the one his boot has left on her hand. "I'm sorry." His quiet voice lingers against her ear. "It was… cruel of me."

"I would have done the same to you," she replies. She would have too, were she in his position.

"Still. I regret it. I regret, too, that while my skills can heal basic injuries, the intricacies of bruises are beyond me."

Reya hums, the sound buzzing in her chest. "I always forget how fragile humans are."

"Don't you remember what it was like?" Kazan asks curiously. "When you were human. Does the transformation make your days as a mortal that fuzzy?"

Reya shakes her head. "No. It's the disparity between the two, I think. That and the passage of time."

"Who were you as a human?"

"Oh, I was no one." She laughs. It's fake, and not a

particularly good fake at that. "I won't regale you with the depressing details. Suffice it to say that I had no prospects and no real opportunity to ever advance in life, until..." She pauses. "Until one day I met Dasar. He took a liking to me and suddenly everything was *glorious*. Titles and money and adoration and everything I'd never had."

"You introduced yourself as the former Baroness of Cairemere. How did that happen, former or otherwise, if you had no station?"

"I married. Dasar could see that I wanted to spend time amongst humans, in all the realms of human society that I'd been barred from. He lent me a disguise, not unlike Adrius's ring, and told me where I could find him when I changed my mind. You must understand, when someone thinks they will never be noticed, never be loved, and then suddenly all eyes are on them..." She sighs, and it's impossible to say if it's tinged with nostalgia or regret. Or both, perhaps. "I married the first person who asked for my hand, the Baron of Cairemere. He was nice and I enjoyed his company, but it was hardly love. After a decade he died of old age while I stayed as young as the day we met, and so it was time for me to disappear."

Kazan reaches for Adrius's hand, currently splayed across her sternum, and laces her fingers with his. "What about you?"

"Hm?" he murmurs.

She turns her head to face him properly and repeats, "What about you? Who were you when you were human?"

"Ah." He hesitates for a long time before replying with a sort of bitter sarcasm, "I'm sure it'll be a shock to know that I was born noble."

"A great and terrible shock."

"I was born in Noreal. Do you know where that is?"

"It's pretty far into the north-eastern mountains, isn't it? What else?"

"My father wanted me to join the Wardens and I suppose I did too," he says. Isn't that a surprise? Who would have thought that she and Adrius had that, of all things, in common. "I was tutored in combat and spent hours in church, everything that I'd need for that life. My mother wasn't quite so insistent." A tiny smile flickers across his lips. "She extolled the virtues of the arts on her children. All I ever managed to become was a passable harpist, but she doted on my younger brother – he was brilliant with a brush and painted constantly." That smile fades and Kazan dearly wishes it back. "Eventually a man named Devon Bartel, the former High Lord of Mooncliffe, challenged me to a duel. He found my skills with a sword impressive enough to turn me, and that was that."

Now that is *quite* different from what Amelia had said, from what the rumors claim.

Ignoring the thought lingering in the back of her mind, Kazan picks something else from his story to inquire upon. "You can play the harp?"

"Passably," he laughs. "And it has been decades." He moves his hand against hers, manipulating her fingers to fold against her palm. "As one's fingers come off the strings, they tuck into the palm. I frequently didn't bother, and my mother despaired of my technique."

An image of Adrius sitting before a harp, nimble fingers plucking at thin strings, forms in Kazan's mind. She wouldn't have guessed it of him, but when she watches the image unfold, it feels right. That elegant dexterity translates seamlessly into the quick movements that mark his masterful swordwork.

"Kazan…" Reya presses a light kiss into the crook of her neck and asks quietly, "May I ask a question about you and your human frailty?" Ah. The inevitable. "How did you get that scar?"

Let's see now. What would Reya find most interesting? She's told a version to Adrius, so it would be easy to simply repeat that. But where's the fun in telling the same lie twice? Does she want Adrius to know she was lying, though? Or has he already heard one of the many iterations of the tale she told to Dasar and Isidora? She prepares to tell the same story as Dasar's and then stops. Licks her lips. Tries again with the version she told Adrius at Rask's party and *stops*.

"I lied to you," she blurts out. "When you asked at Rask's party, Adrius, I lied to you."

He sighs, gently letting go of her fingers, although not relinquishing her hand. "I'm not surprised you did."

"I told you that vampires attacked our village, and I hid." Her throat is oddly sore. "That was true. I told you a vampire came across my hiding place and touched my face. That was also true. I said that a vampire pinned me down, that I couldn't move because they were too strong."

"Yes, I recall."

"But there I was lying," she admits. She swallows and lets herself get lost in his golden gaze. "I couldn't move, but it wasn't because they pinned me down. I could have run. Could have screamed. Could have done so many things, but I didn't. I didn't move because I was *fascinated*."

It would make her laugh, were it not the most important secret she has ever kept. What was she supposed to go around telling people? That she simply sat there and let a vampire caress her cheek because she'd been too entranced by them? All she can remember is cold skin and the vague silhouette of a face in the moonlight, but she remembers the way they held themself. The way they moved with the grace of a lithe panther and the strength of a mountain river. The sheer, undeniable *power* of them.

How could she have moved away from such pure intensity? How could she do anything other than stare in wonder and allow herself to be swept up in that aura? And how could any human understand that?

"I'm fascinated," she confesses, a whisper in the quiet room.

"Did this vampire do it?" Reya asks. "Did they have the audacity to cut such a beautiful face?"

"Not precisely. A Warden burst in to save me. The vampire was surprised, they moved unexpectedly. It was an accident."

Reya kisses her once more. "Thank you."

"For what?"

"Telling us the truth when I asked."

"Yes, well." Kazan chews on her lower lip and can't bring herself to look at either of them. "Don't become overly accustomed to it."

Fondness radiates from Reya's eyes. "I hope I never become completely accustomed to it. Listening to your obfuscations, picking out the meaning behind them, determining what is and isn't true – I would never ask you to sacrifice that. It's as endlessly fascinating to me as our kind is to you."

"How unexpectedly complementary," Kazan eventually replies.

She lets her eyelids droop shut. Her limbs are heavy and languid, and she allows herself to embrace that, slipping into a slow, post-sex drowsiness. Eventually her breathing evens out and while she doesn't truly sleep, she finds herself in a comfortable reverie.

The bed shifts. Adrius gently moves Kazan's arm so that she's not disturbed as he slides out of bed. Reya lightly kisses her bare shoulder before similarly leaving.

"I'll try to keep Dasar occupied for a while," Reya whispers. Were Kazan actually asleep, the words would be far too quiet to wake her.

Adrius is just as quiet, if not more so. "Does anyone else know where she is?"

"Probably not. That handmaid, Isidora, she's not particularly bright. But Kazan's not strictly needed until the final feast, I'm sure we can give her some time. She's…"

There's a silent pause, and Kazan doesn't open her eyes. Some deeply curious and perhaps slightly masochistic part of her is desperate to know what they'll say about her when they think she isn't listening.

Adrius's sigh is slow and soft and almost regretful. "She deserves some peaceful sleep, at the very least. I would be disappointed if we had to wake her just yet." She can hear him kiss Reya on the forehead. "I'm glad you liked her too."

"Of course I did. She's beautiful. And she can be beautifully violent."

Kazan hears the movement of fabric. They must be dressing. The noise of Reya's skirts swishing is unmistakable, as is the silken sound of Adrius tying his cravat. Violence, Kazan thinks. Of all her qualities to find attractive. The worst thing is that she can't decide how she feels about that. Is she angry that they value a trait so many humans would find ugly or intimidating? Or is she pleased that they desire the ugly parts of herself that she refuses to hide?

It takes a great deal of effort for Kazan to remain still as Reya's light fingers trail across the bedsheets, brushing over Kazan's calf. "She doesn't…"

"I know," Adrius replies, equally tender.

Doesn't *what*?

"She would be so…" Reya whispers again.

"I know."

Be *what*?

"Help me with this pin?" There's a *clink* of metal as he presumably finds the pin and fixes it into Reya's hair. "If only you could paint too, Adrius. Then you could immortalize her and hang her portrait next to yours."

"Reya…" Something in his tone makes Kazan risk cracking a single eyelid open. She watches them through the blurry curtain of her eyelashes. Adrius's hands are frozen in Reya's hair, staring at her reflection in the mirror affixed to the wall. Or at *his* reflection, Kazan can't tell. There's a strange, faraway look in the lines around his eyes and the set of his brow. "It's been a long time since you were with a human, hasn't it?"

Reya doesn't answer. Kazan supposes silence is confirmation enough.

"We have our solution in hand. If she leaves after the party is over, it wouldn't exactly be surprising," Adrius continues when no reply is forthcoming. He's quieter, too, forcing Kazan to strain her ears to hear him.

"I know. Do you know where Amelia is?"

"If what I've gleaned of her plans is correct, she's supposed to rendezvous with Ezelind and Weisz in the main gallery, although I doubt she'll show up without the sword in hand. I'll go and watch, see what happens. You should be able to keep out of her way easily. Go. Make your clever excuses to Dasar."

Reya moves to leave. "Adrius..." Reya sighs, pausing with her hand on the door. "I'm sorry. I shouldn't have said that about the painting."

With his back turned, Kazan cannot see his expression, nor can she hear one in his voice. "It's been a lovely evening. Let's not tarnish that by discussing this."

"Of course."

Reya vanishes into the main room, and a moment later there's the sound of the door to his chambers opening and then closing behind her. Kazan holds still and waits. A few minutes later Adrius leaves as well, though he certainly takes a lot longer doing so than Reya.

Kazan waits until she hears the solid wooden noise of the door closing again before she fully opens her eyes and rolls out of bed. Her bare feet hit the floor and her legs feel a bit unsteady at first, as the pleasant ache between her thighs slowly fades away. She cleans herself up and dresses as best she can, taking her sweet time and allowing herself to linger in her relaxed haze for as long as possible.

Tying her hair up into a loose bun, she wanders into the main room only to see that the desk compartment is open.

And her sword is gone.

Running over to the desk, she rummages through the stacks of papers and supplies, tossing some of them over her shoulder in her haste. She drops to her knees to check under the desk and under the chairs; she throws the cushions of the couch onto the floor to search beneath them; she kicks up the corners of the rugs, yanks open the curtains, but it's *gone*. It's fucking *gone*! She pounds her fists against the desk.

Her lips pull back from her teeth and she wishes she had fangs. "Adrius, you *bastard*!"

Chapter Twenty-Three

The door slams shut behind Kazan as she storms out, running in the direction of the main gallery.

Chimes ring through the Citadel, tolling eleven bells. One hour to midnight. One hour until the potential last day of her life.

Gilded halls shift into dark, ornately carved wooden paneling, which shifts into walls filled with ancient paintings. Portraits of vampires with peeling faces and sharp golden eyes stare accusingly at Kazan as she whirls past. She turns down a corridor and finds herself looking at a large open landing, almost a foyer. Two staircases descend from a balcony, mirroring one another as they curve down to the floor below. A tall window stands where they meet, the glass somewhat dirtied in the corners but letting in the moonlight. Glowing rectangles fall on the carpeted stairs. Her heart skips a beat and she hides behind a plinth, covering herself in the shadow of a porcelain vase.

Three figures stand just ahead of her on the balcony. The moonlight casts long and soft shadows across the floor, illuminating the three. The first is Weisz, his blonde hair an eye-catching spun gold. The second is Ezelind, her trailing dress spread out on the floor like an ink stain. Then there is the silver hair and dark coat of Adrius, who carries in his arms a long object, wrapped in a length of cloth.

"...apologies for my tardiness," Adrius is saying softly.

"No need," Ezelind replies, and Kazan risks leaning forward another inch to better hear the woman's cool tone, peering around the edge of the vase. "I was expecting Amelia, but you're perfectly on time and I really don't care which of you delivers our prize. Did anyone see you?"

"No," Adrius replies, just as coldly.

"Where did you find it?"

"Does it matter?"

"Hm. Perhaps not. And where is the queen?"

"Having a glass of wine with Dasar in the statuary parlor," he lies. That can't be the excuse Reya came up with. Why is Adrius telling Ezelind otherwise? What's he playing at?

There's a pause as Ezelind thinks it over. "Good. If she's in the same location as Dasar, it will be even easier to pin his death on her. The marks on his body will point to her actions regardless, but having her standing over his corpse will be a final bite in her flesh. We can keep her locked up until the last feast."

"And if she blames us? Will she need to be eliminated early?"

Weisz laughs. "Why don't you drag her out before we get to the messy business? I'm sure you wouldn't have any trouble hauling a single human around."

Adrius inclines his head ever so slightly. "Of course. Well then…"

For Kazan, the seconds drag out into an eternity as he pulls back the cloth covering what lies in his arms. A hilt of rowan and silver peeks out. His shoulders tense as they would before striking out, but she barely notices. His gloved fingers wrap around the rowan hilt as he frees it, revealing the beautiful crossguard and a smooth, perfect blade of shining steel. It all but glows in the moonlight and it's hers, that's *her* sword. And she *snaps*.

Fury throws her out from behind the statue, a scream tearing its way out of her throat –

"Give that *back*, you *BASTARD*!"

She grabs the first thing she can get her hands on – the porcelain vase – and hurls it at him. It shatters on the carpeted ground when he turns away just in time, there's shock behind his gold eyes, as if he honestly didn't expect to see her here.

"Highness," he says in a distant voice, like he hadn't kissed or fucked her, "I think you had best –"

She lunges for him, fist drawn back, nails digging into her palm.

Cold fingers wrap around her wrist and it's Ezelind yanking her backwards; Ezelind claws against her skin, dangerous eyes burning with sheer irritation. Not anger, not true rage. Irritation. Because Kazan is just that far beneath her. With overwhelming vampiric strength, Ezelind yanks Kazan's arm aside and grabs her by the neck. Those sharp claws pinch the skin of her throat, her pulse racing. She scrapes and punches and slaps at Ezelind's arm in a desperate attempt to free herself, but it does nothing at all.

"It would seem you've done a poor job of keeping an eye on her," Ezelind says to Adrius, though she doesn't look away from Kazan. "Congratulations, Highness. You're now a liability."

A feral snarl vibrates in Kazan's throat but doesn't make it past Ezelind's grip.

"Ez," Weisz whines, like this is barely an inconvenience. "We can't just kill her. It would destroy the Citadel."

Ezelind's gaze bores into Kazan. "Her blood remains in the crown and will remain until midnight tomorrow. That gives us a full day to come up with a solution and prepare a different sacrifice before the Citadel comes crashing down."

"Oh, I didn't think of that." Weisz shrugs. "Go ahead then."

"If you kill her," Adrius warns in a low, quiet voice, "then the wounds will make it obvious one of our kind did it. Dasar will lock down the Citadel to find the killer."

"There's more than one way to kill a human," Ezelind says calmly. She steps forward towards the edge of the balcony until Kazan's hips are forced up against the railing. Those icy fingers tighten, and Kazan can't breathe. She chokes, gasping, throat burning. "Ways that point to nothing more than an... unfortunate tumble."

She releases Kazan's throat. Air rasps into her lungs as she gasps for breath and then Ezelind, a corner of her mouth curling upwards, places both her hands on Kazan's shoulders.

And she *shoves*.

Kazan's feet slip off the ground and all of a sudden, she's staring up at the ceiling and she reaching out, trying to grab onto something. But she can't. There's just gravity and wind and a weightlessness in her stomach as she falls from the balcony.

She doesn't know what hitting the ground feels like. One moment there's terror and falling, and the next she lies on the landing below. For a second, there's nothing. Her vision is white, her lungs are empty, her body devoid of all feeling. It takes a minute for her brain to work well enough to recognize that she's in complete agony. When the pain returns, it returns with a powerful vengeance. She can't move, can't scream, can't breathe. Her spine is on fire and her legs feel as though someone has smashed a hammer into them; her ribs have turned her entire chest into a set of rapidly compressing bellows.

Moonlight swarms above her. So bright. So cold. So distant. Darkness sinks into her vision once more as the effort of keeping her eyes open becomes too great.

Are those footsteps? Or her straggling heartbeat?

"... damn Adrius, running off at a time like this... Check her," Ezelind's voice orders.

Fabric shifts. Someone kneels next to her. "She is awfully pretty like this," Weisz casually remarks.

Cold fingers touch her limp wrist. Weisz feels for her pulse, and he will find it and know she's alive. Then they'll finish the job and that will be it. It will all be over. His fingertips press against the same spot where Dasar had dug his fangs into her flesh. Against the thick layer of scar tissue that formed when Adrius healed her. Weisz waits. Her sluggish pulse isn't strong enough to make it past that layer of gnarled tissue.

"She's gone," Weisz declares.

"Then let's pick up that damn sword and eliminate Dasar before someone finds her body."

The footsteps leave.

Kazan finally musters the strength to open her eyes and once more finds herself swimming in moonlight. Caught in an ocean of it, lines of it streaming in through the window, bathing her in silver.

A single breath slips into her lungs. Her ribs scream in pain, but she breathes. She lives. Time passes and she keeps breathing. Her fingers twitch. She must get out of here. She must make them *pay*. All of them. She may have promised Adrius that she would leave Ezelind to him, but all promises were swept off the board when he stole her sword. Ezelind will die by her hand for daring to try to kill her.

Time passes. She tries and fails to move more than a single muscle.

Eventually, she manages to shift her arm. For a mercy, she didn't hit her head, and the carpet is plush enough that, while she's certain she has broken more than one bone, her body hasn't completely shattered. She turns onto her side, like a dead fish rolling over in a barrel. Her palms press into the carpet, fibers rough against her skin.

Inch by inch she pushes herself up, gritting her teeth against the agony and forcing her body to *move, damn it*. As soon as she's even slightly vertical, her left leg gives out and she catches herself on the nearest banister before toppling over. Tears well up in her eyes and she feels them roll down her cheeks, hot and slick and stinging.

Her own anger will burn her to ashes before she lets them win. A boar, clawing its way onto a hunter's spear, quickening its own death in its thirst for vengeance.

She takes a stumbling step forward. Another.

Ezelind, she thinks, she will behead – cut her throat open in retaliation to her chokehold of Kazan. Weisz fed her blood as a joke, thus he deserves to have her blade plunged into his stomach. Dasar, she'll carve his heart from his chest and let him bleed. And Adrius... Adrius who lied to her and let her think he was going to help before turning right around and reneging on their deal... Oh, she knows what she will do with him. She only has half a claim to his life after all. Someone else has the other, and he can die to the consequences of his own actions.

Scraping, rattling breaths whisper through the gallery halls. Her useless leg drags behind her, foot tangling in the hem of her dress. Strands of sweat-damp hair stick to her forehead. Hot tears drip from her chin.

The faint image of a decaying young man fades into view. She finally comes to a swaying, pained stop in front of Adrius's portrait and the dead geist in front of it.

Twelve bells toll throughout the Citadel.

She bares her teeth and rasps, "Alphonse De Vere, you were murdered by your brother, Adrius. Now pay your debt to me, and I'll help you pay him back."

DAY THREE

Chapter Twenty-Four

Life ignites behind Alphonse's eyes with a rush of green light.

Geist possession is different than Kazan always thought it would be. There's no pain or conflict, no gritty struggle like the stories Wardens bandy around when they tell tales in taverns over pints of ale. Alphonse flows into her like cold sunlight. The pain drifts away. Her body is distant, limbs floating in a cocoon of mist, soft and indistinct whispers aimlessly curling around her in a fog. A film settles over her eyes, shadows and lights that she never would have imagined existing creeping in the corners of the hall, making the candlelight around her sing with a sickly green tint. If she didn't know what was happening, she would think she was drunk on the most transcendent and hallucinogenic of liquors.

"Who do you wish to find…?"

A weight is now behind Alphonse's words, a strength and body that wasn't there before. The words appear in her mind, and when she concentrates, she can feel a presence hovering around her like a cloak. She expected possession to be horrifying. Instead, it feels like a friend wrapping their arms around her. A shield against isolation. A companion as close as her own heart.

"Ezelind. Weisz." Her own words, venomous and reedy, sound strange in her ears. There's an overlap. An echo. "After them, Dasar."

"Then to my murderer. My brother."

"I want to talk to him before we kill him. Just long enough to find out if I must add Aishreya Sutcliffe to my list."

"And then freedom?"

She breathes in with lungs that no longer hurt. Even though she knows her body is still physically broken, she revels in how far away it all is, how trivial. There is strength in her limbs that overwhelms the pain, shrouding her from the world. Mist coats her tongue as she agrees, "And then freedom."

"Together?"

"Together."

"Think of Ezelind, and I will do the rest."

After being thrown from the balcony, she has no difficulties conjuring up an image of that cruel face. Her lips crack open. "Let's hunt."

The lights and shadows wavering over her vision shift, gathering up like a thousand threads coalescing into a cord of smoke. It hovers before her, undulating with the sleek, twisting motions of a snake moving through tall grasses. Things are… less solid, than they were before. A transparency to the walls and ornaments and chandeliers, and when she squints, she thinks she can see shifting, ghostly shapes in distant rooms. Is this how geists see the world? As though they aren't properly a part of it?

She follows that ephemeral cord of shadow.

The strange half sight lets her avoid all others in the Citadel. She can see them from rooms away and she sways into different corridors before they even know she's nearby. Some people look different from others. Most are that same sickly green-gray that geists are made of, but some have what look like a red, pulsing core in their chests.

"Vampires," Alphonse's voice whispers. "And red are the hearts of humans."

She isn't here to concern herself with the affairs of other humans. She doesn't care about them. She's here to exact vengeance. She's here to kill, cut, rip, and stand over the ruined bodies of her enemies so that, before they die, they will know it was *her*.

Alphonse helps her move her body through the halls and up the stairs and into the glistening statuary.

The light streaming in through the tall, narrow windows makes the marble statues displayed around the wide room shine like the moon outside. Dark shadows shroud the carved faces like a widow's veil. Cold mahogany floors and wall paneling blend into the night, turning the statuary into a dichotomy of sharp, hostile black and white. And in that frozen tableau, two figures move.

She sees the green-gray overlay of Ezelind and Weisz before she actually sees *them*. Their features shift like she's looking at them through oil slick water. One of them holds something that shines in Kazan's ghostly vision, a long object that leaves an impression of quicksilver, dangerous and slithering. A vein in her throat tightens, her body tenses as Alphonse pulls his sight off her eyes with the fluttering fluidity of a silken curtain sliding off her.

And then her enemies are standing clearly before her. Their backs are turned. They cannot see her. But she can see *them*. And she can see her sword in Ezelind's hands.

"Get Amelia," Ezelind snaps to her brother. "De Vere may have proven himself a traitor with this little lie, but at least your seneschal has some measure of loyalty, even if she lacks reliability. Someone in this damned manor must know where Dasar is."

Kazan takes another insensate step towards them. Towards her sword.

"You know, it's funny…" Weisz's voice drifts through the statuary like dust motes. "I almost thought De Vere was going to kill you earlier."

"What?"

"Oh, you know. When he was handing over the sword. I almost thought he was going to cut you with it."

"De Vere doesn't have the audacity to kill me."

Kazan stands right behind them, her throat numb, and rasps, "But I do."

Lightning strikes outside the Citadel.

For a moment, the room is lit up in sharp relief. Ezelind's eyes are narrow slits of furious amber and Weisz's fangs are crystal clear in his gaping mouth. Silver glows in the Damascus ripple of the sword's blade as the bright flash of light fades back into cool, watery moonlight.

The world slows down with that strange geist sight. Weisz slides a foot backwards as he turns away, blonde curls and green coat rippling with movement, sharp claws extending into deadly weapons. Ezelind adjusts her grip on Kazan's sword, her thick gloves wrinkling where her fingers bend, and for a moment she is holding the cloth wrapped around the blade instead of the hilt. And Kazan is close enough that she can simply reach out and wrap her fingers around the smooth silver and rowan hilt of her sword.

It burns.

Unearthly strength and speed forces her body beyond its natural limits as she pulls the sword free of Ezelind's grasp and beheads Weisz.

Blood sprays onto her clothes and face and splatters on the floor in a perfect arc, painting Ezelind's dress. The head tumbles to the ground a second before the body, those blonde curls slowly staining crimson. Smoke rises faintly from the severed neck. A heartbeat later and the body falls too, that elegant coat splayed out beneath the unmoving corpse.

The same smoke wisps out from between Kazan's fingers. The silver and rowan burns her skin, but it won't stop her. It doesn't stop Alphonse either. It is such a tiny price to pay compared to everything else that has been stripped from her.

Ezelind stumbles. Her brother's blood drips on her lips, staining her teeth when she speaks. "You *can't* be alive."

"Your brother made a mistake," Kazan growls right back.

"No – no, you *smell* dead."

"What's the matter? Afraid of the dead?" she says, and that's *all* Alphonse.

Ezelind falters, staring at her in shock. She can hear that overlay, can't she. The voice of the dead young man hovering around Kazan. For the first time, a vampire hears a geist.

"How does it feel to be helpless?" Kazan sways on her feet, the tip of her sword brushing the mahogany floor. "Adrius proved to be a liar. Amelia has abandoned you. Your brother…" She nudges Weisz's head with her toe. "Well. You lot are all so focused on destroying one another in your petty games, aren't you? Nothing beyond shortsighted bloodlust."

"Her Highness is a hypocrite," Ezelind snaps.

With a sharp flick of her wrist, Ezelind extends her claws. She draws her flexed fist back, preparing to strike, and it's so… slow.

Kazan slips deeper into the embrace of the geist sight; the rowan hilt retaliates with another burst of scorching pain against her skin. Her rage is too great for this form of bone and flesh she inhabits, and with Alphonse spurred on by the promise of revenge, more and more of his power pours into her. Power, energy, life. He's burning up what remains of himself just as she's willing to let her own body break.

Ezelind slashes her claws out and Kazan turns her head to the side, those sharp nails brushing straight past her. Snarling, Ezelind tries again and again, faster and faster as she lunges with a fury that rips away her usual austerity. Yet she's not fast enough. Kazan's muscles shouldn't be able to move as quickly as they do, not without hurting her own body, but that's not a concern anymore. She moves and she ruins herself and she wins.

Silvered steel slips between Ezelind's ribs.

Blood oozes down the fuller to smoke on the silver, down the rowan hilt, and between Kazan's fingers. Ezelind's body bows over the blade. A thin, reedy gasp chokes in her throat.

A single strand of hair tumbles out of her tight bun and sticks to her brother's blood, coagulating on her cheeks.

Death smells sweet and ferrous on her breath. Without being consciously aware of it, Kazan finds herself leaning in, drawn in by some strange resonance between Alphonse's nature and the half-life draining from Ezelind. She leans close enough that she could kiss Ezelind, taste her as she dies, lick the blood from her fangs. Still fascinated, still enthralled, even by someone she despises. Drunk on her own obsession.

With a final desperate attempt to slice Kazan, Ezelind dies.

Kazan lets her body slide off the blade and her gold eyes stare up at nothing as she lies on the floor in a bed of blood.

"And now, Adrius..." Alphonse's whispering voice reminds her.

In a minute. She is still reveling in this victory. Is reveling the right word? Or is it more like drowning? Drowning in the moment, letting herself memorize every curve and line of Ezelind's and Weisz's faces.

Something shifts in the darkness at the other end of the statuary. Luminous orbs flash like firelight sliding over silver coins.

It's the black cat that kept following her.

The cat *shifts*.

For a split second, less than a single heartbeat, its fur becomes black smoke, a pitch that grows and roils like storm clouds. As she struggles to breathe, the smoke takes solid form once more, reshaping into layers of heavy satin and smooth, brown skin, and tumbling curls of dark hair.

And then the cat is no more, and Reya stands before her.

"Kazan..." Horror has contorted the lines around Reya's eyes but there's no grief. No love lost between her and the two rulers. "What have you *done*?"

"I gave them what they deserved," Kazan replies. Her tongue darts out to run across her lower lip. Blood trickles from between her teeth. Has she cut herself? Is there blood in her lungs? Is it Weisz's? She cannot tell. It's all numb. "If you two wanted to keep Ezelind's death for your own pleasure, you shouldn't have double crossed me. You knew Adrius was going to meet them, didn't you? You knew he would steal my sword, didn't you? Tell me how complicit you were, and I'll decide how swift a death I will give you."

Reya holds up a warning hand. "I think it would be best if we all just calmed down. I didn't know Adrius would snap and go after Ezelind. We went looking for you, Adrius told me Ezelind pushed you – Kazan, we were coming to *help* you."

"If Adrius stole my sword, what else were you lying about? Why should I believe a single word you say?"

And then…

She can *feel* someone behind her. Sense someone. A presence lighting up the geist sight, calling to Alphonse like a lodestone. He writhes around her, twisting in anger and agony; there's a rotten wound inside him that she feels so keenly, as though it tears apart her own chest, opening up her ribcage, pulling out her heart.

She knows who is at the other side of the hall before she turns to look.

Adrius stands in the moonlight. There's a gladstone bag in one hand and his other now rests on the hilt of his rapier. He is not shocked like Reya. Jealousy curls his mouth and pinches his brow, and she luxuriates in the knowledge that she stole Ezelind from him.

"Murderer…" Kazan rasps. And that's not her. That's not her voice. Alphonse moves her mouth and forces her vocal cords to sound.

"Kazan," he says, so very careful and so very worried, "you're severely injured, you shouldn't be moving. I have supplies –" he gestures to his bag "– but I can't do anything to help until you drop the sword…" He trails off, staring at her hands. Her smoking, burning hands.

"Oh, yes." Her mouth moves without her will and Alphonse's voice rings out clear as he makes her say, "We're not alone."

Adrius's eyes blow wide. *Now* there's the horror. "That's impossible."

"You remember my voice, don't you?"

Alphonse makes her body take a swaying step forward. That green light floats over her vision again and Adrius stares just above her eyes. Alphonse is gaining form. Substance. Hovering around her body as he drains her strength and her human life to force his way back into this plane of existence.

"You're dead," Adrius insists. "You're – Kazan, whatever you think –"

"This *isn't* Kazan!" Alphonse roars, sound filling her head and the statuary. "You murdered me, didn't you? I remember now. You snuck up on me, murdered me, you *traitor*!"

There's a *thud* as Adrius's bag slips from his fingers. He stumbles backwards, swallowing before realizing, "You're a geist."

"Slower to the punch than usual." Alphonse's voice is louder, and Kazan hears it as if through distant water. "Did you really think I'd just vanish once you killed me? Is that why you did it? You had just been elevated to your higher status, a brand-new vampire, and you wanted me out of your way. Did you think that I would somehow be a threat to you? Or were you simply always this vicious, and vampirism merely brought it to the forefront?"

Adrius's shoulders shake. "That wasn't it."

"Did you hate me? Did you hate me like I now hate you?"

"No! It was an *accident*!" The words pour out of him, ringing with truth. He all but screams back at Alphonse, "I didn't mean to do it! I was just – I was turned and woke up like *this* and wanted to tell you what had been done to me, what I had become. Damn it, I wanted you to help me! But I was just – I was just so *hungry*!"

"An *accident*?" Alphonse's fury burns like the sun. "I died because of *an accident*?"

"Yes!" Adrius snarls back. "You *did*, and I am so very sorry. But it's been almost a hundred years! I've spent a hundred fucking years being feared and isolated and cast out of my own society because of what I did to you. I've never drunk from another human, I've subsided off the edges and scraps of my world, and it's what I deserve, but I will not let you kill Kazan for your own vengeance!"

"I'll do whatever I damn well please!" Alphonse screams.

He raises her arms, and the tip of her sword is pointed straight at Adrius's head. In a flash, Adrius has his own rapier drawn, muscles tense and ready to strike out if she so much as moves. If Alphonse makes her move.

Then Adrius glances behind her shoulder and shouts, "Don't!"

Reya grabs her.

Instinctual fear pushes Alphonse out of the way and it's all Kazan again, heaving against Reya's grip. She tries to jerk her sword free, but Reya's embrace is a cage and Kazan's arms are pinned to her sides. The blade still burns her and without Alphonse riding her body she feels all that pain and screams again. The sword falls from her hands, and she scrambles to free herself, grabbing onto Reya's arms and pulling to no avail.

"You have to calm down," Reya insists, her voice right in Kazan's ear. Moving lower. "I'm really sorry about this."

Reya's fangs sink into her neck.

"Reya, *no*!" Adrius cries.

Kazan is back in that billiard room, Dasar leaning over her, filling her veins with that paralyzing venom, turning her into an obedient doll. That same fiery venom pumps into her, pouring out of Reya's fangs and deep into her flesh and she can't let this happen, not again.

She expects it now, she has a moment to fight. That feral, animalistic fury that had overtaken her in the Vildenmarr returns with full force. She claws at Reya's arms, tearing against the silken sleeves. Her legs flail, kicking backwards, stomping on Reya's heeled slippers. Nothing, it does *nothing*.

Another scream grows in her chest, and she thrashes in Reya's iron grip, nails digging into cold skin. When Reya adjusts her grip to cover Kazan's mouth and silence her, she bites down *hard*. She bites and bites and doesn't let go, iron flooding over her tongue, and she wants it to *hurt*.

And then suddenly, Reya releases her.

Kazan falls to her knees, impact jarring her legs, and she paws at the bleeding wound on her neck with shaking hands. Reya is staring agape at the bite mark on her palm. It heals swiftly, but that doesn't make the shock vanish. Ever so slowly, her eyes slide to Kazan's.

"Oh dear..." Reya whispers.

Something's wrong, something's fading – Alphonse's presence is vanishing. She tries to grab onto the last vestiges of his power but he's fading away into nothing, pushed out by something *new*. Something *cold*.

Cold like the blue-white center of a blade being pulled out of the forge. Cold like the worst of the winter rains, when the water droplets scrape the skin until it's red and raw. It's scraping her even now, scraping out the inside of her. Claws digging through her arteries and into the marrow of her bones.

In the back of her mind, she can hear Alphonse screaming, the sound smothered by that freezing heat. What remains of him is being drowned out, and despite everything, she tries to pull him back, to return to that painless haze, but she can't. What little is left of him is dying.

"I'm sorry!" Reya's not talking to her, she's talking to Adrius, quick with panic. "I didn't know what to do, she was going to stab you!"

"I could have handled it, even with a geist's power, she hasn't the skill!"

"Well how was I supposed to know! But what are we supposed to do with her? We can't just – I –"

"Stop her!"

Kazan's attempt to drag herself away from them ends as they both grab her, pinning her down and stopping her from escaping. That ice is scorching her body and she finds she can barely move, her limbs refusing to cooperate. All she can do is writhe pointlessly as Adrius catches her arms and holds her wrists down above her head, and as Reya straddles her waist to keep her legs from kicking out.

"We still have until midnight before the Citadel will require the final blood ritual," Reya says hurriedly, "so Dasar won't know what we've done right away."

Adrius shoves Kazan back down with a warning, "This will hurt more if you keep moving."

"Adrius," Reya continues, "we have two dead bodies and now we're about to have a newly turned vampire on our hands. What in the name of all those human saints are we supposed to do? If any of us gets caught by Dasar, we're all dead."

Adrius glances down at Kazan. "Then none of us get caught. Kazan, you have less than one minute to strike a new deal with us."

"F–Fuck you," she spits out. "I'll – kill you. Kill Dasar."

"That can be arranged," Reya replies. She bends over to cup Kazan's cheek, dark hair tumbling over her shoulder. In a low, rushed voice, she says, "From here on out you do *exactly* as we say. No more deviations on anyone's part. You keep our secret, we keep yours. Agree, and we'll get you out of here and cover this up. If you don't, we'll leave you here and let Dasar do what he wants. Do we have a deal?"

Does she have a choice?

Kazan's mouth is full of blood as she gurgles out, "Deal."

She can barely hear them anymore. Everything is a blur. Buzzing fills her head, and she can't feel her own limbs. She can't...

"Ah right," Adrius says distantly, "I remember this part..."

She's unconscious before he can finish his sentence.

Chapter Twenty-Five

"... I can't stall Dasar for much longer."

Kazan absently registers Reya's voice as her eyes blink. Softness envelops her. She's warm. She can hear again, she can see again, her body doesn't hurt anymore. Nothing hurts. Not the bite on her neck, not the broken bones from her fall, not even the various bruises that have littered her body for the past two days.

A fly buzzes past her eyes. Her gaze snaps to the movement automatically before the fly zooms away past the window. Rain pours down outside.

"We don't have to." Adrius's voice this time.

Reya, again. "He'll come looking for her eventually."

"Ezelind and Weisz's disappearance will be noted before long. Once that happens, all eyes will be turned towards locating them. And from what I hear, Amelia's vanished too. No one has seen her since Ezelind and Weisz died. For all we know, they'll blame her. I would, after all."

"I admit, I wasn't expecting Amelia to simply flee," Reya intones.

"She must have picked up on something. For all her faults, she's always been good at sensing which way the wind is blowing."

"You're certainly not."

"Reya, I'm sorry. I simply..." He snarls in frustration, even as he sounds apologetic. "I had the perfect opportunity; the sword was *right there* and I've waited so *long* to kill Ezelind –"

"If you hadn't been so impulsive, everything would still be going according to plan."

There is no tiredness in Kazan's body as she sits up.

She's in Adrius's rooms, in his bed, the door to his bedchambers closed. The light looks strange, somewhat brighter perhaps, despite the heavy clouds. She can focus on the individual raindrops more easily, her eyesight better than it's ever been.

Oh, thank the saints she's alive. She's more than alive, she's...

She brings her hands up to her face and stares. There's a translucent quality to her skin, a paleness, almost pallid, as though caused by illness. Her nails are longer, sharper, but they return to their former length the longer she looks at them. Her stomach drops when she sees that the scars and calluses she has built up over the years have vanished from her hands. Those, she did not want to lose. They showed her work, her years.

The passage of time has stopped for her now, hasn't it? Because she's...

Her feet are bare when she slides out of bed, but her slippers have been helpfully placed nearby.

There's a mirror on the dresser. She has to see.

She stumbles towards it, grabbing it, and the mirror cracks in her hand. Shit, she's stronger now. She can't forget that. She looks into the shards. The scar bisecting her face is still there. Of *course* it is. She wonders if it remains because it was made by a vampire or if it's simply too old to have been purged like everything else. The white of her eyes has turned black, and gold – piercing gold – has shot through her irises completely. When she opens her lips, sharp fangs jut out.

The mirror slips from her hands and hits the floor.

"Is that...?" Reya asks, the question trailing off.

"She must be awake," Adrius replies.

Kazan goes still. They know what she looks like now, don't they? What must they think of her? Does she even care?

"Give her a moment to properly wake up and… adjust to her new body," Reya is saying. "I can't speak for you, but I remember what it was like for me, and it was disorienting, to say the least."

Adrius's voice is bitter and tired. "Oh, I more than remember."

"You would, wouldn't you," she remarks absently. There's a pause before she asks, "How are you? With Alphonse's geist…"

"I don't know what it was like for him, clinging on as a geist for so many years, but for me, that time passed," he says, each word like the stroke of a sharp pen nib scratching against paper. "A hundred years is a long time to mourn someone. You know that as well as I do. I did my penance. I buried his body as close to a church as I could manage to get. Do you have any idea how difficult that was? I didn't destroy his paintings, I merely kept them in the Citadel. I never turned a human or even bit one, despite the expense of bottled blood and the additional damned stigma of it. And Ezelind ensured that neither I nor anyone else forgot what I'd done, even if they believed a distorted version of the truth. I think I'm entitled to no longer hate myself for what a newly turned vampire in the throes of first bloodlust did a hundred years ago."

"You truly feel that way?"

"Most days."

Is that what's going to happen to Kazan? Will she end up going the same way as Adrius did all those years ago, starving from hunger to the point of delirium, to the point where she cannot even tell if she's drinking from friend or foe? Is she going to have to rely on Adrius or Reya to tell her which is which? They've already promised to help, but it will come at the cost of her utter obedience, and she doesn't know what they'll demand from her. They could ask for anything, at this point.

Out of habit, Kazan finds herself scanning the dresser for anything she can use as a weapon, hoping for a hat pin left behind by Reya or a hidden knife of Adrius's. Then she catches sight of her nails in a shard of the mirror. Ah. Of course. She already is, quite literally, armed. She flexes her fingers and there's a sudden stretching sensation in her fingertips as her nails extend a solid inch until they're ragged and sharp. Staring into that reflective shard, she presses the tip of one of her claws to her forehead and drags it down, lightly brushing over the length of her face as she traces her scar.

She shivers and can't pinpoint the emotion prompting the reaction.

The room is suddenly too small, the drapery suffocating, the furniture angular and hostile. She has to get out of here, she has to. She all but lunges for the window and throws it open.

Rain pours down, gloomy and gray. At least Adrius and Reya had the respect not to undress her, and so her bloodstained gown tangles around her bare legs as she climbs out the window. A small ledge runs around the outer wall, and a nimble grace that she has never possessed before lets her walk on it with ease. She stops a couple of feet away from the window, curling up in a niche dug into the stonework. Ornate knotwork and a carved angel loom above her. Water drips from the angel's wings and its head has been removed, either by the passage of time and weather, or perhaps it was never there to begin with.

She has to tuck herself up to fit into the protective space, her skirts draping down below her and rain soaking the fabric.

"Alphonse?" she asks tentatively into the rain, as quiet as she dares.

There's no response. He's gone. Truly gone. Her transformation must have burned him out of her. It feels strange, to miss someone who was dead from the moment she met him, but she does. They had an understanding between them, vengeance driving them both. Not a friend, not exactly. An ally. For those brief moments, she hadn't been alone.

The niche protects her from the worst of the downpour, but drops of water still cling to her hair and roll down her face. The rain is cold. Not as cold as it should be. Not as cold as it used to be.

In the cold and the rain and with a long drop beneath her, she realizes that she's *starving*.

So this is what she is now. Is it better or worse that it was an accident? Is it better or worse that it's half her fault for biting Reya in return? She never wanted this. Never wanted to be some animalistic thing that tears humans apart and indulges in every base instinct without thought. Never wanted to be uncaring and flippant about life like Montanari or happy to while away the years with bloodsport like Dasar. Never wanted to be like that entrancing vampire who had caressed her face in a moonlit barn all those years ago. Right? Certainly she's never wanted that?

But she did know how a vampire turns a human. Gia Montanari had told her how it works. When Reya had bitten her, all she could think of was escaping before that intoxicating venom could enthrall her. Right? Or had she been subconsciously hoping for this? Had part of her seen a chance to become what she has been obsessed with for so many years? She touches her scar again, tracing it over and over with her new claws until she can convincingly tell herself she's desensitized to it.

A raindrop splashes onto her forehead. It drips down from the headless angel, and she wonders if it's guarding or condemning her.

"I'm sorry," a voice says, words falling with the rain.

Reya has appeared at the window, looking out but not climbing towards Kazan. It's impossible to imagine her scaling the outer walls or allowing herself to get soaked in the downpour. Not with her innate elegance. How much of it is vampiric and how much is simply Reya's cultivated poise?

"I owe you a great apology," Reya continues. "It wasn't my intention to turn you. I cannot make you believe me, but I promise I have never turned a human before and had no desire to start now."

An apology isn't enough. Even if it were soothing in any way, she could never bring herself to utter the words 'I forgive you' or even 'Apology accepted'. It is not accepted.

"You must be hungry," Reya tries again. "I remember being absolutely famished after I was turned."

Although she had no intentions of speaking, Kazan finds herself admitting, "I'm *starving.*"

"Come back inside. Let us help you."

The long drop beneath her yawns. Somehow, it's more prominent now than it was when she was human, when it would have actually killed her. "I'll fall."

When she looks, Reya has disappeared from the window.

Kazan closes her eyes and tilts her head up, counting the drops of rain that fall on her. One, two, three... The fourth runs down the line of her scar, kissing the disfigured skin. Her stomach deeply protests its emptiness.

"Kazan."

She opens her eyes. Adrius is half out of the window himself, one boot on the sill and his hand extended towards her. Rain slicks his white hair and runs off his coat, his gold and black eyes shining through the gloom.

"Take my hand," he tells her softly. "I'll ensure you don't fall."

When she lays her hand in his, she finds that he's no longer cold. Not warm either, still distinctly inhuman. But not that same acute coldness from earlier. She allows him to help her out of the niche and guide her along the narrow ledge. He ushers her through the window, and when she drops down back inside, she finds herself once more between him and Reya.

Reya gently holds her and guides her into the main room of Adrius's chambers. There's a black glass bottle on the table that Kazan doesn't remember being there before. When Reya tosses it to her, her eyes track the movement – the bottle falling in an arc through the dust motes in the air. It doesn't slow down, not exactly, but it's as though she can now see where the bottle is going to be before it arrives. It lands in her hands easily.

It's actually a clear glass bottle, she notices. The edges shine red in the light. She reaches to break that wax seal and then pauses.

"Where did this come from?" she asks.

"Look at the seal," Reya tells her.

The wax is stamped with an hourglass and a secondary mark has been stamped over it to display an 'R'. One of the bottles Adrius has purchased from Madam Rask. Thank the saints, she can drink it.

Her new claws make quick work of the wax, popping the cork out with a faint *hiss* as the preservation magic disintegrates. In her sudden desperation, she throws the cork over her shoulder, pouring the contents of the bottle down her throat. It tastes so good, better than anything she's ever tasted in her life, better than spun sugar from Luthow, better than winter berry pies, better than... She can't properly compare anything to it. It's pointless. Her vocabulary simply doesn't contain the words to describe it.

She drains the bottle in the blink of an eye and as soon as there's nothing left, she all but begs them, "Is there more?"

Adrius silently hands her another bottle.

When that bottle is empty too, she runs her finger around the inside, picking up the last few drops, desperate for even the slightest bit more. Somehow, it leaves her hungrier than she was before, in the same way a snack before a meal only whets the appetite. She still wants *more*, but she comes to her senses enough to wrest back a measure of self-control. Adrius drank a human dry by accident. Surely, she can be better than that.

She licks her lips and places the empty bottle down on the table. "Does it always... will I always *need* it like this?"

"No," Adrius replies. There's still that frown on his face as he looks at her, as if she is a complicated knot that he's struggling to undo. "Of course, you cannot simply cease drinking for months on end or you will die of starvation. Craving the taste instead of sustenance is a less intense experience. Or at least, it should become less intense as you grow more accustomed to it."

She refuses to let herself ask again if they have any more. "What time is it?"

"Three hours past noon," he tells her.

Reya gently lays her hand on Kazan's arm. She guides Kazan to the settee and sits next to her, taking her hands in her own. Adrius drapes a soft towel around her shoulders, soaking up the water in her hair.

"Where's my sword?" Kazan asks flatly.

"Lying next to Ezelind and Weisz's dead bodies," Adrius informs her. "Their wounds would have pointed to your sword regardless, and by leaving it behind we don't further incriminate ourselves."

She rises to her feet. "I see. Goodbye."

"Kazan, no!" Reya grabs onto her wrist with desperation plain across her face. "You can't simply *leave*."

"You made a deal," Adrius reminds Kazan.

She scoffs. "And you should know better than to trust me to keep my word."

Before she can make it to the door, Adrius continues, "I don't trust you to keep your word. Reya might prefer to get her way with sweet whispers, but don't forget that I've spent almost a hundred years as Ezelind's enforcer."

Hidden in her bloodied skirts, her fingers flex, claws extending. "Are you threatening me?"

"If you wish to think of it that way. You could also say that I am simply prompting you to recall a few pertinent facts." He's far too calm and collected and cold, and she finds herself shivering once more at that unwavering look in his eyes. "Firstly, you reek of Ezelind and Weisz's blood. Of *vampire* blood. I highly doubt that you'll manage to make it very far if you leave without changing into fresh clothing. Secondly, if Reya and I do decide to inform Dasar of your crimes, he's certain to believe our word over yours. Even if he has his own personal doubts, you make far too convenient a scapegoat. And thirdly, I'm the only person in the Citadel who can help you pass unnoticed in your new form."

The speech scatters her thoughts so thoroughly that it takes her a long minute to gather them enough to compose a reply. "If I do leave undisguised, everyone will know that someone broke the party rules in turning me." Turning her. Even saying it sounds so wrong and so complicated. "I've spent a lot of time with the two of you and Reya's recently given me a convenient alibi. I'm sure someone will be clever enough to point an accusing finger in the right direction."

Reya, of all things, laughs and then says, low and heady, "You really are gloriously sharp."

The intense admiration makes heat rise in Kazan's cheeks. Damn it, she doesn't have time for this! "I'm also your most recent dirty secret."

"Which," Adrius continues, "is why we all have no choice but to work together on this."

"You lied to me," she snaps.

He bristles and draws himself up to his full height. "Yes, I did. Let me be frank. I stole your sword to kill Ezelind, an event you rather rudely interrupted last night. I then left to get my medical bag so I could attempt to heal you, and the moment – yes," he insists, when she rolls her eyes, "the *moment* I saw you were gone, I sought Reya's assistance and went to find you because I was under the impression that you were injured and in desperate need of help. I've been craving Ezelind's death since the day I met her, and your sword provided me the perfect opportunity to get away with it. I won't apologize for taking advantage of that."

"And how does it feel," Kazan drawls, "to have me steal that glory from you? I killed her and I killed her brother too, and you will never –"

Reya clears her throat with more elegance than should be possible. "If the two of you are quite finished trying to rip each other's heads and clothes off, then I think we had best figure out what, exactly, we're going to do about all this."

"Kill Dasar," Kazan declares. "It's not that complicated."

"Ah-ah." Reya wags her finger. "I think you're forgetting the terms of our deal. Before you run off and kill Dasar, I need to ensure that the Citadel will carry on. I have a method; I merely need to prepare the magics for it. I'll fully admit that my skills lie mostly in transformation, not blood magics."

"The Citadel's survival is contingent on my death," Kazan says.

"Not anymore. Your human blood was needed, but that's obviously no longer possible. We must look to other methods."

"Such as what? Killing some other human?"

"Yes, if needs be," Reya snaps back, unexpectedly fiery. "I have worked too hard for too long in this place. I have no intentions of losing my prize simply because both of you are too quick to kill. I want Dasar's throne, and I want everything that comes with it. I want it and damn it, I've *earned* it. Tell me honestly if you're capable of that. Do you really value the life of some random human so highly or are you merely determined to tear apart everything and everyone that you perceive as an enemy?"

Kazan recoils.

Mouth flattened into a surprisingly firm line, Reya rises to her feet. "I'm going to figure out how to change the spells to adjust to your new condition and ensure the Citadel remains in its current state of glory. Dasar will be looking for you shortly. It will be easier if he discovers you before he discovers Ezelind and Weisz. Adrius..."

Some unspoken understanding passes between them, and he nods. "Good luck."

With one final, incomprehensible glance at Kazan, Reya glides out the door.

Chapter Twenty-Six

"Ensure you remove all traces of blood from your skin." Adrius opens up his wardrobe and a dresser for Kazan. "Take your time. We need you to return to the party, but if you show up with a single drop of blood on you, the game is up. Leave the ruined clothing here. No one comes into my chambers to clean without my permission, and I can ensure they're disposed of by then. Oh," he adds, opening a drawer, "I believe Reya left some of her things here over the years. I'll... give you some privacy, shall I?"

Kazan swallows and looks down at her soiled skirts. "I would appreciate that."

He steps out of the bedroom, closing the door behind him.

As soon as he's gone, she strips as quickly as she can, shedding the damp and ruined dress like a snake wriggling out of its skin. Some of the blood has soaked through to her shift and she removes that too, taking everything off until she's completely nude. She nips into the washroom, perching on the edge of an absurdly large copper footed bathtub while she scrubs her body clean.

Her toenails are perfectly, unnaturally smooth. It unnerves her.

Then, still naked and slightly damp, she addresses the matter of clothing. What Reya has left behind is mostly underthings, a few chemises and corsets and smallclothes. Nothing in the way of dresses. Kazan will have to improvise. A corset against her bare skin will be distinctly unpleasant, and so she puts on a linen shirt and laces a corset on top of that. She steals the smallest pair of Adrius's trousers she can find and stuffs them into leather boots. Then a coat, heavy and dark crimson.

Adrius knocks on the door. "Are you decent?"

"As decent as I can be, given this... limited selection."

The door opens and Adrius enters carrying a jewelry box. He opens it, holding it out and offering her the contents. "This may help."

Inside the velvet box are two things. The first is a pair of black leather gloves – they cover her palms and only barely go down to the backs of her knuckles, in a fashion that she's vaguely aware is popular. The other item is his glamor ring, the very same he had been wearing when they met. To think it was only a few days ago. She dons the gloves and over them goes the ring, which she can only fit on her left thumb.

"How do I look?" she asks.

He doesn't look at her when he answers, his back turned to put the jewelry box on top of the dresser. "Human," is his short reply. "Again."

So long as she doesn't pass a mirror. Or touch her sword bare handed.

She twists the ring around her thumb absently. With her glamoured fingernails, the gloves feel strange, not too tight, really, but she's more aware of them than she would be otherwise. "Do you really think Reya is right? In her efforts to save the Citadel, I mean."

Adrius gives her a strange, almost jealous look. "I don't mean to be rude, but you robbed me of my long-anticipated vengeance last night. And last night *your* desire to escape the Citadel as a human was destroyed. One of us deserves to get what they want, and I care about Reya too much to simply..."

"Never mind," she says hastily. "You needn't explain further."

Another peculiar look. She's getting rather tired of receiving those from him. He asks, "Did you actually tell us the truth about your scar, or was that a lie as well?"

"If you didn't believe me then, why would you believe me now? I could just lie again."

"So it *was* the truth."

That single, certain phrase strips her bare. She recoils from him, shrinking away from the sensation of being *seen*, being *known*, having the truth of her pried out whether she wants it or not. Reya said she delights in the lies, in the entertainment of it all, and Kazan thought she could play the same game with Adrius. But if he knows her, does Reya know her too? How many people can see straight through her? How paper-thin has she become? How vulnerable has this place made her?

"Kazan," Adrius says, "you might not need to breathe to live anymore, but you may want to consider doing so, if only to practice the illusion of being human."

She sucks in a deep breath.

"Better." He holds out his arm in a tentative peace offering. "Let's not keep Dasar waiting. I'm sure you're eager to spin him an elaborate story."

Surprisingly, that does make her feel better. She slips her hand into the crook of his arm and lets the illusion take over. She is human, and one of the vampire seneschals is escorting her back to the party, as is his duty. Nothing more. Where had she gone, she wonders? Did she attempt another escape, or was she simply drunk? Surely enough people saw her tipsy the other night that she could weave a convincing tale of being in a drunken stupor?

Those musings save her from saying anything further as Adrius leads her out of his rooms, through the northern wing of the Citadel, and down to the main party.

Partygoers start to pop up again as the pair approach the center of the manor. They all light up when they see her and then hastily turn away in fear when they see Adrius. Every time they pass by a vampire in the halls, she can't help but feel under a magnifying glass. She knows, intellectually, that they can't tell she's one of them so long as she wears Adrius's ring. It still makes her tense up until the vampire has passed them by.

Kazan finds herself on one of the balconies overlooking the main sprawling banquet hall. Below, the party is in full swing.

"Where's Dasar?" she asks.

"Look," Adrius says under his breath. He gestures with a single finger to the hall beneath them, to the whirl of people and color. "Let your instincts take over. Your eyes can track movement in ways they never could before. Allow yourself to do that without *thinking* too much about it."

She stares into the party and tries to do as instructed.

Blue slippers flash out from beneath shimmering skirts as a woman dances, her partner bending her into a low dip. Gold strands in dark brown hair reflect the candlelight as a man passes by one of the thousands of candelabras lighting up the hall. Dark, viscous crimson swirls in a glass, a droplet of blood left behind on a man's lips after he drinks. Each stitch of color or movement draws Kazan's gaze, yanking her across the room in a never-ending stream of distractions.

"I can see you frowning," Adrius whispers. "You're overthinking it."

Bronze hair, ostentatious purple coat, gold jewelry. Dasar. The image fills her mind and when she opens her eyes, she allows them to take in the entire room and *look*. Within less than a minute, her gaze has landed on that bronze hair.

"There." She subtly points to Dasar. "By those two women in green. He's drinking."

"Well done. Go rejoin the party. Play along. I'll be there before the next ritual begins."

She thought he would be staying. "Where are you going?"

He relinquishes her arm and steps back into the recesses of the balcony. "It would be better if we're not seen together any more than we already have been. Just because we are co-conspirators doesn't mean we need to let others know. I'll make an appearance as the ritual starts, but I'll let you speak with Dasar on your own first."

With that, he's gone. The edge of his coat vanishes around the corner of the corridor and she's alone on the balcony. She draws herself up and adjusts the too-large coat she's wearing. Time to deal with the last of these horrid rituals.

She descends into the fray.

Within moments she finds herself being accosted from all sides. Someone pets her hair and tells her how pretty she is, someone else remarks upon her clothing with a patronizing laugh, another takes her hand and kisses her wrist. It's both better and worse now. Worse because she can see what they're all doing with clearer sight now, worse because she can smell the blood on their breath, worse because she can't let herself react visibly to any of this new stimulus for fear of giving herself away. Better because she's in on the joke and they aren't. Better because she's stringing them along, putting on a show, letting them think she's still some pet. Much better because they're in for a wonderfully nasty surprise.

"Ah, Highness!" Dasar spreads his arms wide open with a beaming smile upon seeing her approach. "I was so hoping you'd make it in time. It would be a pity to have to call you here."

She ignores the vampires hovering around, even though they coo over her like she's a colorful parrot. "Yes, well," she says acerbically. "I'd hate to miss my own party."

Dasar throws his head back and laughs. "Indeed, Highness! I'm so glad to see you getting into the spirit of things." His claws curl around her coat and he tucks her close to his side. "You look quite eccentric; I do adore it. Now, let's adjourn to your throne, this afternoon's event is about to begin. Oh, worry not, it will be nothing compared to the midnight feast. You're still the star of the show."

"Thrilled to hear it," she mutters.

Revelers part before Dasar with expectant smiles, allowing

him to glide towards the head of the banquet hall with her still wrapped in his grip. The long table in front of her so-called throne has been cleared, save for her crown of gold and blood, and four empty goblets.

"Hm, a shame," Dasar remarks, pushing two goblets to the side. "Ezelind's absence doesn't surprise me. She can be such a churlish bore on occasion. But Weisz usually enjoys these events."

"Perhaps they're indulging in their own bloodsport," she suggests sarcastically.

Another of those careless laughs. "Her Majesty is in high spirits tonight, isn't she? I'm thrilled to see that some rest and visitation did you good."

Ah, so that's what Reya told him. That she was sleeping and chatting with other vampires? It's not a bad lie, all things considered. It's almost entirely true.

This event doesn't seem to be the same extravagant display as the earlier mock duel. Vampires crowd around them to be sure, but it's not too different from the usual curiosity and cosseting they burden her with. No grand audience, no apparent need for her to give a strange, spoon-fed speech. No magic, just... their enjoyment.

Across the hall, her eyes land on Adrius's pale hair. He's close enough to watch, but far enough away to be at the edge of the crowd, a small circle of space around him as no one wishes to get too close.

Still holding her against him, Dasar passes her a bottle and then picks up one of the goblets. "Pour me a drink, Highness. I didn't get to see you enjoy my best vintages at Weisz's earlier tasting."

She pulls out the wax-glazed cork and nearly swoons.

Never before has she had to restrain herself to such a degree. Iron and meat fill her nose and run down her throat to taunt her stomach. She had drunk before but that was travelers' waybread compared to the luxurious, imported chocolate of this bottle. It had not been nearly enough to tide her over. Her body burned through its stores of energy during the violent transformation, and it left her hungrier than two mere bottles could satiate. The scent of fresh, arterial blood wafts around her, not unlike the wonderful, warm smell that envelops a person upon stepping into a bakery.

"Pour, sweet thing," Dasar murmurs, his hand on her hip tightening.

She pours.

It takes all her self-control to avoid inhaling a deep breath of that scent. To avoid showing her thirst, the near arousal surging inside her. To avoid putting her lips to the smooth glass bottle and downing its contents.

Dasar drinks. She has never been more jealous.

A drop of blood slides down the corner of his mouth when he finally finishes the goblet and sets it aside. Delicately, reverently, he wipes it away with his thumb, leaving a streak of crimson on his skin.

Perhaps he catches her staring or perhaps he simply wishes to torment her further. Either way, he says, "Oh dear, where *are* my manners?" He raises his thumb to her lips. "Care for a taste, Highness? You never know, you may even enjoy it."

It would be so easy to pretend that she's simply indulging Dasar. Or that she's trying to do as he asks to get away from him sooner. Or, or, or… She could come up with a dozen lies to excuse her action, couldn't she? Wouldn't the suspicion be worth it, be worth savoring every remnant of human blood on his skin? There hadn't been that identifying 'R' on the bottle, but that doesn't mean it *wasn't* one of Rask's, or another bottle sourced from someone who doesn't kill their human suppliers. Right?

She parts her lips. Her tongue runs over Dasar's thumb.

The rich taste of blood hits her all at once, intoxicating even though she's unfortunate enough to only drink a single drop rather than direct from the source.

More, she needs *more*. She wraps her lips around his thumb and licks off every bit of blood, chasing that taste, that unbearable craving that makes her aching and wet and heated. He stares at her, eyes blown wide and a thrilled smile tugs at the corners of his mouth. He moves his hand to cup her cheek and leans even closer. She thinks he's about to kiss her.

His mouth will taste of blood.

A scream shatters through the ballroom – *"MURDER!"*

Chapter Twenty-Seven

Dasar pulls away, leaving Kazan suddenly bereft and struggling to return to her senses. There is movement around her, swarming in front of her enhanced vision. Someone cries out in shock. Another gasps.

A vampire runs down the stairs, frilly skirts gathered in her hands and her hair all out of sorts. "Come quick!" she cries. "Lady Ezelind and Lord Weisz are dead!"

Screams and shouts and all manner of beautiful panic fill the banquet hall. Kazan throws herself into it, lets it draw away her bloodthirst. Colors blur in her vision as people run, crowding the woman who bore the message, rushing to Dasar to beg for instruction, fleeing in the foolish thought that a killer would come for them next.

"Lord Dasar!" a man begs. "Who did this?"

Dasar has already abandoned Kazan at the head of the hall, and he ignores his subjects too, instead speaking in hushed tones with the guards nearby. Eccentric and odd he may be, but not an idiot.

"Get De Vere," she can hear him order, "and send for Lady Sutcliffe. If someone is targeting our rulers, they may be next. Where's Amelia? Rumor has it she's vanished, but if she remains in the Citadel, I want her found." A soldier wearing House Rockford's colors shifts nervously and Dasar rounds on him with a toothy smile. "Oh, my dear, I do understand not wishing to think ill of your newly deceased lord's seneschal, but if she has vanished, then she has unfortunately made herself into a suspect."

"Yes, my lord," the guard replies with a salute.

Dasar continues, "Have this lovely lady – Miss Presley, was it? – show you where precisely she found the bodies and then secure the area. Keep everyone out. I know we will have many curious eyes swarming, but any interference cannot be tolerated."

"Lord Dasar." Adrius has appeared in the middle of this, quietly and without fanfare. "I apologize for not being here immediately. I was on the far side of the hall to... avoid interrupting the festivities with my presence."

"Of course, dear, how thoughtful and courteous of you." Dasar seems to have ignored Kazan entirely, which suits her just fine. It allows her to listen better. "I do hate to ask, but needs must. Where have you been tonight? I know you've been a dutiful servant of Lady Ezelind and I know only her kind protection has kept you amongst us all these years, but I can imagine that your... *tendencies* may have understandably gotten the best of you?"

While Adrius keeps his expression perfectly stoic, Kazan thinks for a second, she can see through him as he saw through her. Straight through to an angry, hateful, unbearably lonely part of him. An exhausted storm that has replaced his dead heart. It's no wonder he and Reya have fallen together. Reya admitted that she needs to be loved, and it's clear that Adrius needs the same. No one has loved Kazan since her father, and she can barely remember what that felt like. She doesn't need love. She *doesn't*.

"I did a customary patrol of the area around Lady Ezelind's rooms yesterday evening. At midnight, I went to Lady Sutcliffe's study, and we spoke at length about the latest Warden patrols leaving the eastern lands. At noon, I briefly slept, and when I awoke, I came here for a drink," he seamlessly lies.

Dasar pats his arm. "Fortunately for you, Lady Sutcliffe

is an honorable woman and I trust her word. Don't you agree?"

"I wouldn't know, my lord. I don't speak with her more often than once or twice a year." He inclines his head towards the woman who cried murder, the Miss Presley, presumably. "Shall we? I have a duty to uncover my Lady Ezelind's killer."

"Of course, of course. Ah!" Dasar grins and turns to face a woman who is shyly standing at the corner of this circle. "Darling Isidora! Keep an eye on Her Highness for me, won't you?"

Isidora curtseys with a flop of bows and ribbons and messy hair. "Yes, my lord."

"Let her enjoy the party while we deal with this messy business." Dasar gestures to one of his guards. "Jean, find Lady Sutcliffe and make sure she's safe. Hawkins, do keep our guests from causing too much fuss. The rest of you, with me."

Adrius does not so much as glance Kazan's way as the group hurries off towards the stairs, and the grisly statuary. Miss Presley is ushered along, Dasar escorting her in the same manner he employs with Kazan, that of a polite spider luring a fly. Though Presley is far safer than Kazan; she doubts the woman is even a suspect, despite having found the bodies.

In the mess of people and noise, no one pays much attention to Kazan, and so she turns to the staircase.

"Highness, you can't," Isidora protests, scurrying up to her. "Lord Dasar said to stay here."

She looks at her lady in waiting, at the meek, soft vampire. Someone who survives in this world of greed and violence by keeping her head down and her thoughts to herself. "No," Kazan replies, "I think you'll find he didn't. All he told you to do was keep an eye on me. Which you'll be doing. I'll go, and you can come with me, and that way you'll be doing exactly as he instructed. Isn't that so?"

Isidora sputters, "Well – I mean. I suppose?"

"Come along then."

With that, Kazan practically flies up the stairs, two at a time. The clatter of guards running in full armor banging through the halls guides them. Or, more accurately, it guides Isidora. Kazan must be careful that she doesn't go too quickly or with too much surety in her direction, never giving away that she already knows where the bodies are.

A small crowd has already formed around the statuary doors by the time they arrive, partygoers from around the Citadel having heard the cries and come to investigate. Kazan weaves her way through the crowd, tugging Isidora along like baggage. No one notices her, all eyes on the scene ahead, all noise whispers or shouts of shock.

"Is it really them?"

"Are they sure, maybe someone got it wrong..."

"Who could possibly have done such a thing?"

"Are we safe?"

Dasar's soldiers have set up a perimeter to keep the crowd at bay. Kazan pushes to the front and watches through the metal armor and brandished spears.

With evening swiftly approaching and the heavy rain continuing, the statuary doesn't look much different than it did earlier. It is gloomier now, those stark shadows replaced by a gray, misty light. She cannot see the bodies clearly. All she catches is the splay of Weisz's blond hair and the layers of Ezelind's skirts. And her sword, lying on the ground, still splattered with blood. She can smell it. Where human blood is the most decadent scent imaginable, vampire blood smells more... familiar.

She waits for a guard to glance in the other direction and then wiggles under their arm, leaving Isidora behind. The girl's head whirls around as she frantically searches for Kazan, calling out her false title to no avail. Kazan slips behind a man far larger than her and then weaves between two women too preoccupied with spectating to notice. Before anyone can spot her, she darts between two particularly towering statues and kneels, hiding beneath them.

"… had it last?" a soldier is asking.

"It was *meant* to be in my armory," Dasar replies. He nudges the hilt of Kazan's sword with his boot and winces. "Such a nasty *pretty* little thing, isn't it? What a prize, but it certainly has tempted more than a few these past three days, has it not? No one knows it's better to leave my things alone."

There are footsteps to Kazan's right and she holds her breath as a soldier approaches.

"My lord," the soldier says, saluting. "Lady Amelia is not anywhere in the Citadel."

Dasar's eyes narrow. "*Well* now."

"I have gathered a number of reports on her last known location. My Lord Dasar, I did not see this myself, but yesterday, Petyr Rankin was on guard duty in front of the armory. He hasn't been seen since. And one of the stablehands reported that just past midnight, Amelia saddled her horse and claimed to be going for nothing more than a short ride. She hasn't been seen since either."

"Oh Amelia…" Dasar muses. "What a pity. I did quite like her, you know. Shame that she blundered and killed *my* guests at *my* party."

Were Kazan not hiding, she would laugh. Had Amelia stayed at the Citadel, Kazan would likely have tried to kill her before the day was done. Adrius was right that Amelia clearly sensed which way the wind was blowing and decided to flee, but in saving her life, she incriminated herself in the murder of her lord and his sister. Out of the forge and onto the anvil.

Adrius glances in her direction and for a second, she wonders if he can see her. Or smell her? Then he asks Dasar, "My lord, should we send a raven to Saltrock Keep?"

"Mm, I think we had better. The rest of House Rockford needs to know that our dear Amelia isn't to be given a hero's welcome upon her return home. *If* she returns home. It's more than possible she will vanish elsewhere. Oh, and I suppose they will need to figure out who's next in line to replace Weisz, since his seneschal is no longer up to the task. I suppose you may want to send a message to Glassdow Castle. Your House will need to do the same, won't they?"

A muscle twitches in Adrius's jaw. "I can serve passably well for at least a short while, I assure you," he grits out.

Dasar merely waves him off. "Yes, yes." There's another shuffle as partygoers try to peer into the room and he huffs, "Oh would *someone* close that blasted door? We are attempting to conduct *business*."

The soldiers hop to and push everyone out, shutting the doors behind them.

Leaving Isidora standing in the entryway, fidgeting.

"Isidora..." Dasar's light mood has turned into a low, honeyed venom. "Now, correct me if I'm wrong, my dear, but didn't I ask you to keep an eye on Her Highness?"

It takes several tries before Isidora can properly speak. "Erm. Yes, my lord. I was..."

"You were what, exactly? Letting her run off after there has been a rather bloody attack inside our walls? Run off *again*, might I add. I must say, when I assigned you to be her lady in waiting, I didn't expect you to constantly be letting her out of your sight. Numerous escape attempts, vanishing into others' rooms, and now, once more, she's slipped from your nervous fingers." He spreads his arms out and asks, mockingly, "Tell me, where *is* my queen?"

"Erm. I – I don't know. My lord," Isidora admits, in a voice so quiet it's barely audible.

Oh, Isidora...

Dasar claps his hands a single time. Without hesitation, a soldier grabs Isidora's shoulders and shoves her, throwing her to her knees before Dasar. The soldier raises his spear, the metal point flashing in the light. Kazan presses her mouth tightly shut to keep silent. Isidora cries, tears and snot running down her rouged cheeks and pink lips.

"Please..." she begs Dasar. "My lord, I –"

The soldier stabs his spear into her throat. A faint, sickly light slithers across the blade, revealing the spelled inscriptions.

Isidora's eyes are wide and terrified, and the soldier wrenches his spear up, opening up a gory gap in her neck. Then he shoves his clawed hands into that gap and *rips* her head off. There's a crunch of bone, a splattering noise from the blood spray, and a *thud* when the soldier tosses the head, letting it roll across the floor to stop at Dasar's feet.

"Shame," he says. Then, that's it. That's all the recognition Isidora's death gets. "Someone take these bodies to the tombs. I'm sure Ezelind and Weisz will be moved back to their estates eventually, but for now the Citadel's humble catacombs will suffice."

The soldiers finish wrapping the bodies in white sheets and begin lifting them. Adrius reaches into his pocket and slips on a pair of gloves before bending down and picking up Kazan's sword. There's an ease with which he handles it, no hesitation despite the dangerous nature of the weapon.

"Ah... Are you certain that's a good idea, De Vere?" Dasar asks, and it sounds almost like a warning.

Adrius doesn't relinquish the blade. "When I was human, I trained to be a Warden. I assure you, my lord, that I have far more experience safely handling rowan and silver than anyone else in this manor."

"I *do* prefer to avoid being burned," Dasar admits. "Very well, good thinking."

A small black cat slinks between the gap in the statues and sits in front of Kazan. Reya. She blinks up at Kazan but doesn't make a single sound.

Another guard slips into the room, this time wearing House Rockford's colors. "Lord Dasar," he says, "the..." He trails off at the sight of Isidora's headless corpse. He clears his throat. "The guests are becoming restless. News of Ezelind's and Weisz's deaths has spread through the Citadel, and many are asking questions. A killer needs to be announced and addressed. And the queen is still missing."

Dasar nudges Isidora's head with the tip of his boot. "Yes, so I've heard."

"I'll locate her," Adrius volunteers. He glances down at her sword. "After all, I have something she wants."

"Just don't kill her. We need her for another few hours. Return that pretty blade to my armory once you're done. Wait. On second thought, have it placed in my menagerie instead. A bit more thematically appropriate, isn't it?" Dasar turns to the door. "Come along everyone, let's go address my party."

Kazan flattens herself against the base of a statue as the group strides out, taking the corpses with them, leaving only bloodstains, statues, and the sounds of rain outside. Reya remains sitting at her feet, staring up at her with blank eyes. As though accusing her. Reya would have seen her let Isidora die. Had Kazan stood up and said something, it might have saved Isidora from Dasar's wrath. But she didn't. She let it happen. All she did was watch.

In the quiet susurrus of rain, Adrius's voice is clear as he calls out, "Kazan, you can come out now."

Chapter Twenty-Eight

Kazan rises to her feet and slowly steps out from her hiding place. "How did you know I was here?"

Adrius inclines his head towards her feet, where Reya winds between her legs, tail curling around her ankles but noticeably not purring. Reya slinks out and shifts back into her usual form – dark fur into dark hair, lithe tail into the trailing hem of her maroon dress. She's not accusatory like Kazan had thought. Instead, she looks almost... enticed. Not proud but *impressed*.

"Are you going to give me back my sword?" she asks.

"Not yet," he replies. "If I do, Dasar will know right away that we're collaborating."

Reya places her hand at the small of Kazan's waist. "We should go. This room isn't safe, given that anyone could come back to continue the investigation."

No one approaches them as they leave, Adrius leading them out of the statuary and Reya delicately guiding Kazan. She doesn't allow herself to pause as they walk past the crimson smear of Isidora's blood on the dark mahogany floor.

Adrius slowly heads away from the statuary and towards the central spires. A steep set of stairs and a few turns and then they are in a secluded room of a tall tower. Thin windows, too small for Kazan to squeeze through, allow fading light into the manor's gloom. It's close quarters, Reya and Adrius only a few inches away from her. She stands between them, leaning against the wall, her head next to the window and the tapping of rain against the glass comforting her.

While Reya's voice is soft, it is no less steely than when she'd snapped at Kazan earlier, "I've finished preparations. Your blood will fade from the crown shortly after midnight, and if you're not sacrificed and eaten by then, the spell won't be renewed and the Citadel will collapse. However, if we add another human's blood to the crown, then we can replace you with them and go through the rituals again."

Another three days of this farce, but with a different human stuck in Kazan's place. "You'll just... keep doing this damn party?"

"No. No, I'm not fond of this party. It's an insult to humans and to our kind. We would bring in another human as the sacrifice but we wouldn't do all –" Reya gestures to everything around them "– *this*. I know what is and isn't necessary, and this isn't necessary."

"Then what?" Kazan demands. "Another year, another sacrifice?"

Adrius shakes his head. "If we have a full year without interference from Dasar, Ezelind, or Weisz, we can figure out a different way of maintaining the blood magics, I'm certain of it. There are spellcasters we could contact, rare supplies we could import."

"Someone else will still die," she protests.

"Humans always die," he says, flat and matter of fact. "One last human or an endless parade of Dasar's parties. In my opinion, that's rather an obvious choice."

"And if I refuse?"

"With Dasar dead," Reya says, "I'm sure there will be any number of people suddenly claiming they never liked him to begin with, and Adrius and I already have a plan in place to take over Gambit and Mooncliffe. But those plans will need to be... adjusted, to accommodate everything that's happened. And," she adds, in a stiff, painfully frank manner, "if you refuse, my plans wouldn't include you."

"Or," Adrius continues, "perhaps they'll kill you for destroying the Citadel and everything inside it. There are any number of people who would be willing to hunt you down, either for revenge or because they've been paid to do so."

Reya gently cups Kazan's cheek and there's a genuine plea in her eyes. "I know this is difficult for you. But you barely need to do anything; we'll take care of it all and then you can have everything you've ever wanted. We'll arrange it so someone else takes the fall for having turned you and you can have your pick of my estates, if you so choose."

"You wanted this," Adrius softly reminds her, "when you were trying to sell your sword to Madam Rask. I could see it in you, that desire. All we're asking of you is a few minutes of inaction, and in exchange, we can grant you an eternity of comfort."

So little, for so much.

Are they right about her? She has already killed to secure her own survival, and she let Isidora die to keep herself hidden. And if she had to do it all over again, she would. Vampire lives. Human lives. What's the difference, in the end? How different is she now that she's been turned into one of them? Apart from her hunger, she's the same as she's always been. Nothing in her mind feels different, no part of the transformation made her particularly monstrous.

She wets her lips. "Alright," she whispers. "One final sacrifice."

"The last year," Reya agrees.

Outside, the rainclouds darken as the sun dies.

Reya kisses her, soft, sweet lips almost warm against hers. "I turned you," she murmurs. "It's only fair that I share with you all the gold in Mavazem. I promise, I will not give you cause to regret this."

She finds her head turned towards Adrius as he too kisses her, in a way that tastes like a promise and an apology at the same time. "Nor will I," he swears.

"Will I still kill Dasar?" she asks quietly.

"I don't care to do that sort of bloody work myself," Reya replies.

Adrius adds, "And I don't want him dead by my hand as I wanted Ezelind. He's yours, if you wish."

The murder she's craved most of all, the prized jewel in her crown. She wraps her arms around herself, around the clothing she's borrowed from them. "Thank you," she says, the two tiny words so difficult to force out when they're sincere instead of a manipulation. "I–I… really do…"

Reya kisses away her uncertainty. "We know."

Now Reya knows her too. How many lies do they see through? If the answer is all of them, they can see she's not lying now. That she *will* go through with this. That she *will* let someone die. Didn't she let dozens of humans die in the Vildenmarr? She could have at least tried to save Travers, and she didn't. She saved her own life and while it may not have been as… direct, as it is now, it was still a choice and she still made it. As Dasar once said, even inaction is action.

When a housecat runs off into the woods, it does not become a lion. But when a pig escapes its pen and leaves that veneer of domestication, it does not long remain a pig. Its thin fuzz grows into thick fur, its teeth swell into rough tusks, its eyes turn savage and vicious. In mind and in flesh, once it spends too long in the wild, it becomes a boar. She has been removed from the domestication of human society, and now look at her. Feral.

"Now I believe it's time for you to be miraculously located by Adrius." Reya leads her out of the alcove with a light pull on her hand.

Adrius removes one of his gloves and gives it to Reya so she can safely take the sword. "Of the two of us, you're the one with unrestricted access to the party's preparations and organization. Hide the blade under the head table so that Kazan can easily reach it."

Taking the sword like it's a poisonous insect, Reya uncomfortably holds it away from her body. "I hate how reasonable that is. Oh, it's beautiful, but I'd rather not let it accidentally brush against my skin."

"A scar wouldn't suit you," Kazan remarks.

Reya bites down on her lower lip before slowly agreeing. "No. No, I suppose it would not." She takes a deep breath and heads down the stairs with a final, "Good luck, dear ones."

Nothing is said between Kazan and Adrius as they return to the center of the Citadel. There's nothing to say, not really. What hasn't already been said?

Adrius leaves her in front of her chambers, and while he holds onto her hand for a moment longer than is proper, he doesn't kiss her again. The chance of prying eyes is too great, too risky.

"You can do this," he assures her, and then opens the door.

She enters her chambers, and the door shuts behind her, depositing her properly back into the world of the party's farce.

A woman waits for her. She's wearing a plain gown and little to no makeup, a taciturn frown pinching her eyes. The bed has not been made. It has been stripped bare, the sheets and blankets and pillows removed, mattress ready to be aired out. They're preparing for her death already, removing traces of her from the Citadel. The woman has laid a dress out on the settee and the vanity remains untouched, but the rest is slowly being sanitized of all things human.

That taciturn expression remains as the woman sees Kazan enter. "Ah, Highness. I'm Marta Garner, your new lady in waiting." Clearly selected as the exact opposite of Isidora. "I've drawn a bath for you."

Of course, she'll be tastier if she's scrubbed clean. "I don't need your assistance," Kazan says as she strides towards the washroom.

She kicks her boots off and drops her coat on the floor for Marta to pick up. By the time she reaches the washroom door, she's undone the laces on her corset and throws that over her shoulder too before slamming the door closed.

Steam rises off the tub, filling the room and immediately making her clothes and hair stick to her skin. She strips off her remaining garments, taking extra care to ensure that she removes neither her gloves nor the disguise ring sitting atop them. She doesn't know if Marta will burst in or if a brief moment without the ring will make her smell vampiric.

Washing with gloves on is uncomfortable, but preferable to being discovered. She scrubs herself clean in water that now feels closer to scalding than hot, dowses her hair in rose scented soap and pours lavender oil over her skin. Maybe if she smells too perfumed, it will briefly stave off overzealous appetites.

Eventually, she must leave the refuge of the washtub, wrapped in a towel but still leaving dripping footprints on the fancy wooden floors and elegant carpet. Marta purses her lips, but that is the only reaction Kazan gets. The woman treats her like a doll, drying her off in the manner of someone cleaning a counter instead of a person. She pauses, briefly, at the gloves, but doesn't appear to give enough of a damn to comment on them. Unlike Isidora, she doesn't give Kazan any input in her clothing and shoves her into the many layers and pinnings of a gold and black dress.

She pulls out the vanity chair. "Sit, Highness."

With far more efficiency and far less delicacy than Isidora, she brushes and dries Kazan's hair and pins it up. Varying cosmetics are applied to her face, with only the briefest of commands, telling her to close her eyes or move her lips or tilt her head up. A gold necklace is draped around Kazan's throat, and she's grateful that the bite wound on her neck healed during her transformation. That would be rather difficult to explain.

"Done," Marta finally declares, and then places a pair of heeled, black shoes in front of Kazan's chair. There are tiny pearls sewn onto them, stitches so small they must have destroyed the seamstress's eyes to make. "Put these on."

"Marta, did you ask for this job?"

"No. But my Lady Ezelind no longer needs her lady in waiting, so here I am." She points at Kazan's feet. "Shoes, Highness."

She slips the shoes on.

"Follow me, Highness. It's time."

Chapter Twenty-Nine

Never before has Kazan seen the halls of the Citadel churn like this. When they do not see her, they whisper amongst themselves, endless gossip about the murders. When they catch sight of her, they become a flurry of fanged grins and disgusting glances. They're less restrained with touch now, too – smelling her hair, tugging at her dress, patting her hand. Marta barely gives a damn what they do, and one of them gets close enough to pluck a strand of her hair as a morbid memento.

Wine and blood flow freely, everyone drinks and laughs as they drift towards the banquet hall. The only thing Marta does do is clear a path through the revelers so that she can continue her no-nonsense march through the halls.

Kazan passes an open door and her enhanced gaze snaps to the room behind it. It's just a parlor, empty as everyone heads to the main event. But there *is* a mirror, and through the door, she can see her reflection.

Her *real* reflection. Not the guise of humanity she wears. The silver backing on the mirror strips away that illusion and reveals what hides underneath. Pitch black sclera and golden irises. Fangs when she parts her lips. A bloodless tinge to her skin. Wrapped up in silk and jewels and powders, truly made into the perfect image of the Queen of the Vampires. Beautiful and terrible.

Nothing human remains in that person.

Just a vampire. About to do what every single vampire in this manor, at this party, does. Sit back, relax, and watch a human be slaughtered. And then enjoy the luxurious benefits of that blood price. Maybe Adrius and Reya will find a solution within a year, maybe they have overestimated themselves and they can't. Maybe people will insist on keeping the tradition alive regardless, maybe they will go along with a bloodless version of this spell. No matter what happens, an innocent, random, utterly unimportant human is going to be torn apart and eaten. Just a human. Just like her. Like she *was*. No one of consequence, except to themselves.

Then Marta clicks her tongue and the illusion breaks. She's back in a hallway surrounded by vampires. "Come along, Highness."

She drags herself away from the mirror. The Queen of the Vampires, escorted to her throne.

Riotous color and warm light fill the banquet hall. The night sky shines down through the high glass ceiling above, rain sliding over the dome of it and wavering the moonlight. Even after the abundant display of wealth and beauty over the past three days, it was nothing compared to this. The fine satins and delicate strings of pearls, the trailing ribbons and bejeweled shoes, everything turned up to a level of opulence that beggars belief. A thousand times more ludicrous than Madam Rask's soirees could ever dream of being.

It all glistens around her as she's led down the center of the hall towards the head table. She tries to look for Adrius and Reya, but there are far too many people in her way and Marta can barely part the crowd as it is.

The head table comes into view. Dasar stands behind it at his seat, a wide and toothy grin stretched from ear to ear. To his right is an empty seat, though plates and cutlery have been set. For Reya, perhaps? On the other side of the table is Adrius, sitting where Ezelind should be. He looks in her general direction, but not at her directly. Weisz's seat is filled by the distinctly uncomfortable Jacqueline Dawson.

"Welcome, Highness," Dasar says, spreading his arms wide.

Marta makes Kazan sit in her throne and then makes herself scarce. That crown is laid on the table before Kazan. A gorgeous, finely crafted circle of gold; that fat, crimson jewel filled with her own blood resting right in the center of it. She notices details she didn't before. Filigree spirals in the design, tiny rubies cradled in the whorls. An elaborate engraving brackets the blood jewel, a detailed animal on either side. A pair of wild boars.

Dasar delicately taps a metal spoon against the side of a crystal wineglass and a perfect chime rings out through the hall.

An anticipatory hush falls over the crowd.

"Good evening, one and all," Dasar begins, projecting masterfully to the entire hall with the air of a great performer. "I will admit, never have we had such an eventful party. After all that has happened, it can be a challenge to see past the sorrow and tragedy of our losses and remember to celebrate this joyous occasion. Lord Weisz and Lady Ezelind were beloved by many. Never before have Rockford or Mooncliffe had such dedicated leaders, so devoted to the good of their House and those who lived under their just and magnanimous rule. We may never see their like again."

Cheering ripples out through the hall. All hatred of various leaders briefly forgotten in the scandalous wake of a double murder. The party will end, and they will go back to their separate manors and grumble once again, but in this moment, they adore the show Dasar puts on for them more than anything else.

"We have suffered difficulty before," he continues. "And I do not doubt we will do so again. But our murderer has been chased from our grounds and our dead have been laid to rest beneath stone. So tonight, we mourn as we celebrate. We will lament all that we have lost as we renew the walls around us, our home, our Citadel. We honor our dead. We honor our traditions. We honor our queen's rule!"

A jeering roar rises from the crowd.

Dasar raises his goblet high, an enthused grin on his face. "And now, we feast!" Amidst the cheers and cries, he turns his grin to Kazan and asks, "Do you wish to say a few words, Highness? I think we'd all be delighted to hear from you."

With limbs made of lead, Kazan stands.

Across the hall, a small door opens. Unnoticeable, except to someone who stares out from the head table instead of towards it. Reya silently slips through, followed by another.

A human. A blonde man, lines around his mouth, and a flat, almost dead hollowness in his eyes. He's dressed in a simple servant's uniform, still wearing an apron that has a smudge of flour on the front. Kazan can see every detail, every blink, every stray hair. His hands are held stiffly in front of him. Left thumbnail chipped. His chin tilts downwards as he stares at his shoes. Yesterday's stubble on his jaw.

No one of consequence.

Is that what her father looked like? She can barely remember his appearance beyond a blur of senses and vague sounds. His hair was dark like hers, she thinks. Does this man, this random stranger, have children? Sons like him perhaps, a loving spouse? Does he have a daughter?

Slowly, as though in a trance, Kazan picks up her crown and stares at the gold and the blood resting in her hands.

"What am I *doing*?" she asks herself under her breath, staring at her reflection in the polished metal.

Dasar cocks his head, still smiling. "Hm?"

Her voice returns to her with the gradual softness of a fire warming a cold room. "You never treated me like a person." Louder now, for all to hear. "None of you have treated me as though I'm a real, living, breathing person. If I am not afforded the courtesy of humanity, then in turn I will act inhumanely. So here we are, with my inhumanity. I've schemed and deceived. I've stood back and let people die on my behalf. I've killed, in self-defense, in anger, and in cold-blooded, premeditated murder. And every single one of them *deserved* it."

The grin on Dasar's face has frozen still. "Highness... that's enough."

Her hands tighten around the crown until her leather gloves creak and she declares to the entire Citadel, "*I* killed Ezelind and Weisz!"

A wineglass drops from someone's hand and shatters across the floor. Gasps ripple through the room, frenzied, disorganized, chaotic. She can hear Adrius's sharp intake of breath, can see Reya's face slowly begin to fall as she realizes what Kazan is refusing to do.

Someone in the far back of the hall cries out. "Eat the human!"

She screams, louder than the outrage and the panic she's incited, "I am *not* human! Not anymore!"

Fueled by spiteful adrenaline, she steps onto the table, knocking a goblet over. She raises her hand and slowly slips the ring from her thumb, letting the illusion thin and then vanish entirely. And thus, she sweeps into a mocking bow.

She has earned their outrage and now she has forced them into shock. These few moments of complete stupefied silence as every single one of them must rethink everything that has happened over the past few days, everything that they thought about this party, everything that they thought about her.

"And I," she declares, "am abdicating my throne!"

She throws her crown onto the marble floor like tossing a gauntlet, and with a glistening shine of crimson, the blood stone shatters into a dozen shards.

Twelve bells toll throughout the Citadel.

Midnight.

Chapter Thirty

As the last bell fades, the floor beneath them shudders. One small, tentative shudder, as if in warning. Everyone in the banquet hall holds their breath.

Crrrrrrrrack...

In unison, they all turn their heads to the sky.

A thin, hairline fracture has appeared in the glass-domed ceiling. As they watch, it grows, spiderwebbing around from the center and extending its reach to the very edges. A small handful of glass dust falls, like glittering snow brushed off eaves. Something creaks as the glass begins to shift. Her eyes latch onto a single raindrop, a survivor of the deluge outside. It runs through the cracks of the ceiling, weaving its way through the glass, and slowly lets go, falling down into the banquet hall, landing on the edge of a tablecloth.

The entire glass ceiling shatters.

Screams ring out as huge panes of glass crash into the banquet hall, descending upon the revelers. Someone, Kazan doesn't know who, is sliced in half by one and has to crawl their way out from underneath it, their body stitching itself back together as they writhe.

Is Reya...?

On the other side of the hall, Kazan catches sight of Reya and exhales in relief. She's fine, she's not been hurt, and she's trying to get everyone out. A vampire stumbles near her and she grabs him by the arm, pulling him to his feet and all but throwing him in the direction of the door. The second he's safely out, she slings an arm around a woman whose table collapsed atop her, dragging her to the door while the woman's broken leg snaps back into place.

The shock at the head table has worn off and Kazan feels the weight of dozens of eyes on her.

Dasar's fangs lengthen in his frozen grin. Almost sweetly, he orders, "Kill her."

There's the *hiss* of steel as every soldier draws their sword, a chorus of armor shifting as every guard points their spear at her. Jacqueline Dawson has cleverly vanished. Kazan's body tenses, enhanced eyesight sharpening, muscles preparing for a fight like raising a hammer and lining up the downswing.

Everything seems to move in slow motion as a half-dozen enemies get closer and closer, and there's a whole banquet hall of vampires to contend with even after she gets through this. She kneels to slide her hand under the table, hoping that Reya came through for her, gloved fingers groping blindly for the hilt of her sword.

Fast as the Citadel's guards are, Adrius is faster.

He unsheathes his rapier in a flash of movement, flicking his thumb against the nick, a splash of his blood drawn down the fuller. The spell burns crimson for a split second as it activates and, before anyone can realize that he has not turned against *her*, he decapitates the nearest guard.

The head falls at Dasar's feet.

Dasar's grin fades into nothing but fangs. "Oh, I should have known *you* would –"

Wood brushes against Kazan's fingertips. It's her turn to let a grin split her lips open as she grabs onto her sword, rips it from its hiding place, and swings at Dasar. Before it can connect, he stumbles backwards, just out of her reach. He draws himself up in the manner of one who is not only offended, but offended that she dared to offend him.

"You're paying attention to *me* now," she snarls.

Behind them, Adrius cuts down another two guards with two swift, brutal strokes of his blade. Like a painter with a brush. Dasar steps backwards and reaches out as one of the guards falls. Before the body can hit the floor, Dasar has snatched their spear from their dead hands. For someone so pompous and ostentatious, he handles the weapon with surprising ease, adjusting his grip on the shaft into something that speaks of decades, if not centuries, of practice.

He slashes his thumb open on the small spike near the base of the socket. Blood wells up on his skin and rolls down the thin fuller. A hum of light as the spells activate, the red glow briefly casting macabre shadows under Dasar's face.

"I assure you, *Highness*," he drawls, fury oozing off each word, "you have my full and undivided attention."

Her lip curls back and she runs the tip of her tongue over her new fangs. "*Spectacular.*"

The perfect marble floor cracks open, carving a line between them.

With a growl, Dasar moves. He's fast for a gilded lord, rushing forward and slicing a brutal cut towards her neck. Steel meeting steel rings in her ears as she brings her blade up and pushes the attack just the slightest bit off course. He slides backwards, adjusting his grip on the spear to keep the blade up. She leaps in to take advantage of his brief retreat, stabbing her sword forward to pierce his guard. It fails as he twists his torso out of the way, as though his ribs aren't even there.

He slashes his spear across her body with a vengeance, smashing into her sword and breaking her guard. Those spells are closer than she'd like them to be, and as they slice in front of her vision, she can make out every menacing etch and crimson scrawl. Distantly, she hears another crack of the floor splitting open, but to her, the Citadel and the fleeing revelers might as well not be there.

On a bitter whim, Kazan kicks her leg out and plants her foot through the wooden table. Her new strength snaps the massive plank of solid oak in two and splinters fly through the air in an explosion of needles.

Dasar's mouth hangs open in a horrified, angry maw. "That's *mine*!"

"How tragic."

She barely sees his next swing coming, and the hefty wooden shaft of his spear smacks into her stomach at full force. Winded, she stumbles backwards, down the step that elevates the head table from the rest of the room. She finds herself in the middle of the banquet hall, surrounded by destroyed tables and abandoned chairs, the last of the revelers crushing themselves against the doors in their haste to get out. Soldiers are pushing towards her like fish struggling to swim against the current.

In the Vildenmarr, she'd been herded and circled, trapped for their amusement. She will have to take them on one at a time to avoid getting pinned down again.

"Kill her and bring me her heart!" Dasar cries out, spear tip pointed to the ground as he strides forward. "I intended to eat her tonight and one way or another, I *will*."

Kazan brings her sword up into a guard, wrists crossed, hilt held near her face, point of the blade aimed straight at Dasar. A soldier breaks through the crowd, sword raised as he makes his way towards her. She snaps her gaze to him and then there's another two behind her, spears held out and ready to attack. Dasar or the soldiers? She has to pick one to go after first, but she has a feeling Dasar's going to be a bit harder to kill.

A soldier gets an inch too close and then a blood-slick blade erupts from his throat.

The body falls. Adrius stands behind him, and a sharp flick of his rapier pulls it from the corpse, painting an arc of blood across the marble floor. Before the next soldier can attack him in retaliation, he ducks under their spear and, with a fluid wrist movement, slips past their guard and pierces their heart. Spells flash red and that acidic magic scours their insides and leaves them to crumple.

While Adrius dispatches another enemy, Kazan swings her sword at a soldier trying to stab him in the back. Blessed steel and silver buries itself into their gut. She yanks the blade back, sliding it from their stomach, letting it burn its way out.

"You didn't need to stay," she remarks, standing back-to-back with Adrius as she raises her blade again, preparing for the next wave. "I thought you would have run off the moment you knew I wouldn't go through with it."

Adrius stabs a soldier in the eye and sarcastically snaps back, "You're welcome! Where's Reya?"

"I saw her by the far door –" She pauses to cut a spear shaft in two and open up the wielder's chest. "When the roof shattered. She was helping people get out. I don't know where she is now."

He blocks a strike aimed at her head and then slides forward to decapitate the attacker. "You still want Dasar for yourself?"

"He wants to eat my fucking heart. Of course I want him for myself!"

"I'll take care of these soldiers and find Reya. She'll be fine, if you still care about that. None of Rockford's or Mooncliffe's forces are staying and half Dasar's folk are more loyal to her than to a collapsing building. *Duck*!"

Adrius grabs her by the waist and throws her to the ground. Just in time. One of the stone archways decorating the ceiling has broken off and smashes into the marble floor right where they were just standing. A faultline opens beneath it, spreading out towards a nearby plinth. The plinth shatters and the golden vase atop it rusts in the blink of an eye, warping like damp clay, until it's nothing more than a ruined lump of metal.

A soldier leaps over the hunk of fallen stone and brings her spear down on them, only to fall upon Adrius's blade as he rises to his feet with swift elegance. Kazan grabs the woman's spear and tosses it into the stomach of an approaching soldier before the vampiric blood spells on it have time to fade.

"Get to Dasar!" Adrius tells her, killing a soldier with an

intensity that makes her wonder if he's enjoying this. "Kill him as quickly as you can and then get out before the Citadel collapses completely."

"It's not as though it'll kill me," she replies.

"No, but being crushed won't be pleasant, and it will take you rather a long time to reform your entire body and climb out. Once you do, who knows who'll be waiting with a weapon trained on your head."

Her eyes lock with Dasar's across the mess of soldiers and shattered stone. "I'm on it."

With her free hand, she grabs a fistful of her skirt and *rips*. Her new claws catch at the seam and tear the fabric up to her midthigh, and she tears again until she's similarly shredded her petticoat. She kicks her heels off, taking more than a little pleasure in watching them hit a collapsing pillar, a brick falling and crushing them. She hopes those silly pearls are turned to dust.

Her bare feet dart over the cracked ground with new agility, her eyes fast enough to keep up with the increase in speed. Light glints on the tip of Dasar's spear as he readies the weapon.

They collide. In the manner of one delivering the headsman's axe, Dasar brings the spear down. Kazan throws her sword above her head to block it, the impact rippling through her muscles in a way that feels distinctly off. Steel against steel, the both of them pushing with all their strength in a battle of pure force. It can't last. He knows how to use his vampiric strength in a way she's still adjusting to. Already, she can feel herself straining under the effort, her fingers tightening around the hilt.

Fine then.

She drops the tip to the ground and all the momentum Dasar had been throwing sends his spear sliding down into the floor. She surges up to slash diagonally across his body, but is not quick enough. He adjusts his grip and slams the blunt end into her chest. Something *cracks*, pain stabbing through her. Did he just break a fucking rib? And then it *snaps* back as swiftly as it broke, with another flash of burning hot agony. She stumbles back and prods her torso with her free hand. Nothing out of place.

But that second of distraction costs her. Dasar's spearpoint slices too close to her head and she falls backwards in her haste to avoid it, losing her footing and falling to her knees. With a smug smirk, he takes a step closer.

A slab of stone twice the size of her body crashes to the ground between them.

She tilts her head up to what's left of the ceiling. Not only has the glass gone, but nearly all the stone itself too. The higher buttresses and arches have entirely crumbled, the upper stairs cracking and breaking before her very eyes. As she watches, a tapestry tatters and rots and then disintegrates into nothing more than faded scraps.

When she rolls over to push herself up, a body lies not two feet from her. One of Dasar's soldiers. Adrius's work, going by the thin, acidic burn that has opened up the dead man's throat. There are more bodies the more she looks. If the soldiers are all dead, then Adrius and Reya must be safe, right? She reaches for her sword, the tip scraping against the cracked stone as she rises to her feet.

Across the hall, she sees a flash of Adrius's dark coat. He bends down as he rushes towards the exit and extends a hand. A small black cat darts across the uneven ground and scampers up his arm until it rests on his shoulders.

A second later, and the two are gone.

Relief that she will never admit to runs through her. Then another tremor rumbles across the Citadel and rocks fall, collapsing that final exit.

When she turns back, Dasar is perched atop the stone slab.

"So audacious, my queen," he growls, stalking towards her, tip of his spear snaking along the floor. "It's a shame you had to cross me."

She settles into a low stance, blade held in a fool's guard. "Technically," she snaps back, hoping to rub his face into his failure, "Aishreya Sutcliffe crossed you first. After all, she's the one who turned me."

His upper lip curls as though she's just poured spoilt milk between his teeth. "De Vere *and* my darling Lady Sutcliffe. How *did* you manage that?"

"Honestly, it wasn't exactly a challenge," she taunts. "Nearly everyone in this place who isn't a sycophant, a lush, or a coward has been chomping at the bit to betray you."

Something in his eyes sparks with anger, fury enough to break through his poise and reveal a wrath that almost matches her own. Anger is her friend. Her lover. It has made her clever, made her quick, made her *strong*. Dasar's game is all vanity and ego. He doesn't know anger as she does, hasn't let it kiss the very marrow of his bones as she has. Where anger sharpens her, it blunts him.

An entire balcony crumbles above.

With an enraged cry, he stabs his spear towards her heart.

Kazan's new eyes slow the movement down, allowing her to follow the perfect line of his spear, the spellwork that begins to faintly light up, the individual strands of his hair that drift across his face. The muscles in her arms tense, the leather gloves creak around the hilt. She brings her blade up in a circle and the silver shines cold in the midnight light as the final candelabras extinguish.

Her radiant blade collides with the blood-magic spearhead.

The spear *shatters*.

Dasar's irises are tiny pinpricks of gold against wide black as he stares at the shards of steel glistening in the air.

In that second of distraction, she plunges her blade into his chest.

Or she tries to. Right before the strike can connect, his body turns into wispy, black ink, pouring out of the way of her sword. The wisps pull back and transform exactly as

Reya transforms. Only Dasar doesn't become a cat. His body shifts and splits until that shroud of ink has become a flock of bats.

Leathery wings flap around her in a storm, high pitched laughter swarming in her ears. She swings her blade at them, a frustrated hiss on her teeth, but the damn bats are too fast and agile for her to so much as nick them. All she can see is the flashing of their wings and the way they flick raindrops on her as the last of the roof cracks open like an egg and lets the rain and wind in without any further obstruction.

Then the bats are gone as suddenly as they attacked her. When she drops her arms, she sees them fly to a nearby fallen bust and swirl around themselves in a whirlwind. They shift back into that black ink. A heartbeat later, Dasar stands atop the cracked bust, his coat tugged by the wind like the wings he had donned.

He curls his fingers, and his claws extend outwards into wicked weapons. "Very well, Highness. If you want to do this the old-fashioned way, then I'm happy to oblige you."

She barely sees him move before she has to throw herself sideways to dodge his strike, palms open, claws out to slash her face into ribbons. Part of the Citadel collapses overhead and a spike of stone spears the broken ground. Dasar leaps up onto it, tipping it over and landing with all the deadly rage of the predator he is.

She does not need to wait more than a heartbeat before he strikes again.

Everything about his movements screams of training and skill, yet he abandons all of it in reckless anger. He slashes at her with his claws, and she twists away. He lunges towards her, one hand wrapping around her sword arm to keep the blade away from him, and she brings her knee up to smash into his gut.

He pulls back, claws scraping her arm as he retreats, flecks of blood splattering over his sleeve like a trophy. She grits her teeth and swings her blade again, and this time she opens up a thin, burning line on his shoulder.

"You –!" He touches the wound, as though in shock that she actually managed a hit. "You *cut me*."

She bares her fangs at him. "Hurts, doesn't it?"

His claws lengthen even further, cuticles splitting open, tips of his fingers blackening as though burnt. He draws back, preparing to lunge. Then he glances up.

Once more his form shifts and he transforms into a cloud of bats, surging away from her. Is he running? Why? That doesn't make any –

She looks up and sees a pillar falling down upon her.

Shit.

She tries to run, tries to throw herself to the side, but the pillar is too huge and the rush of wind and stone dust wraps around her. Right when she's almost free, the marble in front of her collapses, plummeting down into the lower floors of the Citadel. She skids to a halt before she falls who knows how far down, and then there's nowhere to go. She closes her eyes and reminds herself that at least it won't kill her.

The pillar hits the ground and knocks her flat on her stomach.

She coughs on dust and rain, grinding her claws into the ruined marble beneath her and scraping her way out from underneath the cracked stone. Agony suddenly smacks into her. A scream tears at the inside of her throat as pain envelops her legs. She does everything she can to stop herself from hyperventilating, gingerly turning onto her back to see that the pillar has fallen on her legs.

Her own blood is smeared on the wet stone.

When she retches, it's a dry, sandpaper heave, nothing but human blood in her system, and that refuses to leave her body. She holds her breath instinctually before realizing that she doesn't actually need to breathe. Something inside her sings, not confidence exactly, not determination, but the untouchable desperation of a caged animal ripping its shackles off with its teeth.

She drags herself out from underneath the stone as her legs snap and slither their way back into place. Her reforming feet tingle as though filled with needles.

When she's hauled herself out, she reaches for…

Her sword.

Now she well and truly stops breathing. Splinters of rowan stick out from beneath the broken pillar. Shattered pieces of steel. A bit of silver wire. The pieces of her broken sword lie at her feet as the Citadel falls around her.

Another scream fills her chest like lava and she tilts her head back, letting the sound slash its way out of her throat and surge past her fangs and into the rush of wind and rain. Every ounce of her newfound strength surges into her reformed legs and her sharp eyes lock onto Dasar across the ruins.

She *runs*.

Her feet push her over uneven stone and broken statues until she's lunging at Dasar, scream still on her lips and claws extended. Laughing at her misery, he twists to the side, slashing at her stomach as he goes. But that doesn't matter, the pain doesn't matter, it'll be healed in a moment anyway. When he leaps at her, she turns her back to him and drops low. Her hand snatches his arm out of the air, and she throws him over her shoulder like a sack. There's a crash as he hits the floor on his back, his face torn into a breathless, pained gasp.

With a vengeful cry, she flings herself on top of him, straddling his waist, drawing her fist back.

She plunges her claws through his throat. Beneath her, he chokes, trying to slash at her ankle, his lips forming soundless shapes. Blood trickles out of his lips and she claws at him again, ripping at his arm this time again and again. Slippery muscle snakes under her claws until she grabs at the solid length of a bone. She *wrenches*. The noise is horrible at first, and then deeply satisfying as she rips his arm out of its socket and hurls the useless limb across the ruins.

The open wound starts to twitch. It will reform soon, and without her sword or a spelled blade, there's no way to stop it. Is there?

Human instinct tells her to breathe, to avoid injury, and blink. But it's vampiric instinct that fills her now, a scream pouring out and that ancient instinct flowing into her in its wake. She tears at him again, reopening his throat and letting the rain drip into his trachea. It starts to reform as soon as she removes her claws, but she doesn't need to rip his head off.

Instead, she stabs her claws into his solar plexus, piercing straight through his shirt and his skin. She keeps going. His body writhes beneath her but he can't throw her off. Trapped, fates at last reversed. She grabs onto bone, claws scraping over the hard surface, and with a furious burst of strength, she rips his ribcage open like the petals of a flower. Gore splatters her and she finds herself reveling in it. Lungs, kidney, intestines all open to the night sky.

She grabs his undead heart. Cold, wet flesh squelches around her fingers. Veins and arteries rip and dangle from the organ when she tears it from his chest. Her trophy.

She watches his aghast eyes twitch and declares, "*Mine.*"

Fangs lengthen as her jaw cracks open like a snake, and she sinks her teeth into Dasar's heart.

Meaty, rich blood bursts on her tongue and dribbles out of the corners of her mouth. It's thick and oozing down her arms, and then slick and watery as the rain saturates her skin and tattered dress. Everything becomes shades of crimson. A mouthful of flesh tears off and she chews and it's *good*. She swallows. That same fervor that overcame her at the first taste of human blood rises up once more and she bites again, swallows again. She shoves more of the heart into her mouth as she devours it, ignoring the sounds of the Citadel's foundations cracking, the tremors in the ground.

Flesh slides down her throat and she feels it sitting in her stomach. When it's gone, and Dasar's body is unmoving beneath her, she begins licking her hands clean of any remaining scraps.

She's still licking as the ground collapses beneath her, and she falls into the depths.

DAY AFTER

Chapter Thirty-One

"…zan!"

Weight shifts overhead. Pressure being moved.

"Kazan!"

The pads of Kazan's fingers drag across wet stone. Her head aches but even that pain is fading quickly as she grabs onto rock and pulls her body upwards. Something in her shoulder snaps back into place and there's that gut-churning slither of her own flesh stitching itself back together. A hand snatches her own. A moment later, she finds herself heaved from underneath a boulder, on her knees in front of Adrius.

Blood and dirt stain nearly every inch of Kazan's skin. It's not her blood though – all that is back inside of her. It's what remains of Dasar. Her dress is tattered and barely hanging on her body and she pushes her sopping hair out of her face, its elegant styling long since dropped.

Moonlight bathes her and Adrius. The Citadel is gone and they're surrounded by nothing more than ruins. The remnants of an arch over there, a collapsed base of a tower over here. Some walls are standing, but not many, and while there are the barebones of some upper levels, she can see where the ground floor has caved in down to the dark basements. Anything that hadn't been reliant on the blood magic has surely been ruined entirely by the collapse. The lowest basement and its spiral of blood magic, gone. The library, its geists and human trophies, gone. The portrait of Adrius, gone.

"So," Adrius says, hard as iron. "You made it out alive."

She can only nod, her head heavy.

"You do realize what you've done, don't you?"

Another nod.

He sighs, staring down at her even as he calls out, "Reya! I found her."

When Kazan glances to the right she sees Reya just beyond a mostly collapsed archway, pacing back and forth as though trying to wear a new floor into the ruins. At Adrius's alert, she turns to them and climbs through the archway. Her image blurs as she moves and Kazan's pounding head struggles to track the motion.

"Tell me at least Dasar's dead," Reya demands as soon as she's close enough to Kazan to speak without having to yell. "We need to have gotten *something* from this."

When Kazan can't bring herself to respond right away, Adrius takes over. He shakes his head, eyes still locking with Kazan's. "His body is missing. For whatever *that's* worth. I've been doing what I can to keep others away from –" he gestures to the skeleton of a building around them "– what's left of the banquet hall. But few of them trust my word and not all are afraid of me enough to stay away for long. They're combing through the ruins, searching for whatever they can find."

"Has anything been uncovered?" There's no small amount of hope in Reya's voice.

"Not much. Bits and pieces, nothing more."

"Bits and pieces. Saints forbid *we* get to keep anything," she mutters. "Well," she adds, bitter sarcasm leaking into the words, "I hope the human servants escaped, hm? I'm sure a couple of humans makes *all* the difference, doesn't it? What's our history and possessions and home in comparison?"

Kazan can't bring herself to rise to the bait. Exhaustion has sunk into her along with the rain. They have every right to be angry with her. She lied to them, and unlike every time she's done so in the past, she didn't mean to. Every lie she's ever told has been a deliberately constructed fable. This time, like Adrius running after Ezelind, she simply couldn't stop herself. She lost control of her control.

"Where is Dasar?" Adrius demands of her.

The sharp sound of his voice is like a knife through Kazan's temples. Finally, she manages to speak, her throat sore and raspy. "Dead..."

"You stabbed him?" Reya grabs a fistful of her skirts as though she means to run around the ruins in search of his body. "Where is he? Where did you leave him?"

"My sword... it broke." Kazan can barely keep her eyes open as she mumbles, "I ate him. Ate his heart."

Reya blanches. It would seem her willingness to eat others, in comparison to Adrius at least, doesn't extend towards eating her own kind. *Their* own kind.

It takes a long time for words to work their way around the lump in Kazan's throat, but when they do, they surprise her. "I'm sorry," she whispers, so hoarse that she doesn't even know if they can comprehend her. "I meant it when I promised that I would go through with it. It wasn't a lie. I just... I couldn't. I thought I could, and I couldn't, and I'm sorry."

"Why?" Reya's voice is quiet and sharp as a whip on velvet.

Kazan blinks in confusion, raindrops flecking her lashes.

"Why are you sorry?"

"I'm not sorry for what I did," she defends. "I couldn't let someone die, not even a stranger. Not to that ritual. But I'm... I'm sorry that..." She wets her lips and tastes Dasar's blood again. Her stomach is full but she's empty, something inside her fading out as she stares up at Adrius and Reya, as a supplicant beneath a silvered saint. "I'm sorry that I hurt you. I'm a liar. I guess I'll never be able to stop being a liar. Even when I tried to be honest with you, I ended up lying in the end..."

Footsteps scramble up the rubble near them. When Kazan looks, a familiar woman is approaching. Jacqueline Dawson.

Dawson's eyes narrow into slits upon seeing Kazan. "*You*," she snarls.

"It would seem our time for debate is ended," Reya mutters under her breath. To Dawson, she says, "Calm yourself. We're here for the same reason you are."

"To kill this filthy –?"

"To sort out this mess," Adrius hisses, cutting her off.

Everything is so fuzzy for Kazan, it takes her a minute to feel Reya grab hold of her and haul her to her unresponsive feet. Dawson doesn't cease glaring as Adrius leads them through the ruins towards a swimming blur of color. Vampires, Kazan realizes, once her vision manages to focus for half a minute. Or… people. Her mind is straining as it is. The crowd is overlaid with a riot of noise that's beginning to get swept away by the rain.

A man in a torn shirt stumbles forward as soon as they approach. "Lady Sutcliffe! I demand to know who did such a vile thing!"

As Adrius walks forwards and passes Reya, he whispers in her ear, "*Lie.*"

Kazan can see Reya swallow. Then Reya squares her shoulders as much as she can with Kazan still struggling to stand on her own, and declares, "It was Dasar."

It's impossible to distinguish the individual shouts and cries with the rain still pouring, but Kazan doubts they say much of interest.

"Dasar violated the rules of our celebration." Reya appears to grow taller as she speaks louder, ensuring that everyone in the crush of people can hear her. "He turned Kazan Korvic, our former queen, thus condemning the Citadel to ruin and destroying the ancestral home of House Gambit. He was a traitor to his bloodline," she says, even louder as the shouting increases, "and to our kind! As one of his sole remaining heirs, I stand beside his other progeny in defending our society against his heinous actions!"

Dawson's mouth falls open and then she snaps it shut. "He fed her blood," she remarks softly, and then louder when someone in the crowd makes a noise of protest, "we all saw it! He fed her human blood in the banquet hall, right before Ezelind and Weisz's bodies were discovered."

A different vampire, similarly dressed in Rockford's colors cries out, "But she murdered out Lord Weisz! And Lady Ezelind, for that matter."

"On Dasar's orders," Reya lies. "He promised her salvation if she did the foul deed —"

Her falsehood is drowned out by furious shouts.

Adrius steps forward, one hand resting menacingly on the hilt of his rapier, and that simple motion is enough to instill silence into half the crowd. The other half is silenced by his sharp declaration, "We all know the depths of the animosity that ran between Dasar, and Ezelind and Weisz. I can confirm Lady Sutcliffe's story on these matters, as my own investigation into Lady Ezelind's death revealed the nature of our former queen's involvement. I spoke with her before the final feast and impressed upon her the importance of staying true to our bloodlines. As we all saw, she too realized that our bloodlines are of greater priority than one man's petty grudges."

Not a bad lie, Kazan thinks. Vaguely. Her thoughts are as slugs crawling across the inside of her aching skull.

A man dressed in the blue and silver of Mooncliffe strides up to them and spits on the rubble at Adrius's feet. "I refuse to listen to *you*, De Vere. We all know what sort of person you are. And if Sutcliffe is working with you, then she is just as rotten."

Reya bristles. "And do you fancy yourself an adequate successor to Mooncliffe, Sir Gamison? I shudder to think of what would become of our northern bloodlines if you —"

Her words are cut off as Gamison pulls a knife on her.

Kazan staggers away and nearly falls, while Reya gasps, seemingly frozen in what is either fear or sheer indignation. As if in slow motion, Kazan's new vampiric eyes watch as the blade gets closer. He means to stab Reya, and Kazan can barely stand let alone do anything about it. The blade will not even kill. It's not spelled. This is simply to prove a point.

In a quick and silent flash, Adrius snatches Gamison's arm and snaps it like a twig.

The knife tumbles from Gamison's grip as he cries out, falling into the rubble and vanishing in the mess of stones. Casual as anything, Adrius allows Gamison's arm to slip back into place and begin the healing process before yanking said arm behind his back and forcing him to his knees before the assembled crowd.

In that same cold, calm voice, Adrius tells him, "Raising a weapon against one of us only proves that you would be ill-suited to rule Mooncliffe."

"What are you going to do?" Gamison grits out. "Kill me?"

"Even I can tell that enough blood has been spilt today." Adrius nods politely to Reya. "As the attempt was on *your* dignity, Lady Sutcliffe, I shall give you first claim to dictate his punishment."

Her smile is a slight, sharp thing. "No harm was done. Besides, he disgraced your House, not mine."

"Banishment, then," Adrius decrees. There's an unsettled murmur from the crowd. His reputation is one of murder, after all. "You are banished from all parishes that Mooncliffe vampires walk across. Flee to the east, if you must, and hope that you can escape the eyes of the humans and their Wardens. In fifty years, you may return to Glassdow and petition me for clemency."

"You truly believe you'll be High Lord in fifty years?" Gamison spits.

Adrius breaks his arm once more with a *crack* that hurts Kazan's ears. Then he tosses the man aside like trash. "I am High Lord *now*." His upper lip curls into a sneer. "Get out of our sight."

A man dressed in Mooncliffe's colors hauls Gamison out

from beneath Adrius's glare and pushes him away with a series of rough shoves. Kazan tries to see if Gamison leaves, if he continues walking away from the ruins, but the rain blurs everything and darkness is falling over her eyes in a hazy shroud.

"Our world is in danger, we all know it," Reya declares, and as much as Kazan was queen, it is she who truly fits the crown. "De Vere and I will work together to ensure the safety and glory of our bloodlines whilst we recover from Dasar's treachery. If we allow ourselves to be further divided, the Wardens will fall upon us with the same fervor that we fall upon humans. While I know not where Lady Amelia is, we will welcome her with open arms should she chose to return to our fold. Our bloodlines shall not be further diluted."

Rocks are suddenly hard and cold and damp against Kazan's knees. Oh. She's finally slid far enough down Reya's rain-slick dress to have hit the ground. That's probably not good.

There's a pale blur in front of her vision and then pressure on her upper arm. Adrius bends down to grab her. She feels like rocks herself, her body heavy and noncompliant with his attempts to bring her back up on her feet. Skin shifts against hers. More pressure, this time on her wrist, seeking out her pulse.

"She didn't eat enough earlier," Adrius tells Reya. He sounds as solid and clear as distant clouds. When she blinks, she can no longer hear him. She opens her eyes and there are snatches of words. "Her body is struggling... strain of regeneration..."

Reya's voice drifts and then is entirely swept away by the rain as Kazan passes out.

Chapter Thirty-Two

When Kazan wakes, she doesn't know where she is. By now, she should probably be accustomed to such circumstances.

Soft pillows are tucked beneath her head and a blanket has been drawn up over the lower half of her body. At least whoever put her here is friendly. Brass knuckles are still rapping against her temples and her limbs are stiff as timber when she tries to move. Her mouth is dry as dust, her throat begging her gums for the slightest drop of moisture.

Obviously she cannot be in the Citadel, but this room only reinforces the knowledge that she's in a house nowhere *near* as grand as that building. She lies in a relatively large bed, and while the sheets are clean, the wooden posts are scratched and lacking shine. The carpet is beginning to appear threadbare and the colors are faded, but it has been recently dusted and aired out. Three trunks are stacked near the door, not yet unpacked. A brass candlestick sits on the desk, caked in old wax, a pristine new candle stuck on top of the mess with a fresh wick burning. Someone must have recently come in and hurriedly tidied. When she looks towards the nearby window with chipped paint on the wooden frame, she sees nightlight and leaves of overgrown ivy peaking over the edges of the glass.

The window is open a crack, and outside are the sounds of people moving and muttering and shifting luggage and the braying of horses.

It takes her a solid five minutes to bully her body into

moving, and when she pushes back the sheets, she notices that someone has taken away the rags of her ballgown and dressed her in a simple shift.

Then she sees her legs and stops.

Purple, rotting bruises cover every inch of her skin from her thighs down to her feet. Her toes are blackened, shriveled stubs, nails missing entirely, the bones on her ankles jutting out like spokes. Nausea churns her stomach, and she quickly pulls the sheets back up, clutching them to her waist in the desperate hope that if she just doesn't look, they will fix themselves. She's a vampire now, isn't she? Shouldn't she have healed?

There are whispers outside the door.

Squaring her jaw and shoulders, she throws the sheets off and slips out of bed without looking down. Pins and needles assault her feet as she forces herself to tiptoe towards the door and press her ear to the crack.

"...easily over a hundred either inside or about to arrive," an unfamiliar voice is saying. Deep, gravelly. A man? "Cairemere can't sustain so many for longer than a day or so. While some of us understand that things are in chaos, most are complaining that they don't have their own rooms and soft beds."

The second voice is Reya's, "Remind them that we don't need to sleep. I'll sort this out as soon as I can."

"Of course."

"How many have returned to their own estates?"

"Easily half of those under Gambit," the man replies. "We are still in the southern parishes, and unlike those of us in the north or west, it's a far shorter and easier journey back to their homes. Those that stay await your orders."

"Well at least that's something," Reya grumbles. Kazan gets the distinct impression that the grumble is to cover up nervousness. "Send a raven to the steward of my Pearlwood house and to Giltend River. Oh, and Wesson; please bring up a couple of bottles."

A set of footsteps approaches them, and this time Kazan

hears Adrius say, "I hope you've been receiving better news than me."

Wesson squeaks out a hasty, "Er – excuse me. My lord. My lady. I'll just – ah… send those ravens. And bottles. That too. Of course. Excuse me."

Kazan hears him scurry away.

"Wonderful," Adrius mutters. "Glad to know that my reputation is even more fearsome than it was before. I'm certain that won't hinder my attempts to rule without challenge whatsoever."

The door handle turns. Kazan jumps, and in her sudden haste to get away before they can find out she was listening in, her legs spasm and she collapses to the ground.

The door opens.

Adrius stares down at her. "Why am I not surprised?"

He bends down and grabs her arm, helping her up to her feet and assisting as she staggers over to the desk. She sinks into the chair with as much dignity as she can muster, wincing at the sight of her feet.

"Where are we?" she asks, coughing around the words.

"Cairemere Hall," he replies. "One of Reya's estates."

"I thought Reya was the *former* Baroness of Cairemere."

Adrius raises an eyebrow in disbelief. "And you're under the impression that she wouldn't have found a way to keep at least one of her entailed estates?"

"Ah, of course."

As if summoned by the sound of her name, Reya waltzes in through the door a moment later. Adrius leans against the desk, arms crossed over his chest. Reya paces.

"Welcome to Cairemere," Reya says. It doesn't make Kazan feel particularly welcome at all. "I don't suppose," she says with that same soft sharpness, "that either of you had a plan beyond destroying what was to be my castle?"

Adrius draws himself up in his seat and snaps, "Either? You think *I* wanted this?"

"If you hadn't gone off and tried to kill Ezelind, then we could have done the swap without Kazan knowing and ruining it all!"

A lump sticks itself in Kazan's throat. "So, I needed to be lied to for you to be happy? No, that's not... I understand the falsehood was necessary for all of us," she admits, her hands tightening around the fabric of the shift in her lap. "I'm only a hypocrite when it suits my desires."

"I didn't tell you," Reya stresses, "because I wanted *you* to be happy. If I'd told you, you wouldn't have been. You would have hated me for it."

And Reya does so *need* to be liked. Kazan doesn't say it aloud, but it rests right underneath her tongue.

Adrius pinches the bridge of his nose and reluctantly allows, "If we all want to tally up the various injuries we've done to one another, I'm certainly not going to protest. But we will be here for some time if we do. And time has now become a very precious commodity."

Reya's pacing slows. "I suppose you're right. Ah, I'm sorry, I hate arguing like this. I don't intend to be horrid."

"I know," he assures her.

There's a knock on the door.

Reya allows it to open a mere crack, just enough for her to reach out and grab something from whoever's on the other end. When the door shuts, two dark wine bottles are clutched in her hand, fingers laced around the necks.

She holds one out to Kazan and orders, "Drink."

That dryness in her throat rises up again, powerful enough to choke her. With grateful desperation, she accepts the bottle. Her new claws extend, break the wax seal, and dig into the cork by the time she realizes that this bottle is stamped with a golden crown, not an 'R'. It's not one of Rask's. It could have come from anywhere. Her body stops moving, unable to withdraw her claws from the cork, fighting the screaming voice in her head that insists she can't drink it.

"Oh, for the love of –" Adrius snatches the bottle from her unmoving hands.

He yanks the cork out, drops it onto the desk, and then drinks deeply. Before she can figure out what he means to do, he's tilted her chin up and is kissing her. The surprise is enough for her not to protest as he slides his tongue between her lips and then there's *blood*, warm and divine. It fills her mouth, rich taste running over her teeth and overwhelming her senses as he kisses her.

Thirst consumes her, and she takes the bottle from his hands and drinks without further reluctance. A faint smear of blood colors the corner of his mouth, satisfaction burning in his eyes. Deservedly so, she must admit. She drinks and her throat sings in relief. She finds that she's too hungry to be concerned about where this decadent meal came from anymore.

By the time she's drained the bottle and licked every last drop from the rim, the bruises on her legs have faded into nothingness and fresh, delicate keratin crowns each toe.

"You hadn't eaten enough," Reya tells her, handing over the second bottle. She's not smug, nor is she gloating at Kazan's misfortune. Would it be better if she were? If she weren't so obviously helpful, even after everything? "Reforming after being crushed by stone takes power, and power takes blood."

Adrius wipes his mouth with the back of his hand and then runs his tongue over the blood that he's cleaned off. "You did ask if we could be starved," he reminds her with the faintest touch of sarcasm. "I hope this has satisfied your curiosity."

It *has*. Deeply so. Is that terrible?

After tossing aside the empty bottle, Reya continues to pace. "You're lucky to still be alive," she says, her siren's voice sharpened into a needle, though she doesn't seem poised to stab Kazan with it yet. "Dasar could have killed you. If you'd just followed my plan then you would have been fine, and Adrius and I wouldn't be in this damnably messy position."

Kazan merely winces.

Anger has drained out of her with Dasar's death, curled back into her chest like a satiated cat that refuses to wake until after a long slumber. Instead, it has been replaced with a thought that scratches at her brain, digging nail-shaped trenches in her skull. She said she could go through with it. And then she didn't. It was a lie, and it was a lie she didn't mean to tell. She *always* means it when she tells lies, and she always knows when she's lying.

Except this time.

She speaks up, "What are we to do now?"

"We make for Glassdow Castle," Reya says. "With Amelia still absent and the Citadel in ruins, we must return to the only ancestral home we have left."

"I'll force Mooncliffe to bend to my rule," Adrius promises her. "Glassdow *will* be ours."

Reya stops pacing entirely and the look she gives Adrius is so soft and loving that Kazan physically shies away from it. "I'm sorry. I'm sorry I couldn't give you what you wanted."

"I'm sorry I took this away from you," Kazan murmurs.

That's mostly true. She is sorry Adrius lost the chance to prove that he's not what everyone thinks he is, and she's sorry her actions resulted in him being stuck leading people who don't respect him and treat him like a loose cannon. She's not sorry that she broke the magic and let the Citadel be destroyed, however. The moment when Dasar looked at her, properly *looked* at her for the first time, and saw her as a person and as a threat, is a moment she will savor for the rest of her unnaturally long life.

Adrius stares at her, black and gold eyes piercing through her already shredded defenses, as he did before when he realized she was telling the truth. "You are, aren't you?" he muses. "Despite your actions. You never cease to intrigue me."

Is that a compliment or a condemnation?

When she doesn't answer, Reya gently pets her messy hair.

"Rest, Kazan. Your body is still new and needs to rebuild. We will take care of everything else. You need only accompany us when we depart for the north."

Can it truly be as simple as that?

Chapter Thirty-Three

Preparations are all abuzz around Kazan and yet none of that energy touches her. It swirls around her and slides off her skin like water off leather. Despite remaining in the room where she'd awoken, several vampires have come and gone. A mélange of meaningless phrases murmured at her. Some ask for confirmation that it was Dasar who turned her, some say they're glad a fighter of her skills has now joined their self-proclaimed superior ranks. Some simply look at her, as though searching for confirmation that she's still around.

Kazan spends hours curled up at the window, staring out into the gardens and watching rain drip off the leaves that have grown up along the outer walls. Her mind turns over uncountable memories, examining each of her lies. Were there other lies she told that she didn't intend? How wrong about herself is she?

Eventually they leave Cairemere, in the early hours of the morning, as the sun begins to rise sluggishly over the trees surrounding the manor. Kazan has been hastily dressed in plain travel clothes and a black veil is draped over her face as though in mourning, the lace so thick that she can barely see out of it. As Reya and Adrius hustle her out to the awaiting coach, she catches a glimpse of Cairemere Hall. The manor is closer to the city-bound grandeur of Rask's estate rather than the sprawling palace of the Citadel, but it is still undeniably beautiful. Warm stone forms carven pillars and narrow windows, ivy and waxy vines twisting up the walls leading down into lush hedges. And then Kazan enters the carriage and the view vanishes behind the heavy curtain covering the window.

Adrius takes a seat across from her, the disguise ring on his finger once more giving him the illusion of humanity. Outside, she hears Reya exchange a few muffled words with the human driver. The man must be suspicious, but Kazan hears a frequent *clink* as more and more coins are handed over. A moment later, Reya climbs inside the carriage as well, her customary elegant ballgowns exchanged for an equally elegant travel gown, and a similar lace veil covering her features.

Adrius raps his knuckles on the roof. The driver snaps the reins, and the horses begin to pull them away.

Only after an hour on the road does Kazan feel comfortable enough to lift her veil and peer through a gap in the curtains. Endless woods and picturesque fields stretch out before her, taunting her. She spent all that time locked up inside the Citadel, cut off from the outside world, and even now she must only look at it through slightly dirty glass panes.

Day one passes in silence. They stop at a coach house where driver and horses are traded out and then they ride on through the night. Further ample quantities of Reya's coin are apparently enough to quash any questions.

Day two is still filled with silence, but at least now Kazan knows where they are – the southern part of Mavazem. They are closer to the east than she had expected, and she wonders if that proximity to the human-dominated lands is what mostly keeps Reya away from the estate. They change drivers and horses at another coach house and Adrius and Reya go through the guise of grabbing a quick meal to make a few noticeable comments to staff, feigning normal, human exhaustion.

Day three, they reach the Vildenmarr. They don't bother taking the Faebower as Kazan's caravan did, and instead skate around the forest via Rivervale.

Kazan naps a bit, for lack of anything better to do rather

than actual desire for sleep. Near the end of the wide Rivervale road, she is roused from her light nap by the sound of galloping horses approaching.

Adrius straightens up in an instant, as though struck by lightning, and reaches across the gap between them to pull Kazan's veil back down over her face. "Wardens," he hisses urgently, laying a tense hand on the hilt of his rapier. "If they stop us, I'll do the talking. Kazan, you're ill and can't speak. Reya, the driver knows there are three of us here so if you transform, that discrepancy may put us at risk. You know how to avoid having to lie."

"Be demure, I know." Her attempt at humor is betrayed by the way her voice wavers. She tugs her own veil down as well.

The carriage rattles to a stop.

Despite the potential for this to end in bloodshed, Kazan still can't make a spark of anything burn in her chest. Not apprehension. Not concern. There is only that sleeping cat where anger should be and the scraping inside her skull.

She hears rough voices outside, indistinct through the carriage walls. Then the slightly higher voice belonging to the driver they hired.

A horse trots up to the window. Adrius contorts his expression into one of pleasant banality as he pulls back the curtain and opens the glass. A Warden sits upon a steed outside, a woman in armor.

"Can we help you?" Adrius asks in a charming and slightly confused voice. "I wasn't expecting to be stopped so close to Upper Welshire."

"Sorry for the delay, sir." The Warden peers past him, eyes sliding over Kazan and Reya's veiled faces. "There's been increased vampire activity in these parts, and we've got to stop everyone. Routine, you see. You haven't seen any signs of vampires on your way north, have you?"

Adrius shakes his head. "Why no, we haven't. We're headed just past Upper Welshire. Is it safer there, do you think?"

"Should be." She tips her hat. "I'll send you on your way."

A flick of the reins and her horse gallops away once again. Two of her fellows rush after her a moment later, all three of them heading south to the ruins of the Citadel and whatever they may find there.

After a minute, the driver spurs their own horses onwards and they continue along the Rivervale.

"What would have happened if they'd tested us with silver?" Kazan asks as she closes the window once more and raises her veil.

"I would have killed them," Adrius flatly states.

She supposes that was a given, and settles back into her seat with a simple, "Ah."

Reya tilts her head to the side. "Aren't you going to protest? I would have thought you'd care about them."

She shrugs. The motion makes her skin itch. "Not particularly. It isn't as though I know any of them."

"But you *would* care if you *did* know them?"

"Perhaps. I don't know." She squirms uncomfortably in her seat. "Why does it matter?"

"You've not asked even once about whether or not your intended replacement survived the Citadel's collapse." There's a sharp look in Reya's eye that makes Kazan distinctly nervous. "You threw everything away for some random human. I would have expected you to ask about his survival. But you haven't. Nor have you asked about any of the other human servants who were in the Citadel when it came crashing down. Don't you want to know if you saved any of them?"

When she was in the Vildenmarr, she didn't save anyone. During her entire time in the Citadel, she never once attempted to help a human servant and she left Travers to die for a second time. The only people she helped were vampires and geists, and she did it only for her own sake. So why *did* she save that one man at the very end?

"I... don't know," she says. She rests her head against the window, staring down at her feet, her boots accidentally intertwined with Adrius's. "I don't think I... care."

Though she cannot see Adrius, his incredulity is plain when he asks, "You went to such lengths to avoid one human's death and now you don't care?"

Fixing her gaze on a single speck of dust on the windowpane instead of facing him, she quietly brings herself to admit, "I'm not... a good person."

"None of us are," he says, unexpectedly soft.

"No," she quietly agrees. "No, I suppose not."

"Then why?" Reya presses. "Why did you do it? Why did you let him go?"

Why *did* she? She didn't care, and still doesn't now, about who she was trying to save. Perhaps, she thinks, she only saved him to be selfish. "You said you lost your first husband to old age. I've never lost anyone that way. Everyone I know who has died perished on the road or in the streets or beneath fangs. I lost my mother to starvation and my father to vampires. I don't remember her, and I barely remember him, but... I refuse to become what killed him."

Reya exhales. Her shoulders sag. "Why didn't you *say*?"

"I didn't know," she promises. "I didn't know I wouldn't be able to go through with it."

All her life she's been fascinated by vampires. But the ones she fell in love with first weren't the distant and shadowed figures that ran wild through the village she'd lived in as a child, slaughtering the inhabitants, drinking their fill. It was a deadly, beautiful predator, a moonlit vision in a barn who caressed a child's face instead of simply killing her.

"We took away your life, didn't we?" Adrius murmurs. "Neither Reya nor I see it that way, but..."

Kazan can only nod.

Reya exhales. Her eyes shut and her red lips part in a sigh. Drawn together by a familiarity that almost makes Kazan jealous, Reya and Adrius gently rest their foreheads together. Stored tension releases from his jaw as he lightly cups her cheek, her hands resting against his coat, their expressions a soft and resigned mirror of one another.

He closes his eyes. "You know we must..."

"Selflessness doesn't become me," Reya replies, and it is light enough to be a laugh while heavy enough to echo.

"You think I'm any different?"

Never before has Kazan been so aware of the years between the two of them, the decades they've had together, the way they know one another, the way they can speak only half a conversation and still understand it even as it's incomprehensible to her. She yearns for that, for a brief moment. Yearns to be able to pick them apart and see the intricacies of them bare before her eyes, to know them completely as they seem to be striving to know her. Maybe that's the greater part of it. She wants to know them as they want to know her. A craving for reciprocity.

That strange yearning still churns her thoughts as Adrius pulls back and raps his knuckles on the carriage wall again.

Outside, the horses whiny and the carriage rolls to a halt.

Kazan frowns. "What are you doing?"

"Giving back what little of your life we can." Reya leans across the carriage to delicately kiss Kazan. She chases the kiss, lets it linger, and when Reya pulls away, she laments the loss. Reya caresses Kazan's hand and says, "I truly hope it brings you happiness."

"I don't understand."

Adrius slides the disguise ring off his finger, gently takes Kazan's other hand, and puts it on her left thumb. "Never take it off," he warns her. "Live as long as you can as peacefully as you can in this human life you want."

She can feel the illusion of humanity settle over her. "But if I take it, you won't be able to seek refuge among humans anymore."

"Then I shall simply ensure I no longer need that respite from my own people."

Adrius opens the carriage door.

Mist rolls over the wet grass and a cloudy evening sky tints the entire world a cool, grayish blue. They've left behind the gentle road of the Rivervale and the twisted trees of the Vildenmarr and now Kazan looks upon the fields and paths that lead up to the walls of a large town in the distance. Lamps are being lit along the gates, bright as stars to her new eyes. A few wagons roll past the gates, a handful of town guards are tiny wandering specks.

Upper Welshire.

Adrius kisses her, a soft goodbye kiss. "If you ever want to come north to Glassdow, the invitation remains open."

"Thank you," she says, surprising herself with her own sincerity. "I... appreciate the offer."

Her fingers linger on the doorframe as she steps out of the carriage. Grass crunches beneath her boots, dew brushing against the leather. She's surrounded by the fresh smell of wet earth and the still, moist air.

She gives Adrius and Reya one final, bittersweet smile. "Goodbye," she says, and closes the carriage door.

The driver snaps the reins, and the carriage rolls off, continuing down the main road that will lead past the town and up the slow incline towards the mountains that mark the northern lands of Mavazem. Away from her and back into their now cracked society. A society that she has one foot in and one foot out of.

She walks the final few minutes to Upper Welshire. This is her home. The only home she ever had after her father's village was ruined. Strong walls and as much safety as a large town can muster. A business she can reopen, a loft over her shop that's comfortable enough, associates, though no friends. Her home. Shouldn't she feel... more?

The familiar face of Emil the guard stands at the gate,

checking a wagon full of barrels that reek of barley. "Miss Korvic." He gives her a pleasant nod. "Welcome back."

"It's good to be back," she says.

She wonders if it's a lie or not.

Chapter Thirty-Four

Kazan's shop is as she left it. The spare key hidden away in a niche underneath the side windowsill remains and no one looks twice at her as she unlocks the front door. She hasn't been gone long enough for dust to start accumulating in the front room, the forge, or her small rooms upstairs. It's untouched. Unchanged. She walks through each room like a geist, waiting for the house to reject her. It does not. As though it doesn't notice the difference, as though there is no difference to see.

Night falls and she is not tired. She washes and puts on a shift, lies down in her bed, and closes her eyes, but nothing happens.

In the morning, she dresses in her old clothes. They still fit, but they don't feel quite right against her skin. She's hungry and out of habit finds herself standing in the small kitchen for ten minutes, doing nothing. There's nothing here that would satisfy her. Is this going to be her life? A starvation diet?

She opens her shop. With her sword gone, she must make up the lost revenue from her time spent away, and that means selling whatever she can. So much for her dreams of grandeur. It's time to start from scratch.

She turns back to the forge and dedicates a day to crafting a single knife. It's not her best effort. New strength means her muscle memory is thrown off, and she ends up swinging the hammer with too much force. Her first try results in a single blow flattening the billet into a thin sheet. The hot air from the charcoal fires is tempered by the chill air outside, no wind to blow away the smell of smoke, metal, and oil. Her new eyes trace the path of the sparks that puff up from the charcoal forge, the red-white flickers that catch her gaze with more intensity than ever before. She wonders if it would hurt to stick her hands in the fire now.

Half of her forge is dedicated to silver wire and tools dusted with rowan shavings and buckets that have been filled with blessed water so many times they radiate cruel heat when she so much as walks past them. She stays away and thus only has half her craft. She throws a sheet over the small silver mirror in the front of her shop. The only glimpses of herself that she catches are on a particularly polished piece of steel. It shows human eyes and human teeth, and it sits hollow inside her, an emptiness in her stomach that's not mere hunger.

A customer shows up on the second day. They buy a simple paring knife and leave. Kazan weighs the gold coins and feels nothing.

On the third day, she leaves her shop and simply walks.

Upper Welshire hasn't changed. Something deep inside her feels as though there should be *something* different. She's different so the town should be too. Her life should be different. For the love of the saints, she's a vampire! She's living a lie, she doesn't belong here, so why does it feel the same as it always did before?

She ends up in front of the city's cathedral.

There's an unusual crowd swarming into the building, people gathered outside and pressing themselves up against the windows to look in. An usher pins a notice to the wooden board hung up on the wall, and Kazan maneuvers her way to stand next to him. She peers through the stained-glass window. Inside, between the pews of people, she can see several priests in a circle around some sort of relic. They're not doing anything, just standing there. She can't even see their mouths move.

She politely nudges the usher to distract him from his work. "Sorry to bother you, but what's going on?"

"Oh, you haven't heard? It's been quite the wonderful occasion. Priests from Lower Welshire arrived this morning, bringing Saint Lumain with them." The usher points through the window. "See?"

All she sees is a circle of emptiness around a relic.

Saints are geists, as she'd so confidently told Adrius all those days ago. She'd even *seen* Saint Lumain before, from a distance, yes, but they'd been visible. They had been visible, and she had been human.

She's filled with the overwhelming urge to carve her eyes out of her head with her claws until she gets back the sight she's lost. But there's nothing for her to see. There's nothing for her here.

She flees.

Habit takes her to the corner pub two blocks from her house. In the past, it had been filled with the warm and hearty smells of food and drink, the chatter of patrons and sometimes bawdy music if anyone tried to earn a few coins with an instrument or their voice. Despite the afternoon hour, there are still plenty of people packed in, most eating rather than drinking, but a few already red in the nose from alcohol. None of the old smells, sounds, or sights have changed. But now the first thing that hits Kazan upon entering is the rich, meaty smell of human blood pumping in human veins.

Hunger pangs growl in her belly. A shudder runs through her entire body, her jaw aching to extend fangs that shouldn't fit in her mouth. The disguise ring trembles on her thumb, and she leans into that as much as she can, relying on that magic to keep her fangs at bay. Spellwork begins to make the metal burn hot and she clamps her other hand over it to prevent anyone else from seeing or feeling the heat radiating from it.

In a truly depressing move, she orders a cheap ale and then

goes to lurk in an empty booth tucked away in a corner. The more she drinks, the thirstier she gets.

Someone plops down in the chair across from her.

It's her old friend and former lover Spencer, her blond hair even brighter now that Kazan's eyes are sharper, the scars on her bare arms pronounced and familiar. She places her own mug down on the table in a way that declares a conversation is now open.

"Didn't think I'd see you back here so soon after Rask's little soiree," Spencer says, eyebrow raised. "Thought you'd be gone for weeks."

Kazan hides the lower half of her face behind her ale and mutters, "So did I."

"And...?" Spencer prompts.

"Trouble on the road." That's only partly a lie, so she elaborates with a complete fable, "We were intercepted by a messenger. Turns out the Wardens guarding us were desperately needed elsewhere, and without them accompanying us, half of us decided to turn back instead of risking the journey alone, on foot."

Spencer scratches her chin. "Oh yeah... now that you mention it, I have heard that there's something going on with the Wardens. They're all in a panic. Did you know more of 'em are coming to camp out in Upper Welshire for a bit?"

"Oh?"

"Yeah, only for a few days before they keep scouting south."

They're running south to the Citadel as all the vampires are fleeing north straight past them, or further south out of their path. Ironic, really. "Speaking of, I did have a favor to ask of you."

"And what do you mean to bribe me with this time?"

"Come now, you don't even know what I want. Let's talk bribes *after* I've told you what I need."

"Fine, fine." Spencer waves a hand for her to continue. "What's the matter?"

Taking a sip of ale spurs her on. She's *so* hungry. "Remember Adrius De Vere? From Madam Rask's party? I..." She leans in and whispers, "I know he's a vampire. I know he was there to buy preserved blood from Rask. Don't deny it, I know *you* know. What I need from you is really quite simple. I need the name of Rask's supplier."

A flash of anger curls Spencer's lips down. "Seriously, Kazan?"

"What?" She wasn't expecting this kind of resistance. "It's merely a name."

"First," Spencer says pointedly, putting her elbows on the table as she leans in too, "going around telling everyone the details of Rask's supply chains would break her rules on confidentiality and get me fired and kicked out on my ass. Second, I'm not an idiot. You *hate* vampires. If you find out who they're trading with and hunt them down, you're going to get yourself killed, and I don't really want to have that on my conscience."

"Damn it, Spencer, it's not like that, I'm not going to try to kill them –"

Spencer shoves her chair back and rises to her feet. "Don't try one of your lies on me. I'm done with doing favors for you."

"But..." she murmurs as Spencer stomps off, "it's not a lie."

It doesn't matter that she's not lying. Spencer leaves anyway, vanishing out the door and slamming it shut behind her. The bartender gives her a glare as the various bells on the latch rattle. So much for finding a safe source to eat. What's Kazan supposed to do now? Go directly to Rask and expose herself as a vampire?

She drowns herself in ale and stumbles back home after midnight, gloriously, depressingly drunk.

On the fourth day, she tries her hand at a knife once more. She puts on a pair of thick leather gloves and risks pressing silver ingots through the die to turn it into thin wire. The wire gets inlaid in the knife's fuller and it feels... fine. Is that it? Just *fine* and nothing more, forever?

On the fifth day, her stomach filled with rocks and aches, she does something she would never have done before. She pulls on a coat instead of a dress, slips her new knife into her belt, and goes to Madam Rask's manor without an invitation.

She pounds her fist against the front door until a harried butler opens it.

"Do you have an invitation, ma'am?" he asks tersely, looking her up and down, clearly finding her unimpressive.

"Yes," she lies. "But I've lost it. Tell Madam Rask that Kazan Korvic is here to see her about a matter of great urgency that can't wait until her next soiree. If you turn me away," she warns, hoping this might spur him to action, "then Rask will be very displeased. Go ask her, if you like, or simply show me to her office."

The butler sighs, staring up at the ceiling in exasperation. "Very well..." He stands aside to let her squeeze past him into the manor. "Stay in the foyer. I'll go and speak with Madam Rask."

Even without the glowing bustle of a party, Rask's manor still oozes opulence. It is quieter, however, and as Kazan waits, the back of her neck itches. Her foot taps a furious rhythm on the thick carpet. It is a relief when the butler finally returns and gives her a polite, short bow.

"Madam Rask will see you now," he says.

She stays right on the butler's heels as he leads her through the ballroom and up the staircases to Rask's office. The door is unlocked, and she's once more ushered into the dizzying splendor of the room.

Rask sits at her desk, adorned in silks with her golden hair piled atop her head, strings of pearls winding through the curls. A pair of bejeweled spectacles rests on the tip of her nose, and she looks down at a piece of parchment through the lenses.

At Kazan's entrance, she places the parchment down on a glass music box that must cost a truly extraordinary amount of money.

"Kazan Korvic." Rask straightens up and gives a tiny flick of her wrist to dismiss the butler, who closes the door behind him. "An unexpected pleasure. How can I help..."

She trails off. Her eyes narrow as she peers over the rim of her spectacles to stare unerringly at the disguise ring on Kazan's thumb. Of course, she would have seen it before on Adrius, and like Kazan, she knows enough about magics and spelled objects to recognize it, to see beyond the simple outward appearance.

Acceptance washes through Kazan. Alright. Rask knows. Rask will expose her. Rask will end the lie. Because it is a lie. This is all one big lie. Every part of her life is a lie now.

No, she realizes suddenly, in a way that makes her feet heavy and her chest empty. It's always been a lie. She has spent her entire life obsessed with vampires in a way no other human has been able to understand, spent her life hiding and pretending as though it was nothing more than professional curiosity. But it never has been. It's always been *more*. No wonder she's so good at lying. She has been unconsciously lying since she was six years old.

Isn't she *tired*?

"I'm here to make a trade." She had intended to ask about blood. That's all. But her mouth moves without her permission. "My house for a horse."

Rask removes her spectacles, folds them, and delicately places them down on her desk. She taps a perfectly manicured nail on the wood. "Well," she says calmly, staring at Kazan with a layered and contemplative curiosity. "On a technical level, it's a fair trade. Your forge will have decent value, and if your house is in good upkeep then I see no fiscal reason to deny your offer."

"Then you agree?"

"Yes." The confirmation is said painfully slow, as though she's waiting to change her mind in the middle of it. That curious look only intensifies. "I'll send someone to your house tomorrow morning to collect the keys. They'll bring a new horse for you with them."

"I'll have my belongings packed by then. Anything I leave behind, you may sell."

As she turns to leave, Rask stops her with a quiet question. "I hate to pry, but for the sake of my own inquisitiveness... Was it De Vere?"

"No." She amends, "But it wasn't quite *not* him. In a way."

"I see," Rask says in that same slow tone. "Good day then, Kazan. If you're ever near Upper Welshire again, keep in mind that I'm indiscriminate with whom I do business. Oh, before you go – is there a message you'd like me to convey to Spencer?"

Kazan smiles for the first time in days. "Tell her I wasn't lying."

Chapter Thirty-Five

Morning dawns with a ray of stunning light. Kazan has spent the night packing a rucksack with anything she may want. Clothes, mostly. Her lucky hammer. No keepsakes. She tucks knives into her boots and her belt, the best ones she has after she lost most of her old ones in the Vildenmarr. An enthusiasm that she hasn't felt in what feels like years fills her blood as she takes the steps two at a time down to her main shop.

One of Rask's men waits outside, holding the reins of a dark brown mare.

Kazan holds out the key. "All yours."

He gives her the reins. "Thank you for doing business with Madam Rask."

The mare is cooperative as she mounts up, saddling her bag and sliding her feet into the stirrups. She spares a final glance at her shop. Forge dead and windows dark. She turns away and nudges the mare towards the city gates. The horse's shoes click against the cobblestone streets as she winds her way through the crowds of traders and merchants setting up for the morning market.

Emil is nodding off at the gates and doesn't notice her leave. There is a cloudy sky overhead and the taste of rain on the air, roads and potential stretching out before her.

She boots her horse and gallops forward without looking back.

Acknowledgments

I would like to thank all the usual cast and crew at Angry Robot for enabling me to inflict this hot mess upon the world and allowing me to put "sexy vampire threesomes" on my list of published works.

Huge thanks also goes to Andrea, for providing the original inspiration for Reya, and to Dee, for providing the idea of Gia Montanari.

I owe the most gratitude to my incredible agent, Lauren, who read this book back in 2018 before she ever signed me on, and somehow remembered it fondly enough to suggest that I revisit it years later.

And the final drop of thanks goes to 2018 me, for writing this and going, "Damn, I bet I could sell this." Congrats, past me, you absolute lunatic.

CHAPTER ONE
Red Dock

"Twenty kydis says you can't hit that!" a patron yells over the raucous cheering.

Rig stands on top of a chair that's leaning precariously against the bar, gun in one hand, mug of she's-not-sure-what in the other.

The neon lights of Red Dock shine brightly through the haze. When Rig breathes in, her lungs are thick with a mix of crystal smoke and a colorful assortment of gases from the refineries built into the outer walls. In the packed atrium, the air presses in on the thousands of people milling about on this floor alone, to say nothing of the twelve other floors of the spaceport.

The dense shopping area is filled with the sounds of bargaining, gossiping, and drunken slurring, all in a cacophony of different languages beyond just Deit-Standard. Even from her stationary perch inside a publica, she can smell three different types of sweet pastry being fried up, one made with pickled Ascetic plums that have an almost sickly aroma.

Maybe she can bribe one of the many *ludicrously* drunk people around her into buying her one.

"You're on!" she cries in response to the challenge. "Prepare to eat your words and also my cute blue ass!"

The crowd cheers. Half of them are so far into their cups they don't even know what's going on. They cheer simply because everyone else is. The beauty of drunken solidarity.

Her accuser is a hulking Oriate with what must be twice the

usual number of spikes growing out of his skin. He crosses his
arms menacingly. "Your mouth is writing a check your gun
can't cash!" he taunts. That's not even how that phrase goes;
yeesh, what an idiot. "Do it with both eyes closed and then I'll
pay you!"

Rig throws back her drink, tosses the mug over her
shoulder – there's another gleeful cheer as it smashes into
something – and aims her weapon. The target is a can on a
shelf at the other end of the crowded publica. Its patrons part
faster than the wind.

Rig lines up the shot.

Closes her eyes.

Her gun is steady in her hands, familiar, a good weight. All
it takes is a gentle squeeze of the trigger and...

Crack!

The excited cries hit her ears before she opens her eyes and
sees that her bullet has pierced the can.

"Hah!" She points a finger at her accuser. "Eat that, you
bastard!"

A frown curdles on his face. He grabs someone's glass out
of their hand and balances it on the top of his head, spreading
his arms in triumph because he must surely think he's called
her bluff now.

"Double or nothing!" he declares.

A murmur runs through the crowd and Rig pauses.

"You know that's risky, right? We're talking insides on the
outside, blood, murder, death, deathy-ness... deathing?" she
asks. "Just pay up already and admit I'm fabulous."

He laughs, clearly drunk off his ass. "You said you could hit
anything! You a liar?"

Someone in the press of people yells, "Just pay up!"

"Come on!" he insists. "Do it!"

If she misses, she's doubtful anyone in Red Dock will want
her hide for it. This place isn't exactly known for tight security
or a desire to obey the law. Besides, she's good at what she

does. Or at least that's her usual brag. She double-checks her grip, makes sure that she's aiming steady, and scrunches up her face in concentration as she gauges how sober she is. Sober enough.

Alright then.

Let it never be said that she is a coward. Actually, many people *have* said that, but not today. She raises her gun again and takes as careful aim as she can manage.

Crack!

The can is blasted off the Oriate's head and the publica descends into a roar of cheering and mindless noise.

With a sour expression, the Oriate pulls out his link and opens up a kydis transfer. Rig's link is similarly mounted on her wrist, attached to her glove, and all it takes is push of a button to exchange the money.

Her link chimes as it goes through, and she tips an invisible hat at the Oriate. "Pleasure doing business with you."

He just glares. She'll take that as a compliment.

"Next round is on my good friend here!" she declares to the crowd before slipping off her makeshift throne and vanishing into the throng of people.

She slides into a stool on the far side of the bar, next to an older woman who's sipping a glass of something that smells like a swamp mixed with silverite fumes. At her signal, the bartender passes Rig another round of whatever it was she had been drinking previously. She'd ordered an ale, but she doesn't actually know her ales that well and she'd just pointed at the nearest tap without looking.

"You were *quite* loud," the old woman next to her says, sniffing disdainfully into her glass.

Rig winces. "Sorry, ma'am."

She gives Rig a long, stern glare before finally conceding, "But you are a good shot. What faction are you?"

"Er. Pyrite." *Formerly*.

"Hrm. Do you know why you call yourselves Pyrite?"

"…Cause of the god? Cause pyrite crystals spark fire? Cause shiny things are cool?"

"Because you're all fools digging for gold where there's only dirt." The woman gives her another hard look. "I'm from Ascetic. We could do with a shot like you, if you ever felt like joining up with a *proper* faction. You know, one that doesn't spend all its time in spires, mindlessly tinkering."

"Thank you for the offer, ma'am," Rig replies, because although she's got a blanket dislike of factions, this woman in particular hasn't done anything worthy of rudeness. "But although I can't defend Pyrite, tinkering as a whole can be quite respectable, if you do it with enough smart-assery. And I'm happy right where I am."

Which is nowhere in particular.

Plus she's got no desire to go back to any one of those three galaxy-conquering, warmongering, merry bands of bastards. Ascetic, Ossuary, and Pyrite. Lying bastards, terrifying bastards, and bastards out to get her. In that order. They've been cutting the galaxy up like a pie for ten thousand bloody years and she's much happier kicking them in the shins whenever the opportunity presents itself.

The bartender scooches over and takes away Rig's drink, instead passing her the tab. "Mohsin is ready for you, miss. Best not to make him wait."

"Thank you very much, good sir."

She transfers the proper amount of kydis, with a tip, before giving the old woman a casual salute. It's no crisp, militaristic, proper factioned salute, but it's good enough for a place like Red Dock.

The bartender jerks his thumb towards the back door.

Rig steps through and instantly finds herself in an elevator. She rockets up maybe five or six floors before stepping out.

This place has none of the clatter of the main publica, the noise replaced by softer music and a low buzz of less rowdy conversation. Wall-to-wall carpeting, hovering chandeliers, and the sound of cards being shuffled for gambling addicts, all dimly lit with red light fixtures. There's a game of Ascetic roulette being played at a green velvet table to her left and a man setting up holo-pong to her right. A grin spreads across her face as her boots cross from the metal elevator floor to sink into the plush carpets like candyfloss.

She weaves her way through the fancy-shmancy super-secret back-upper room and takes a seat across from a man dressed in a brown leather duster.

"Heya, Mohsin," she says. "Good to see your ugly mug again."

He snorts in amusement. "I see you haven't changed a bit."

"I've gotten prettier."

He snaps his fingers at the bodyguard standing by his side. The guard is a Zazra, sporting the distinctive pointed ears and black facial markings of that species. Makes sense. She's seen Mohsin beat the crap out of enough people to know that he doesn't need *protection*. But Zazra have other specialties.

The Zazra man holds out one of his hands. How polite of him. "May I read you?"

She nods and tugs her sleeve back, sticking her arm out. "Yeah, go ahead."

Zazra hands are shaped the same as Rig's basic five-fingered set-up, but the skin on the backs of their palms is black as the stripes on their faces, rough and leathery, designed to protect their sensitive palms.

This Zazra places his palm gently on her wrist.

His eyes flutter closed. There's a soft brushing feeling in her mind as the Zazra uses his empathic abilities to read her emotions and see if she's here to stab them in the back. Or he wants to know if she's really as charming as she pretends. Six of one.

Damn those abilities are useful. All Rig gets from her Kashrini blood is blue skin and no hair. Not that she's anything less than proud of her species, but abilities like the Zazra have would be appreciated. Mohsin is half Kashrini as well, and he shares similar sentiments. There's a blue tint to his skin and he's got the purple eyes to show for it, but his blonde hair is all human. Makes it easier for him to get contacts sometimes. A lot of humans are too stuck up to deal with anyone who *isn't* human. In their minds, human equals faction. Faction equals good.

Yeah, *right*.

"She's clear," the Zazra says, pulling back and letting her fix her sleeve.

"Are you really surprised?" she asks with a smile. "We've known each other *how* long?"

Mohsin relaxes ever so slightly in his seat. "I didn't think so, but it never hurts to double check. Policy, and all. Drink?"

"You paying?" she asks. "If so, yes."

There's a decanter of Ascetic whiskey sitting on the table, and he pours out two small glasses, sliding one across the table to her. Not her favorite – too carbonated – but she'll drink it. Honestly, why does Ascetic carbonate nearly *everything*? Highly unnecessary, in her opinion.

Mohsin sets his glass down and licks the last of the gold liquid from his lips. "So what do you have for me?"

She produces a thumb drive from her pocket and slides it across the table towards him. "As promised. One stolen freighter filled with refugees. Those are the coordinates right there. Should be easy for you to send someone to escort them out of the Dead Zone and to a safe moon somewhere."

He snatches it up, holding it to the candle fixture on the table and getting a good look at it. With a wave of his hand, he dismisses the bodyguard, who goes back to lurking around their table and glaring at people who look like they might try and approach. "Are they safe?"

She nods. "Yeah. Last I checked in, anyways. Most of them are just refugees fleeing the war, but there's a couple of kids that ran from a factioned agriworld."

The Nightbirds, the group she and Mohsin work for, mostly work in people-moving. Getting refugees fleeing the ongoing war to safe planets. Helping former indentureds – like herself – smuggle themselves away from faction homeworlds and agriworlds. Hiding people from the law for as long as need be. When they're not moving folk from one end of the galaxy to the other, they're sabotaging every piece of faction tech they can get their hands on, stealing faction intel, breaking up faction bases. Just generally doing everything they can to slow the all-consuming, three-way war that so often puts their people – the Kashrini people – in the line of fire. Each member only has a handful of contacts so that if one of them gets caught they can't bring down the whole network – a set up that works just fine for Rig, who always has a good deal of fun pretending to conveniently forget things.

The thumb drive disappears into Mohsin's jacket pocket. "We can get some people to them as soon as possible. It should be secure, so long as we wait for any annoying patrols to calm down a bit first. If they've got kids with them, I don't want to try anything before we know we can get them out safely. How many of them were indentured?"

"All of 'em. Twenty-one. We got their tracker chips out before we moved 'em onto the freighter, but Ascetic is going to be *pissed* at us."

"It's not like we're taking more heat than normal here. *All* the factions are *always* pissed at us for freeing their indentured–"

"Or for sabotaging their supply trains," Rig breaks in. "Or stealing their weapons. Or for coding a virus that got into Pyrite ship systems and made every sound speaker play 'Rainbow Asteroid Party' on repeat."

He chuckles in a rare show of non-grumpiness.

"Hey, it was worth it. Anything to piss them off. Keep them distracted, keep them off their game." If a Pyrite ship spends one hour pulling their hair out and trying to fix their broken communication systems, that's one extra hour the Nightbirds have to evacuate a Kashrini settlement that's about to become a war zone. Rig leans back in her chair. "So what's my next job? You mentioned that I might actually get paid for this, and to be honest, I could seriously use the kydis."

Her ship isn't going to fix itself, after all. There are bad scrapes in the hull, the cannon is a bit roughed up, and the engines are running on nothing more than fumes and what little she can scrape out of the depleted fission chargers. The old girl has a couple more hops left in her, but unless Rig can fill her up soon, she's going to end up dead in the black. No power means no heat, no oxygen circulation – a combination that makes one very dead Rig.

Fortunately for her, Mohsin isn't the sort of person to leave her high and dry.

"I've got a job lined up for you," he tells her. "It's not quite the usual thing. Friend of a friend told me about it 'cause I mentioned you needed cash for ship upkeep. Crate full of merchandise needs to be shifted into Ascetic space."

While she doesn't like Ascetic, she has to admit that it's the enemy territory she's most comfortable in. She can get in easily, get out easily, and usually has a fun time while she's there. "Where *exactly* in Ascetic space?"

"Heart of it. The Ascetic homeworld itself."

"I know someone there. Haven't seen her in two months."

"So I've heard. I also heard this *friend* of yours," he says with a wink, "has hooked you up with a nice set of clearance codes to get onto the homeworld. Figured you'd be the best bet for this job."

"And this is... legit?"

"It's solid. I know lawful work isn't usually our cup of tea, but I heard your wallet was in a sad spot and thought you might make an exception for this." He gives her a lazy smile. "I know artifact reclamation is a side project you dabble in."

He's right. When Rig has time, she frequently hunts down the bits and pieces that factions have stolen from the Kashrini over the millennia. Jewels that were plucked from the necks of corpses, statues pulled from every place of worship they used to know, all the precious things from stories and legends. She figured that since she'd managed to steal her own research three years ago, then she'd make a pretty good thief.

She'd been right.

She'd gotten a taste of reclaiming things from Pyrite three years ago, and she's wanted more ever since. They tried to take everything from her, and they're trying to take everything from the Kashrini. Stopping them, even in small ways like this, is an indescribable satisfaction.

"Where am I picking up the goods?" she asks.

"I can have one of my guys drop the crate off in your ship right now, if you want. I'll assume you've changed the damn passcodes again?"

"You know me so well. Give me the info on who I'm taking this to, and I'll give you the new codes."

Mohsin has his link attached to his wrist, the small flash of metal almost hidden in the leather of his gloves. He presses it and a small holographic field pops up, displaying a series of coordinates and what looks to be a letter of introduction. "Transfer done." He taps a key, and her own link vibrates. "No deadline, but don't take too long or else he might get skittish and find someone else. You know how these types can be."

"I'm not green around the ears, Mohsin."

"It's why I save all the best jobs for you."

"*Aw*. You really do care."

"You're one of the best I know. You've proved that time and again over the years. It's less caring and more… practicality?" He shrugs. "What can I say, you're good at getting the job done."

How sweet. "Do we need anything from Ascetic space that I can get while I'm there? You know me, I like to linger on that giant garden they call a homeworld."

"Not that I–" Blood drains from his face as he stares at a point over Rig's shoulder. His hand automatically reaches into his jacket, wrapping around the pistol he has holstered under his shoulder. Not drawing, just waiting. "Ah shit."

Rig freezes. "Are we blown?"

"Yeah, and not in the fun way." He lowers his hand. "Turn around, but slowly. Anyone you know?"

With a forced casual air, as if she's only getting a look at the bar's menu, she tilts her head at just the right angle to get a glimpse of the unwanted guests.

Two humans are loitering at the edge of the bar, armored and armed. Bounty hunters? No, they're too – for lack of a better word – *clean* looking. Clean and *shiny* armor at that; they're not worried about standing out. Her eyes narrow as she scans them, looking for a symbol. A flaming gear is emblazoned on their chest plates.

Shit.

"Pyrite," she hisses under her breath.

Rig is longing to leap out of her seat, ready to draw her weapons and shoot when Mohsin gives her a stern look. It as good as glues her back to her chair.

He shakes his head. "Don't."

"Mohsin, if they're after us–"

"Are they? And for the sake of the gods don't draw attention to yourself. They might pass us by if we stay seated and careful," he mutters.

"I wasn't followed, okay?"

"I didn't say you–" He curses under his breath. "How would you know if you were followed *anyway*? The whole point of someone successfully following you would be *stealth*. You wouldn't have noticed."

"Weren't you *just* the one telling me all about how great at my job I am?"

"Yeah, when it benefited me to say it, sure!"

"Well yelling at me isn't going to help any, now, is it?"

"*Neither* is yelling at *me*!"

"Okay then!"

"Okay!"

Their whispered shouts cut off as the music in the chattering bar slowly wells down. They weren't the only ones to notice that Pyrite showed up. Funny how faction soldiers can really kill the mood.

She knows that if she can get behind some good cover, she can probably outshoot them. Pyrite armor has weak spots, and she knows them all. The real question is how much back up they've brought. Dealing with thugs is a whole different numbers game than dealing with one of the *factions*. Factions have *armies*. For all they know, Pyrite forces could have the entirety of Red Dock surrounded by now. She tries to run through scenarios in her head – how many can she take out, how does she best run from them, what's the fastest way back to her ship?

"You shoot now, and you'll get a hundred civilians caught in the crossfire," Mohsin sternly reminds her. He jerks his head towards his Zazra bodyguard and says, "Give them the standard welcome greeting and see if you can find out who or what they're here for. I'm getting her out of here before bullets start flying."

"Good luck," the Zazra replies before striding over towards the two enemies, drawing their attention.

The waiting is the worst part. Rig doesn't turn around to look at the Pyrite soldiers again, she doesn't want to attract their attention, so she just has to sit here. Like a stump. While Mohsin watches discreetly over her shoulder until his Zazra bodyguard has done a sufficiently good job of distracting the targets. She wants to sit perfectly still, but even that would be a tell, so she casually sips at her drink. The alcohol sours on her tongue.

Her mind unhelpfully dredges up memories of Pyrite torture instruments, and she has to kick the thought away before it makes her sick.

After an eternity, Mohsin slowly stands up, his posture forcefully relaxed. "I'm going to go ask my bodyguard what the trouble is," he tells her, each word calm and deliberate. "Wait forty seconds after I leave before you head to the bar.

Tell the bartender that I'm ordering a crystal shot and she'll get you out of here."

"Got it," she replies, her hand so tight around her glass that one twitch of her fingers would shatter it into dust.

He leaves.

She counts down the seconds, resisting the urge to turn her head around and see what's going on. Mohsin will be fine. The guy practically runs this place, he's carved out a business for himself here over the years. Half the usual punters that come through here know who he is and would whip out a gun in his defense. There's nothing unusual about him stopping a couple of Pyrites who've wandered into his bar.

She tries to tell herself that this is going to be fine.

Finally the allotted time passes. She grabs her glass and stands up, holding her head low so that her face isn't easily visible.

She heads to the bar, making sure she doesn't move like she's in a hurry, that she keeps her steps nice and even. She doesn't want to attract attention by appearing as though she's running. She only glances over her shoulder once. It looks like the Zazra and Mohsin have successfully drawn the soldiers' gaze towards a security monitor on the wall, as if they're actually trying to help them. Knowing Mohsin, the monitor doesn't actually work – or if it does, it's rigged.

The woman tending bar gives her a smile as she steps up. "Anything I can do for you?"

"Yeah." Rig sets the empty glass down on the counter and hopes that this works. "I need a crystal shot for Mohsin."

"Sure thing."

With a professional smile, the woman steps aside to let Rig behind the bar. She presses a button hidden on the underside of the countertop and a hidden hatch on the floor slides open, revealing a ladder.

"Thank you," Rig tells the bartender, slipping a few kydis into the woman's hand. "For your troubles."

Then she jumps down onto the ladder.

CIEL PIERLOT   343

The hatch above her head is closed again and her world is plunged into darkness.

Only after her eyes adjust can she see the dim light fixtures built into the sides of the vertical tunnel. Her footsteps on the ladder rungs echo in the metal corridor as she descends, keeping her eyes firmly on her hands to avoid slipping. She doesn't know how long this tunnel is or where it leads, and if she falls she very well could die. Still, better a fall to her death than the slow tortures Pyrite will come up with. They have no moral boundaries, no scruples when it comes to violence, and no shortage of fancy devices to play around with.

She knows better than anyone what they're capable of.

All their overclocked guns, clever bombs, doomsday buttons – she had a hand in all of them at some point or another.

Relief floods through her when her feet finally hit solid ground and she can step off the ladder. Short-lived relief, however. She's not out of the asteroid field yet.

Noise and lights flicker in from ventilation grates set into the floor. This tunnel must be in the airways. She pries open one of the panels to let herself pass through, putting the sheet of metal back in place once she's crossed through into a separate ventilation shaft.

She's pretty sure she's nearing the starboard lifts; all she has to do is keeping heading in that direction and then she can start making her way down towards her ship.

The noise of people talking and moving about fades as she moves through a more cramped section of air vent. Good news for her. It'll be better to drop down from the ceiling in a relatively deserted part of the spacedock than land on top of some poor folk who didn't sign up to have a random Kashrini woman hit their faces with her boots.

She reaches down and starts prying open the grate beneath her feet. It's stubborn, but she gets it all the way off, shifting it to the side and looking down to make sure the area below is clear.

She drops down.

She lands in the middle of a quiet section of the spacedock. Only a few people are milling about; they quickly look the other way and pretend as though they don't see her spontaneously appearing in their midst. In a place like Red Dock, most just want to mind their own business and ignore what isn't either profitable or hilarious.

The elevators are nearby, and she gets on the next one heading to the lower levels.

Every second she's in the elevator is a second at which she's convinced those Pyrite soldiers are going to jam its controls and it's going to stop and she's going to be trapped in this because it's such an obvious kill box – she takes a deep breath.

She hits level five with her palm on one of her guns, the cold grip of the semi-auto pistol pressed so tightly into her hand that it'll leave a pattern imprinted on her skin.

No one's here – not for her, at least. It's packed to the next galaxy and back, of course, just with tourists and criminals and the standard bunch of ne'er-do-wells. No sign of the two soldiers from Mohsin's bar, and as she scans the throngs of people, she can't see anyone else wearing unusually clean armor or the Pyrite symbol.

Her heart pounds.

As she walks through the crowded atrium again, she does another check of her body language – still relaxed, still inconspicuous. She tugs her headscarf up, just a little bit. Enough to make it difficult to get a closer look at her face, but not so much that she looks like she's actively trying to hide her appearance. It's an art form, one that she is usually better at. She pinches herself. Freaking out isn't going to help her. What *will* help is keeping her cool and staying focused.

All she needs to do is get to her ship without incident. Then she's in the clear.

Pyrite has sent people after her before, she reminds herself. They've never managed to stay on her tail for very long. She's got a dozen friends with safe houses and hidey holes scattered across the galaxy. They'll never pin her down and they'll never take her back. She can make it.

Color flashes in the corner of her eyes, the red and blue of Pyrite's symbol.

She freezes in her steps, her hand a moment away from drawing her weapon, cursing herself for letting them get so close–

Click.

A rifle is pointed at her head.

"You are under arrest."

Even her lungs seem to stop moving. Her eyes dart to the man pointing a weapon at her and she can see the shiny red armor underneath a civilian coat. They're hiding in the crowd; of course she didn't notice. Why couldn't she use her brain for one minute and realize that's what they'd be doing? It's what she'd do, after all. After so long chasing her, she should have expected that they'd pick up on a few of her tricks. Half her usual kit would take civilians out in a burst of fire, and she refuses to drag a bunch of innocent people in her mess. All she's really got are her guns.

What can she do?

Two thoughts filter to the surface. Firstly, that they are going to take her alive. If she's dead, she can't give them the research – *her* research – that they want. And second, that there are more than just this one.

"I understand," she tells the soldier.

Deep breath in.

She flashes her left arm up and wraps it around his wrist, digging into the soft spots between his armor until she hears something *snap* and the gun drops. Her right hand goes for one of her guns. She spins on the balls of her feet, pushing the man to his knees and yanking his arm back until the slightest movement by him would cause it to dislocate.

She puts her gun to the back of his head.

"Shoot me, and your friend dies!" she calls out. They're listening. She knows they are. "I'm not messing around!"

A scream goes out through the atrium and people begin to panic.

"Stand down," a new voice says.

Three more Pyrite soldiers emerge from the crowd, weapons in hand and aimed straight at her. The crowd scatters like a school of fish facing a shark, but there's nowhere to go. The atrium isn't designed for mass evacuation. There's no flashing sign marked 'exit.' The crowd parts away from the confrontation, sure enough, but they can't get far.

One of the Pyrite soldiers reaches out and snatches a civilian.

Fuck.

He holds the woman in one arm, and with the other puts a pistol to her temple. "Release our comrade and stand down. Or else we'll kill her. You're opposed to civilian casualties, are you not? We were told you no longer have the... *taste* for that sort of thing."

Rig's hand is shaking.

The civilian woman opens her mouth. Rig braces for her scream, but instead the only sound that comes out is a calm:

"I suggest you release me."

Rig blinks.

The Pyrite soldiers glance down at the woman, their helmeted faces reflecting her dispassionate features. The roar of the crowd quiets. Everything seems to fade away as if the galaxy is focusing on the unfamiliar woman. Does she not know what sort of things Pyrite will *do*?

The woman – a Zazra, like Mohsin's bodyguard – looks down at the arm across her neck with apathetic disdain. "I *won't* ask again."

She glances between the soldiers, one eyebrow arched in a silent question. Their blank helmets turn to look at one another and Rig can only imagine that the confusion on their faces is a mirror of her own.

When none of them reply, the Zazra lets out an exasperated sigh.

"Fine."

She moves.

Her body is almost a blur as she grabs the soldier's arm, drops to one knee, and throws the large man over her body like a sack of feathers. His back smacks against the ground with the sort of bone deep *crack* that would have made Rig wince if she weren't staring, slack-jawed, as the woman brings her boot down on the man's helmet. There's a metallic groan of the helmet giving way and then a wet squelch that makes Rig gag.

The Zazra turns to the other two soldiers.

One shoots – she's already dodged before he pulls the trigger. She twists around his gun to grab the barrel and then uses it to yank the soldier towards her, letting him fall into her fist. The chest plating caves into his solar plexus with a sickening crunch beneath her hands. She spins around, using the body she's holding to block the rain of bullets that the last soldier unleashes upon her, and then she tosses the corpse onto the remaining soldier.

He throws his dead comrade to the side – just in time to get a spinning kick to the head.

The man goes down.

Blood as red as his armor splatters the ground beneath his shattered helmet.

Fuck, Rig thinks, and then again for good measure, *holy fuck*.

The Zazra woman bends down to pick up a black duffel bag that she must have dropped when the Pyrite grabbed her. Smears of blood dot the silvery gauntlets she's wearing. The red shines as she moves her hands.

"Well?" she asks Rig.

Rig tries to make her mouth cooperate. "Uh."

She sighs, bends down to pick up one of the dead soldiers' guns, and then shoots the man that Rig has pinned.

Rig feels strangely detached from her own body. She lets the corpse fall without taking her eyes off the woman. Who *is* she... how did she... Rig has never seen *anyone* face Pyrite – or any factioned soldiers, for that matter – and come out without a scratch, let alone take out four of them without breaking a sweat.

A siren screams through Red Dock.

"Damn it." The Zazra spins around, holding up one hand in a loose fist.

Bright red lights start to flash as a monotone voice comes through the speakers, demanding they cease and desist. Another squad of Pyrite soldiers is pushing through the atrium, weapons raised and ready to fire as soon as they clear the crowd. Rig's eyes dart to the walkways overhead and counts another team shooting grappling hooks into the steel beams overhead, preparing to jump down.

The Zazra slings her bag over her shoulder. "They sent for backup. Why are those bastards after you, anyways?"

"That's a long story," Rig replies, wide eyes staring at the approaching Pyrite soldiers. They need to run. She's screaming at her legs to move, but she can't quite manage anything more than a tremble. "Really long."

"I see."

The Zazra slides her feet into a low crouch, one armored hand brushing against the floor like an animal preparing to pounce. She's not going to – she *is*.

Although Rig doesn't know if this woman *can* fight off dozens of Pyrite soldiers, she also would really prefer not to find out. The Zazra can do what she wants with her life, but if Rig doesn't get the fuck out, *now*, she's going to die. Or, more likely, be tortured until she sings to Pyrite's tune and *then* die.

In a burst of desperation, she grabs a handful of the woman's shirt and tugs her away from the rapidly approaching enemies.

"*Run*!" she yells. "I have a ship – we can make it!"

For a moment she thinks the woman is going to protest, and then she's running after Rig.

They crash through the atrium, Rig with far less dignity than her strange new associate. Bullets crack past them as the Pyrites open fire – one tears through Rig's shirt, and another cuts a hole in her headscarf. At least it isn't her *ear*. She jumps a crate and then turns down a corridor, crashing into the wall in her haste. Her palms slap against the metal before she's off again, her heart beating wildly against her rib cage.

"Left!" she calls out to the Zazra, who's already a number of feet ahead of her.

They skid left down a smaller corridor.

"I hope you have a plan!" the Zazra yells over her shoulder as they book it down the corridor, dodging bullets from a group of Pyrite soldiers chasing after them.

"Plan? I'm running for my life! What part of that says 'plan'?"

"You dared three Pyrite soldiers to face you and you *didn't* have a plan?"

"The extent of my plan was to hit them with Panache and Pizzazz!"

"This isn't the time for theatrics!"

"No – my guns!"

"You *named* your guns Panache and Pizzazz?"

"Yeah, what did you name your guns?"

"I don't have guns!"

"Well that sounds like a mistake–" Rig ducks a bullet as they turn another corner, "–considering the circumstances!"

Rig slams to a stop in front of the right set of doors and throws them open to reveal a small hangar bay. She slides in first and then slams the doors behind them.

Her ship sits in front of them, and behind it, a vacuum-guard field paints a glowing blue tint over the star-filled blackness of space. Normally she'd love to stop and admire the pretty picture her bucket of bolts makes. Instead, she dashes up the gangplank with the sounds of Pyrite bullets shooting the door down on her heels.

A blast of fire – grenade – takes down the hangar bay doors.

Rig almost fumbles, slamming her hand onto the lock and punching in the code just as the soldiers step over the ruined doors, their limbs dragging lines through the debris and smoke-filled air.

Shwoosh.

Rig has never been so relieved to hear the sound of her ship's hatch sliding open.

"Get in!"

She and the Zazra leap through one after the other, and then she's able to shut the hatch behind them. With a touch to the wall-mounted security panel, a glowing holographic panel springs up at her fingertips. The floors rumble as a blast rocks the ship – the Pyrite soldiers have opened fire.

She almost trips over an unexpected crate. Mohsin must have come through and had his people bring the merchandise on board before everything went to shit.

Adrenaline and panic send tremors down her fingers.

She redirects all the power to the shields. Just in time. The next few blasts fire off and the ship groans under the strain.

Collisions send Rig stumbling into walls as she runs through her ship towards the bridge. She built near every feature of those shields, and while she knows that they'll save her life, she also knows that they won't last forever. They won't be safe until she can get away from Red Dock and enter luminalspace.

"Can you shoot a cannon?" she calls out to the Zazra.

She slides into the pilot's seat, slamming her palm down on the controls – a *shwish* as the lock scans her fingerprints and powers up the ship's basic systems for her. Panels and screens flicker to life on the console.

The Zazra woman is right behind her, jumping down

beneath the main cabin and into the co-pilot's seat where she can access the ship's cannons, her head just a bit below Rig's feet. A quick series of punched in commands from Rig gives the Zazra control of the weapons and overrides the main system lock.

"Hard light or particle?" the Zazra asks as she straps herself in and grabs the controls.

"You've shot a particle cannon–" Nope, ask questions *after* they're out of here. "Never mind! They're hard light."

The next burst of bullets comes for them as the Zazra quickly spins the lower mounted cannon around and opens fire. Rig glances at the rear-view holographic screen and watches as the Pyrite forces scatter.

Some of them throw up hard light energy shields for cover, kneeling down behind the walls of light and continuing their assault on the ship.

Neither her pistols nor her ship's guns can do much about those, other than trying to bash them down. Her bullets are made of hard light too. Hard light can't penetrate hard light.

Fingers moving fast as light, Rig flips off the brakes, pulls the gangplank up, and engages the subluminal engines. Her ship comes alive with a roar of power, the engines singing with the promise of freedom and survival. With another blast of fire from the Pyrite soldiers, a quick glance at the holo screens shows more soldiers pouring out of seemingly nowhere. How many of these bastards did they send after her? She picks up the pace, flipping on the artificial gravity and powering up the luminalspace bubble generator. A red warning light goes off in the corner of her vision. Shields down to fifty percent.

Rig switches on the lower repulsors and then the ground falls out from under them as they lift off, hovering above the hangar bay floor.

Her engines whip up a dangerous wind, pushing at the soldiers that are too close to the ship. A hum runs through every inch of the vessel, making her bones resonate – the thrum of her ship preparing to activate the warp bubble, which will propel the ship in to luminalspace at her signal.

The Zazra hisses in annoyance. "Pyrite dreadnaught."

Fear makes Rig's breath crawl back into her lungs.

A massive ship drags itself into view outside the hangar bay forcefield. Massive, elegantly sleek in that stupid way Pyrite design favors, and along the prow is the flaming gear sigil of that faction, painted larger than the entirety of Rig's ship.

"If they shoot, they'll hit the station. All we need to do is dodge their mooring cables and make sure their fighters can't pin us down. Easy-peasy." Rig's under attack, she's being shot at, and she's grinning. "Strap in."

"I'm *already*–"

Rig punches it.

Rig puts her ship into a steep nosedive, hurtling underneath the belly of the Pyrite dreadnought, hoping to move fast enough to avoid getting caught by mooring hooks. It won't buy her much time, not with those damn clever targeting systems Pyrite has. A dark cloud is released from the ship's belly above their heads. Rig's monitors freak out. The cloud gains clarity as it approaches. It's maybe fifty fighter ships, all screaming towards her, guns blazing.

"Oh, lovely," the Zazra grumbles, even as she spins the cannon around to fire on the Pyrite ship, their shots quickly absorbed by its shields. "Any bright ideas?"

"Just the one bright idea," Rig says. Her hand grabs hold of the luminalspace ignition. "We run. Clear us a path!"

There's just enough time for the Zazra to blow up one of the fighters – *good* aim. It leaves them a pinhole of a space to fly through, almost nothing at all, but Rig is *very* good at what she does. She aims her ship towards the gap.

And yanks on the lever.

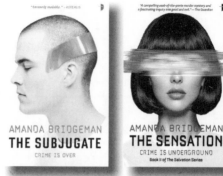

ANGRY ROBOT

We are Angry Robot

angryrobotbooks.com

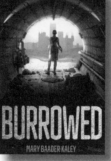

Science Fiction, Fantasy and WTF?!

@angryrobotbooks 📷 🐦 📘

We are Angry Robot

angryrobotbooks.com

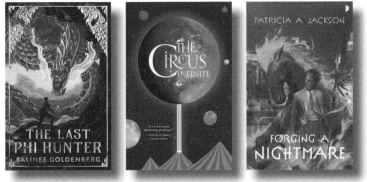